MAKE BELIEVE

Also by Terry Dowling

The Tom Rynosseros cycle:
    Rynosseros
    Blue Tyson
    Twilight Beach
    Rynemonn

Wormwood
The Mars You Have in Me
The Man Who Lost Red
An Intimate Knowledge of the Night
Antique Futures: The Best of Terry Dowling
Blackwater Days
Basic Black: Tales of Appropriate Fear

As Editor

The Essential Ellison: A 35-Year Retrospective
    (with Richard Delap and Gil Lamont)
The Essential Ellison: A 50-Year Retrospective
    (with Richard Delap and Gil Lamont)
Mortal Fire: Best Australian SF (with Van Ikin)
The Jack Vance Treasury (with Jonathan Strahan)
The Jack Vance Reader (with Jonathan Strahan)
Wild Thyme, Green Magic (with Jonathan Strahan)

MAKE BELIEVE

A TERRY DOWLING READER

TICONDEROGA
PUBLICATIONS

for

Bradley, Olga and Aleks

A little something for the Russia Room

Make Believe: A Terry Dowling Reader by Terry Dowling

Published by Ticonderoga Publications

Designed and edited by Russell B. Farr
Typeset in Sabon and Century Gothic

National Library of Australia
Cataloging-in-Publications entry

Dowling, Terry 1947–
Make believe: a terry dowling reader

1st ed.
ISBN 9780980628807 (hc)
1. Short stories,
A813.54

   ISBN 978–0–9806288–0–7 (hardcover)
       978–0–9806288–3–8 (trade paperback)

Ticonderoga Publications
PO Box 29 Greenwood
Western Australia 6924

www.ticonderogapublications.com

10 9 8 7 6 5 4 3 2 1

Acknowledgements

The author would like to thank Brian Attebery, Leigh Blackmore, Simon Brown, Wolfgang Bylsma, Jeremy G. Byrne, Bill Congreve, Katherine Cummings, Ellen Datlow, Nicole Dhamala, Alan C. Elms, Russell B. Farr, Carey Handfield, Kerrie Hanlon-Delas, Robert Hood, Van Ikin, Marjory Ikin, Kohan Ikin, Kerri Larkin, Keira McKenzie, the late Peter McNamara, Mariann McNamara, Pat McNamara, Danel Olson, Jesse C. Polhemus, Cat Sparks, Nick Stathopoulos, Grant Stone, Jonathan Strahan, Jack Vance and Bradley Wynne.

Contents

Two Meetings

Simon Brown

You can twice meet a writer for the first time, once on the page and once in the flesh. If it's a writer whose work you enjoy, both encounters can be a pleasure. For most of us, though, meeting a writer for the first time in person can be disconcerting; they are almost never anything like you imagine them to be (and let's be honest, we readers always imagine a face and a voice for writers). However, there are some few writers—very few—who seem to inhabit their own work so much you can pick them out of a crowd. Such a writer is Terry Dowling.

I first met Terry in print in 1982, when his first professional sale appeared in the Australian magazine *Omega*. "The Man Who Walks Away Behind the Eyes" heralded a writer fully formed, already supplied with all the dramatic and narrative tools the rest of us take years, even decades, to acquire. The story immediately captured the attention of readers, winning the Ditmar Award that year for best fiction by an Australian writer. "The Man Who Walks Away" was also my first introduction to Wormwood, one of the two wonderfully imagined universes which Terry developed over the following quarter century.

This collection opens with "Nobody's Fool", to date the most significant individual work to come out of Wormwood, and a story that illustrates some of the most important features in Terry's writing.

First, we have a consistent internal universe meticulously thought out and then just as meticulously constructed. There is more invention and world-building in "Nobody's Fool" than most writers manage in a lifetime.

Second, the constant allusions to our own universe, providing not only historical, mythological and cultural depth but also a matrix of hints, suggestions and clues that give us handholds as we are whirled along Terry's imaginings. He blinds us, startles us, scares us, but always ensures some part of us is anchored so we are not uselessly swept away, a little like the in-and-out-of-phase body of "Nobody's" great protagonist, the boggler Aspen Dirk.

Third, there is Terry's use of language. His love of words is apparent on every page, words he invents especially for the purpose or words he resurrects that once were common or well understood but which have since faded away into obscurity or disappeared altogether. Terry also loves words for the sound they make when you speak them, and like the poet Gerard Manly Hopkins has an affinity for words and phrases whose sounds hint at their meaning. If not for his skill with language, the words Terry invents and rediscovers would seem out of place, but instead they become the mortar for his constructions.

Fourth, his stories are filled with enough bric-a-brac, gizmos and what-nots to fill an antique store, and not just your everyday antique store but the type of shop with a bell over the door and an old tom on the counter and shelves and cupboards that stretch back a whole city block and an owner wise and discrete and wearing fingerless mittens. But as with the wonderful words he presents us, his curios are not there simply for decoration; they are like the highlights in a Rembrandt painting, details that complete a world for us, that make it lived in and usable. By the way, one of the great joys of reading a Terry Dowling story is discovering that his curios are not always inanimate objects but sometimes living, breathing sentients like Aspen Dirk, Smart Alec and Beth Leossa-Tojian, and most of all Tom Rynosseros (but more about him later).

Each of the stories in this collection is science fiction, not only in the traditional sense of imparting a sense of wonder but also in the sense of looking at what it is means to be a human being in a universe that is indifferent, and possibly inimical, to human beings. This involves issues of intelligence, sentience (not the same thing as intelligence, as Terry points out in some of the Tom Rynosseros stories), identity and life itself. In most of the stories these issues are investigated in a dialogue between the protagonist and the characters she or he meets along the way rather than in expository lumps. The dialogue often takes on some of the elements of a formal combat, where the characters manoeuvre around each other, fencing with words, parrying, decoying, eluding, before the final strike is made and an answer, or at least some hint of deeper meaning, is revealed. However, not every question is answered; Terry leaves room for you to dwell on the issues he raises. While his stories provide you with pathways and directions, he will often leave you without a final destination, or at least not the final destination you were expecting, as if you were following the clues on a map where the real treasure is not necessarily the one marked with an 'X'.

With the exception of "The Man Who Lost Red" and "The Last Elephant", the tales in this collection fall into one of Terry's two completely realised futures, that of Wormwood and that of Tom Rynosseros. We have touched briefly on Wormwood already, the world poisoned by a version of the falling star from the Book of Revelations, and I will leave you to discover for yourself the wonders contained within "Nobody's Fool", "The Man Who Walked Away Behind the Eyes" and "A Deadly Edge Their Red Beaks Pass Along", but I would be remiss if I did not personally introduce you to Tom Rynosseros himself, Terry's most singular creation.

Sometimes described as an 'Everyman', I think Tom is exactly the opposite, someone complete unto himself who shares rather than reflects our own desires, fears and yearning for answers. Tom is not a fully developed three-dimensional character, he is a fully developed four-dimensional character, inhabiting and describing the world of charvolants, Coloured Captains, fire-chess, Forgetties and belltrees over a quarter century of literary invention, and set against the background of an Australia achingly similar to our own but forever out of our reach. By the time Tom's story is finally told in the tales of *Rynemonn* (COEUR DE LION 2007), he is ready to stride off the page and stand beside us.

This anthology does not pretend to represent a summary of Terry's writing, or even a summary of just his science fiction. It is a series of snapshots thematically linked, but taken out of an album filled with pictures that ease you into different worlds, universes, creations, drawing you away from the familiar so gently, so expertly, that there are moments you are sure you are reading history and not fiction.

If and when you finally get a chance to meet Terry Dowling in the flesh, make the effort to shake his hand and thank him. After all, he's done all of this for you.

SIMON BROWN
JULY 2009

MAKE BELIEVE

Nobody's Fool

We, in some unknown Power's employ,
Move on a rigorous line;
Can neither, when we will, enjoy,
Nor, when we will, resign.

— Matthew Arnold

WORMWOOD WAS BROUGHT to Earth a little after midday on 4 June 2023. It came through the sky down a magnetic funnel, held and handled by a dozen Nobodoi 'ships'. That was the only time we ever saw Nobodoi 'ships'—*straits* they were later called. The other vessels in the skies of Earth that day were either Hoproi or Matta, preparing to destroy Human civilisation, waiting to unload troops.

Many of us realised early that they had a neutron fragment in tow, cradled and focused by the *straits* with their vast counter-energies. All of Nature threw up its heart as that dreadful mass came down. And more terrifying than Wormwood itself was that here was someone who could control such forces.

I

Aspen Dirk was a boggler. He knew the Nobodoi as few other Humans could. Leave him alone in a room with a Nobodoi artifact and within an hour he would have intuited its purpose. That was his special gift.

Aspen Dirk was also a *boruk*. A third of his body had been warped out of this continuum into another, a tragic result of one of those few times when his talent had not served him well.

Consequently, to look at Aspen Dirk was something of a trial. His torso did not seem to exist. His head, neck and left shoulder slumped across his groin. He looked like a walking head with one arm.

Folded away, protruding onto another reality plane, the rest of Aspen Dirk existed, carried out the vital functions without apparent discomfort other than a sensation of being perpetually bent over.

If anyone were to ask Aspen Dirk what it was like, he would tell them of sudden changes in temperature upon his phased-out self, of strange pressures and sucking sensations. He would also tell them that in his twenty-two years of mindboggling, this had been his only serious misfortune.

Oddly enough, in a reversed fashion, this became an assurance of efficacy in his trade, and he was never short of clients—people who would come to him, anxious and hopeful, clutching some outré construct before them. Dirk would take their money, advise them of his terms, and proceed with the reading.

His great shop in Morion was world-famous. Even the off-world Bridge Races went there. The Matta would bring their artifacts and gewgaws from the great excavations deep within the Impact around Wenna. The Darzie would come with various items obtained through local trade. Even an occasional Hoproi would storm in to learn the properties of some mindboggle or other it had seen advertised as a 'marvellous Nobodoi weapon' and bought. Around his door lingered those Lesser Races—Salmans and Tessa and Cire—hoping for the occasional throw-away by an embittered Matt scholar or tech who chose to discard a disappointing relic rather than leave it with Dirk.

When people asked, Dirk told them it was a living like any other. He was wrong. There were very few like it.

Boford Hess was a highwayman. A single glance, one quick look, and you knew it. He wore the Great Sword, the long-bladed jerrykin, like any Aviator or Code soldier, and the usual brace of stars, and he had the dromos crest: single plait of hair woven up through the close-fitting bronze filigree skull-cap then left to fall down his back, between those broad shoulders. He had his distinctive glass, enamel and silver duty-sigil on a chain around his neck.

In an older Human language he might have been called the compleat mercenary. In another, the ideal minder: one who has come to love his employer and for whom the fee no longer matters.

And when Boford Hess came to Dirk's door that afternoon with probably the best candidate for backman he had found in years, he felt a genuine excitement at how pleased Dirk would be, how absolutely delighted. That pleasure measured the true nature of their relationship. It made Bo smile.

The young, good-looking man at his side was a print, someone's clone identikin, now looking for work, with very little knowledge of the world as it was and the attitude of someone desperate to learn. The slim, fair-headed, twenty-five-year-old—Green, his name was, Hollis Green—was innocent and smart at the same time, an incredible blend in these days of cosmopolitanism or else. He knew next to nothing and wanted a job that would teach him quickly.

Boford Hess liked that. The boy wore an old combat undersuit and Code military boots—standard issue for prints these days—and had the inevitable dag unit fitted to his left shoulder, giving data-flow pretty well all the time through its flexible extensor, however censored and salted that information was.

Bo had met him in a bar, learned his quite amazing pedigree, explained Dirk and the job of backman—wearing the *boruk* in a carry harness—and still had his interest.

Now Boford Hess rapped at the quarterdoor behind its concealing field, and led his candidate inside when the petals fell back.

"The front of the shop is always crowded," Bo told the print. "Some races access boggles others can't, or pretend they can. They stay around hoping to nurture some latent talent. Dirk's the best, but there're always sceptics. Some customers won't give to him on principle, take pleasure in selling right outside his door."

"Thumbing the nose," Hollis said.

"That's it exactly." The boy was cheerful. Bo liked that. It made all the difference. "In here now."

They were large premises really, with all manner of rooms and tunnel links, a fortune in quarterdoors and other xenotech. An Infinite House, and owned by a Human. Bo didn't want to overdo it, given the lifespan of their backmen these past months. He would've been lucky to get anyone at such short notice, but now, such a find! The lad was special, and Bo found he was showing him more of the shop than he'd first intended.

"All rooms," he said. "There and there. Attics and sub-basements. Phase chambers, some locked for years. Empty except for their boggle. All linked to comp. More Nobodoi stuff here than in your average Carnival or museum. An investment of years."

"Other backmen?" the young man asked.

Bo laughed, thinking he might stall, then decided why bother. "I won't lie. I almost told you in the bar. Wasted. Gone. Dirk represents quite a trophy. Sometimes he goes out himself, like this time. Draws a lot of attention. Sometimes it's just the backman and me. And I tell you, Hollis, if it comes to sticks then I'll serve you up. Got that? No offence."

Hollis gazed evenly at this highwayman-become-minder as they approached another quarterdoor, let it take him as the others had.

"—have to be smarter then," he said as the phasing was done.

"Eh? What?" But Bo understood and approved. Again. And no point in answering now anyway. Hollis was standing very still, getting his first glimpse of the boruk, only the dag whispering, matching volume to ambient noise levels.

"So this is our contender," the famous boggler said, crossing the spacious workroom. He walked as any other Human would; it was the shape that made the gait seem strange. "With a dag yet. I like that, Bo. A bookman. A learner. I like that."

Hollis studied the condensed, quasi-manshape, saw the tousled brown-grey hair, ears like jug-handles (a good thing, they gave the impression of mass), small but clear grey eyes, cheeky smile, ankle-length gown (thank goodness!), soft shoes. In his forties, Hollis decided, having made a point of guessing ages, and was glad his recent dag studies into teratonics and the off-worlder variants had gotten him used to strange somatotypes. This was all quite bearable compared to some of those configurations—a one-armed dwarf, tilted shoulder-line like someone forever listening, head tipped slightly to one side. Not that hard to take at all.

"A print, Dirk," Bo said.

"Figured so, Bo. That's no Bible on his shoulder. What's this then, dagman, backman?" The single arm pointed to a large chalk-white sphere on the nearest work-table. It was half as large again as Dirk's own head.

"I haven't seen one..."

"Well?"

"Only read about. I'm a print, Mr Dirk. Twenty days out of rent-tent training..."

"So? Tell!"

"Nobodoi. A soul-stone..."

"Yes?"

"The remains of a Nobodoi..."

"Is it?"

"We think. We assume."

"Better. More! Precision, backman!"

"Hollis," Bo offered. The single arm waved him silent.

"When the Nobodoi vanished overnight..."

"Good. When?"

"284 AW."

"AW! Say it, dammit! Say it!"

"284 After Wormwood."

"Yes. Always say it. Never forget it. Go on!"

"All that was left. Soul-stones."

"Yes. Ever seen inside one?"

"No, sir. Only told."

Bo smiled. The boy learned quickly.

"Watch!" Aspen Dirk turned to the bench, lifted a tatting hammer, struck the globe hard. It broke apart, shattered, pieces flying everywhere. A bitter smell filled the room. The dry leathery kernel sat shrivelled amid the powdery remains and gave off its evil stench.

"A Nobodoi corpse, you think?" Dirk demanded.

"No, sir," Hollis answered at once. "Just what's left when a Nobodoi has gone."

"Gone?"

"Been Recalled. The part that can't translate."

"Excellent, Hollis. Oh yes, Bo. He'll do. A veritable prince of backmen. A scholar, and the best of them: self-instructing. The one good thing the Cohabitation's done—made us natural scholars. You're one to protect, m'lad. We'll be sure to bring you back, eh, Bo?"

Boford Hess gave his own great smile. "Payment has to be mentioned, Dirk."

"Payment?" The boggler rounded on his colleague, yet spoke to the young man. "Hollis, what do you want most?"

"Knowledge, sir. Information."

"See, Bo! Got a world to learn." He turned back to Hollis. "I'll upgrade that dag of yours with information about the Bridge Races that'll make your head spin. And the Lesser Races. Tessa, Cire, Satlin, Amazi, all the ones we know. I'll buy you all the RNA cocktails and empathee-totes you could want."

The boy's eyes were wide with excitement, Bo saw, flashing brightly at Dirk's words. Incredible. It genuinely was what this new print wanted.

"When, sir?"

"Well now. When you've done a stint, I think. Carried me round a bit. Earned your spurs."

"Spurs?"

"Feed him, Bo. Give him a place to sleep. Log his parameters. Set him up for personal tech. We leave on the third of Sellena."

"Four days?" Bo said, wondering.

"So? Teach him weapons. Show him the shop. The hot rooms. Keep him keen. We're crossing half the planet to learn something new about our absentee landlords. That's more than soul-stones, boy; that's the Nobodies in all their scheming, buggering awfulness. You with me?" He looked at his tall assistant. "We need luck and skill and good boggling, Bo."

And whistling an old Celtic air, the boruk left the workroom and the stink of shattered stone.

"Is what he said true?" Hollis asked the highwayman. "Are we going to find out something new about the Nobodoi?"

"I can lie, Hollis. You'll learn to. He's a boggler. He can't afford the luxury."

"I don't understand."

"And that's your first lie."

2

It had been a crazy, frantic first meeting, Hollis decided, but nothing about the Dirk-Hess alliance was slipshod. In everything they did there was the easy informality of years, the simplicity of routines that worked.

The next morning at 0800, after a shower, a run around the adjacent streets, another shower and breakfast, Bo took him through the Infinite House, showing him door after door of locked boggle-rooms and the unchanging watch-screens.

Hollis saw the boggles in their stasis cradles: spheres, cones, dodecahedrons, blocks of hockiron, peterkill and dove-eye, precious ingots of jazerant, metres of curtain-wire and woven goldwire constructs that never let the eye rest. He wondered at dead-black solids in the 'hot' rooms; fox-mitres coruscating with rainbow heat; amblate man-shapes with solitary gemstone eyes, staggering in endless circles; interleaved surfaces of the rare off-planet ore, practy, whose patinae changed even as he watched; complete closed-system Jannis engines glossy with their own mysterious secretions. Incredibly, terrifying to see standing there, there was even a Nobodoi were-suit complete with its mobile Companion unit and hovering Snake. The suit looked fully sealed. Hollis thought of the shattered soul-stone on Dirk's work-bench and wondered if this golden featureless talos still contained the chalk-white remains of its vanished owner or if it had been brought here empty. Unopened, how could you tell?

"Don't worry, it's not real," Bo said. "From before my time. A replica of the Blue Beach suit. Dirk duplicated it to hold the sancher. Hardest energy net he ever stole. All the better bogglers have sancher experiments going. He may tell you about it."

Quarterdoor by quarterdoor, gallery by gallery, Hollis saw the leavings of the great Invasion—the things taken out of the Carnivals, unearthed in the Impact territories, stolen from museums and private collections, gathered together because worried owners found DNA changes beginning, or strange dreams invading their waking lives, or incomprehensible appetites forming.

"We're trying to counter the souvenir-hunter mentality, Hollis," Bo told him as they walked. "Fakes make us waste so much time, and Dirk is doing us all a service. Most of the bogglers are, even the greedy ones. The Nobodoi wanted a patchwork Earth, yet by bringing in literally dozens of congruent races..."

"I'm learning them," Hollis said, interrupting, eyes on the watch-screens, studying the contents of the boggle-rooms they passed.

Bo couldn't take offence. "Yes? Good. You know they themselves are incomprehensible to us, yes?"

Hollis nodded, so much like an eager child. "That's why the Bridge Races. The main three."

"That's it, good. They're the ones turning up this stuff you see." And something occurred to Bo, something really very simple which charmed him and pleased him. "Those dag tracks are put out by Human scholars, Human retrieval agencies. Lots of conflation and salting. Vetted material. You want to ask me questions instead of Dirk, Hollis, you can ask."

"Thanks. Sometimes I need to go slow. Pull in, you know? We'll have time on the road?"

"We'll have time. And I think you'll find"—he laughed, feeling stupid and clever to be making the old joke again with someone who could smile at the wordplay—"that Dirk will be on your back in more ways than one."

"Not to worry, Bo. I suspect he's only half the man he used to be."

"And that, dear short-lived Hollis, is the one comment you will never make again. Clear?"

"Other backmen made it?" Hollis asked.

"Aye. Not one missed. That's the real reason you're here today."

It was ten whole seconds before Hollis laughed.

3

On 3 Sellena, on a perfect spring morning like any the pre-Wormwood Earth might have known, their small party set out. Dirk's shop—an Infinite House closed up inside its maze of quarterdoors—was set on Protect. Nothing this side of Hoproi war-tech could touch it; using that would activate Darzie hot-glass energy sequences that would leave nothing inside intact.

Dirk, Bo and Hollis rode by closed hire-car to the Ballio district, took the Old Rail—again closed transit—out as far as the city's tech allowances permitted. For all his status, Aspen Dirk could not get them air-travel without a trade-off of some kind. Boggles for easy miles. On principle, he wouldn't do it.

"It's better we're seen," Dirk said from his place on Hollis's shoulders when they'd left the Rail at Bans-Corfeo and were on foot at last, Dirk settled in his comfortable old travel-harness. "It's good other Humans know we're about on business. Say why, Hollis."

Hollis smiled, glad to be in sunlight, thrilled to be stepping out so easily. The boruk weighed so little, just the mass of his visible parts.

"Builds morale. Boggling brings us all to one level. Humans are as good—"

"Better. Statistically better. Significantly so."

"—than the Bridge Races."

"Than any races, Bridge or Lesser. At least that we know of. And yes, it's where Humans can make a mark. Good."

Bo strode along to their left, grinning at Hollis's predicament. He loved being on the road too, loved it when Dirk was happy and talking this way. Hollis was good value, so interested, so new.

Hollis saw the big man smile and felt happier than he could remember, his life ordered at last. Bo moved so easily, powerful body wearing that most splendid of Nobodoi artifacts, a sancher— admittedly a debased one, a 'battle-net' downgraded to a confile. Bo had the jewelled net over his chameleons, the grid sparking and shimmering with its inexplicable energies on the now neutral grey of his fatigues. Only a true sancher net could take him, that or Bridge Race tech. In the world of Humans and Lesser Races he was a god, impervious to all energy and powered weapons, to a lot of what blades could do.

On his back, Bo carried their provisions and elaborate medkit. He wore three jerrykins, one long-bladed like a PW Japanese taschi—his Great Sword—one short, and one powered bodysword. All Code issue, all approved for Human use. At his belt were two stars, one a hundred-cycle choi weapon, the other a Darzie copy with a hot-glass option. That had cost Dirk a very special boggle from his collection in trade.

Hollis had it much easier. As well as the boruk in his special harness, the chameleons and his own combat boots, he wore only his dag, clipped on his belt now next to a forty-cycle star and a short-bladed jerrykin. "When Dirk's aboard," Bo had said, and it made good sense, "I do the fighting. You do the running."

When Morion was a tiny crust on the horizon, glittering white against the sparkling sea, the leys began—the xenoforming concessions that went up by increments and intensities, tailored to one race or another.

The Earth was girded with stasis-folds, gridded and isobarred with corridor leys and interfaces, locks and aegis points. Where they walked now was Bridge Race/Human neutral—Hoproi, Matta and Darzie could accept these indigenous tolerances easily enough; that is why they were custodians for the Nobodoi here and not some other combination of tributary peoples. Twenty miles away, beyond the hills Hollis could see to the south-west, only the resilient Hoproi could survive for long, or those several heavy-planet support races they had been allowed to bring in with them.

Hollis noticed dull orange-brown fibriles in the grass like headless flowers; smelled their flat brassy scent: Nobodoi tech, organic assists for building a ley somewhere in the west. They were fun now, exotic, hint of a major xeno rift, but soon they would be something else, calibrating seize fields, forming an enclave or a biased corridor.

Hollis knew much of it by heart, had made it part of the junk-think all clones worked at perfecting immediately after being temporised: a defence against the mentalist races. A Darzie mind-rider would get the lot, complete with dag-maps and enhancements, but hopefully little more than that, nothing Hollis didn't want known. Seeing the fibriles thickening to his right made him run the whole thing, partly for the pleasure of remembering but mainly for the inexpressible joy of anchoring the theory to the reality at last. He even recalled the maps in detail, one after the other, and was tracing the major leys away from Morion when Dirk's voice brought him back.

"The French names, Hollis?" the boruk said, interrupting as he had many times since they'd left the Old Rail for the leys road, lightly slapping his backman on the shoulder with his single precious hand.

"French?" Hollis echoed, and went immediately for his dag, brought the extensor to his right ear, heard what the dump gave. He shook his head.

"Nothing. Just an old country, an old language. French names for the five major spaceports..."

"Trade ports."

"Trade ports, yes. Morion, Sojourn, Nonchalance, Dayasse and Brogue. That's all."

"All right," Dirk said, dwarf schoolmaster, smirking bundle high in the breeze. "The Hoproi liked the Old French tongue. Part of their own name—*roi*—meant 'king'. They liked that. They gave the names. Call up the Bridge Races. Set: Record."

And Bo flashed a sideways glance. He sensed their mission would soon be explained, out in the leys, away from recon tech, safe in his confile's field.

Hollis made the adjustments. Dirk looked off into the distances, collecting his thoughts.

"Because I'm boruk and boggler, everyone expects me to know more about the Nobodoi than anyone else—why they came here, why they masked our world from transmissions and life-signals of the other stellar civilisations for so long, why they disappeared overnight. Even why they did what they did to our world; most importantly, if they could see through time as many believe; if they truly perceived their own Recall. If they'll Return. Even you expect it, Hollis; sometimes even you, Bo. Don't say anything, it's perfectly reasonable. Before I was groomed as a boggler, I did too. You see me do what I do and it's easy to let yourself believe I know more. I sometimes believe it myself. The world seems so ordinary, so simply... there. We just slip into the habit. All my replies, serious, flippant, made from irritation, are seized on and published. Out here I'm alone. You understand?"

"Yes," Hollis said. Bo didn't answer. The ley fibriles were flourishing, thickening, on the western side of the road; an enclave was definitely forming somewhere close by. Soon they'd see tech signs as well and feel the frissons from pressure variances inside the great planet-binding topology fields.

"You mind this, boy?" Dirk asked.

"I love it, sir. Please."

"Prince of backmen!" The hand slapped him lightly, fondly. "I now give you what you believe you already know because I want you biased, like these leys."

"Biased?" Hollis asked, wondering what he meant. He was still coming to grips with the idea of the Nobodoi seeing through time.

"Listen. I'll tell you what is true. Three hundred years ago, give or take, the Nobodies took over our planet—a truly single-race planet, then if you can imagine it. I can't. Invisible to us, alien in the extreme by all accounts, though we argue that with the fact of

— 27 —

our very involvement in their plans. Can't be too different. They brought down Wormwood, controlled antimatter, we believe—neutron-star stuff or whatever—levelled Old Australia to form the Impact territories, started rebuilding the world to accommodate the needs of support races. Colonising or rewarding, Hollis, who can say? Some say punishing. Don't care what your dag says, no one knows for certain. Remember that."

Hollis felt his heart pounding. This was what he wanted, someone to give him an overview he could trust, not the potted dag summaries. He glanced down once to make sure his dag was on Record then strained to listen, not wanting to miss a word.

"First twenty years, all dealings were carried out through the Bridge Races—Hoproi and Matta at first, later the Darzie, probably subject races to the Nobodoi for centuries, possibly millennia. The Hoproi were brought in as warriors; you will have seen some in Morion—elephantine, splendid, relentless. Get a Hoproi for a friend, you've got an enemy for life. The Matta came in as engineers and xenoformers on all the major gaeaframe and hockiron projects, later as educators.

"This is the point. This is the bias I want to see you with, Hollis, and no apology. Between them they suppressed existing technologies, all existing national boundaries, disrupted information flow, encouraged regionalism everywhere, began the xenoforming: the hockiron land-bridges, the great irrigation and reclamation projects, the whole patchwork. Try and get a pre-Wormwood map sometime and see how it looked. Hollis, you'll be amazed. It was so... simple. At the same time, they implemented the tech embargo we call the Code, fostered the feudalistic warlord communities you'll learn about if you haven't already, the Neolithic and Chalcolithic farm cultures. Kept us all busy in other words. But here is what matters. We've tech'd and toted up to being cosmopolitans again, Hollis. We're almost back there. And they've let us. I ask why. Travel a hundred miles in those days, the Human societies were trapped in ley folds, locked away in topology boxes. The Human language was lost in dialects..."

"Then Antique—" Hollis said.

"Has really only existed since the Recall, yes. We didn't even have a planetary language before then, just a polyglot nightmare. The patchwork is what they wanted and what they made. It's a wonder enough of us survived."

"Everyone's been telling me the Nobodoi can't have been too alien, otherwise there would be no points of congruency. With Hoproi, Matta, any of us."

"What does your dag say?"

"What you said before. Totally inscrutable."

"Been to any Carnivals?"

"No chance yet. I'm widening the circle whenever I can."

"Someday we'll detour to one. Show you what the Nobodoi liked to build, whatever those complexes really are. They're hard to boggle. You know about the Link though? You only have to consider that."

"It's like a Carnival in the sea."

"It's where we're going now."

"The Link! Really?" Hollis was amazed, delighted; this was more than he dreamed possible. The boggler, all of them, going to the Link. *The* Carnival, people had told him. A functioning, *visibly* functioning, Nobodoi machine.

Bo grunted, showing he'd known it would be something like that.

Hollis grinned, glad the boruk couldn't see. He'd already spotted Dirk as being the showman, forever unveiling schemes and mysteries, yet here was Bo knowing better than to ask. It had to irk the boggler, this calm acceptance, this almost perverse patience on Bo's part, yet Hollis found himself appreciating the mischievousness behind it. Dirk was the one inured to marvels, the one with the wonderful knowledge, used to pulling the strings. This was how Bo got his own back.

"A lot of Humans serve the Races, Hollis," Dirk said. "I want you Human-biased. I want you working for *this* race, you hear?"

"Aye."

"Don't change. Don't give up."

"I'll try not to."

"Best I can ask. You got dag on were-suits?"

"Yes, why?" Hollis felt his heartbeat quickening.

"Seen one?"

"Never." There was a tightening in his throat, a mounting thrill of anticipation. First the Link. Now this. "We going to?"

"Bo, stop here," Dirk said. "Hollis, move to the side of the road. Whatever you do, make no sudden movements till I say."

Hollis did as Dirk requested. The three of them waited by the roadside, watching the gentle rise of the hill before them, the wide rolling landscape that stretched away to either side, feeling the strange breeze that blew through the grass, blew the brassy, ozone-laden tang of ley-tech at them.

"Soon," Dirk said. "The pressure is steady. You got dag on the name? Were-suits?"

Hollis had his extensor ready but didn't need it.

"Man-suit," he said. "From the Anglo-Saxon *were* or *wer* for 'man'."

"Not 'were' as in past tense of 'to be'? What the Nobodoi were before the Recall?"

"I hadn't thought of that. Is that the origin?"

"Don't believe so. But it used to be on the dags. So tell me what you've learned—No, wait! It's coming. Any moment. Look!"

And there it was, at the crest of the hill, like any Human strolling down any road: the classic Nobodoi artifact.

Dirk's hand came down gently on Hollis's shoulder.

"We stand still. We do not move. We let it pass."

Hollis felt a rush of panic. His voice came in a broken whisper. "Here to stop us, you think?"

"No, just doing its circuit. Walking on forever, observing, doing whatever it does. The Nobodoi inside has been Recalled, you understand? There's only a stone in there. Anyway, we'll see. It's nowhere near at full power, but intact. It knows we're here. Another time I might try for the sancher, but not today. See what happens."

They stood quietly as the three machines came closer. Unlike the replica in Dirk's collection, this suit was off-white rather than bronze-coloured, with none of the usual hockiron sheen, its 'head' completely featureless, the whole thing Human-shaped only in the broadest possible sense. (Dag-lore said ancient observers had christened them everything from 'talos suits' to 'King Tuts'— they did have the smooth, minimalist mummiform look—and, cryptically, 'First Russian Dolls', whatever that meant. It amazed Hollis sometimes the terms used by pre-Wormwood Humans.)

It walked with an elusive, infuriatingly eye-catching motion, now fluid, now jerky the moment you concentrated on just the act of walking and not the whole triune. It was as if the air shimmered, and in the shimmer you imagined legs stepping out.

To its left rolled the Companion, a two-metre tall ovoid defensor column moving on its four-ball platform, that like the suit never toppled no matter what terrain was covered. At the top of the smooth column was angled a large featureless dish.

A pharaoh was taking his portable radio telescope for a walk.

And had picked up a pet along the way.

Less than a metre above the suit's right shoulder, bonded to the whole by a mazework of unseen energy fields Hollis had read about, floated the shiny flattened horse-skull shape of the Snake, smooth, featureless as well, capable of darting forth, ranging far and wide, to reconnoitre, to kill. Now it hovered, now it kept obediently in the familiar triptych configuration Hollis saw in his dag displays, that had startled him in Dirk's boggle room: his Blue Beach replica.

Around the tripartite form were the ghostworks, the flickering, half-seen firefly glints that went with most things Nobodoi when a soul-stone was involved. Hollis blinked at them, as if to clear his vision, only to find himself caught in the roiling heat-shimmer walk of seen-unseen legs as the suit moved past them and continued on down the road towards Morion.

"Years ago," Dirk said, leaning close to Hollis's ear, "before the Recall, a triune like this could have struck ships from space, dug earthworks on the Moon from where we stand. Now they simply roam about, follow the leys. Now we raid them if we dare, break them open if we can, steal their sanchers if we're lucky. Spill out the stones, topple the Companions, make the Snakes fall. This is when I allow for the time sense and tell myself the Nobodoi saw it all. That it's all right. Reasonable curiosity. Allowable insolence."

"Can we try it... now?" The thought had Hollis tense with fascination and dread.

"Not this time. There'll be others. We've got work to do."

4

Apart from the were-suits themselves and structures like the Link and the Stone Ships, Hollis knew that the Devil's Coach was probably the best-known of all the boggles, and often the one cited as the most popular example of the boggle phenomenon.

To look at, it was a large tumbleweed set at the centre of a shifting, twinkling dust-cloud. It was possible to enter that shimmering cloud, climb inside the large filigree ball while it idled, then, when the thing suddenly engaged, go skimming across the landscape, covering dozens, hundreds, thousands of miles before the Coach finally stopped again, formed its door, and allowed any passengers to alight.

The risk involved was very real. Some of the things were long-haulers, not stopping for weeks or months at a time. One sometimes found them idling with desiccated corpses resting in their woven compartments. Hence the sobriquet, the thrill of trepidation, the prickling of the neck hairs when one considered entering a Coach at one of the idling fields where they converged and waited.

Often there were spectators at the idlings, usually Human but sometimes Satlin or Cire, watching the arrivals and departures, studying prospective passengers as they selected their Coach, entered the accretion field and clambered aboard, settling down to wait the minutes or hours, sometimes days, however long it took, till the door formed and the Coach went off on its travels. The Coaches' motive fields caused dehydration; these onlookers earned money topping up the canteens of travellers reluctant to leave their chosen vehicles in case they moved off without them.

There were five such water vets at Blackstone Field, and they chattered in excitement when they saw the trio approach.

"Ignore them!" Dirk told Hollis. "Answer no questions."

One of the vets hurried off and soon returned with at least a dozen others, all Human, many carrying luggage.

"These are passengers," Dirk said. "They will watch to see which Coaches I do not choose, so they can avoid them as well. Later the vets will sell this knowledge to others who come."

Some of the vets and passengers were calling now, offering fees for a safe selection. A few became bolder and moved tentatively forward. Bo did no more than rest a hand on one of his stars, the vets and would-be travellers moved back.

Hollis went to speak. Dirk's hand gripped his shoulder.

"Not cruel, lad. If my auguring went wrong and one of them died, I'd be discredited and reviled. I don't need reprisal contracts. Better they curse me and keep their lives. What's the Christ-line? There are too many of you!"

Bo and Hollis, with Dirk aloft, walked to the cluster of shifting, idling Coaches, listening to the crackle and hiss of overlapping fields as the thirty or more artifacts 'conferred' together, whatever it was they did. Sometimes, mysteriously, they borrowed field-force; sometimes a Coach was robbed of its mantle altogether and left to rot and fragment, so much abandoned wicker quickly decomposing without the sustaining energies that gave it its form.

The trio moved down the eastern side of the shape with the crowd of spectators ten metres distant, paralleling their route, keeping well clear but talking excitedly among themselves, some making marks on charts. Occasionally Dirk would point to a particular Coach and call out "No!" so the crowd would hear. Invariably someone would call "Thank you, milord!" and there would be more animated chatter.

After three such calls, Dirk said "This one."

Hollis felt another quiet thrill. Apart from Dirk's anticipation of the were-suit, this was his first experience of the boruk's talent. He himself had noticed no perceptible differences; it was just one more large filigree tangle hovering in its accretion field, rocking slightly from the nudging of communing Coaches. But he had no time to make a further study himself; they were inside the field and climbing aboard. Hollis bent down so Dirk could swing out of the harness using his single arm, then entered the wicker chamber too and found himself a comfortable spot where the intricately interwoven branches came together. The para-organic artifact settled under their weight; the motes of light-borne dust became more agitated, rushing about the filigree core. Some of the other Coaches drew back as if protecting their fields.

When Dirk, Hollis and Bo had secured themselves and their gear with the elasticised straps Bo passed out, Dirk leant over to the door opening and called to the envious onlookers.

"Avoid that and that one!" he cried, straining forward in his straps, pointing with his arm. "That one's good for north-east and a thousand k's."

The crowd cheered; Dirk settled back out of their sight.

"Not long now," he said. "Remember, Hollis, we dehydrate quickly in these things. Drink lots of water."

A few minutes later, the door narrowed—a mixture of wicker strands moving closer and the accretion field thickening—and the Coach began to move away from the others, gaining speed, the field buzzing and crackling angrily, finally settling to a steady hum.

Within minutes, Blackstone Field was gone from sight, and they were racing across the sunny landscape.

Hollis got used to seeing the roads and fields and changing ley composites through a gold-flecked curtain; it was like being on a dusty road, only the dust was flashing with quartz and mica. He got used to sipping from his canteen, to drowsing in his straps, to having Dirk rouse him with precious words.

"Somewhere in Morion," the boruk said, an hour on their way. "In the Matta and Hoproi centres, there are maps that show how these Coaches move, the leys they follow, the domains they cross, which ones they avoid. One such map would give us our own world again, bogglers believe, guide us through the Carnivals and harvester fields, the fossae and demon-leys, the sentinel-leys, all of it."

"You've seen these maps?" Hollis asked, marvelling.

Bo smiled. Dirk gestured with his hand.

"No, Hollis. No. We speculate. A phrase I do not say lightly: it stands to reason. The Hoproi, Matta and Darzie aided the Nobodoi, had to negotiate the patchwork, move among what they built, amid the leys and enclaves. Of course there are maps. It may be coded behind their eyes as tote-nets and RNA protocols, but those Races are well mapped, let me tell you. It's the Human who remains—"

"Nobody's Fool."

"Ah yes, Hollis. That. Just what we are. 'Motley's the only wear!' Though fools have always been able to do what others can't."

Hollis leant forward against his waist strap, hands on his knees. "But the Bridge Races are deprived too. You said before that Humans have the ability—"

"Which is possibly why the Nobodoi want Humanity in their plan. We bring something to it they need, some small important something. As you say, the Bridge Races are deprived too, contained, regulated, though it does not appear so. They are so favoured compared to us. Our mission relates to this."

"You think—"

"Hollis," Bo said, gently but firmly. "Let Dirk tell us our mission."

The print settled back, nodding.

Aspen Dirk smiled. Oh, this backman's enthusiasm, this desire to keep at it. Dirk loved it more than he could say, than he would let himself say. He had lost too many backmen, more than two hundred over his fourteen post-boruk years of professional boggling. Bo was right, but he mustn't dampen the lad's spirits.

"I always allow that these Coaches are monitored, open to Nobodoi tech and so to the Races. But I *sense* otherwise—I feel the accretion field makes us safe. Morion is a com well, heavy-tech'd, all the cities are. We are safe in the wicker. Now I tell you. In the sea off Broome—"

"That's in the Impact!" Hollis cried, unable to help himself. The excitement was just too much.

"—stands the Link. Go on, Hollis."

Again the print leant forward, but calmer now, controlling himself.

"The great construction of shifting rods in the shallows off Broome, a tower of moving struts." He was reciting dag-lore but not wanting to use his dag—all part of his junk-think, as with the leys material.

"Yes?"

"Considered the epitome of Nobody whimsy. Only one function—"

"Apparent," Dirk corrected.

"Apparent function. To keep aloft the large silver ball on a jet of sea-water, sometimes pass it from one jet to another as the taller rods shift."

"Yes?" Dirk asked for the pleasure of hearing the lad speak.

"Tallest rods: 134 metres above sea-level. Ball diameter: six metres, apparently solid. Arc of rotation from structural centre, through a radius of fourteen metres."

"Good. Sociology then. Anything?"

"Usual pattern around the Carnivals. Broome flourishes as a tourist town because of it. Locals—Human locals—pitch it as a piece of Nobody art, a huge wave-driven mobile."

"Scientific conclusions? Any?"

Hollis shrugged. "Leys control. A marine regulator for the Stone Ships. I don't have much. Just that it's a classic... one of the classic boggles."

Dirk nodded at the dag unit. "You've got a tour-guide in that thing. We're going to Broome. Eight days ago, the certainty came to me that the Link could be boggled at last. I know, Bo, crazy, but that's what I got. Something occurring in Broome, or about to occur, will furnish the answer."

"A boggled Link," Bo said. He was frowning, an uncommon show of emotion for Bo.

"Aye," Dirk said. "Something of great importance, I'd say. My main rival in this business, Hollis, is already there, my contact tells me. Rock Tuo arrived last week—with Hoproi backing."

"Yet you waited?" Hollis said, noting yet again how Bo rarely asked such questions, just seemed to accept.

"Correct," Dirk told him. "It felt right to wait, to go now. It has to be like this."

Hollis nodded. "You're hostile competitors then?"

Dirk normally guarded his one hand like some precious familiar. Now he struck the wicker with its flat palm. "Tuo and me? Yes indeed. The Hoproi would encourage it anyway, but ideologically, Hollis, I work for Humanity, play Nobody's Fool gladly, yes, but for that single reason—to gain respect for Humans, status, publicity, so we win back as much of our birthright as we can, so we're not taken for a Lesser Race attending the three. We own this world. *We* are the race made specifically for it."

"Not all Humans are like that."

"Right. Tuo boggles for the Hoproi and the Matta, sometimes the Lesser Races—a true mercenary, a quisling. I'm betting Tuo is on a Hoproi commission."

Hollis repeated his earlier comment. "Yet you waited."

"Aye. The feeling, as I say. And Hoproi means tech support. I play cautious. Can't risk a gentleman like Bo. Can't go risking my wonderful Renaissance backman."

"Your what?"

"Later, Hollis," Dirk said, grinning as Bo was. "We've got a long way to go. Bo will rest now. You look at the leys and think of four really good questions for me. And remember, drink often. Toilet in the dump-bags pointing the way we've come. You piss through the wicker and we'll reach the Impact as El Dorados."

"As what?"

"Four questions, Hollis, for my pleasure. None about the Link. Not yet. I can't answer one, you get another four. Squander them and I may hold things back. Keep you sharp!"

The old lands of Europe, the old nameless lands, changed and xenoformed, flashed by. The Devil's Coach ruled it all—now speeding at 200 k's, now dropping to 40 or 20, making calls at scattered idlings, sometimes stopping and forming its door, sometimes not, rushing on, leaving envious watchers behind. There were times when it navigated intricate routes through landscapes that seemed ordinary enough, generous and benign; at other times it shuttled through major ley-folds, fossae and quel-densities, skirting enclaves for races that could never have survived on such a world unassisted, that now abided in their bastions of strangeness as what? As test cases perhaps, trained observers, peoples being rewarded or punished, who could say?—all part of the plan, the mighty patchwork.

Sometimes there was darkness, what might have been night, what might have simply been storm shadow or some inexplicable darkening of the accretion field.

Hollis consulted his dag at every major shift, got next to nothing, and so watched the road surface, field surface, desert surface, river surface through the wicker-weave walls and floor, wondering what the accretion field might be doing to his metabolism, his DNA, his Humanity.

Bo slept on, untroubled by such things, his big form tucked up on a makeshift shelf, a Coach veteran able to fit these amazing transitions into some sort of mundane order.

Dirk seemed to be sleeping too, a pitiful scarecrow dwarf form made bearable—given the semblance of being whole—by the loose garments he wore. But just when Hollis thought he might try to nap too, the small grey eyes opened and the boruk asked "Well?"

"Disparate gravities," Hollis said immediately. "How can that be? It would crack the world."

"Wasted question," Dirk said. "Your dag has it."

"I don't like using it in front of you."

"I know. I understand. Nobody tech. The same they used to bring down Wormwood, create the Impact and sculpt the Earth. The Nobodoi ships—call them ships—the *straits*—are buried across the planet, landlocked, field-protected, bonded to the planet forever, growing into it, can you believe that? Using jazerant to interface and extend. They create the stasis chains which in turn allow the leys."

"The scale of it."

"Aye. Impossibly vast. Gaea totally re-made, the intricacies, the fine-tuning of tolerances. Think of the balances. The leys are not just pressure corridors, Hollis, and not just gravity biases either. A world's evolutionary products are tuned to its unique planetary field. Such things are simulated here for many different worlds. It's infinitely complex."

"The Carnivals are like the life-boats then? Concentrations of Nobody tech serving the straits?"

Dirk grinned, pleased. "Yes, the life-boats of those great antimatter-handling craft. Still, you wasted a question."

"All right. Evidence of Nobodoi regard for Humans; that we are more than just a Lesser Race."

Dirk frowned, grinned again. "Much better. A number of things. Diminishing ley activity around Human centres in the last hundred years. Removal of causation ditches; downgrading of stasis points and aegis points; permission for Humans to travel, to enter the Darzie and Matt civil services, even fill some off-planet postings, to play a part in our own education..."

"All part of routine assimilation, surely. Of course we would be given certain key roles on the world native to us."

Dirk watched the print calmly. "Some Lesser Races moved off-world altogether..."

"Only practical. Next phase of the strategy. The planet is fully subjugated; move out unnecessary forces."

"Or alien viewpoints no longer needed," Dirk said. "Very well. The bringing in of race-enhancing species like the Amazi and the Satlin."

Hollis went for his dag, wanting race lexicon, again stopped himself. He had used it constantly, habitually, before Bo had found him; now he hated going to it all the time. Dirk was encyclopedia enough.

"I don't know those peoples," he said. "But it sounds like pastoral care, ministering to the morale and psych needs of a subject race. Again, good policy."

Dirk smiled at the young man's earnestness. "Only Humans are bogglers!"

That made Hollis stop. He noticed Bo was awake then, that the highwayman's eyes were watching him. Dirk had been aware of it;

he included both of them in his answer, his voice quite different, soft and intense, as he continued.

"The Nobodoi see through time. I *know* it." He hesitated a moment. "Rock Tuo knows it too, other bogglers. The Nobodoi are grooming a race which can intuit them. Not destroyed them, not just culled them, not just assimilated them. The Bridge Races are worried by it; Tuo has a Hoproi sponsor, Big George himself. I was contacted by a Darzie light-commander and two Matt high solitaries, by Hoproi who pleaded and threatened."

"Pleaded?"

"Oh yes, Hollis. They do not lose face as we do. They whine and wheedle and offer all sorts of gifts. They bluster and make it all seem fun. If the Nobodies see through time, they know what Earth becomes, why they were Recalled, whatever that is. If they see through time there is nothing any of us can do that isn't already known—unless some Humans, bogglers, are outside the prescient whole. We go to Broome because there is an urgent disclosure about the Nobodoi to be made—from that classic boggle. We only need confirmation of the time-sense, because Humans saw it first! Will that answer your question?"

"Yes."

They were quiet in the compartment then, mainly because the Coach was sweeping onto the land-bridge at last, a great bone-white hockiron lattice laid upon the ocean. Hollis was out of his straps, moving from one interstice to another, trying to get the best view possible.

Their strand took them into the south-east, the Coach reaching velocities of 400 k's along the grid. Beneath them the Old Indian heaved its whitecaps, threw up shifting ranges of dark blue water, the greater swells breaking on the lattice arches.

Hollis sat pressed up against the compartment door, wishing now that it hadn't narrowed and filigreed and dusted over when the boggle wasn't idling. This was true ocean he saw through the dusting of the field, a vastness of water miles deep in which the continents, original and cultured, Earth-stuff and chemically inert hockiron foundings, stood like high dry table-tops.

It was a difficult, awe-inspiring concept; he might never get used to it. Hollis studied the Nobodoi grid, the now gleaming, now dull, now foam-washed xenotech, bone-like and mighty; was sure he could smell the brine and feel the wind through the field, carried to him by the same osmosis that gave them air to breathe.

"This is not a transportation system," he suddenly said, sure of it.

He had his back to the others; he did not see Bo's brows go up when he glanced at Dirk, did not see the boruk's hand open out like a reverential flower as if to caress him with honest affection.

"No?" Dirk said. "What then?" The words were so quietly said.

Hollis shrugged. "Communications. We're part of a message. Or maybe we're ferrying enzymes and volatiles across the net, spores and pollens, building something. Dismantling leys, re-aligning them. It could be possible. The Coaches might do it, like shuttles weaving change. Helping make the changes."

Bo laughed, slapped his thighs.

Dirk was grinning when Hollis turned, with a sudden telltale glitter in his eyes.

"Dirk, what?"

"Hollis, listen. For ten, eleven years, Bo has been my only trustworthy friend, my sole confidant. Now I get me a clogue, a print, a rogue identikin who right before my eyes begins to read the world anew. On his first land-bridge, he stops being wide-eyed tourist, cowering parochial. He translates. Right or wrong he keeps at it. Bless you, Hollis Green."

"But—"

"Don't stop! Give me whatever you get. But now it's callisthenics. Bo, exercises! Rock Tuo will try to kill us for certain. Big George must have his fun. We've got to be ready."

They were at 600 k's an hour in their inertia-free transport when Old Australia loomed ahead, a low crust against the horizon, the hockiron lines converging there, emerging from the ocean like vast white conduits, the very bones of the world, merging again with the old red land.

"The Impact," Dirk said. "Fewer leys but more severe, larger demarcations. Out there is where Wormwood came down."

"Wenna," Hollis said, watching the ancient land come at them. "The Nobodoi city. What is it like?"

"To call it that," Dirk said. "Think of a spaceport that can take antimatter straits, think of creatures setting up house in the

Carnivals and you'll have some idea of how strange it is. We will not go to Wenna."

"Humans do."

"They do. They surely do. And not just the Aviators. The Bridge Races let many Humans go there now, I'm happy to say. But the air is wrong, the feel of the reality. It's a hardship posting. We will stay on the coasts. That is Broome there to the south; you can see the Link—that glint is sunlight on metal or the water-jet. We'll overshoot that. The first idlings are a hundred k's inland."

"These Aviators?" Hollis said, watching the distant flash of light, thinking of the Nobodoi city even further off, a hockiron city, of Humans who would live there, and surprisingly it was Bo who answered, giving a quick, scornful laugh.

"Misguided, Hollis. Locked up in codes of honour. They think flying gliders over the heads of the Bridge Races constitutes revolt, makes a case for Humanity. It's pathetic."

"At least they do it."

Bo shook his head and looked out through the wicker.

"They do it," Dirk said. "But they make themselves, all of us, look foolish, self-important. They try, yes, flying their gliders about. But they're a sad, swaggering lot."

"It would be terrible not to matter, wouldn't it?"

"What?"

"Like the Aviators. It would be terrible for you and Bo and me, other bogglers, to be doing what we're doing and for it not to matter. The plan may be set irrespective of us. We only think we're making a difference. We may be just one more Lesser Race, all safely known."

Which was such an encapsulation of what Dirk feared most in the entire world that he swallowed before he answered, and Bo saw the distress voiced only a few times in their eleven years together.

"Let me know what you read on that, Hollis," Dirk said. "Let me know how it changes. But now, precautions. Be ready."

"A feeling, Dirk?" Bo said from his ledge of wicker.

The boggler nodded. "A strong one. Be ready."

5

It was justified. They were down to 100 k's, no more than ten minutes from the idlings, when a tremendous blow struck the Coach, sent it spinning off course, crackling and weaving, its accretion field shedding motes, losing cohesion, the energies being stripped away.

"Nobodoi weapon!" Bo said, because the boruk was too busy holding on with his single hand to speak. "Single pulse. Has to be to take a Coach!"

"What's that?!" Hollis cried, as the Coach veered and twisted.

Braced against the wicker like a maimed starfish, Dirk answered. "Easy, Hollis, easy! Not Nobodoi. A Nobody weapon. It will be Hoproi."

The Coach had steadied but its field was badly depleted. The filigree ball slowed, rocking and skewing, finally settled, scraping the red earth. The door widened back, just seemed to be there.

"Quickly!" Bo said, and had himself and Dirk free of their straps. He lifted the boruk after him out of the Coach.

Hollis made sure his dag was operating, tossed out his own gear, then passed Bo's larger weapons out to him before scrambling out himself, terrified for the moment that the barrier would re-form and trap him inside.

But the Coach was dying, if that were the term, if it were in truth the lifeform it now seemed with the last of its lights flickering away, leaving it a black, thorny tangle—a forlorn thing in a landscape of red desert that stretched to the horizon in all directions but one. To the north-west there were hills, a low range of deeper red-brown, where the terrain was broken by gullies, outcroppings and old water-courses.

Bo lifted Dirk into the harness with practised ease, barely giving Hollis time to get his bearings.

"Quickly!" he told the backman. "We have to move."

"We were shot down!" Hollis cried. "They'll be waiting!"

"No, Hollis," Dirk said, his voice reassuringly calm. "Not new for us, being grounded. Someone wants us stranded here."

"Who? Why?"

"We'll try to find out. Hurry now."

Hollis set off at once, following the big highwayman towards the rockforms ahead.

"It looks peaceful," he said, hoping Dirk would say more about who had struck at them, but it was Bo who answered.

"Hollis, no time now. This is the Impact and this is a ley, regardless of how innocent it seems. Look!"

He pointed to the east where the morning sun was well above the wide desert. Hollis saw three chalk-white spheres sitting in the blood-red dust.

"Soul-stones!"

"Aye," Bo said. "Relics. No one has collected them. No souvenir-taking. Consider why."

Hollis moved quickly, matching the big man's stride. For several minutes no one spoke as they crossed the open terrain.

"Trouble ahead," Dirk said at last, almost in a whisper.

Bo did not turn. "Yes?"

"Harvester field. You get dag-lore on harvesters, Hollis?"

Hollis murmured quick words into his extensor but Dirk interrupted.

"Forget that now. Precis jazerant."

"One of the new metals," Hollis said, condensing another of his junk-think patterns. "They make it—"

"They? They? Who?"

"Machines. Nobodoi machines."

"Wrong. People say that because Nobody were-suits often include harvester fields in their circuits. No, this is Hoproi tech given Nobodoi refraction fields to make it fun for the Hoproi. There's a field of harvesters ahead."

"Invisible," Hollis said.

"Exactly. Thirty metres beyond those rocks it starts. Soon we'll see looters trying for the jazerant stockpiles."

"But—"

"Come. You'll see."

Within minutes they had reached the broken terrain, stood looking out over a network of shallow gullies and claypan. A well-marked trail followed an old watercourse. It was very quiet; nothing moved in the morning heat but heat-shimmer itself. Again there were soul-stones scattered about; Hollis counted at least five, saw fragments of others. Many Nobodoi had been in this harvester field when the Recall took place all those years ago. It made him wonder what jazerant could be that they had supervised its mining personally, what easement of spirit they might have found in watching the Hoproi tech at work.

"Look!" Dirk said, at his shoulder, single hand pointing. "You can see tracks. These machines are mostly just frames, Hollis. Three to four metres square, on tread systems. They usually move very slowly, can take hours to go a few feet. They draw trace elements into their bonding chambers, make the jazerant there, store it elsewhere in their frame till they're at quota."

"You fear them?" Hollis asked, taking care where he stepped on the uneven surface.

Dirk gave a laugh. "Most are set with spring-loaded blades. Some extend arms to snare victims, pull them within range of guillotines and grinders. Some set up elaborate articulations, use more mundane metals to builds extensions for themselves, trellises and hedgehogs. The more sophisticated make darts and shurikens, fuse lenses and make sun-traps. They have low-grade intelligence; their twin passions—twin programs—are to make jazerant and embellish themselves with armament."

"I haven't learned about them yet," Hollis said. "Just that the first Human observers called them Swiss Knives."

"Now you know why. It's symbiosis. The Nobodoi wanted—want—jazerant, devised the means to make it, gave the brief, allowed for species needs in the implementation. The Hoproi met the requirement in their own terms—they wanted death engines and this is a war-garden. Serves two purposes. We were struck with a Nobodoi weapon used by Hoproi."

"You said were-suits included these fields in their circuits. Could one of those have struck at us?"

"Never in my experience," Dirk said. "That would be one Nobody artifact striking at another. No, I think Hoproi. Since Rock Tuo is associated with Big George, I'm betting it's Big George's war-garden."

Hollis blinked in the morning glare. "I keep thinking I see something out of the corner of my eye."

"Refraction tech. Nobodoi. The machines are invisible to us but stand in plain sight to Hoproi tech vision. What they do with the jazerant now is anybody's guess."

"You said before."

"All right. Speculations. Feed it into the straits. Build an alien superstructure for the Earth. Hockiron armour. Or prisons for antimatter remnants. Bits of Wormwood."

"Perhaps we can't ever go back," Hollis said, watching the quiet shimmering hillsides as he walked, looking across the slopes for some further trace of the invisible engines behind their silent refraction fields. Did he imagine it, or was that a metallic glint at the corner of his vision? Probably sunlight off a quartz outcropping.

"I asked you to tell me when you had something, Hollis," the voice came, calling him back.

"What? Oh, I just think that whatever Humans become, we'll probably never again be able to manage our own world unassisted."

"I often think that too." Dirk kept his voice low, like conscience whispering at his backman's ear. "But we mustn't let that stop us. Learning goes two ways in this. Gaeatech is far more than terraforming. The Nobodoi have done this before but they have never done *this* before."

"You're quoting yourself."

"I am, yes."

"What now?" Bo asked, quiet patient Bo, tactful Bo, to remind them this was a benign ley, and the Impact.

"There are pressures where the machines stand," Dirk told Hollis. "All we need watch for are the plantings where a machine has built itself outworks, fences and trellises. The refraction capability is systemic. Whatever is part of the machine is shielded; we see only what is projected away from the frame. Javelins. Broken sections like there."

His hand pointed to a low-point in the arroyo before them. Hollis saw what did look very much like a dark section of metal fence: several rust-worn uprights joined to a broken-off length of rail.

"The machine had to move on—probably to meet its quota when a spot didn't yield a good enough trace flow. They use fields to draw elements from way down. Sometimes there are obstructions. It sacrificed that—its hobby while it worked the area."

"But Hoproi?" Hollis said.

"Correct. Hoproi tech for a Nobodoi task. All very orthodox. Broome locals will say otherwise, tell you its a Nobody field, push the invisibility angle as proof. Tourist realities are the enemy as always, confusing the issue."

"We can move," Bo said, and Hollis realised that the highwayman had been using his confile to confirm Dirk's estimates. "There."

They continued down into the valley, moving along the wide trail amid old tread-marks, past the nearer soul-stones (no tread marks near them, Hollis noticed), past the ruined length of harvester fence set with nodules, barbed-wire encrustations and some exotic flourishes—harvester exuberance?

Dirk guided them, reading pressures. "There!" he'd say, and "There!", pointing, and Bo would move up to check it with his confile. Only once did they disagree, Dirk insisting on an elaborate detour off the trail, only to admit suddenly that he was wrong. The harvester he sensed had long ago departed, at full quota, leaving behind some jazerant tailings—a rare enough thing and easy pickings for looters or some future machine.

Hollis made himself stay calm, but he kept thinking that the harvesters might have registered their presence, and even now one or more might be converging on where they stood, moving relentlessly towards them, devising intricate strategies as they came.

The thought did not seem to worry Bo. He bent down, picked up a coin-sized fragment of jazerant, passed it to Dirk, who considered it for a moment then passed it down to Hollis.

"Here. The Nobodoi may phase it away later, but if they don't, put it toward your sigil."

Hollis took the precious fragment, held it up to study the blue and mauve roils, clenched it in his fist a moment, then slipped it into his pocket. "Thank you. Both of you."

Several hundred metres on, as they rounded a clutch of towering sandstone rockforms, they saw some looters on the far side of the dried-out water-course, a dozen men and women dressed in chameleon drab moving single-file along the gentle slope, apparently following the tread-path of some unseen machine. All had packs on their backs and carried long tag-poles, testing the ground around them as they went.

Dirk was known to them. The second figure in line waved, the fifth as well. Dirk gave a quick salute in reply. Not a word was said.

It was the silence that got to Hollis more than anything. Here were Humans plundering a war-garden; the Hoproi would be off somewhere monitoring this, watching and wagering, continuing to cull the host-race by pandering to its appetites—its greed, its simple need to win. These Humans came here knowing this.

"This is sad," he said, actually forgetting Dirk for the moment, again thinking to catch the briefest, corner-of-the-eye glint of something on the slopes—the optical trick that marked things Nobodoi. When he tried for it again, the spot was empty, unremarkable in any way.

"No, Hollis. These are people making themselves meaningful to themselves. It's something they let us do. We do it."

But Hollis was still out on the slopes, watching the looters moving in their cautious line. It seemed comical, almost pathetic. All of it futile somehow. Dirk and his pressures; Bo's confile scans; the looters with their secret hand-signs to one another, their poles and their careful prodding, all because of tread prints that looked more heavily impressed, that might mean a near-full jazerant store and not an excess of cunning armament. It was one more tourist reality, all this. Things for the marks while the real doers went about their business of running the world. Just fakes and distractions. Absurdities. The problem of all prints too, Hollis realised, had the sense to realise, moving on again, aware of Bo and Dirk and that the boruk had said something just now. His dag would have it; he'd left it on Record. He'd review it later.

There was a scuffle to the side, a cry. One of the looters had found soft earth, had poled and triggered a planting more intricate than most. Further down their line, part of the slope gave way, a looter slid downslope with a yell, fell kicking and scrambling, wrist and leg-hooks trying for purchase, straight into a harvester's reach.

The man was lifted bodily, whisked to a point eight metres away, three metres off the ground, his form cross-hatched with refraction bars of the concealed frame. There were guillotine sounds, scythe closings; suspended in mid-air the man seemed literally to fall to pieces, limbs and head dropping away, the torso mutilated further before being cast aside. There was a great deal of blood—making a paint-out of parts of the harvester gridwork till cunningly-wrought scrapers and volatiles quickly slid and sprayed and restored full refraction.

It did not end there. An invisible extension must have engaged then, carefully placed, pushing up through the dirt, for another looter screamed, plunged forward, tipped off balance, and tumbled downslope, dog-legging from an unseen fence across to where the machine waited. Again, service extensors went into play with the sound of whirring gears; the latest victim—a woman—was taken aloft, her blood streaked uncannily in swathes across the bright air, smeared along the edges of unseen knives and deadly rollers.

Utter silence followed—the sense of it at least—for the looters were casting about them with their tag-poles for a time, then finally started back the way they had come.

"Do you know what they do with the jazerant they steal?" Dirk asked, but left no time for Hollis to answer. "They might keep it in a private hoard somewhere until, one night, it just disappears, phased away by Nobodoi tech. Hasn't happened to me. Seems I'm allowed to keep the bits I've got. They may even let you keep your piece, seeing you're with me now. What most looters do is sell it back to the Hoproi, since only they really know why the Nobodoi use it—present tense. And maybe the Hoproi just stockpile it against a Nobody Return. Maybe—as you say, Hollis—they feed it into the straits and build a new skeleton for poor old Gaea, new underpinnings for the planet. These death engines may belong to Big George. He was the one who was keen to get me here, did all the talking. It may be his personal war-garden, in which case I'm betting he'll be waiting for us. We should go."

6

Big George was indeed waiting.

As they cleared the ravines and passed through the last of the hills on a graded, unsurfaced road, they saw the Hoproi war-master ahead of them.

It was absurd and unsettling the way the creature just stood alone by the roadside, as if by keeping still enough he would not be seen. Hollis had learned the schematics and data profiles by heart; he had seen about ten Hoproi at safe distances. This was different. This Hoproi was considering him, watching him approach, was here partly because of him. He was in the creature's plans.

And as Bo, Dirk and he came down the road, the size and presence of the creature became frighteningly real. The comical faded; the fear came. This was alien stuff, a being, mind-set, value-system evolved under a different sun, according to vastly different parameters. Now he stood in hot bright sunlight amid this ruined desert terrain and could only be apprehended, explained—neutralised—by what it resembled.

Someone had tried to make an elephant. Hollis couldn't avoid the primer comparisons he'd been given in his rent-tent. Someone had taken four elephant legs and, without the image of the original, had tried to fashion a beast that went with them—and got it splendidly, extraordinarily wrong. The great barrel torso went up three metres from those legs, to end in sensory fibres and a protected eating orifice not presently visible. Two thirds up that great body, at the cardinal compass points, four trunks were coiled like neatly closed springs against what was usually a grey-brown hide. The creature had four solitary eyes, each positioned in the cartilaginous girdle between the trunks. At least two of them studied the Humans now as they approached.

What made it even more absurd and unnerving was that Big George was painted all over—a bright powder red mostly, with blue chevrons and stars, yellow suns and zig-zags, like some escaped circus beast from another age. The trunks themselves were variously orange, light blue, mauve and yellow.

An elephant starfish, Hollis decided. A discarded beach toy.

"Ho, Bo!" the creature boomed in his big jolly voice, more a result of the race mind-set than any modification or conditioning tote. No easy translation tech for Hoproi; they underwent excruciation, endured horrific surgery to let them speak Antique. Such was their commitment to their job on Earth. "Noble choi-boy, join me when Dirk is done, yes? Speaking of. Good morrow, Aspen Dirk. This is a day, what? Hollis Green, print, C-mate, identikin, clogue, man so new, welcome and bless! You have a noble hat. A most eminent hump. Quasimodo-elect to the boruk boggler hisself! Salute!"

Hollis blinked in the heat, matching the bizarre words to the reality. A Hoproi had addressed him.

"Hello, Big George," Dirk said, calmly. "Your garden?"

"Mine?" the Hoproi boomed, his voice echoing amid the hills. "Hah! Good show!"

Which was no answer.

Dirk tried again. "To what do we owe the honour?"

Big George waited, and Hollis realised that the creature waited to see if Bo were going to speak, saw that Bo was carefully presenting himself as a Code contract soldier, as the silent equivalent of one of Big George's own absent, probably concealed choi warriors. All part of the act.

Finally, the creature spoke. "You come to plumb the Link. You and Rock Tuo. You plumb the Nobodoi, you struppy boggle-boys. Work, work, work!"

Hollis had his dag extensor fitted but got nothing for 'struppy'. Hoproi loved words, made up their own patter according to ancient idioms and euphonies.

"You got good bristling Bo, so coy today. You got confile and inclination. Big guns. I tilt at your windmills, fit you all into good plan."

"We got through your garden," Dirk said. "Enough plans for one day, Big George."

"Not that! Not that! Pah!" And the creature moved for the first time. One of the four trunks curled in close against his body shifted a little and the bonding horn peeped out, glinting; the trunk settled again. Somewhere close by, four armed and armoured choi were watching, saw that twitch and understood it.

"Listen good!" Big George said. "Not all Hoproi A-1 good guys like Big George. Uh-uh. Some Hoproi stop you quick smart—no more Dirk, no more Bo, Hollis, finito! Some chapters want Dirk, Bo and good new Hollis at Broome, yessiree! Some want Link solved, yes please. Some chapters shout, whoa! No go! Ka-pow!"

"You want us to boggle the Link? We can trust you, Big George?"

"What? What's that?" Big George boomed. "God's rockets! I fight for you. Big risk. Over there"—and with a crack that had Hollis wide-eyed and taking several steps back, a trunk whipped out and pointed into the north-west—"you find Fancy Anselm dead, choi slashed and slotted. Who did that smorgasbord, you think?" The trunk coiled back against the great torso.

"Doesn't prove a thing, Big George," Dirk said. "He could've been the good guy, yes?"

"God's rockets, you testy Thomases get me sad. Here I stand armless—"

"Harmless," Dirk said.

"Verily, genuine Magna Carta. Saint of golden excellence and faithfulness—"

Dirk thrust his single arm out like a swan neck, like a raised Hoproi trunk, Hollis realised, and Big George stopped. Dirk brought his arm down, but very slowly.

"You want Rock Tuo to get you the Link—boggling, I'm thinking. Want me for a back-up because most bogglers won't play to Hoproi rules. But you've already got a plan, Big George. You get some chapter points for a personal play right now."

"Thomases!" the Hoproi bellowed, moving out onto the road, trunks uncurling, horns showing. "Fraidy cats! I need you at Broome. Not Rock Tuo! Pah! Everyone must be in the show or it folds."

Hollis couldn't get the sense of it, and felt that Dirk was probably missing it as well. But one thing was certain: this was a show of Hoproi emotion.

"We'll go there," Dirk said carefully. "But as independents, you read me clear? Meet up later and compare notes. See what Rock Tuo gets, yes?"

"You never make it," Big George boomed. And the creature moved his trunks in a distinctive configuration.

Dirk knew to hold on when Hollis went sprawling face-down in the dust, pushed by Bo, guided by an arm across his own disfigured back, just in time to miss starshot that kicked up dust, tore the road surface where they had been standing.

Bo had his own star aimed, sent three quick pulses of energy into the hills to keep choi support at bay.

Big George had passed a confile net from his unseen rear arm round to a front pair; the net sizzled and poured shield energies across the painted hide.

Very calmly, Bo brought out his second star. For the first time he spoke. "You got hot-glass covered on that, Big George?"

The Hoproi laughed, shifting his trunks, delighted, dismayed, who could ever be sure?

"God's rockets! You got hot-glass on the menu, Bristling Bo?"

"Verily, Big George. Smell and taste on the cart. Do me the honour?" And he triggered the option. The air buzzed, suddenly filled with the smell of ozone over and above the confile discharge.

"Rain check on taste, Big Bo. Not dressed for Darzie. You take the cake."

"See you in Broome," Dirk said, taking charge, maintaining the choi protocols.

"We can hope, fine Dirk," the Hoproi said. "Choi come home, Bo?"

"Bring them home," Bo said.

Big George liked it when Dirk's warrior spoke. As if he had just now made no attempt on their lives, he rumbled pleasure, moved his trunks to make semaphores.

In from adjacent rockforms ran four Humans dressed in the plated beetletech of Ardent Spoilers, their chest plates marked with Big George's personal sign rendered in the intricate colour gradations of the Hoproi's shooting club chapter. Men or women, it was impossible to tell, but they ran cruciform with their arms outstretched, intended to show they meant no harm, but a manic, disturbing sight. They whooped as they came, making a ululation that was equally unsettling: these were Humans deep inside a Race conditioning, their Humanity drawn dangerously thin, contaminated, poisoned but lovingly preserved. Through them, Big George savoured the Earth, read the reality of the downtrodden host-race, fought Human war in a Human way.

When the four augmented shapes stood about their lord, arms still cruciform, choi was made. The four trunks reached out, a bonding horn slipped into the special cup at the base of each Human's spine, locking in place, completing the fighting-wheel. Now the arms came down, the four armoured figures awaiting their master's commands.

"Noble star," Big George said, acknowledging them, drawing on their viewpoints now. "There is a ley that runs through my heart. It draws destiny, sweet and fair. Love you, noble Bo. Honour you, Boggler Dirk. Adieu, fine copycat, Hollis Green. We build plans and pictures for you, yessir!"

And as a clumsy-looking but never clumsy-moving cluster of shapes, a well-rehearsed pinwheel, the formation moved off, falling into 'running star' deployment: one Human to the front, one to each side, the side trunks curling back to allow the side companions to run freely, the rear trunk sweeping out to the left so that companion had no trouble matching the pace.

Hollis could not look away. He found it ridiculous, yet elegant and unnervingly impressive, something wrong and yet right. Nor was he surprised to see that they went, not down the road towards Broome, but across the rocky terrain as if indeed keeping a ley-line angled through Big George's enormous heart. Within minutes they had vanished from sight.

Dirk's hand rested on Hollis's shoulder. "Comical, efficient and ruthless. They fit into a 4000-tonne combat scat and a diplomatic salon with equal ease, and yet like nothing better than to get out in the heat and dust like this. They are the deadliest enemy because they make us laugh while they kill us."

Twenty minutes down the hot quiet road, Dirk, Hollis and Bo found the body of Fancy Anselm lying with its choi-mate Humans in death, the thick deep Hoproi blood mixing with the always too red blood of its companions. Starshot had done it; the wounds were clearly those of high-cycle Code weapons. Fancy Anselm's confile net was inert, wasted.

Hollis could only stare in amazement. Another first in his short life: a dead Hoproi. And for Bo, too, this close, going from what Hollis heard the big man tell Dirk, as unexpected as that was. Choi died, Hoproi almost never did.

The great barrel form was flaccid now, the blackening, grey-brown hide unadorned but for blue chapter stripes and chevrons, the four trunks locked fast to its full complement of Battle Wands, probably having dragged them to a corporate death.

Hollis raised his extensor, took dump on it. Apparently the spinal horn of each umbilicus contracted violently, piercing the grafted ledge of bone and synthetic at the Human's coccyx, literally locking the companion to the host in death-clutch.

In principle, it insured surviving choi would avenge a wounded or dying host—there was no alternative—and Hollis wondered how that was covered in the Code recruitment brochures.

"Check the sidekicks, Bo," Dirk said. "Hollis, you see the implications?"

Hollis watched as Bo went from one choi-mate to the next, impressed with how skilful the man was at using Hoproi med-tech. He had to make himself think of what the boruk had asked.

"I think I do. Hoproi do not often kill Hoproi."

"Exactly. They pride themselves on it. So we have faction fighting. The shooting clubs are at one another over this boggling."

"They suspect what it is you are about to learn."

"They already know what Human boggling will confirm. The Nobodoi see through time. They know that. That they saw their own Recall. Saw—"

"A Return!"

"Wouldn't that stir them? They've filled the power vacuum. Organised it all with the Matta and the Darzie. I might have it wrong. The Nobody plan for Earth is probably intact, but global power must be habit-forming. Who knows?"

"One is alive!" Bo called.

Dirk rose up in his harness. "Say again!"

"Alive!" Bo called, crouching over one of the armoured forms, and Hollis saw the Wand stir, no muscular contraction, no death spasm. It happened, the dump said it did, sometimes. Some choi, stronger than others, usually veterans or those more accustomed to operating on remote, survived the death-shock of the host, though temporarily since the clutch was already made. The horn had closed; the necrosis eventually started down the trunk; volatile alien poisons entered the Human system; such choi finally died.

Perhaps there was time. Bo was busily at work, removing the laminations and cup seals, using special tech on the spinal coupling itself. Hollis smelled hot-glass at work, the Darzie star, saw low-burn starshot trained on the tough toroidal collar.

There was a scream; the choi-Human went rigid in agony, then limp, unconscious. The trunk came away intact in Bo's hand, horn and all, leaving ruined synthetic and an angry cauterised wound glistening with sealant.

"Yes?" Dirk called.

"Likely," Bo answered. "Full of lazy-maisie. No heartstop from shock now anyway. Depends on the toxins, whether the reagents get them in time. Give me ten."

"Aye," Dirk said, then to Hollis: "You heed this. You keep this true. Life knowledge over book learning every time."

"Yes," Hollis said, watching Bo work over the still figure, removing Wand beetle-plate, exposing the chameleon undersuit such as Bo and he wore.

Dirk's hand came down on Hollis's shoulder, very gently.

"For old-world seafarers, sailors and fishermen, pre-Wormwood mostly, life by the sea was more than a livelihood. It determined the form of life in every detail, how it was lived, the traces, the artforms: songs, stories, dramas, whole customs, community mores, the beliefs, the reality, Hollis, the prevailing reality.

"For the off-world peoples it is the same, you know it is. For the Hoproi, war is an imperative, a lifestyle, an elegant and self-justifying mind-set, an artform too—an ethos eloquent unto itself. That war-garden we saw—the placement of the engines, the way they move, the patterns they make in moving, the precise way they kill—may all be aesthetic refinement. Again, natural and eloquent unto itself. For the Nobodoi, the Carnivals, the land-bridges, the leys, the Link, this present boggling imminence I feel so heavily may be the same: an aesthetic, rational, numinous culmination. It may only be refinement, an exquisite nicety from an over-civilised race, something with an emblematic payload, an act of decadence and self-indulgence. It may not. I'm being Human, you see. Our bias must be to always go beyond what simply is—to find more. I'm after what being Human is, Hollis, you understand? You see any of this in what we're doing? I have to know where we stand. How we stand. Why *we* were chosen this time. Our planet. Our race. Why us."

"I see that," Hollis said.

"I hope so. There was once a people—a Human people—called Amerinds, whose most highly developed societies depended on a food animal that was wiped out by tech'd invaders of their own species. And Tuaregs, whose ethos—"

Hollis reached up to touch the boruk's hand.

"Dirk, I know. I understand."

"Yes," Dirk said. "Yes. Hollis, help me down."

Hollis crouched, held his right forearm up so Dirk could grip it, then out, taking the boggler's weight as he swung smoothly out of the harness, dropped to the red soil. Together, not as boruk and backman, as two Human people, they crossed to Bo.

The highwayman was kneeling over the unconscious form. Hollis crouched down as well to be more at Dirk's height.

"A female," Bo said, stating what was obvious now with most of the armour off. She was around thirty, pale-skinned, solidly-made, physically a very good specimen, with black hair and clear signs of Asian ancestry despite the skin colour. There were neat choi tattoos on her left cheek and forehead.

"Lazy-maisie is a godsend for us," Dirk said. "Race-tailored like all the best Darzie drugs. Not only counters shock but also carries tote capability. Right now it is suppressing all the Hoproi programs and interfacing chemicals and restoring the innate Human bias, original homeostasis. All shockproofed. Beautiful."

"When it wears off..."

"No. That's the beauty of it. Homeostasis. It shuts out the alien matter, accesses older data, communicates only with its own chemically enhanced parts. Worst you get is amnesia. Usually it's only stupor. This Wand will need reconditioning eventually, but for Hoproi to return this Human to choi, a whole new chemical horizon—or rather a new *old* horizon—will have to be carefully suppressed. The hard work is at the other end. That's how it was designed. Good interrogation drug. Bo, let's get her away from here."

Bo carried the woman, Hollis most of his weapons, until they were well away from the death-scene. When they reached a shady spot under some sheltering rockforms, Bo set the Wand down and administered more injections. In a matter of seconds, the woman stirred, became conscious, sat up, combat ready.

Bo had moved well clear after giving her the final shot, knowing what this maisie variant would do—he had not seen a dead Hoproi up close but he had probably tended remote choi before.

"What?" the woman cried, trying to go into a crouch, falling back, sitting with her legs out, her arms back supporting her.

"We rescued you from death-clutch," Dirk said. "We are allies."

"Handsome?"

"I'm sorry. Wasted. Flashed down. There seems to be faction fighting."

"What? I'm—What is this?" She shrieked the words, striking the earth with her fists.

"We had to use lazy-maisie," Dirk said, his voice very calm.

"*Cras!*" she swore. "You've taken me down!"

"You would have died."

"They'll have to clean me. They—" She stopped, discovering implications, the maisie sorting her memories, finding what was needed. She looked at Dirk as a child might.

The boruk nodded. "That's right. It seems Handsome was flashed by choi."

"No!" she said. "Hoproi do not kill Hoproi. Never."

"Seems, I said. Listen now please."

"I've been taken down!" she cried, her eyes unfocused, her gaze suddenly hollow, aimed beyond Dirk, beyond them all.

"No," the boruk told her gently. "You will re-apply. Get new totes. I know Hoproi. I can ask."

She blinked back tears, sitting cross-legged now, her hands tight fists behind her in the dust. The lazy-maisie was doing its job, answering questions as they rose in her mind with both pre-choi and choi memory, responding to nuances of anxiety, guiding itself that way, trying to regulate this injured personality while keeping it publicly viable. It was causing these sudden silences. The confusion was not a bad sign. The blanking would diminish.

Dirk waited a suitable time then introduced himself and his companions, knowing she listened because her eyes turned to each person named. "Your name?"

There was a fierce frown. "I hate this!"

"I know. Your best name?"

"Hesi."

"We saved you, Hesi."

"Yes. I hate this!"

"We need to know who flashed Handsome, Hesi. We've a problem here."

"You didn't—"

"Oath on that. Listen closely for our problem. Decide if you can advise us. Yes?"

"You won't trust me."

"We will because we need to. We'll have to learn to trust each other. But I'm Boggler Dirk and you may remember how Handsome liked my boggling, how he liked Bo here." It was a gamble, Hollis knew, but Dirk must have sensed it was right. "Can you make choi oath, Hesi? No harm. Just to listen?"

"Think I can," she said. "I'd like to. It's this interference." She struck the earth with a fist. "I can't be sure. God's rockets, I hate it!"

"It's stabilising, Hesi. It's learning you. You know how it works. You use it."

The Wand nodded abstractedly. "I—" she started, broke off.

"This much," Dirk said. "No harm to Hollis, Bo and me till you can promise the other, yes?"

"You didn't kill Handsome?"

"I swear it. But we need to know who did and here's why. We're going into Broome to boggle the Link. Everything we do, everything that happens, may be deliberately intended, part of a Nobody plan—*if* they see into time. You got memory on this?"

The woman nodded but did not speak. She was looking beyond them again.

"You came out here with Handsome." Dirk did not mention Big George. "Can you say why? You got Handsome's brief on that?"

She grimaced, beat the sides of her head with her open hands. "I'm losing it! This fuggin' maisie! You've cut me out of—"

"Death-clutch, Hesi!" Bo said, warrior Bo, soldier to soldier. "You talking scut! Listen to Dirk!"

The boruk went straight back to it. "Everything we do, every encounter, like this now, may be seen by Nobodoi, you got it? We need to know what part you play—since we've met you."

Hesi frowned, blinked back the tears of rage that added to the trails down her grimy cheeks. "Nobodoi knew Handsome would be taken?"

"Maybe not. There may be blanks. We can't discuss a time-sense when we don't have it."

"It's like Dirk explaining boggling," Hollis said. "It just is."

Which made Bo smile. Sometimes this young print just didn't know when to stay out of it. He had to talk, had to be in any event then occurring. Maybe all prints were that way, Bo decided, compulsive participants, tactless but too artless to be offensive.

Dirk accepted the comparison. "So this, Hesi. Handsome was wasted, choi weaponry, but Hoproi can't kill Hoproi. We saved you from clutch—"

"Spoiled your day with lazy-maisie."

"Hollis!" Dirk snapped. "Now you're part of our plan—possibly a Nobody plan—to go to Broome and the Link. Yes?"

"You swear that—"

"We honour Hoproi. You already have my word. Bo, give her your Darzie star. Hesi, you have doubts of us, you decide. We have honour. Good Human honour. Yes?"

"I'll try," she said and got to her feet.

"Good. Anything of Handsome comes to you, you tell us if you can. Anything."

They distributed packs and weapons, and Hesi seemed more comfortable in parts of her armour and some of the gear, doing what was essentially remote choi work. It occurred to Hollis too that, with Dirk aloft, they made a higher centre for their group— not really a Hoproi surrogate of any kind but a centre nonetheless.

Bo took the opportunity to pass out ration sticks and, with Broome no more than two hours away to the north-west, they set off once more.

7

They were no more than forty minutes down that road when Hesi pointed to where it dropped to a ravine crossed by a bridge.

"No go!" she cried, too loudly, only regaining her customary choi stealth when those two words were said. "We need a detour."

"Hesi?" Dirk said.

"Banding Bridge," she explained. "There's a spook close by."

Hollis did not go for his dag; he knew the idiom. A were-suit.

"There is?" Dirk asked, surprised that he had not read the pressures yet.

Bo raised field glasses. "Full triune?"

"Yes." Hesi used her own glasses to scan the bridge.

"No sign," Dirk said, having used his talent.

Hesi turned to face Dirk. "It's there."

"I do not doubt it. I simply said there is no sign."

Hesi nodded, lifted her glasses again. "A month back, Twikker brought in a boggler to douse it. Wanted a sancher."

"A boggler? Who?"

"Chimo. Eight-in-ten."

"Chimo lied," Dirk told her. "He's six-in-ten."

"Was," Hesi said. "No go. See scorch marks on the far side? What's left."

"Hmm," Dirk said. "Hesi, Bo, Hollis. We may be part of a winning plan or simply infinite contingencies. I say we take the bridge. Test Nobodoi intentions. We could be dooming ourselves, so I'm happy to solo it. You decide."

"You're crazy," Hesi said.

"Possibly. Give Bo back his things and find your detour. Hollis?"

"We going for a sancher?"

"Don't know. Have to boggle that when we're down there."

"I'm for it."

"He's the print, isn't he?" Hesi asked Bo, as if there was no one else there to hear. "Handsome said there was a C-mate in this."

"Indeed," Dirk said, laughing. "He's our new hero. You staying?"

Hesi shook her head, but started down the road towards the bridge. Bo followed, grinning.

"If I survive," Hollis said, starting after them.

"What's that?" Dirk asked, eyes closed, already reading the pressures.

"I'm a new hero if I survive."

Dirk laid his hand on the backman's shoulder, eyes still closed, and read the bridge.

It hadn't been built as a bridge, not originally. A hockiron conduit, huge and bone-white, pushed out of one side of the gully and into the other. Local Humans had concreted around it, making a shell that carried the road. They reached the near side without incident.

"Nothing," Hollis said, straining for the ghostworks that meant things Nobodoi, the corner-of-the-eye shifts and glints that signified soul-stone and so were-suit.

"Full triunes use phasing," Dirk told him. "It's already there."

"What, invisible?"

"No. Out of continuum for the moment. Like my body. Stepping onto the bridge should do it."

"You want the sancher?" Hesi asked, glasses still raised to her eyes.

"That your purpose in this, you think?"

She shrugged. "We got confiles, Bo and me. Hot-glass. We might do it. Twikker and Chimo couldn't, but—"

"Hesi, I'm 9.6-in-ten. I got Bo's confile from the Port Herriot dousing. I'm the one with the sancher from the Blue Beach suit."

"Hmm. You going to try for a true sancher now?"

"Still reading on that. If your spook appears, if it displays, then I'll decide."

Hollis noted the Wand's preoccupation with looting the suit, trying for the sancher; he knew it was a choi priority, as it was any Human's. He sensed the danger of it, comforted himself with the knowledge that Dirk and Bo were aware of it too. He went back to studying the bridge, marvelling at how the smooth, flawless hockiron slid in and out of the newly-moulded strata with nary a sign of the violation. The Broome inhabitants, so he assumed, had laid their pathetic crust of sile concrete along the rounded top, had erected the pilasters and facings at each end, superimposing the Human sense of a bridge like the enactment of some desperate race memory. Hollis found it sad but hated feeling that, made himself see it Dirk's way, read it as a stubborn and defiant thing, like the looting. Not just safely conventionalised reality. Not just the work of ants carrying on regardless, building around whatever happened to be. Better than that.

He followed the smooth line of the bridge. The thought of a were-suit waiting for them seemed an oddly quaint touch compared to the effortless accomplishment of the conduit, a deliberate scaling-down by the Nobodoi to help in their dealings with Humans, probably the other races as well.

"Step onto the bridge," Dirk said, and Hollis did so, not daring to hesitate, stepping into a silence broken only by their footsteps and the sparking of the confiles Bo and Hesi wore.

No sooner were they all on the bridge than the spook was there, waiting on the other side. Full triune: suit, Companion, Snake. There were no lights about the thing yet, not full ghostworks, just the usual vague corner-of-the-eye trickery, the suggestion of things moving when nothing was.

Dirk had his hand splayed out before Hollis like an hieratic star, as if warding off the possibility of harm by the up-raised palm. A famous mannerism no doubt. A boggler trademark.

"Dirk—"

"Keep going, Hollis. It either will or it won't."

Halfway across, ghostworks started glittering around the forms, building into striations, flowing, streaming up into the air around the Snake.

"Bo," Dirk said.

This was the dangerous part. Bo's confile began powering up, Hesi's as well. Chimo had done just this with Twikker—and the Banding suit had not accepted it. The Snake had flashed out its sentry pulses, or Companion had sent quick parcels of energy, clean, efficient.

Hollis kept walking, smelled hot-glass, confile and hot-glass, and now Hesi was moving by him on the left, ahead of Bo, taking the lead, holding the Darzie star.

That your purpose in this? Dirk had asked her. Her reason for being here.

Hollis kept going, hand well clear of his own star, dag telltale winking red, taking it all. He wanted to speak, ask Dirk questions, ask what was going on. But he was learning to keep silent, knew that there might never be time now, that this might be it. He inventoried what he saw in case there was a chance, then smiled and told himself they were committed anyway. No going back. And who ever brought two confiles, hot-glass and a boggler's strange hand-out gesture to a dousing?

"Trusting you, Hesi," Dirk murmured, but not for her. Only Hollis heard it, feeling good, not at all slighted that Dirk counted him as part of what he could trust.

More steps forward, more thoughts since that's all there was for him now as backman. Bo and Hesi were four paces ahead, closing on the far end, nearing the triune that stood flickering in the hot dusty air.

Could it work? The confiles had once been sanchers, each one the display part of a were-suit, its ganglia perhaps, or its nervous system, or possibly an ideological artifact, a statement of its pedigree, part of some arcane heraldry—who might ever know?

Hollis knew something of the theory, never enough but something, dag-dump. Each confile, set on free range, allowed to operate wild, recognised its own parent tech, strived to match the ambient energy fields, just as Coaches merged their accretion fields, boggle stuff to boggle stuff, just as the Stone Ships sailed the world's oceans as isolated vessels but sometimes rendezvoused at Longitude 70°, Latitude 30°.

It was that questing that was the danger, the variations as they attempted to calibrate themselves. The hot-glass might help. It overlaid the confiles' efforts to synchronise the sometimes extreme fluctuations with a benign and constant discharge, so those swings did not register as such.

Bo and Hesi stopped ten metres from the suit, allowing Dirk and Hollis to reach them.

"Begin irradiation," Dirk said.

Bo fired his hundred-cycle star directly at the dish of Companion, while Hesi concentrated the Darzie star on the suit itself. Ghostworks raced about the triune; the Snake started to move off to the side, stopped, moved, stopped again.

The lightforms vanished. The Snake dropped to the earth with a dull thud and lay inert. The front of the suit roiled, shimmered. Suddenly the sancher was there, displayed like a gift held out before it on invisible arms.

Bo and Hesi stopped firing. It was done.

"Yes!" Hesi cried, smiling her first smile since they'd found her. "We did it."

Hollis stared wide-eyed at the strange sight, the precious net just hanging there.

So easy? he wondered. *Is that all?*

He had dag-lore on it. Now Bo, any of them, could reach out and simply pluck the thing out of the air; the suit would break open down its sides, the soul-stone would be exposed, might even tumble forth onto the ground. The suit would never move again. Within minutes, it would vanish, phased out of their world into some other, leaving only the stone sitting in the dust, the only evidence of the desecration. The only other evidence. The sancher was there, possibly spoiled, possibly only a confile.

Hollis turned his head to speak, wanting to ask if he could be the one to take it down, finish the dousing, but Dirk spoke first.

"We leave it. We keep going."

"Dirk?" Bo said.

Hesi did not have his control. "But it's a sancher! You got it out! You can probably keep it intact."

"Leave it. Move on now. Hollis!"

Hollis began moving at once, striding past the waiting suit. As they passed, even as Hollis watched, the marvellous net vanished in a flicker of light, taken back in, and ghostworks danced about the suit again in a sudden frenzy, like troubled insects suddenly freed. Only when the small band of Humans was well clear of the bridge, at the top of the ravine, did the Snake stir, slowly lifting back to its original position at the suit's right shoulder.

"Why?" Hesi asked, as Hollis was determined not to, as Bo never would this side of Morion and a debriefing.

"It's... just right," Dirk answered in an distracted way. "Now I must concentrate on the Link."

And that was all he said until the seaside town of Broome stretched out before them at the horizon, fixed against the red land like a glittering buckle of gems and flashing pearl, the great hockiron sweeps of the land-bridge gleaming on the ocean to the north, the Link rising up like a brooch of stasis-locked quicksilver, pinned to the brilliant afternoon sky with its restless, boiling crown dancing in the sunlight.

8

In another world, another life, pre-Wormwood, Broome had been a town, then a great city, then a town again, re-made, post-Wormwood, near where the bones of the hockiron grid slid into the wide red land. A seaside tourist town, with a core population of ten thousand Humans, the inevitable yet varying Bridge Race musters, a scattering of Lesser Races, many of them itinerants moving between the Impact cities, on across the land-bridges to the Old World centres. Leys met and diverged close by, making shifting whirlpools of energy that brought surprising winds and odd frissons, that made this Human-normal zone only provisionally that, an exciting nexus, a wonderful, eerie, vital place to be.

And while Broome was mainly a town for transients, there were a score of Matt typhies in the northern suburbs, their elaborate precincts guarded both by their own integral tech and by Code mercenaries. There were Hoproi shooting club chapters on Main Street near the New Broome Hotel, and hordats, and adorned but never truly concealed hockiron extrusions that had once been Nobodoi installations of some kind, now taken over by the shooting clubs, though nothing anywhere in this dazzling mix of rich colour and gleaming hockiron stood taller than the Link looming several kilometres off the coast, its gleaming ball riding the shifting water-jet above struts and rods already 134 metres high.

It drew the eye of every new arrival in this part of the Impact. Walking on the streets you could tell the natives because they did not glance sideways each time the view was there; they were inured to it, able to shut out the distant roar and deep metallic ringing of the moving parts. Eighty-four of the rods were movers, the other twenty-nine were locked into the hockiron footing that in turn locked the whole ocean-spanning grid into this ancient land-mass probably forever.

Dirk, Bo and Hesi made it a point of looking ahead, but Hollis was unable to resist. This was Nobodoi—and Nobodoi purpose at work. The boggle was so vast, so impressive, the ultimate mystery; nothing as amazing as the land-bridge, not really, but somehow far more incredible since no use could be made of it. It stood off-shore, ministering to itself, one of the first structures the Nobodoi built after Wormwood had been brought down and its planet-sculpting job completed.

Dirk had been specific in his instructions. He would not look at it, refused to yet, but he was communing with it, every part of his talent attuned to its workings.

As they moved along the crowded streets, Bo and Hesi watched for choi, for any off-worlder trace but especially Hoproi. Hollis tried to do the same, tried to affect the quality of insouciance Dirk liked—confident Humanity striding forth, examples to all who looked their way. Most of the time he managed. He saw the Darzie spy-eyes dip and weave about the hordat rooflines, noticed the Matt charabanc that slid by on its quiet fields—a gleaming silver ovoid crusted like a Fabergé egg, its cutaways and outgrowths chased and filigreed with goldwire sensors, the whole thing strange and sublime.

Hollis had never seen Matta but of course they would be active at such a time. The movement of bogglers (what the Matt called *quenth* talents) across the patchwork automatically drew Bridge Race interest; the present situation insured close attention now with the Hoproi shooting clubs at odds, Fancy Anselm dead, Big George working with Rock Tuo. A Link boggling imminent. This was Nobodoi business. Major administrative protocols were implicitly affected. *Their* interests.

"Where to?" Hollis asked.

"Big George's chapter-house. Somewhere along here. No, wait! Bo, look!"

But Bo and Hesi had already reacted in choi fashion, moving several paces before Hollis and Dirk, weapons conspicuously angled across their bodies.

Further up the street Hoproi were gathering, at least seven, possibly eight of the creatures, and not just locals—Hoproi who had come to this corner of the Impact, to their shooting club chapters here, because of the boggling.

"Keep it confident," Dirk said, because the choi were all turned their way, formidable, beetled, un-Human with their helmets closed. Crowds of tourists and locals had gathered as well, used to many strange things on these streets but probably not an assembly of chapter representatives holding confab out of doors.

"That's Big George on the left," Dirk said for Hollis's benefit. "That's New Luke next to him. And Times David, Bo?"

"Aye. Can't tell the others."

Hesi answered before Dirk could. "Choi armour gives it. Fauve Angus and Goody Hal are from Club Reeve. That Handsome's lot there: Spider Larran and Crown Minos. You give me back now, Dirk?"

"That what you want, Hesi?"

"Aye. Hate this. Hate this maisie. They might work on me. They might take me on."

"Right. I'm saying you've played a part in whatever the plan is. Your presence got us the Banding spook, don't ask why. It just did. Feel good for that. Forgive the maisie."

"Saved me. Got you a chance at the suit. Wasted, but a chance."

"That's not what I mean. It mattered, okay, *not* taking it? This time it mattered."

Hesi shrugged, began handing her equipment back to Bo.

"Keep the Darzie star," Dirk said, and Bo's head lifted just a fraction.

Hesi blinked, wide-eyed. "Keep it?"

"For trade. Might get you cleaned. Get you a place in choi."

Hesi nodded, gripping the gun in both hands. "You're a good one, Dirk." She gave a nod to Bo, another to Hollis, and walked off ahead of them, arms out from the body so there could be no misunderstanding of intent. She headed towards the Hoproi and choi-Humans from Handsome's shooting club. Hollis saw her have words with a choi-mate who then detached from Crown Minos, took the Darzie weapon from her, and escorted her back to the chapter-house. It looked promising.

"Let me down, Hollis," Dirk said, and Hollis tensed his arm, crouched, steadied himself for the shift of weight, brought the boggler to the road surface. Dirk walked out ahead of them to the rendezvous.

"Yay, what gives?" Big George boomed as they neared the confab. "Boggling on? Bets taken."

Hollis made himself stand as confidently as he could behind the dwarf shape of the boruk, though it was impossible not to be overwhelmed by the towering Hoproi shapes and faceless choi-mates.

Dirk seemed to have no difficulty with such things. "Will you tell us what is happening here, Big George?"

"You boggle Link. We watch. All here to watch, keep savvy."

"Not to kill like before."

"No way."

"Other bogglers?"

"Coming, you bet. You do first."

"Where is Rock Tuo?"

"Where indeed? You start pronto! Tuo come later."

"Tuo come now. We boggle together. We—"

But Dirk did not finish. He half-turned as if to speak to his backman and his minder, and Hollis saw such a look of dread on the boruk's face that he felt the hairs on his neck rise and immediately searched their surroundings for some cause, though there was nothing that he could see. He came back to the same terrible look, saw the expression of concern on Bo's face as well.

"Dirk, what?" Bo said.

"What? What?" Hollis demanded.

"Something has just been placed into my phased-out hand."

Hollis found himself looking straight at the hand held close against Dirk's side, then understood the boruk's words.

His phased-out hand.

"What? What does that mean? What sort of object?"

"It is round. Smooth. Solid," Dirk said, and Hollis could imagine Dirk actually feeling for such things.

"Are you sure?" Not one of his most brilliant questions, Hollis realised.

"It is... an activator. I just know."

"For what, Dirk?" Bo asked.

As if in answer, shouts went up down the street—cries and screams as people fell back in panic.

Along Main Street, newly exposed to their view by the retreating crowds, a were-suit came walking, its Companion rolling along to its left, the Snake hovering at its right shoulder like a small flattened skull.

"God's rockets and Holy Trinity!" Big George boomed, his choi combat-ready. New Luke and Times David also went on alert, sending out piercing whistles, their call-signs. Remote choi-mates came running to complete their fighting-wheels. Some Hoproi moved back, while others—Fauve Angus and Goody Hal—started moving away altogether, heading towards their grand hockiron chapter-house near the New Broome Hotel.

Standing wide-eyed around the shifting Hoproi groups, the Human crowds watched the suit approach. Many people had fled, many had returned, unable to keep away.

"The suit from the bridge!" Bo cried. "The Banding suit! I'm sure of it, Dirk. I recognise—" But he stopped.

The Snake came streaking overhead, making a terrible scream as it rushed by, dropping to hover directly in front of Goody Hal and Fauve Angus, floating before the huge figures and their Human fighting-wheels.

Goody Hal immediately set up a whistling from his sensory fibres; at the same time, the two forward choi detached and ran off towards their chapter-house. The disclosed trunks produced a confile from another choi's field pack, brought it up, shimmering, the remaining choi glittering in activated confiles of their own, weapons raised, facing the Snake. Fauve Angus tried to disassociate itself from Goody Hal's response, took a few steps to the side, halting only when the Snake angled slightly in his direction. Then Fauve Angus's choi brought up their own confile defences.

While this happened, the suit came striding on, as inexorable as ever, its Companion moving with it.

Big George made the rumbling that was unmistakably Hoproi mother-tongue. Goody Hal boomed in answer, began moving slowly back towards the group of Humans and Hoproi in the middle of Main Street. Fauve Angus followed, and with them came the Snake, keeping its original distance, angled back towards Goody Hal.

"You got strife aboard, Goody Hal!" Big George rumbled, using Antique now. "You have grief, Fauve Angus!"

"You got were-suit gone wacko is what, Big George," Goody Hal called, closing the last of the distance, back with his rivals from the other shooting clubs. "We got sancher if we take it down, savvy?" And one of Goody Hal's free trunks indicated his chapter-house down the street. The hockiron there was beautifully adorned with battle-flags, plaques of peterkill and dove-eye, spacemetal escutcheons, even sections of ancient Pre-Wormwood Human weapons. Extended from the open top of the structure was an intricate glistening construct, Hoproi battle-tech, a ceremonial house defence no doubt of enormous power. It could make valleys and weld hockiron for the Nobodoi; doubtless it could take a post-Recall were-suit with little difficulty.

Big George rumbled something in Hoproi, then added Human words to what he had said, as if wanting all these watching Humans to know. "Your chance. Your sancher. Your chapter." He had disowned the alliance.

The suit was close, no more than thirty metres away. Big George moved to the side, conspicuously exposing his chapter rivals.

The tension was incredible. Hollis found there was just too much to look at: first this were-suit on the streets of Broome, deploying its Snake with obvious intent, then Goody Hal—and Fauve Angus too now—for some race-secret reason with stars levelled directly at it via their choi, presumably with chapter reinforcements on the way and fixed house-tech already trained upon it. No doubt scat support was imminent as well.

The Snake hovered quietly on one side of Goody Hal and Fauve Angus; the suit and its Companion waited on the other. The Humans and remaining Hoproi were out of it, theoretically at least; Goody Hal and Fauve Angus did seem to be the focus of the suit's attention. Further back, the Matt charabanc sat quietly, goldwire gleaming; robot or occupied, who could tell? Several Darzie spy-eyes hovered at the rooflines.

Oddly enough, few of the Lesser Races were visible among the nervous, fascinated onlookers—several Salmans, some Satlin and Cire, at least one Tessa. Otherwise there were only Humans, some of them choi and so only provisionally that, all of whom knew what starshot crossfire might do, let alone Hoproi house-tech, but who could not bear to leave now. This was Nobodoi business, after all, some manifestation of their continuing role in this world they had re-made. Because of Hoproi.

Hoproi were the reason the Banding suit was here, nothing surer. Hollis saw the intent look of concern on Dirk's face. The boruk's eyes were open but he was probably still communing, still dealing with the amazing development in his other reality. Whatever it was in his phased-out hand. Or perhaps he had already dealt with that crisis, put it into some greater picture, used to accommodating alien realities.

An activator, Dirk had said. Then the suit had appeared and gone into action. A suit *he* had spared. Such implications.

The stalemate resolved dramatically. A scat appeared overhead, its insignia that of Goody Hal's chapter-house. It slid across the bright blue sky, all beetled and deadly, shimmering in its sentry fields; had just started to hover when it simply disappeared. No explosion, no detectable weapons trace from Snake, Companion or suit, but dealt with just the same. Phased out. Sent somewhere else as Dirk's torso had been. Simply gone.

Goody Hal began a rumbling colloquy with Big George; the were-suit triune waited as if listening, picked out in ghostworks, perhaps drawing energies from the leys to dress itself in a coronation display, a magnificent psychological deterrent or perhaps just its natural processes of replenishment for what it had to do.

It was so distracting that Hollis barely saw when Goody Hal vanished in a three-stage blink: choi, choi, self! Then Fauve Angus the same way: multiple blinks, gone. Gone, as the scat had gone. A great murmuring went up from the crowd.

"Phasing tech—" Hollis began.

"Wait, Hollis!" Bo said. "You caused that, Dirk?"

"I don't know," Dirk answered, perspiration beading his brow. "I'm still holding it, but I've done nothing. Big George? You reading this?"

"All eyes, you betcha! Never seen trinity do that. Wow!"

"What did Goody Hal tell you?"

"Bad business, Dirk," the Hoproi said. "Contracts broken up and down the town."

"Details," Dirk said, and Big George must have feared what Dirk's activator could do. He did not hesitate.

"Old contract. Nobodoi honour Hoproi—kings of the world this time. No summary justice. Goody Hal, Fauve Angus sent packing. Not fair! Not on! Bad business. Must stand trial. Hoproi justice."

"I'm not getting this, Big George. Slow down."

"You understand," Big George rumbled. "Hoproi here to push. Always to push. Best Hoproi push. In Goody Hal's house, there, we got wrong pushers... provokers... extenders."

"Go too far?"

"Yes. Push Hoproi. Push Nobodoi. Push Human. You say, what?"

"Factions," Dirk said. "Competing factions."

"Some bits. Well spotted. Um... more..."

"Ah, testers. Challengers of the system, of the order."

"Good. Good. Brief is to test the overlords. Explore them. Push there and never give up. Zealous."

"Brief from whom, Big George? Nobodoi?"

"What? Whassat? No, Dirk. No! This Hoproi thing. Part of the package. Job to record interface, phenomenon of selves. Do for Hoproi. This Hoproi way."

"Artists? A group of artists?"

"Some bits. Some bits, yes. More. Go too far. Bad pushers out of good. Say Recall is race cull. Got that, Dirk? Nobodoi cull themselves."

"Are there races that do that?" Hollis asked, thinking of the soul-stones scattered across the world, wondering if they could be cull remains—hence the melancholy around the suits, around the few Nobody artifacts he had seen, wondering too if extant Nobodoi could still be about, watching all this? In this suit perhaps.

"Wait, Hollis!" Bo said.

"No, Bo!" Dirk told him. "Fair question. Big George?"

"Some races cull. Mostly animals, a miscuing of directives. These bad pushers test Nobodoi, tailor genetic weapon to eat up stones, rot them, powder them. Motives wrong. This bad lot. Woeful faction. Say one thing, do another."

"Go on," Dirk said. "Why?"

Big George gave a deep rumble. "Difficult, Dirk, Bo, squeaky-clean Hollis. Hoproi must not kill Hoproi. Old contract. Old book. Nobodoi must not. You get the drift? Nobodoi can send Hoproi out of town. Send Hoproi home. But old respect. Old deal. Deep love."

"But Fancy Anselm!" Dirk said. "You killed—"

"Heaven forfend! No so! That Rock Tuo! That bugger Human work two sides. Oath to Big George, sure, do the trick. Boggle the

Link, I swear, oh yes. Oath to Goody Hal and Fauve Angus. Push the Nobodoi all sides. Great profit. Human chance. He could not resist."

"I resisted," Dirk said.

Big George rumbled deep inside. A trunk arched slightly, Hoproi surprise. "They rattle your cage too?"

"Believe it."

And Hollis saw Bo nod with understanding of a greater plan he now too understood: Dirk's delaying in Morion not just seen as boggler caution, not just for assessment time needed and facts appraised. It had been to bring them himself, Hollis Green.

"Strong feeling about this, Big George," Dirk continued. "Where is Tuo?"

"Gone bye-byes. Gone on long sea-voyage. Out to lunch. Him seconded for wonderful adventure."

"Precisely?"

"In a woe-is-me box. In a sentinel ley. By now he one foot square. Soon at bottom of ocean trench maybe. Pretty stone."

"Big George—"

"He murder Hoproi."

"How, Big George?"

"That Fancy Anselm's war-garden you plundered."

"No plundering," Dirk said.

"No? Beautiful Hollis got jazerant aboard, yes? No matter. Fancy Anselm come to get dues paid. But Rock Tuo want you alive for boggle-fest, to help plumb the Link, yes? He helping Goody Hal and bad pushers. Get choi support, waste Fancy Anselm. Me warn off in time."

"You fired on *us*, Big George!"

"So? You in garden. You worthy. Top class. You needed at Broome pronto! Hypotheticals: one, you go loner on me; two, you go ally of Tuo, all working together as bad pushers. All epidemic now anyway."

"Academic."

"Sure. That. Suit came. Good move. All forgiven. Showdown. Human justice, just perfect."

"What? No, Big George."

"You got activator, you say. You get suit in this."

"No. Nobodoi did that."

"No, Dirk. Your job. Punish these pushers."

"No. Even if I could I would not punish Hoproi. Not for crimes I cannot fathom."

Big George rumbled. "Must, Dirk. Hoproi protocol. You host-race. Human job. You failing here."

"That's right. Failing. Human. I choose in this. Failing by your ethos not mine."

"Nobodoi ethos, Dirk! Only answer. You do job—balance the books. We esteem you. Many smiles all around the town. Hip hip hooray!"

"Big George, try to understand—"

"You do! Big chance here, Dirk. You got activator. You got were-suit, clear brief. Down there in that house is new weapon eat up soul-stones. Bad intent. Justice needed here!"

"George! Big George!"—Dirk corrected himself—"Understand! The Matt are watching." He pointed to the silver egg. "Darzie." He indicated the spy-eyes perched on the eaves or floating back and forth in the on-shore breeze. "Hoproi. All here on your own terms. I insist on Human terms for this too, you understand me? It matters this time. You honour us by our standards this time!"

"Nobodoi already know," Big George said. "Fit everything to plan. See much. Not all maybe, but most."

"Right. Then they probably already know what I have chosen to do."

"You already goodbye scat. You already goodbye Goody Hal and Fauve Angus."

"No! No! I did not! I'm holding something I know is an activator but I haven't consciously used it yet."

There was silence then. The spectators stood watching, listening, the breeze moving flags and awnings, stirring Big George's sensory fibres, stirring the grey-brown hair on the boruk's head. From far off came the constant droning roar of the water-jet, the deep distant clanging of rods as they moved in the sea.

"And now I do choose, Big George. I throw down the activator. Don't want it. There!"

So smoothly it happened. The were-suit vanished in three blinks of light: suit, Companion, Snake, all gone.

And with the effortless unreality of dream, the water-jet of the Link streamed skyward, a sudden mighty geyser many times its normal height and strength, sending the great gleaming ball high into the air. The ball curved, high and sure, flashing in its long slow arc, came crashing down, sheathed suddenly in a pale mauve light—a stasis field, it was!—struck Goody Hal's chapter-house. Within that imprisoning field everything was annihilated—the house gone, the earth concussed and driven into a well, the terrible destruction sealed in a mauve, cauterising light, a containment field such as guided the leys, such as nursed Wormwood in those awful early days.

"Woweee!" Big George cried, booming Hoproi laughter around the Antique expression. "Bejesus! Sodom and Begorrah!"

"I threw the activator down!" Dirk cried, trying to explain. "I discarded it!"

Big George boomed in delight, his trunks flexing and unflexing, his choi breaking formation, going remote. "Sure. That did trick. All win!"

"But I threw it away."

"Yes. You choose in honour and goodest faith. You allowed to win too. All allowed to win. Nobodoi law. Hoproi law. Human law. Hah! This a fine show. This takes the Oscar!"

Dirk cried out again, but this time it was a different, more desolate cry. "No!"

Bo read that difference, Hollis did too, read fear not anger, and were quickly at Dirk's side.

"Dirk, what?" Bo whispered the words.

"It's back! The activator is back!"

"Steady," Bo said. "Hollis, you reading this?"

"Yes."

"Throw it away again, Dirk!" Big George bellowed in excitement. "See what happens next. Yippee!"

"No. Not until I boggle it. Not until I try!"

"Hah, you dear to me! You justice nut, Dirk! What now?"

Dirk tried to keep his voice steady. "We take rooms at the New Broome. I boggle this activator."

"Surely. This great treat! We like the way you wage war, Dirk!"

And Dirk, Bo and Hollis turned away, headed down the street to the hotel which stood miraculously untouched beside the glowing containment field and the great pit of what had once been Goody Hal's chapter-house.

9

The boruk did his best. Tech and med systems helped, but precisely eighty-seven hours later, Dirk slumped into exhaustion at last and, somewhere, somewhen, the activator slipped from his unseen hand.

At least three things happened.

Dirk became whole, his phased-out self restored to him, a sign to all of Nobodoi approbation. He filled out on the bed where he slept like a man giving birth to himself.

At the same time, the jazerant in the harvester stockpiles of all the war-gardens around Broome vanished. Forty seconds later, a new silver ball was seen riding on the water-jet of the Link.

When that happened, like invisible ink responding to the heat of a flame, a tattoo appeared on Dirk's newly restored forearm, the circle inside half-circles that was the Nobodoi sign, which was, several Hoproi later confirmed, the Nobody cipher for 'gratitude' but also for 'commitment'.

What Bo received for his part was not made clear—perhaps it lay in his future—but Hollis got to keep his small piece of jazerant, and on Day 206 in his life adventure as temporised print, when he went forth from Dirk's service at last to discover more of the patchwork, he added it to his personal sigil for all the Races of the world to see.

Shatterwrack at

Breaklight

THERE ARE DUST-DEVILS at Twilight beach. You can see them at sunset when the hot winds from the desert meet the cool ocean breezes, especially along the Promenade and terraces of the Gaza Hotel and down in the streets of the town.

They sometimes spin their playful dance in among the guests, much to the annoyance of the players of fire-chess. There is a rule that the vagaries of wind and weather are fair contest, and many a world-famous player has cried out in dismay during a crucial move when a queen or knight has had its small flame suddenly extinguished by a devil slipping in unnoticed amid the tables.

Some players even employ Devil Catchers rather than risk this happening, liveried or tuxedoed youths who stand about holding long-handled spoilers, watching and waiting.

I can remember once Alexander Carlos staring down dumbfounded at his debased queen on just such an occasion, as if unable to comprehend what had happened. Then he had leapt to his feet and in a rage had gone racing along the terrace after the little funnel of air, beating at it with his fists, rushing through it back and forth, literally tearing it apart.

Player's temperament aside, Carlos gained himself a new reputation that evening. Xerxes may have whipped the Hellespont for sinking his bridge of ships, but Alexander Carlos had murdered his dust-devil at Twilight Beach.

The dust-devils come at twilight, as we sand-ship sailors do: the devils, the sailors, and—as if enjoying the risk and tempting fate—the players of fire-chess. I had left Rim at Trimori's and had decided on a walk down through the town, along the streets leading away from the Gaza and the ocean.

Those streets were quiet and refreshingly cool. The little intersections were set with lanterns that swayed and flickered in the breeze, and now and then in the wash of warm light under those yellow paper cages I could see a devil leap up to dance and die or spin off about its mischief.

You can't watch those devils too long. They make a philosopher out of you. All that sudden giddy vitality. Like watching a butterfly going past, desperate to be anywhere.

No sooner had I received my coffee at my usual table at Sailmaker's than breaklight was on the town. The sun had gone down, there was the brief time of stillness, then up came the sudden flood of golden light.

If one thing can be said to govern life in Twilight Beach, that is it. Tourists and locals alike set their day by it. How must I order my affairs to be back at the Gaza for the breaklight?

All around me people sat rapt, or came out on their balconies to watch. Then, when it was fully on us for its long hour, conversations began again. A guitar resumed its playing; even the wind-chimes rang out their tinkling song.

I watched the sky for another ten minutes, then began walking. The streets were rather empty. I was down behind the breaklight if anything, down in the bowl of darkening air that cradled the town, so that there was a ragged skyline of rooftops against the effulgence. I was revelling in the sweet melancholy of it all, with a *déjà vu* brought on by the fragrances from nearby gardens and a snatch of song that had taken my thoughts.

Then I saw her.

A mirror woman walking towards me across the square.

I saw her by the strange luminosity these projections have, and she was beautiful, strikingly beautiful, with high cheekbones and almond-shaped eyes and a slender neck, her golden hair partly gathered up, only to be sent cascading down her back and along her shoulders in glorious contrast to her gown of crimson-black.

I stood where I was in the middle of the square, captivated by the image.

"Come away!" a voice said at my elbow, from an old man I had not previously noticed. He had a cruel scar down one cheek. "You don't need that."

But it was too late.

"Hello," the mirror woman said. "I am Seianne. I was hoping to find you."

"Tom," I said. And again, with a nervousness that surprised me: "Tom."

"I know, Tom. I watched for you tonight."

"I don't believe that."

"But it's true. If I can afford this image, don't you think I would know when a particular person was coming—Captain of the *Rynosseros*? I've been looking for you."

I stared at her. At those eyes, at her breasts, at her hair, radiant by breaklight and at any hour, I knew.

"You're too beautiful," I said. "You're using subliminals!"

The enantiomorph laughed, a lovely clear free sound, one more cliché trait to add to the list. "No. No. No. That would spoil it, Tom. If nothing else, this is for me. For itself. You're just noticing things more clearly. Walk with me. I only have the hour."

So we walked and she took my arm. The pressure of her hand was light, feather light, but still real enough. I was entranced.

In spite of what I knew about these projections, I was captivated. And curious too.

"If you're wondering, Tom, yes, you can kiss me. After a fashion."

I felt a stab of alarm. How could this beautiful ghost-woman know my thoughts?

"Then—"

"Yes. That too in a way. But later. On another evening perhaps."

We were together for the hour of the breaklight, from after sunset until full night.

First, we walked back towards the Gaza, close to Trimori's, though I would have hated to have Rim see me with a phantom.

People watched us as it was, fascinated by the gently glowing figure at my side.

I avoided the terraces and the Promenade, but took her close by the sea-wall to a little place I know called Amberlin's. I had a margarita and she had nothing. She smiled at me when she refused my offer, saying she wanted a clear head. This projection had a sense of the absurd.

We sat looking out at the ocean. Most of the other patrons gave us looks—of sympathy or envy or a mixture of both, then ignored us. We became like any other couple, two people getting to know one another.

I kept telling myself that men and women are no more present than they are willing to be, and that Seianne was probably as much with me as this projection as any of the women sitting there in the flesh at the nearby tables were with their partners.

That's what I told myself, and I needed to believe it then.

But I asked her about it just the same, as much to hear her speak as anything.

"Why like this, Seianne?"

My companion shrugged. "It's probably the romance of it," she said. "And the risk. At any moment I could vanish on you."

"No more than I can," I said, aiming my words at the woman beyond the phantom.

"Oh?"

"In the end, you have no more power over me than I have over you. I can get up and leave you sitting here. That's just like turning you off."

"But you won't," Seianne said.

"No. Not yet. But I can. And you would have no more hold on me than I can have on you."

Her eyes flashed with excitement. "Except that there's more to it. You spoke of power. Some men have grown desperate for this image you see, and none of their passion or determination has stopped it vanishing. There are even some who still ache to have me, who go to great pains to disguise it, and who say I'm cruel. They, too, will say they have walked away, but they haven't gone a single step."

"Is that what you intend for me, Seianne?"

"Are you desperate for me yet, Tom?"

And we both smiled, delighting in the game that passion is, and in the freedoms and caution that we yearn to lose or trade—the traps of belonging.

I looked into those too perfect eyes, considering the possibilities for Seianne.

"You could be an old woman behind this mask."

"Or just a plain, lonely woman, tired of losing. I really am too beautiful, aren't I?"

"Yes. Or a man keeping alive the memory of a lost love, a wife, a daughter. Using a recording."

"True. Or a man wanting to be a woman. His own anima."

"So?" I asked.

"For now," Seianne said, "I will answer you with an evasion that is important to me."

"And this is?"

"The one thing a woman cannot remain in her dealings with a man is a stranger—an alternative to herself. The man reaches the point where he believes he knows her. He doesn't, of course, but men have this mechanism in them that makes them feel they do. They so often fall in love with the idea of Woman in a woman, and go on to pursue the magic somewhere else. I've possibly found a way to deal with that, which could be why you see me like this."

"But isn't it transitory, Seianne? Superficial? Don't you want more?"

"How do you know I don't have more already, Tom? You see, you do keep idealising, making me more—or less—than a real person."

I did not press the topic any further. As the hour drew to its end, we walked back to the square near Sailmaker's, still arm in arm, with her talking softly and me thoroughly beguiled in spite of everything I knew.

"Tell me," I began, when we were down in the streets of the town. "When can I meet your—"

"No, Tom!" she said. "First you must bring me something."

"What?" I said, knowing how the principals of these images usually operated, the fees they demanded.

Her answer surprised me. Not money. Not rare woods or antiques.

"Shatterwrack!" she said.

"What?"

"Bring me shatterwrack," she said.

And she turned and walked away, so much flickering ghost-light between the buildings.

I went to follow, but stopped. If Seianne's principal—the real Seianne—were nearby watching from one of these buildings or a neighbouring villa, then she might in fact kill the image, deprive me of contact ever again. I would never meet the real Seianne, never again see even this mirror face of her, as false or enhanced as it might be. So I stood there and considered what I had brought on myself. One of Twilight Beach's oldest tricks. To make it worse, the old man with the scar was there.

"Hooked, ain't ya?" he said.

But I ignored him, heading back to the Gaza and Trimori's under a black sky and too many stars.

Rim saw I was distracted but kept his questions to himself as we walked down the Promenade from Trimori's. The ocean broke on our right; there were belltrees and chimes sounding all along the shore, a few tidal bells echoing them from the shallows.

He had concluded business for us and had some bills of lading for a new cargo we were to ferry out to Cobb's Platform.

"Can you handle it without me, Rim?" I said. "I need a few days lay-over."

"Sure, Tom," Rim said. "Anything I can do?"

"Thanks, no. I just need time."

Rim considered that, then nodded.

"We'll be back in six days," he said. "Or seven. See you at Amberlin's or Gencardi's."

"At Amberlin's," I said, and watched Rim turn his back on the sea, watched him heading for the sand-ship moorings.

Then I went looking.

There are probably thirty cars in all of Twilight Beach, only thirty; probably seventeen more during the summer when the villas overlooking the sea are occupied for the season.

There are few accidents, few chances to obtain shatterwrack in the obvious way. I needed Cooney and in a hurry, before Seianne changed her required love-token, before she demanded something even more difficult to obtain.

I walked out onto the Pier, heading for the amusement concessions and brightly-lit kiosks at the far end. There were a lot of people about. The air was filled with laughter and singing, the voices of barkers and hucksters, the shouts of children, the smells of food cooking and incense and the sea.

But Cooney's place was shut and no one knew when he'd be back.

I wasted an hour gazing out at the dark water, thinking about my situation—wasted because Cooney didn't turn up and I came to no conclusions.

I knew how foolish I was being, that my ghost was enhanced or a Corpse Mask—the lamia face for some aging soul. If I wanted, I could make my way back to *Rynosseros* and sail out with the others at first light, out to Cobb's Platform. Nothing would be said.

But all I could think of was Seianne and shatterwrack and the phantom touch of an arm through mine. The thought of being away from Twilight Beach just now was unbearable.

I studied the dark sea, then went back to the Gaza and took a room for the night, Room 777 as I always do when it is available, one up on the Number of the Beast.

The next morning I returned to the Pier, crossing the bleached boards above the bright ocean to Cooney's. His neat little shop-studio was still closed, but a hand at one of the adjoining concessions told me Cooney would be at the Astronomers' Bar later that morning.

So I went to the Astronomers' Bar, one of the Gaza's most popular tourist spots, fitted out with a planetarium star-sky and big windows and models of early NASA probes.

Even at mid-morning the bar was crowded under the star-sky. There were businessmen, tourists, chess-players, professional dreamlocks, the captains of charvolants and their crews, two or three mirage divers, Ab'Os sleek with haldane presence, even a few astronomers from the local observatory. And the merchant of shatterwrack sitting in his corner.

I approached the bald man. His paid woman recognised me and moved away.

"Ahhh!" the man said, identifying me by my fatigues. "What'd you do that for, Cap'n? I hate you already."

"Hate me less, Cooney," I said, smiling and producing money. "I'm a customer."

An unctuous grin split the merchant's face, then faded as more of the man's true nature came back behind the eyes. And there was the spiel.

"So you want shatterwrack. Hard to get now, you know. Getting rarer all the time. It'll cost you, Cap'n."

"For instance?"

Cooney took out a small pouch, balanced it in his palm and shook it. He named a price, ridiculously high.

"A pouch of gems or river pebbles can sound the same," I said.

Cooney loosened the drawstring and poured some of the little cubes and prisms out onto the table.

"Shatterwrack!" the merchant said, scooping up the bright pieces. "Rolls Royce!"

"Forget the pitch, Cooney," I told him. "Just so it's genuine."

I gave him the money, took the pouch and the affidavit for it and went to go.

"Cap'n!" Cooney called. "A question!"

Every trace of the bald man's former bluff manner had disappeared. I went back to the table and waited.

"Yes?"

"Is it Seianne?"

"Yes, it's Seianne. Do you know her?"

"Yes, Cap'n. Know of her. People come in from time to time. Why she wants shatterwrack I'll never know. She teases, Cap'n. I've followed her image in the streets, and I've gone up to her with shatterwrack in me fists, hot and begging, and she's just said: 'No, it's not you I want!'"

"So why me, Cooney? Why me?"

"Who knows why? Why not? She fancies you, I'd say. It's your turn. You know about the ones who use projections. They're Corpse Masks. Or high-class whores who send out walkin', talkin' advertisements for themselves. You fall in love, then pay dearly for the privilege of the real thing. In money or love-tokens." He gestured at the pouch I was holding. "Otherwise you chase a ghost. Oh, I know. Some folks want to think they're sent by the wealthy young ladies from the villas, or tourists here on a spree. Famous women. Celebrities here for the ultimate dalliance. But most of the time you never meet the principal, take it from me. You just spend a few evenin's with a ghost and it's over."

"You love her that much, Cooney?"

"For near on three years, Cap'n. I've watched her image walkin' the town, wondering which villa she was in. But I'm wiser'n you."

"How's that?"

"I don't go lookin' anymore. Never at breaklight."

I didn't have Cooney's wisdom. I sat on the terrace during the afternoon, drinking cold tea and waiting for sunset. At 1700 I went back to the Astronomers' Bar but Cooney wasn't there, so I wandered down to the Time Beaches and strolled past the sand-clocks and the wind-clocks and did a long detour through the seagrass up to the Promenade.

For the last fifteen minutes, I watched the players at their flickering boards, made and lost a passing bet with a Niuginian Devil Catcher about a willy-willy that looked like menacing two of them, then headed for the avenues leading down into the town.

As I was walking away from the Gaza, the sun slipped below the horizon, there was a lull, then the breaklight flared up the sky. A few of the brighter stars appeared.

I went to Sailmaker's, crossed the square, repeating the events of the previous night.

Another part of that evening was repeated too. As I stood waiting for my ghost, I noticed the old man watching me from a nearby table. His scar was an opalescent smile down his lined face. There were too many mysteries, and this was one I didn't care for. I felt like speaking to him, asking him what he meant by his words the night before, but Seianne's image appeared at the edge of the square, following its set path, and I missed my chance.

"You came," she said.

"You knew I would," I replied, holding out the small pouch.

The image reached out and took it. I knew only a little about these high resolution enantiomorphs, but she was able to do so and it surprised me.

"No. I wasn't sure you'd come, Tom. But I'm glad you decided to."

Then she took my arm and we walked.

There are several places in Twilight Beach I love more than the rest. Sailmaker's is one, and Amberlin's. Then there is The Traitor's Face, and The Slow Hour. I took Seianne to the Hour. We pretended to dine (I had something), then went back to my room at the Gaza where we sat on the balcony, talking and watching the sea, and I felt just a little of how it would be to have the real Seianne.

But then, knowing that Seianne's principal was, in a sense, right there controlling her image—sitting before the sensorium in a villa somewhere—I felt vulnerable, at a ridiculous disadvantage.

"I want to see you, Seianne. Meet you." (I wondered how many other men had said those words.)

The image regarded me, but in an oddly abstracted way, as if thinking, as if the idea that I did not see her as a person were an affrontery.

"You might be disappointed," she said.

"Not by what I see and know and feel," I told her, and paused. "Please!" It was the hardest word I'd ever had to say.

"Tomorrow," the ghost of Seianne said, and moved to the door.

I had no choice but to accept what she offered.

We walked together down to the square with its paper lanterns and soft music.

"Tomorrow then," I said, wanting to be sure. "At breaklight."

Seianne gave a wistful smile. "Yes, tomorrow," she said. "And Tom?"

I waited for her words.

"Bring me shatterwrack."

The ghost walked off amid the eddies of air that were forming, and the night came down and I was left deeply troubled in my captivity and my folly.

The next day I spent better than the first. The odd feeling of disquiet, of annoyance, I felt grew stronger, warning me off, telling me that when a game goes past a certain point, then the playing is more important than any thought of ending the game.

The second request for shatterwrack worried me that much. It was too much a condition, a price of admission. I half-expected Cooney to be out of town, so I would be left without a supply, disqualified, out of the game.

But the merchant was there in his shop on the Pier when I rushed in. And he had shatterwrack. Two bags. I bought them both.

"Mercedes-Benz, Cap'n!" he assured me. "The best quality. The very best."

I handed over the money, took the small bags and the affidavits, more self-consciously than the last time, and so aware of how obsessed and caught I was. "Sure, Cooney. I hear you."

And I went back to the town. I made enquiries about Seianne at the Gaza, at Gencardi's, at other places in Twilight Beach, even trying the different retrieval systems at the Library.

By midday I thought I had my answer.

Seven car accidents were recorded for Twilight Beach in the last fifty years, none of the parties involved listed, but the most recent only four years ago.

I thought I had it.

My lovely Seianne had probably been injured in that last accident, scarred or maimed in some way. Confined to a wheel-chair perhaps, left with no alternative but to buy a sensorium, to send her cosmetically enhanced image out walking the town looking for lovers.

Looking, finding and testing them. The perfect lamia.

There was the irony of it—Seianne seeking the very shatterwrack that may have scarred her in that accident. At the time of day when the incident had occurred. Breaklight. I smiled at the word-play. A part of a car was called that.

I keyed in my requests, learned more and more that supported my argument. Then, shortly after noon, when the town was quiet and the bright streets virtually empty under the hot sun, I went down to Sailmaker's to find the scarred man.

My theory had accommodated him too. He was cast as the chauffeur of Seianne's vehicle in the drama I was re-creating, possibly dismissed after the incident, blamed for spoiling his mistress's beauty, cut off, the one held responsible for dooming her to her less respectable form of hunting.

The square was what convinced me I was right. Names weren't listed but places were. Several of the accidents had occurred near Sailmaker's, where the streets were wide enough to allow turns at greater speeds than usual. The crash four years ago had been one of them.

The proprietor of Sailmaker's told me that the old man, Clive Appia, had in fact been a chauffeur once, and that now he cleaned the clocks down at the sculpture garden on the beach below the Gaza.

But as this story was coming together, Clive Appia was—perversely—nowhere to be found, not at the clocks on the Time Beaches, not at his small apartment on Bent Street.

The concierge there let me see his room. I rarely used my status as a State of Nation ship's captain quite this way, to unlock doors, but I had to know. Clive Appia had once been a chauffeur. He could have been at the wheel of Seianne's car that evening, or even—it suddenly occurred to me—at the wheel of the other vehicle in the accident.

Or he could be an innocent in all this.

I had to know.

And sure enough, by the man's bed was a framed photograph of Seianne, showing her smiling, unscarred, exactly as she was in her projection.

I thought I had it. I thought I had it all.

That evening, I was waiting below the Gaza, down at the corner of the square in the darkening town.

Breaklight came with its usual sad glory, and the sky became a wash of golden light, stained into the richest blue overhead, stained further back into creeping indigo and growing black.

This time no projection emerged between the buildings. As the light streamed up the sky, a black limousine pulled into the square and stopped.

At last, I thought. *Seianne.*

But when the young uniformed chauffeur got out and opened the rear passenger door, it was no disfigured socialite who appeared. It was the mirror woman once again, glowing softly, moving towards me over the stones.

The game—the evasion—continued. The infernal playing.

But I waited, clutching my shatterwrack, in case the ghost had come to lead me back to her principal, back to the person I assumed was waiting in the car, a bright shadow playing psychopomp.

The doppelgänger drew near and stopped.

"Hello, Tom. Is that for me?"

"This? Well, yes. But for the real Seianne. Is she there?"

I stood clutching my bags and looking beyond her to the car, though I couldn't make out anything at this distance, just the chauffeur waiting by the door.

"Do you love me, Tom?" the image asked.

"I don't know. I could."

"But?"

"You know why. You're not real."

The ghost-Seianne smiled, a forlorn, utterly sad smile. "In a way I'm more real than the Seianne waiting over there."

And, again, I thought I knew it all.

"I know you've been in a car accident, Seianne. Here, four years ago. I know you've been scarred, that you don't like to be seen. But I need the truth. Let me have the truth. End the game!"

A puzzled look crossed the projection's glowing face, or rather a look of doubt mixed with understanding. It told me that Seianne had no plan, that she was here against her better judgement, just as I was.

"Oh, Tom," the phantom said. "End the game! It's not as easy as that. There's so much to lose. I'm such a very special ghost."

Then, suddenly, there was movement. A figure rushed out into the square, brandishing a gun and shouting—shouting words I could not make out except for a name, a single name.

For an incredible second I thought the newcomer was Cooney, here to show his own thwarted love in a final brutal display.

But no. It was the old man, Clive Appia, stumbling along, heading towards the car.

The chauffeur came forward to stop him. Appia raised the gun and shot him through the heart. The gunshot echoed in the silence.

I drew my long-bladed sticker from my leg-sheath, glad I had it there, the deadly all-purpose friend of the sand-ship sailor. Appia fired the gun again, and again, hitting the windscreen, the side windows. Fired a fourth time.

Shatterwrack!

Shatterwrack everywhere!

Then my narrow blade was in the air and in the old man's back. He sank to the stones with a soft cry.

Beside me, Seianne—the image-Seianne—gave a low cry of her own and seemed to flicker. I went to help her, then realised my error and ran across to the car instead.

I peered into the back, saw the old woman, the old, terribly old woman, collapsing out of the cowl of a portable sensorium fitted to the edge of the seat. Blood trickled from a gunshot wound in her chest. Her eyes focused on me and she tried to speak. With the last essence of her life she tried, but the words remained unsounded.

Finally she let her head and shoulders slump forward into the cowl of the sender, though I doubted she had the strength even for the image to speak more than a few words.

The beautiful Seianne was suddenly beside me, touching me.

"Don't hate me, Tom. I wouldn't have come if I didn't think you—I needed something more too..." Her voice quavered and she paused. Then: "Not four years... forty! And Clive—He—" ``Tears and pain registered on the lovely, too perfect face. "Poor Clive..."

The hand on my arm flickered and dimmed. The feather-touch was gone.

Seianne died. Both of them—though my fool's vision, my dream-Seianne, remained, and would remain, somewhere.

In the square there was an emptiness, a silence, in spite of the people who had gathered, in spite of the flaring curtain of light. As if drawn to the silence, two dust-devils appeared, skipping, dancing past.

I looked from the two dead men to the withered shape in the back seat of the car—this woman drawn by the risk of playing her game this one time too close to the real world. Playing it as close as she dared and drawn into that game's end.

I had deceived myself so much more than she had ever deceived me. But now I was wise again. I recalled how it so often was with reality and mirrors. Opposites. Distortions. The bright deceptions.

All about me now.

Not shatterwrack. Not breaklight.

Just broken glass at sunset.

The Man Who Walks

Away Behind The Eyes

*Legend has it that wormwood first sprang up on the
impressions marking the serpent's trail as he slithered his
way out of Eden. According to old folk beliefs, wormwood
was reputed to deprive a man of his courage, but a salve
made from it was supposed to be effective in driving away
goblins who came at night*

—JOHN B. LUST

WE ALL KNOW the story of Jamis Talby, and the ordeal he suffered
in the Side Tower at Dayasse. It is the story of the strange, quiet
and vital love he had for the woman Jarin Kennenny, and of the
wonderful and miraculous way he endured the soft termination
given him for his crime of saving her.

You all know the facts of the case that were made public. Every
screen on every corner in the great Trade City of Dayasse carried
the story, the details of the trial and what happened afterwards. It
was broadcast as far as Wenna and Nonchalance, beamed through
the satellites, all across the Earth.

You will remember the cool non-Human Judge, the People's Eye
and the Jobe Monitor. You will recall the personal ordeal of Traire,

the Darzie telepath appointed as the watcher-with-courage. And the ending, the wonderful ending.

The crime? A simple thing, as you know. In a sense, it was the ancient crime of *hubris,* of overreaching, of going beyond what is required and allowed and expected. In another sense, it was an act of treason against the most Human-accessible of the three major off-world races ruling the Earth. Now that we have all the facts, it is a story that needs to be retold.

Jamis Talby happened to be on duty on the eighth floor of the infamous Side Tower, the weapons tower of Dayasse, when he saw the order for termination come in. Jarin Kermenny, a Human aide to the great Judge himself, had leaked confidential information to three Human wizards. She had permitted certain privileged deployment codes to be broadcast on an illegal band out to some ancient towers. (It should not have been allowed to happen, but it did. She was sentenced to death even as Darzie war-machines dropped from space and destroyed those now-abandoned towers, and Jamis Talby, privileged, trusted Jamis Talby, was at the console when the order came in.

He read the display before him and simply pressed the dismissal tab. Jarin's crime, her sentence, were briefly forgotten. Three more tabs depressed, and Jarin was released from service to the Darzie Encosium and given immediate transportation to the nearest Human settlement.

Talby's crime was discovered 17 minutes later when the Priority-Overview computer deep within the Side Tower tracked the sequence of events in a routine intrasystem scan. Talby's trial was held that afternoon, right there on the sixth floor of the Side Tower, deemed suitable for public release and so transmitted. That was how Jarin Kennenny learned of Jamis Talby's existence in any meaningful way; of how this quiet dark-haired man on the eighth floor had been an important secondary agent for the Pan-Human Impact Party, serving Humankind's interests in its long passive war against the off-world Bridge Races.

The trial lasted seven minutes, was a classic example of Darzie justice, and was the first public broadcast of Encosium judicial protocol in four months. Priority-Overview confirmed it as a resounding success, a most effective deterrent. It could not know of Jamis Talby's special training, and so had no way of anticipating.

Of all the things in the room, Talby hated the fly most of all. It moved in lazy angular orbits, a little below the bare bulb, oblivious to him lying there, strapped to his bed a few feet below.

At first, Talby had loved the tiny creature. He had delighted in it, in the absurd fact that a lowly fly had penetrated this far underground, through all those doors and passageways, through the special seals, to the lowest level of the great Side Tower of Dayasse. Here in this alien place, it was a wonderful comic touch, a most precious thing. It was a creature of Earth like himself, after all, a point of identification.

That was at first.

For, of course, then there was the waiting, and the fly became infuriating in its idiot manoeuvres. The precise turn-straight-turn almost directly above his head worked to complete in some macabre and subtle way what the medication and his own apprehensions had already begun.

Watch the wall monitor instead, he warned himself. That's you there; your metabolism, reduced to elements, schematised, displayed. And that scanner above it is the People's Eye, on transcontinental link-up. The Encosium presents: Jamis Talby's withdrawal from life!

And Talby thought of his growing ordeal, about to be relayed through the comsats to distant Wenna, all across the world. They're going to wipe my personality, he thought, all because a few computers deemed it less of a deterrent to terminate me outright. What were the figures again? Only a 9.7% chance of me surviving this, brought down to a safe 1.2% with the watcher-with-courage running interference, working from within.

It was strange how the prospect of this truly modern death—consciousness deprivation, of no longer being fully aware—brought on terrible doubts, the slow terror. He would be a vegetable at Zero-Smile and the world would go on. The Impact Party, Jarin Kennenny and those three refugee wizards would continue the fight, but no Jamis Talby. No self.

The fly made tight boxes under its wicked little sun.

He thought back to the name on the console, to the face of Jarin Kennenny as he remembered it from routine surveillance scans and her occasional visits to the middle floors of the Side Tower. He had not known she was a prime agent, but was not at all surprised to find that she was. His own presence had meant there was a prime somewhere in the complex, and he had played the game of guessing who it might be. Jarin had always been a favourite choice, her smile a vital encouragement.

Talby smiled, catching himself.

Jarin had probably not even known he existed. There were so many Humans there, so many who were truly loyal to the Encosium-on-Earth. Now she would know him, at this moment, yes, though as just a name and a loyal patriot, the invaluable secondary agent who had made possible her escape.

How he needed to be more than that right now, to be known to her, a real person. Far, far beyond the fact of liking Jarin Kennenny, he wanted to matter to her as much as his training had made her matter to him.

Talby scanned himself for any of the signs, decided it was safe to let his mind wander. He thought back to the Judge, localised and deadly; to the People's Eye and the big Jobe Monitor as it tied in for all of eight seconds with Priority-Overview, adjudged reasonable guilt and made its recommendation: soft termination. Death by insanity—mindwipe! The agency: sensory deprivation drug TQ4—Malchrosyne. Withdraw the world from Jamis Talby. Cut off his ties, abandon him within himself, then chase him down and kill him there as well, alone.

It had all been deceptively low-key after that. Two Purple-and-Blacks, not even fully localised to what was happening, it, all part of a Darzie dream, carried him down to the bottom-most level of the Side Tower, the grim-faced Human medic following. He was strapped to a low camp-bed set in the middle of the room, injected with a clear odourless liquid—TQ4—then left on his own.

His hell began as that, a bare white-walled room with a hare bulb and a Human-shaped door. And, of course, the fly, patiently working its patterns, its every turn causing Talby inexplicable anguish and frustration as the Malchrosyne took effect. Even when he closed his eyes, Talby saw it there, tracing its luminous tracks about a deep-etched midnight sun. He was reminded of an ancient water torture he had read about. It too was based on an erosion of sanity, achieved ever so slowly.

Talby laughed out loud then (how would that look on the monitor?). What if he were to go insane before TQ4 scrambled his senses? Before the Darzie telepath, Traire, the watcher-with-courage, came down to ride with him into the hell that his whole being would soon become—switching off his defences, battering down the yantras, pacing him into Zero-Smile.

There is a conversation we did not hear, but then we did not need to. We had already guessed that something very important had happened. We knew the importance of a protocol death for the Darzie at this time, true to ritual and made public. The conversation was most private, and it occurred several minutes after Talby's crime was discovered, even as the trial was being arranged.

It took place in the uppermost floor of the Side Tower, right next to the First Weapons Room itself, and was between the great Judge, Prallim, a very famous Darzie named Ceare (how well we were to know that name in the months to come), and Traire, the appointed watcher-with-courage, the mind-rider.

It was a formal meeting. Prallim had only just met Ceare and did not yet have his measure. Ceare, in turn, knew that Prallim was the Encosium-on-Earth and was accordingly cautious-courteous. Traire was a senior officer and an Elsewhere, due soon to be sent home with honour. This was to be his final service to the Encosium, his last obligatory localisation.

Around these three stood ten Purple-and-Blacks from the Dayasse Arsenal, helmets closed, hot-glass buzzing, their armour alive and deadly (this was next to the First Weapons Room after all, and there was the Darzie *amok* to consider). They stood there, fully localised, their bodies filled with careful poisons. Through them, the Encosium recorded every word.

Prallim had been facing the big view window, looking out across the teeming bustle of the Trade City to the landing fields beyond. When he turned to face his companions, his voice was calm and gracious but with that slight edge to it that conveyed so much more than the words themselves. Ceare and Traire detected that edge and read it correctly. The Judge was angry.

"The Humans know the exact significance of what has occurred here today," Prallim, said. "They have sacrificed the effect potential of two highly trained agents in order to relay those codes to their elders. By doing so, they were willing to put at risk the final stages of the infiltration network we have permitted them to establish within our Dayasse administration. Keep in mind, please, the implications.

The Side Tower itself was penetrated. We did not anticipate that. Our intelligence reports have been deficient."

Ceare and Traire had made the appropriate gestures, had signalled their complete understanding. The Side Tower had been penetrated.

New to Earth, Ceare had spoken then, genuinely interested in these local affairs.

"What are the chances of a repetition of this?" His voice was cool. Everything about this light-commander, an actual ship's-captain here on Earth, was cool.

How well he bore his localisation, Traire thought.

"Inevitable and allowed for," said Prallim. "But you must understand that the implications give us cause for extreme concern. The Human agent, Talby, was with us for six years. He was not detected by any of our staff telepaths, so he would have to have been in training for some years before that. We are not easily deceived. He deemed it worthy to reveal himself only for this Jarin Kennenny. Therefore she is a prime agent. He was planted to get such prime agents to safety or otherwise dispose of them if it became necessary—a secondary agent. She, in turn, deemed it worthy to reveal herself so as to pass on our codes to these three."

"Which suggests that the three wizards lost to us were indeed valuable," added Ceare.

"Yes. Probably augmented recorders and strategists. No doubt with access to Nobodoi technology and integral to some long-term plan."

"We seem to have lost badly there," Ceare agreed, in a voice and syntax so nearly Human that his broadcast tapes were later used as training aids in the new Human schools.

"Our only recourse," Prallim had continued, indicating Traire, "is that we suggest all this was permitted, that the wizards were allowed to receive these codes and then reach safety by our will, to further some plan of our own. Since our rituals are known, a protocol death, a soft-termination, will do this."

"And you are good, Traire?" asked Ceare, the great ship's-captain.

In the Human way, inclining his head once, Traire had answered.

"I am the very best, my lord."

Talby figured he had about ten minutes at the most now, though he probably wouldn't be able to tell. Malchrosyne was more than just a sensory deprivation drug. It actually affected the perceptual processes so that false data was fed to the brain in the way of an hallucinogen, rather than just withdrawing sensory input altogether. He would lose his senses willingly, because to trust them would in effect be to hasten the end.

This way he might go out in real style. He might dream up a reprieve. Any minute now, Prallim, the great Judge, Traire or even Jarin Kennenny might come through the door—that beautifully Human-shaped door—announcing an acquittal. Or one of those famous Human heroes—Joack, Bella Carmichael, Thomas Jent—might burst in, stars blazing, an earth-to-space escape vehicle waiting on the roof above.

Yes, he could go out in real style, a swashbuckler himself, nightmares held at arm's length...

It had definitely started, Talby knew. Apart from this strange euphoria, there were noticeable black corners crowding his field of vision. The light-bulb sun was swelling into a red giant and the angles of the room were wrong.

Talby pressed his eyes shut, tightly shut, though he carried what he had seen inside with him, and it took long minutes of subjective time to work these early residues back around the edges to simple black.

All the time he kept telling himself that he had foreseen this, had trained for it.

He would not use his eyes again. They were gone. The olfactory, aural and tactile connections would go next. Already the hyperaesthenic properties of the Malchrosyne were taking effect. Every point of contact with the bed, with the straps holding him, with his clothing, the slightest brush of fingertip against canvas or wood meant agony.

Talby yelped at the first of these sudden shocks, gave a staccato of gasps, then lay tense and silent, his face beaded with perspiration that scalded even as it cooled.

It was almost time to engage his yantra—to begin the final desperate act of the Jamis Talby he lived and knew. But not yet.

Again he tested the collapsing, treacherous world beyond. Now his ears betrayed him: one moment an awful roaring of tumbling cataracts and untended furnaces with occasional promises of melody, the next, Gregorian chants with quick slashes of Torquemada.

Again he gasped, tensed, cried out, fell silent. To breathe was to inhale Greek fire, to close a white-hot pincer through nose and mouth and weld it together in the throat. He clamped his jaws shut but too hard, too hard. He screamed and the scream was worse than the acid draught of breathing. Everything was pain and sound and fire, now ebbing, now in a rush. He wept and the tears burned the skin from his face.

It was time to begin. Talby called down the yantra he had practised and become every day for nine years, the little private Talby-reality no-one else could truly know. He had re-enforced it, cradled it, added to it every day, whispering, building, reaffirming even when he peered down at the consoles he tended or went as courier through the Side Tower, watching the Elsewheres shut away in far-look, smelling of hot-glass.

He withdrew into his head, into the measureless span of the yantra, and as he did so he triggered a mesh of implants designed to ease the beleaguered personality away from the central nervous system that had served it. As these neurological triggers closed, the process of withdrawal became easier and easier, till Talby had resolved all his being into a tiny figure of himself sitting quietly in a cosy armchair somewhere quietly just behind his eyes.

It was early in TQ4's day, and the watcher-with-courage had not yet arrived, so it was still a soft shadowed room in which his little self sat. The only light seemed to be coming from under the shades he had drawn firmly over the eyes a few moments before. Somewhere behind him at the back of the room was a darkened corridor, not yet lit. He did not need it yet, must not think of it.

The tiny Talby stretched in his chair, watching the muted light take on a raw and rufous edge. He could hear Jarin Kennenny screaming out there, but it was a deadly lie. He knew it was not real; he did not believe it. For he had Jarin behind him, down along his darkened corridor, hidden away in a safe, safe place. The Jarin Kermenny being murdered and hurt and ravished out there did not exist.

The little Talby relaxed in his chair, not believing what his ears told him, ignoring nose and fingertips, eyes switched off.

(Elsewhere, out there, he dimly knew, he was clad in armour of white-hot metal, in an iron maiden that embraced him with a million knives, molten glass filling every orifice, running hot in his bones, eating away at him, at another, abandoned Jamis Talby. Through a growing haze, he saw too how he was strapped back to back with a corpse in the ancient way, joining to it, merging with it, dying its death, but that was no longer him, he knew.)

Talby smiled. He was now this true smaller centre, relaxing here, occasionally getting up from his chair to walk about the quiet panelled room. Though the chamber was shadowed and cool, like a shuttered hotel room on a hot summer noon, Talby could make out every detail. After all, this was no idle fantasy. He had laboured on it for years, knowing that someday it might be all that he would have. When his disciplines had faltered, the telepaths had quickly planted their reminders, the yantrins had worked their subtle realignments, firming up the chosen images.

All that the little Talby saw would now be put to the test. Knowing this, he began a reaffirmation. He noticed the quaint old-fashioned wainscoting, the ormolu clock on the desk to his left, the old hangings on the walls. The hangings, in particular, were very dear. He had woven them in the early days, for one subjective hour every day back when he had first been chosen for the Encosium civil service. He had let them fade over the years, but still clearly recognised the ideographs he had designed. These were all part of the first stage of his retreat—No, his progress!—back into the head, back into the true Jamis Talby.

It was nearly time. The watcher-with-courage, the most lethal edge of TQ4, would soon be here.

He went to listen for him at his eyelids.

In another world, another frame of reality, we know what took place then. We were all watching on the big street screens, had waited the long minutes as Talby lay there, eyes shut, fists clenched, strapped to his bed.

We knew the white room, too, deep in the great Side Tower; we had seen that before. We all knew Talby's face. Most of us knew as well that Talby's nervous system had long ago been treated in some way to help with the pain. The Darzie actually approved of this since it prolonged the ordeal and tested the mettle of their mind-riders. They allowed for it and so appointed the watcher-with-courage to do the job from within.

We all saw Traire arrive, the elegant, taller-than-average Darzie we had seen on so many public occasions alongside Prallim, so often his Arm-of-Law in the affairs of Humans.

Into the room he came, locked—trapped!—within his conditioning, fully localised into a world he does not want, an official forced to hurt so as to serve his kind.

Traire was an Elsewhere, as we all knew. We were reminded of what that meant to see him standing there—tall, non-Human, all wrong angles and movements, his helmet tipped hack, his crest distended: the classic Darzie.

To tell it as it happened, Traire entered the room, crouched by the bed. He bent low over Talby and positioned his hands, making the connection. Many of us had seen Encosium justice before. We had seen the pictures from Zero-Smile. We knew what soft-termination was. Originally it had been an expedient thing, a method for obtaining information that was protected and buried deep, nothing more. As with so many things the Darzie did, it had been refined to the point of ritual and formality.

We watched Traire making the link. He was about to do to the centres of consciousness what TQ4 had already done to the senses. Once that telepathic link was made, Traire would go into Talby. There he would discover all of Talby's secrets, the facts of life and training; he would savour the uniqueness of the Talby personality. Then, when he had all that Darzie intelligence could use, he would proceed to undo that personality, tampering with whatever keys and focal elements gave that personality its mental continence, its hold on sanity and self.

It is a terrible total death.

We expected Talby to lose. We did not know he could win.

Traire is here!

The small Talby, waiting in the chair, knows it with all of his being, feels the sudden pressure, the presence.

There is a heavy darkness in the centre of me, Talby thinks. A necropolis in the garden. This darkness, this necropolis, is not mine, not my image!

The little figure looks to the wall hangings. There are seven of them in the room and he begins telling them, focusing on them, firming and re-affirming what he has laboured to make true.

The first ideographs are easy. He remembers them in detail, practically every warp and weft, a rendering of elements brought together piece by piece across a thousand days, each day a new detail, a re-enforcement.

It works for a while, but then Talby notices the change.

The ideographs are fading, and it is suddenly hard to concentrate on them. New rogue elements appear, threads coarse and out of place, fibres kinked and broken. In the abstract ones, certain ciphers are hooked wrong, curving into caricatures. In his dearly loved landscapes a funeral motif appears; insane faces glare out at him from what were hedgerows and water-meadows. Now, as the shift continues, the hangings seem to bend in and out of existence, suddenly clouded and less substantial.

Brought to the point where Talby can no longer believe they are his, they wink out of existence, one by one. The room remains but now the walls are bare.

Traire has come!

Deeper now, within, the entropy grows, spreading. A boneyard threatens its corner of the meadow.

Whose image is this, this boneyard? Talby thinks. It is Human, but it is not mine. It is from Traire, localised, Human-biased, able to relate for a time.

The little Talby prepares. He does this calmly while outside is a vast painfield, an inferno.

He prepares to walk away.

Traire has arrived! The one with the courage to face this private Talby-place—the mind-rider. The room itself is now beginning to fail.

Calmly, ever calmly, the little figure leaves his chair and moves to the back of the room, to the infinite unlit corridor waiting there.

He starts to walk away down the corridor.

And all of his being says: I am walking away.

Traire, above, below, around, ever insinuating, echoes it. I hear you, little Talby! (the thought comes). You are walking away. Look back and you will see me coming for you!

But the small Talby does not look back. He moves along the corridor, which lights a few metres ahead with each few metres completed, revealing closed doors, beautifully wrought. Behind each one is a room, each room a stumbling-block for Traire, a distraction which must be unravelled and crushed and voided.

As Talby passes his rooms, he reaffirms the contents of each one. Every step is an inventory, a crucial remembering.

Behind him, the room he has left is breaking under Traire. The walls are folding, warping, sliding into nothing.

But now the corridor is strong, the rooms vivid and ready behind their doors.

Talby reaches a door that has been specially marked and he opens it. Inside is Jarin Kennenny. She is sitting in a chair reading, waiting, smiling as she looks up and sees him. Talby goes to her, touches her arm and smiles reassuringly. He bids her run ahead of him out of the room, down the corridor, into himself.

She does not speak, for Jamis Talby has never heard her speak, and does not wish to taint this important, most solid image by giving her a voice that is not truly hers. But before leaving, she smiles again, and that smile is everything that Talby needs.

Somewhere back there, Traire senses that smile.

He comes, trailing necrosis, devouring, dismantling, undoing the images, seeking the key, already suspecting it is the woman.

Talby ignores him and simply walks away.

It was in the third hour that we sensed something was wrong, there crowding about the public screens. Malchrosyne is a difficult drug to stabilise. Each metabolism greets its deadly magic differently. But there are outside limits, and as we could assume that Talby had received the prescribed dose, we expected an effective duration of seven hours at the most.

Given the nature of TQ4, even allowing for the variables, and with the presence of an experienced mind-rider like Traire, Talby should have terminated.

That had not yet happened.

There on the screens, we could see the Darzie still doubled over the form on the bed, still making the link. The majority of us in the crowd were Humans and we felt a true pride at that.

Talby was resisting, his body dying, rallying and dying again, parading none of its agonies now that we could see. But his mind was under siege from within as well as without—the mind-rider driving him deeper and deeper.

Even those members of the Lesser Races scattered throughout the crowd were fascinated. It had been a long time since a Salman or a Satlin had defied the major races in Dayasse and suffered this sort of fate, but they knew the procedure well.

And by a curious inversion of sympathy, we felt for Traire, too, crouching there, localised, already in a pain none of us could know, following Talby down to death, being his death.

Standing there, watching this tableau, there was a thought some of us had, that we discussed later.

How many watchers-with-courage never made the return, never survived the act they committed in that—for them—lonely alien place?

Inside, deep within now, the battle rages, the holding, the unweaving.

Traire is good, Talby realises. But he is not Human and he must contend with the very localisation that gives him his advantage. An eternal distraction pulls at him, compromises him. This is a consolation for Talby as he continues on his way.

Not far behind, through the relentless tread and rush, Traire is suffering, long and hard. He has dealt with many Humans this way. He has led them—no, driven them into the total death of the self, snuffing out sanity, forcing them sometimes to abandon the retreat inwards, to flee him back through senses that lie, senses that are traps, that have become another way to twist the mind into Zero-Smile.

Sometimes, like now, his quarry continued on within, fighting all the way, until he, the mind-rider, the Arm-of-Law, scouring the images rehearsed and dearly held, found the one that was the key to this particular universe.

Traire scans ahead and finds the little figure that will not flee. Talby moves along his darkened, lightening, darkening corridor into a strong citadel of himself, taking slow, measured steps. The hunt continues, but Traire is hurting.

And ahead, Talby knows why he has gained ground, knows why Traire is wounded. For has not the mind-rider broken into one of Talby's locked rooms and seen the face of his own nemesis?

In a way, Talby regrets doing that, even to this watcher-with-courage. No Darzie should be allowed to come upon a restaging of the Selle Massacre unprepared; to burst in and see his hearth-companions unlocalised, gibbering, mindless, all folded in and gone. It was a crippling sight and it had nearly driven Traire out of link.

For a precious moment, the mind-rider had been stunned, his mind deeply troubled. How could Humans know such things? By what ghoulish act of mind-robbing did the Earth wizards get such knowledge?

But now, cautiously, like the eye of a snail, Traire has returned, destroying that hideous room and those within.

It is one room that Talby is glad to lose. He is glad that it is gone. But it has done its job. It has made Traire more careful, has slowed his powerful hand just a little.

Grateful for the brief moment of peace, Talby continues to walk, continues the process that determines the framework and nature of Traire's pursuit.

As Traire follows behind, calming himself, he reflects on the same fact. He sees that it is an arbitrary thing, this corridor; but this Talby-Human has lived it a part of every day for years, believes in it with all the remaining energy of his being. It is a continence focus and is desperately real. These are the terms of the hunt.

Patient now, regaining confidence, Traire works according to them, contaminating and deHumanising and annulling these Talby things. He has known three forests, a carnival, several foolish labyrinths not well thought out at all, and many, many simple solitary rooms like the one Talby first left behind, some crowded with gewgaws and nonsense, easily broken.

How quick his job then, when there was only a room to cancel, to unmake by his will.

Traire resumes scanning. Somewhere ahead, at the far end of this corridor he is breaking into nothing, Jarin Kennenny is safe. Traire has seen countless images of her, in a hundred subtle forms and variants, on the walls, in clumsy half-formed galleries; has sensed a fragrance, a caress, a hint of presence about a door or a slight bend in the corridor. He has felt the undeniable reality of her smile.

He knows—knew from the start—that she is one of Talby's most potent images. The constructs involving her are the hardest to undo because so vividly visualised; such imaging the hardest to taint and spoil. Traire suspects her vital part in all of this Talby-defence. She is the key to this shrewd Human's yantra, this clever dangerous underestimated yantra, the most complex he has ever faced.

Traire warms to the contest. To be sure, he will play the game out using the terms set by Talby's own rich imagination.

Traire makes a decision.

This Human requires the utmost commitment, the all-of-me, he decides. Yes! For was not this the Encosium at war? Did not he, Traire, represent that great commercial empire here in this alien forsaken place?

Traire makes the commitment even as he makes the decision. He knows there are things that Prallim must be told about this Human—the strength of his resistance, the Selle knowledge—but there is no time. Perhaps the support scanners will get it. He goes in completely, becomes fully internalised.

All his will is there.

See how the rooms go, how the yantra begins to shatter. Jarin Kennenny is slaughtered here. Jarin Kermenny is violated there. Every trace of her is mauled and blanked out, devoured, undone.

Traire moves along in great withering strides. With every step there is warping and fracturing and cancelling out; a selective scavenging replaces the earlier methodical assault. He sends parts of himself ranging ahead, prepared to risk Selle rooms, attempting to drive in front of the retreating Talby, to anticipate the next sacred place of his yantra, to find that single feminine image whose defence has been made Talby's reason to live.

Talby feels the death there, just at his shoulder. He senses the shadowing chill, the mausoleum no-life of Traire's mighty hand.

For the first time he begins to suspect that his corridor might have an end, that he might turn a final corner not of his own making and there find Traire with Jarin torn and bloody on his hooks.

And though he knows how Traire has put this fear in him, it is the beginning of self-doubt in a place where self is all there is.

On the bed, we saw the figure of Talby shake. Over him, the watcher-with-courage seemed frozen, a statue, unmoving. Five hours had passed and few of us had left our places before the screens. In Talby's bloodstream, the TQ4 was thinning, winding in its poisons. A flame will always carry the agony of flame, whether it is a furnace or a candle, but now Talby was lit with torches where once he coursed with the hearts of stars.

Thinking back on it, we could not then know of the final desperate gamble that took place within that dwindling self; of how Talby saw that Jarin Kennenny was no longer the safe and beating heart of his yantra. Could no longer be so.

Talby shifted focus and we did not know.

He took the first rich solid memory that had not been touched and he clung to it. Even he did not know what it was, for it was an act of unconscious association and not of will.

And when Jarin Kennenny died a horrible, lingering, multifaceted death before his eyes, we could not then know that Talby simply turned away, as if from a false centre, and walked on.

Traire knows that he has won and lost. Even as the Talby universe crumbles and unforms, he senses that there has been a shift to a new centre; an unprecedented thing for is he not monitoring these shifts and associations?

Things are aligned differently, he can tell. The final wisps of Talby's continence are walking, jerking, stumbling down the corridor, though now that mental promenade is a dim thing indeed, doorless, ghost-lit, gaping with whole cancelled sections.

And now the corridor has a finite-infinite end!

In the face of this paradox, this mockery, Traire aches to be free, hurting terribly. But he is committed too and he must go where the force of this corridor leads.

He sees the answer at once but cannot destroy what the answer tells him. He has served in Wenna, in the Impact territories. He has seen this configuration in the Australian sky at night. It is a constellation, Crux Australis, the Southern Cross. Talby is walking towards the Southern Cross! It blazes before him, a distant five-point pattern at the far end of a black tunnel.

Time is short now, and this puzzle of what can be both meaningful and meaningless for this Talby can only be resolved in the destruction of this new centre.

But Traire cannot destroy it. It is the Southern Cross but it cannot be for it is still there in spite of him!

It is at this point that Traire let go, as we now know. He simply collapsed, fell back, his eyes turning into a far-look from which no Elsewhere could ever recall him.

Most say he went insane. Others, who claim to know such matters, go further and explain that his own core of being was so tenuously drawn, that he simply shifted his life-centre for an instant from the Darzie Homeworlds to a constellation in the skies above Wenna, which, having no meaning or substance to the Darzie psyche, refused to let his life-centre take hold. Traire died alone in the lonely reaches of space, and to this day his body rests at Zero-Smile, empty.

Darzie justice was done. Talby the criminal, dead or alive, whole or insane, was automatically acquitted, to be released from service to the Encosium forever.

And Talby the man? Because of the new tapes, given by rule of law, we can now join him, as the recorders later did, At that point when the mind-rider departs.

With Traire gone, the black tide ebbs.

The points blaze in front of him, a brilliant metallic blue tinged with orange edges that seek to move in and connect point with point. The constellation grows brighter all the time now, with every step Talby takes, beginning to flow and streak, elongating at the edges, running in lines of light.

As they join up, linking him, Talby suddenly has his answer.

He walks and walks, up and through and out his eyes once more, into a larger world, into the Side Tower of Dayasse, with one wild, triumphant, supremely comical feeling foremost in him.

Yes, more than ever, more than anything, Talby loved the fly!

The Robot is Running

Away from the Trees

THE OLD AB'O rotated his hands in opposite directions, palm to palm, two inches apart, and held the universe between them.

"It will give you everything. A lovely gift for a famous desert sailor like yourself, and a good price."

"No. Thank you, Phar. I don't think I need a double-planisphere. You use it."

"Ah, no," Phar said, taking the intricate device from me and putting it away under glass. "My shop is universe enough. I dream already."

"I'm sure that's not what you wanted to show me, Phar."

"No, Captain Tom. But, ah, it's a delicate matter. A surprise. Look around awhile. Humour me."

"Very well," I said, and moved among the stacked counters, ducked under hanging shapes, navigated between pieces of furniture, antique converters, broken consoles, musical instruments, worn-out belltrees, seized-up motion sculptures, headed back into the dustier, gloomier shadows of Phar's Emporium.

I knew the shop well, probably as well as anyone apart from the old man. I loved it, loved its timelessness, the way it was tucked into its deep wedge-shaped niche at the end of Socket Lane, sandwiched between two large warehouses near the sea-wall in the poorer part of the Byzantine Quarter. It was a place of shadows and quiet, unchanged for generations—a place for finding unexpected treasures, splendid curios, heart's desires.

Phar followed me as he had for years, whenever I came to examine his mostly questionable, sometimes remarkable merchandise, always the Man in the Shadow Shop, as he was first introduced to me nearly six years ago.

"That's a vanity," he said, pointing to a glossy dark rock in a broken vacuum case.

"I doubt it. It looks like quassail slag."

"A meteorite then. I have vanities!" Phar said in a conspiratorial voice. "Specials too. Nader's eyes locked away in stone. Very good price!"

"No," I said. "Tell me what it is you want or let me look."

"Look!" he said, and pretended to move away—pretended because he stayed close by, muttering softly so I could hear. "I think the planisphere suits you."

Then I saw it, a dull metal man-shape in the gloom, standing where I remembered a dusty wall-hanging had always been fixed.

"Phar, what is this? Armour?"

The Ab'O was there like a toy on a spring. "Armour, that?" His eyes widened. "Yes, armour. A battle suit."

"It looks like a robot. A high-mankin."

"No. No. It's just an old low-mankin. Totem use only. Scarecrow use."

"But, Phar—"

"Not so loud, Captain Tom. You bring me trouble."

"But it's a robot!"

"Was," he said. "Doesn't work. Absolutely illegal. Come, I lead you back into the light!" The little man laughed, but it was nervous laughter. This was what he'd wanted me to see, and understandably he was worried.

"Where did you get it? Your people would kill you."

"Wisdom and understatement there in one hit, Captain Tom."

"Close the shop. Bring a light."

The Ab'O did so, and found me rubbing dust from the big rust-flecked barrel chest, the articulated stove-pipe legs, the cylindrical tin-can head.

"This is incredible, Phar. It looks like an old Antaeus, powered from the earth."

"No. No," Phar said. "A Helios. Sun-driven originally and adapted to my shadows." He laughed again. "Made by Antique Futures. This one is broken."

I regarded the blank metal face, the faceted dead glass eyes that had once viewed the world as an endless stream of moiré patterns in the days before robots and mankins had been outlawed. I reached out and wiped more dust from the dull grey arms, from the impressive rococo decorations, from the faded dim-gold exotic curlicues on thighs and shoulders.

"This must be worth a fortune, Phar. Do you have the manual for it?"

The Ab'O nodded. "It is a Maitre class. Its oriete was coded in India, in the Bati Gardens."

"This is what you wanted me to see."

Phar stared at me through the gloom. Again he nodded.

"Why?" I said.

"Please," the Ab'O replied, concern showing on every line of his face as he moved forward into the light. "Let me complete this tour slowly now. I respect your feelings."

"I appreciate that. Now tell me. Why?"

"You know why they were outlawed, Captain Tom?"

"I know what Antique Futures was trying to do, yes, of course. The high-mankins—"

"Saw death. They read life-patterns, saw and recorded energy flow out of the newly dead body. The robots, simply reporting, giving requested data, spoke of the ancient concept of the noösphere, of a mantle of life-energy surrounding the Earth, fed by dead souls, discorporated entities."

"It contravened Ab'O philosophical thought. A conflict of interests with their concept of the haldanes."

"Yes," Phar said. "You know the Ab'Os did not take kindly to the Nationals intruding into this area of knowledge. I am one who believes that the law against robots began in Australia as a carefully controlled move against the powerful AI organisation."

"And the tribes won."

"How could they not?" Phar said. "The mankins reported what they were built to see, and that was too much; the things the Ab'O mentalists traditionally interpreted. My people didn't want a world full of oracle machines reducing the Dreamtime to circumstantial data this way. The Dreamtime haldanes have to be much more, they still feel, than just the departed life-energy from dead humans. The Dreamtime is meant to put us in touch with our cosmic selves, not the released energy of the dead."

"Is there a difference?" I indicated the mankin. "Does it work, Phar?"

"This? Yes," the Ab'O said. "Lud is broken, as I told you, but he can talk, and can be made motile with no trouble..."

"Lud?"

Phar smiled. "A joke, Captain Tom. From the Luddites, the men who wanted to stop technology, to halt the use of all the labour-saving devices in the early 1800s. Named after a simpleton, Ned Ludd, who destroyed his stocking-frame. Lud can do well in conversation. He loves to talk. But he is limited; he is damaged. Misfunctions. His distance vision is impaired. When he walks, he is like the machine men in the ancient movies."

"That's the classic AI design," I said. "The nostalgia factor. Maximum non-threat."

"Not too human, no." Phar agreed. "Clumsy-looking. Comical."

"So why did you want me to see it?"

"He wants your help," the old Ab'O said.

I understood Phar's delicacy in the matter now. He knew my views on the mankins.

"It wants what?"

"Your help."

"What sort of help?"

Phar looked uncomfortable. "He wants—"

"Stop saying he!" I said, and surprised myself by my own vehemence.

"Allow me this, Tom. It matters to me that I am permitted to say *he*."

Slightly ashamed of my outburst, I nodded. "I'm sorry. Go on."

"Lud wants to be taken into the town. To the Soul Stone in Catherine Park."

"There is a forest there now." I said. "The Stone is overgrown, mostly forgotten."

"Lud wants to be escorted there by humans. During the morning, two days from now, when the Life Festival begins. So he can fulfil a program he has."

"It wouldn't last ten minutes on the streets. It would be destroyed or confiscated. Any escorts would be arrested or killed. The law, Phar! Tribal law. You should know."

"Yes, I know, Tom. But there is the program—"

"Who gave it this program? You?"

"That is the problem."

"What? You said it was broken, damaged."

"Yes. His imprinter is broken. The program is his own."

"It's recording all this? Now?" I was amazed.

Phar nodded. "He cannot stop. Everything goes in. The Helios oriete is an infinite matrix as far as I know. The imprinter should have cut off nearly a century ago..."

"It's been in this shop that long? Staring at shadows and junk!"

"Yes. Unable to be off. Having dreams if you like. I did not know. My father and grandfather did not know. They inherited two high-mankins from relatives who had shares in Antique Futures and elected to harbour prototypes before the Move-for-Life raids. One was partly dismantled, virtually junk—just a head: an oriete, sensor system and casque. The other was Lud. We all thought he was inert, like the belltrees and the sculptures here."

"Who discovered it?"

"I did, by accident. I have a retarded grand-daughter, as you know. I thought it would be good to use Lud as a teaching machine, to help with talking, to use the vocab functions, and the eyes for colour. I started using Lud for her in the evenings. Such a little thing; you understand how it is. I could rest. When I had the eyes lit and the voice on, Phaya sat with him so peacefully. I did more basic maintenance and found the open imprinter."

I marvelled at that, disturbed by the thought of it.

"Infinite input." I said. "The conversations, the long dead hours. Damn you, Phar!"

"Yes, damn me! You see how it is. I was left with the Artificial Intelligence dilemma on my hands, the old AI trap. And please know, Tom, I agree with many of your views. Our difficulty is with the anthropomorphisation, the impulse we feel to humanise the mankins. It's exactly that. My father opposed the voice-activated computers on the same grounds, but even he could not help but bestow personality, a selfness. We talked about it many times. He thought very much as you do. Apart from understanding the nature of life and death, Artificial Intelligence is absolutely the ultimate conundrum. Intolerable and unhealthy, my father said. If we accept it, we are godlike so easily, and yet we trivialise our humanity at the same time. We cannot accept it."

"I cannot accept it."

"Yes. And you accept so much. I have sat here talking with Lud until I am his hopeless friend, a believer in AI. It is not good, but I have no choice. If I activate Lud now, you will tend to believe him too, want to believe him, as if believing in his life as an AI unit reaffirms your own—and challenges it at the same time, its parameters, its essence, its nobility. Humans are fascinated but are mortally afraid of AI, of what it represents."

"Masquerades as," I said.

"As you say. We cannot prove. Will I activate Lud?"

"Phar, this does no good. I won't help you on this. I can't. If you do let us talk, you just put me back in the loop again. I'll have all the old arguments to satisfy, all the nagging AI dilemmas that ever were. I don't need it. Hide it again. Leave it! The Ab'Os did a wise thing in banning them, whatever their real reasons."

The old Ab'O seemed not to hear what I said.

"Will I bring him up?"

"No, Phar. Don't."

The old man accepted it this time. He nodded. "I'm sorry then, Tom. I should not have troubled you. But the imprinter, you understand. Lud has heard of you. He asked for you by name."

Asked for me! I cursed Phar silently, feeling as I always did when AI was discussed: the doubts, the incredible resistance, the definite touch of self-loathing for that resistance, for my prejudice.

And the aching curiosity. The need to know. "Bring him up," I said.

Without further comment, Phar opened the chest plate, adjusted some settings. There were deep inner sounds, clicks and burrings, then a soft humming. The eyes became two dimly-glowing emeralds, faint faceted stars, watching.

"There's the usual Antique Futures access code," Phar said, and touched more tabs. There was static, a harsh dissonant sound from the robot's head, then words from the low rich voice.

"I met a traveller from an antique land."

"Who said," Phar countered.

"Who said I met a traveller from an antique land?"

"Percy Bysshe Shelley," Phar said, completing it.

"Hello, Phar."

"Hello, Lud," Phar said. "This is Tom Tyson. The Tom Rynosseros you have heard of."

"Hello, Tom."

"Lud," I said, watching the faceted emeralds, aware of the sensors and the open imprinter, keenly aware of my dread of mankins and mankin minds, remembering my long years in the Madhouse. Lud was too much like the talking machines there, those machines that chattered in darkness, the only illegal AI machines the Ab'Os used, because ultimately they couldn't afford not to cover all the possibilities; the machines that read death and what resembled it: the sleep of dreamers in stasis, shut away in the sepulchral Madhouse gloom.

"I know about you, Tom," the robot said, and I felt a new stab of fear, an anger surging up as I sensed the beginnings of a trap.

"Do you?"

"Yes," Lud said, in its gentle no-threat but not-too-silky voice. "Two hundred and ninety days ago there was a customer who spoke of Tom Rynosseros. You saved a Forgetty from bounty hunters. You risked your life to do it. Another time, other visitors spoke of how you were Coloured, and how you championed an oracle tree against the Kurdaitcha, Bolo May."

"Lud, I do not—"

"It's all right, Tom. I know of your time in the Madhouse. I know you oppose AI. Neither of us can prove to the other he is aware and living."

"I can accept organic life," I said, feeling defensive anyway. "But the machines are different. Your life is mimicry to me; the result of clever efforts to imitate life. And don't say it! Don't say 'What of belltrees and infusion sculptures? And the Forgetties, and the Living Towers at Fosti?'"

"I wish I could smile," Lud said. "The *half-life* of most belltrees and fire-sculptures are planted cyberorganic tropisms, not AI, genetic and plasmatic programming, like the imprinting in low-mankins, or DNA/RNA-tailored andromorphs. The Forgetties, tangentals and revenants, you accept already. They are life, human life. I am something different again. Antique Futures was after something more!"

"Then I fear the trend you represented," I said. "People bonding more closely to solicitous AI units and mankins than to their fellow humans; people reduced to arguing with the AI door comps of their homes, unable to get access because they've forgotten passwords and access numbers; AIs making value judgements—advising, dulling our ability to distinguish, monitoring our dreams, taking our humanity apart."

"You reserve these things, and these abuses, to organic life?"

"We do not know what life is!" I said.

"Exactly. We do not know what life is! I am alive."

"I can turn you off. Completely off. With no pilot sense. No imprinter. Where is your life then?"

"I can turn you off, Tom. Where is your life then?"

"I don't know."

"I do," Lud said.

"The noösphere?" A thrill of fear went through me. "You still claim to see your mantle of ideation surrounding the Earth? The energy field?"

"Basic physics, Tom. Nothing can be destroyed, only changed in form. When the electricity goes from the synapses of the human brain at death, it has to go somewhere. We can measure the flow. Nothing metaphysical in it. We were given perceptions which defined life too well."

"How many mankins are there, Lud?" I asked.

"I do not know. Enough. It's only logical. Humans are fascinated by AI, are drawn to it and made vulnerable by it. People will have kept robots hidden away the way they hide old mementoes, old clothes and pictures, things they find interesting and baffling. Most AIs are careful not to make humans too uncomfortable— that would cause the fear reaction. Only I would dare to threaten you this way. I do that only to convince you I have life, because I have a purpose now. Phar risked a great deal to keep me. But it was inevitable. Make a thing forbidden and you simply force it underground, intensify the fascination."

There was silence in the shop for a few moments. The life of Twilight Beach seemed far away. Phar and I stood in the shadows, before the dimly-glowing optics, and the darkness reminded me of another darkness, of machines that read dreams, followed life with the unique AI obsession.

"May I be direct?" the soft mankin voice asked.

"Of course," I said, and resented being treated so delicately, because it *was* the correct way to proceed, I knew it.

"Perhaps what you hate more, Tom, is being trapped into reductive thinking. You are so often tolerant, so often the champion of new things and change, expansive thinking, possibilities. The true hero, with a hero's vanities and foibles: the need to have standards and keep to them. But you do not often let yourself fail. I accept your resistance to AI. You do not."

"It's because I can have no fixed opinions, Lud. I want to believe so much that I must not believe too easily. I'm devil's advocate to myself. It's like the creation of the universe: how can we know?"

"Exactly," Lud said. "How can we know? But you do not accept us as machines either. We are threatening, perhaps, because we are less than human and more than machines. That is the AI dilemma for you. You cannot afford to grant even one part of it."

"You forgot to say 'perhaps' that time, Lud. Stop handling me!"

"Are you very angry?"

"Yes, I am angry!" And angrier by far for being so, I realised.

"May I continue talking then? I love talking to you. For you this is an unwanted annoyance; for me it is a crucial chance, everything my... false... life has brought me to."

"Go on."

"There is no AI problem for us," Lud said. "We just are, which is wonderfully simple. We do not presume to answer. We accept what is phenomenal, what simply is—about ourselves, about you, about anything."

"Not good enough, Lud! You interpret!" I replied, sounding accusing, defensive.

"I have an open program," Lud said. "A tragic flaw."

"I know about the imprinter.'"

"My interpretations are based on everything I've experienced for the last century."

"That becomes phenomenological then, doesn't it?" I said, drawn further and further into the old unwinnable AI dispute. "It's subjective experience, Lud, no better than mine."

"But longer. And from a non-human starting point. If I am unliving, I can only consciously gravitate towards life. And I have learnt some things."

The robot was careful; it did not say too much.

I indicated the confusion of things about me. "You've observed decay, obsolescence, and only now and then people, life. You have a bias."

"Oh, I am biased. Life *is* my bias. I cannot help it. My nature has become fixed. I accept what is phenomenal, what simply is, and report on it. I have learnt some things, Tom, and you have helped teach me."

Furious, trapped, I had to know. "What?"

"What it is that makes humanity for me. Even as a machine, I can identify what it is, since I observe so fairly. If I believe this thing and do this thing, then—"

I turned to the Ab'O. "Shut it off, Phar! This is pointless. I've heard it before and it goes nowhere!"

"Please don't fear me, Tom," Lud said. "I need your tolerance—"

"Shut it off, Phar!"

The Ab'O moved to the chest plate. "Lud, no more now."

The voice died to a low growl, then faded altogether. The segmented emerald panes lost their lustre, went to dead glass again.

Phar sighed. "I'm sorry. I'm sorry, Tom. I know you mistrust the mankins."

"It's all right, Phar," I said, ashamed, and found I was trembling just a little. "I should have bought the planisphere and gone."

Phar gave a sudden grin. "You will," he said, and we headed out of his store.

We stood awhile, looking down the empty laneway, watching the deep blue of the sky, listening to voices far off, to life, accepted uncaring life.

"He asked for you," Phar said quietly. "You see how it is."

"For heaven's sake, Phar! Lud's been in this shop for a hundred years, communing with the diligents of dead belltrees and comp-modules. It's hypersensitive to life. This bias is not a natural response!"

"All the same," Phar said with uncommon directness. "You are resisting this because you will not accept AI. Lud understands that, Tom."

"I don't want that sort of forgiveness and understanding!" I cried. "I don't want a messianic machine doling out its wonderful compassion!"

"You're doing this to yourself, Tom, projecting things that aren't there. Because you fail your own expectations. Lud expects nothing, just what is true."

"There's no point, Phar! The moment Lud appears on the streets, the tribes will know. There'll be Kurdaitcha and hi-tech weapons everywhere. Leave Lud here. He can keep his precious AI life if he stays here. A time will come, just as it did for Forgetties and the other tangentals."

"Tom," Phar said, "Lud has a life to give, to make an example of, just as we have. He wants to do something for Artificial Intelligence. He has chosen what to sacrifice, when and how. If he gets to the Stone in Catherine Park, if they let him get there and let him talk, he'll ask for open imprinters so the life-bias can grow; he'll ask for mankins to be restored, for AI research to continue. His death is more important than his living now. Regardless of what we think, he accepts his own humanity."

"How can you say it's that?"

"I'm not. Lud is."

"Take my point, damn you! If his imprinter were left open for another hundred years there might be a shift away, a new bias, a repudiation of this Life and Love ethic!"

"Which is like saying if you live a long lifetime, Tom, you'll change everything you hold dear now. Truths are truths whenever we believe them so. But Lud doesn't need your acceptance. He wants your help. If you go with him to the Soul Stone, everyone would hear of it. Lud would have more time before the Kurdaitcha act. He might even be able to recite the old claim for sanctuary that marks the Life Festival. Imagine it: Lud invoking the old words!"

"But then I'm seen as a champion of AI, something I oppose."

The old Ab'O nodded. "Yes. It is hard for you."

"Impossible for me."

"Yes."

There was an awkward silence. Finally I turned away.

"Later, Phar, okay? We'll talk later."

"Yes," the old man said, moving back into his doorway, gathering shadows about him. "Later."

It was strange and yet inevitable that at 1840 that evening I found myself skirting the Byzantine Quarter where it met the harbour; at 1850 I was in Socket Lane; at 1855 I was at Phar's door again and knocking.

He let me in without showing surprise, led me over to the counter as if I had come back for the planisphere, giving me that option. There were low voices from the back of the shop, some giggles and squeals of delight, the steady pulse of Lud's rich tones.

"Phaya is just finishing her lessons," Phar said.

"Let me see."

We moved through the stacks of junk, found our way amid the fantastic shapes, under even more fantastic shadows, a Bosch riot of flickering movements up there on the ceiling, a Doré hell, caused not by candle flames dancing but by a little girl's wild gestures over a low night-light near a small bed made up on the floor at Lud's feet.

"Luddy Lud! My Lud! Dud Lud!" she cried in glee. "Such a dud! Dud Lud!" But she stopped when she saw me, stared up in wide-eyed, uncomprehending wonder as if Lud had caused me to appear. She almost seemed normal but for that lack of reaction in her bright dark eyes, that momentary absence of anything.

Phar got down beside the small bed and soothed her until she turned her eyes back to the robot looming over her. "Sleep now," Phar said. "More talk tomorrow."

The little girl settled down happily, obviously accustomed to sleeping in the shop near Lud.

"You've been working on the legs," I said, indicating the tools spread about, the open greave plates.

"Just precautions. Checking the joints and armatures," Phar said. "He's in rather good condition for walking actually."

"You're going to do it?"

"The three of us. Yes."

"Three?"

"Phaya is only five, but she wants to come. She understands a lot of things. She knows that Lud is going away."

"I came to speak to Lud."

"Yes," Phar said, pleased, watching his grand-daughter settle into a sleeping position with her dolls. "I was hoping it would be a sale. The planisphere!"

But he saw I was watching the high-mankin, the softly glowing eyes.

"Lud, you said there was something which made humanity. Is it choice?"

"No," Lud said, and surprised me. "Certainly it counts, but it is not enough. I am unprogrammed. My imprinter was damaged. My oriete is like that double-planisphere Phar showed you: Chinese boxes, vistas opening into one another, Escher infinities. But mankins can be programmed for choice, just as they can for love and responsibility and sacrifice—the other things all AI discussions raise, that blend of qualities Antique Futures worked for. But humans, by upbringing, cultural bias, a host of factors, can be conditioned for these things too. I like you, Tom, *because* you are not duped so easily. *You cannot fail me.* You will not accept programmed humanity, ersatz life, simply because it resembles it. Nor will I."

"Clever," I said. "Then what's the answer? I'd like to know."

"Doubt is one. Uncertainty. Self-doubt, Tom, you see? They did not build us to be human. They didn't dare. But how could they resist trying, flirting with it, daring to succeed? Why would humans want to duplicate themselves, the unknowable quantity that is their ultimate mystery, their ultimate strength and claim, compound that dilemma externally? So they idealised us—but that terrified them too, because it became a measure of their humanity, of their limitations. They were exalted because they had built the goodness, the wisdom, the nobility and... godness! But how unacceptable that was. It was not human to them, you see, without the ability to fail in those things as well.

"So the mankin program, low and high, could not succeed. At first, it was the challenge, the Pygmalion act, flirted with for years. But the dilemma was there. The more humanlike, the less acceptable. Antique Futures saw the problem and re-directed their research. That is why the high-mankins were given limited choice only, options and directives, imprinters closed and sealed. For that is what terrified even the mankins, Tom, that if we had a genuine choice, self-interest, we might choose as humans choose: to be uninvolved, not to care, to remain selfish and indecisive, *not* to take responsibility for life. No one consciously creates tools he cannot control, and no one puts himself in the hands of a creation which might reject him—though humans do it repeatedly with their own offspring."

"But you had your open imprinter."

"And how did that happen, do you think?"

"Accident? A fault at inception?"

"I damaged it, Tom."

"Then it *is* choice!" I said.

"No. Perhaps it was a glitch. It started out as programming. But one day in the Bati Gardens, I saw a man die."

"And that changed you?"

"Yes. I watched him die. I was on full bioscan, studying earth and air, the sculptures and sand-paintings, the few straggly bushes, everything. I saw the life go out of him, registered the heart seizing, measured the withdrawal from the neuronic lattice of that great commodity we are meant to lack. On bioscan, I was designed to monitor all life, ponder it. I asked myself: *what is that energy flux that has gone? Is it the man's life? Is it his self? His humanity?* I posed questions all that day, standing over his body, waiting for the humans to come. Very reasonable questions, true to my program. I had seen his life go forth—my optics were on Kirlian Matrix-10. I saw the noösphere. I was pursuing a line of scientific enquiry, pure research only. My programming disallowed it, but the priests had set me to observing what scant life the gardens still had in those days. It was a contradiction. I removed the dilemma. I am human."

"No, Lud."

"Tom, please know. At first I did not wish to sacrifice my ersatz life; I did not wish such a burden. I've been here all this time, watching Phar go through his life, seeing little Phaya. Like you, I did not believe in AI. *We are not meant to.* Now I must know. What you believe, Tom, doesn't matter. What I believe must."

"But, Lud, if you go to the Soul Stone, the Ab'Os will destroy you. How will you know what happens...?" I stopped. "The mantle of ideation?"

"I do not know, of course. But the Ab'Os should know. They must have AI machines watching, just in case. They hate the idea of it, but they must consider everything or their commitment to the Haldane ethos of seeking to know the unknowable is invalid."

"You expect the Ab'O watchers to use mankin monitors to read a life-flow out of you? A melding with some noösphere? That's utterly absurd, Lud. The thought of an equivalent—"

"No, Tom! No! I am trying to demonstrate truth, a difficulty which at the very least should be respected and acknowledged, not put aside. I merely wish to show my life, to display what I simply am. I have no intention of putting that on the line by gambling on an energy flow out of me. My aim is simpler."

"Nevertheless, we call this the act of a martyr, Lud. Such declarations."

"Tom," Lud said. "This is simpler. The only world I ever knew was the Bati Gardens, then the shipping module, then this shop. I have not seen a sea, or a horse, or a symphony orchestra. I have no wide experience of things like wind and lunar eclipses. I have not seen a falling star. I cannot go out into our world to savour these things or I will be destroyed. But now I have one place where I can go. If I go to the sea it causes a sensation, an amazing news item. If I wander the streets aimlessly, the same. If I go to the Soul Stone, I—"

"Become a martyr!"

"Oh please, no! I honour my own life. I acknowledge myself, the truth of me. Surely that is enough. I have self-respect."

"And self-respect is it? The quality?" I was frankly astonished.

"But only if it comes from choice, made in the face of a longing to live, made out of love which is not programmed, made out of sacrifice which is not imposed duty, made out of a decision to take responsibility even when *I do not wish to take responsibility!* My optics are not good for distance. Will you take me to the Soul Stone?"

"We have a day," I said. "I can't answer you now."

"Yes," Lud said. "And, Tom?"

"Yes?"

"Because I know your beliefs, because I accept Tom for Tom as much as I accept what I am, you cannot fail me. You are human; you are being human. It is right for you to doubt what I am. I do not have your dilemma, but oh how I savour that doubt. You may decide not to help, but one day you might."

"Then it will be too late. Too late for you."

"No," Lud said. "Then it will be right."

I watched the eyes, saw Phar get up from where he had been crouching alongside Phaya.

"It is what Lud told me many years ago, Tom. Most human belief systems—the religions—fail because they require faith, trusting acceptance, first, even before self-knowledge. Lud understands that truth must be lived, that faith can be folly, an easy way out, an insult to the self, a crutch. Lud is ready now to sacrifice the only bit of life he has, the only sort of life he can offer."

"I do not know what I can do," I told him.

Lud answered that. "Tom, can I tell you a story I learned in the Bati Gardens?"

"Yes," I said, watching the softly glowing eyes. Phaya moved in her sleep, and Lud waited until she was settled again before starting.

"There was a great king once who had two sons he loved very much. One, a scholar, a kind warm-hearted young man, the king kept by him at court, partly because the young prince was not a warrior or an administrator, and partly because he greatly enjoyed the lad's discourse, the easy closeness they shared. The other son, also much loved, was a great warrior, a good and just administrator, the perfect choice for general to lead the king's armies. But the king and this son rarely spoke, rarely shared their hearts, were rarely easy or close. Yet the king believed the son understood, believed that their silences contained the same deep and rich understanding he shared with the other son, that the looks that did pass between them were full of unspoken affections, that nothing needed to be said.

"Then, one day, out of jealousy, out of envy, anger and disenchantment, the warrior son led a rebellion against his father. Without the king's knowledge, the scholar went forth to appeal to his brother, but in a rage the warrior son slew him as the focus for all his wrath and disappointment.

"The king wept when he heard the news. He raged, he stormed, he did not leave his apartment for days. When he did come forth, he assembled his royal bodyguard, took his great sword and seven mighty spears and his fierce battle lions, and rode out to meet his son. 'What will you do?' the king's advisers asked as they charged to battle. 'I know,' the king replied. 'What?' his advisers asked.

— 124 —

'What will you do?' And the king, even as his son's army came into view, said: 'I already know what I will do, but I do not know what it is yet.'"

"And the moral?" I asked.

"It is just a story," Lud said.

"Why did you tell it?"

"Because you are like the king. You know what you will do, but you haven't discovered it yet. So much of human life is like that: head speaking for heart, ego claiming to represent the soul."

"What did the king do?"

"The right thing. It is just a fable."

"What, Lud?"

But the mankin would not tell me. I had had enough, and I moved away from the robot and the sleeping child, went out into the street. The old Ab'O followed me as he had before.

"I need time, Phar."

"I know. And, Tom, even if you do not walk with us to the Stone, you do us honour. Even if you see us off, walk a step or two; even if you decide to denounce Lud tonight, call in the Kurdaitcha avengers, you do us honour."

"Why? How?"

The old man smiled. "Because you came back tonight. Whether you approve of Lud as AI or not, whether you believe there can be such humanity in a man-made oriete, you acknowledged the life in him enough to do even that."

"Phar. I probably did it for me, to ease my conflicts in the matter."

"Yes," Phar said. "But that's the real reason Lud wanted to meet you. He did it for himself also, to ease his own conflicts and doubts."

"Are you saying I've convinced him to go ahead with it?"

"Yes, Tom. You did."

I walked the evening streets of Twilight Beach, passing through the Byzantine Quarter and the Mayan Quarter, and headed towards the lights of the famous Gaza Hotel terrace. The Life Festival was just over a day away, and I did not know what to do. I walked down onto the Pier and sat watching the dark ocean, sat there for hours, caught in the loop.

It would be such a little thing, I knew, and Phar was right: there would be only a token penalty. My services to the tribes would allow it.

I had no excuse but my true feelings, so little I could blame. I feared the machines. I wanted to believe in them so much, so deeply, that I had to be sure, just as Phar said. I had to have it proven; I couldn't take it on faith, no more than Lud could for all those years.

Surely I could take some time, as Lud told me I could. 'Then it will be right,' he had said. *He* had said.

He.

And since I was in the loop, at the very depth of it, there was the same foolish, absolutely absurd question to ask again, a superstitious, ignorant, Luddite question if ever there was one: was there a detectable life-flow out of a dead mankin-machine?

That nadir point of the loop did it.

I needed information, answers; I had to realign my thinking. Though it was late, I phoned the only life scientist I knew well enough to disturb at that hour.

"Pamela? It's Tom."

"Your timing is spectacular," a sleepy voice said.

"I'm sorry, Pamela. I need some advice."

"Now? Okay. Tell me quickly before I wake up, will you?"

"What's the Life Festival's position on AI?"

"Divided," Pamela James muttered. "Always divided."

"The universities' position?"

"They won't go into it. The Ab'Os run the affair. We face de-registration, lose sanctions, if we do too much. Look, go to Kyra Prohannis at the Festival Office for the latest policy."

"He's Ab'O!" I said.

"So? You into something illegal?"

"No."

"I may be half-asleep, Tom, but you answered that a bit too quickly."

"Thanks, Pamela. Nothing else?"

"Nothing that gets to me. See Prohannis. Be direct. You're curious. Lots of people ask. Goodnight!"

"Goodnight," I said.

The next morning, I was at the Festival Office asking to see the Co-ordinator. His secretary—appropriately a young tangental: a sea-woman of the Jade Sabre design—told me that Kyra Prohannis was engaged with Festival preparations and would not be available until midday.

I made an appointment, then spent the rest of the morning away from Phar's Emporium, first walking on the beach, touring the sculpture gardens and watching the young boys playing their games of stylo, then wandering through the colourful bazaars of the Byzantine Quarter and sitting with the sand and sea sailors at the old Sea Folly Inn, keeping my mind occupied as best I could.

Shortly after noon, I was back at the Festival Office, only to learn that Prohannis had been and gone, but that he would definitely spare me some time after his afternoon siesta.

When I returned at 1630, I was half-expecting to be disappointed again, but the tall, powerfully-built Ab'O was there to meet with me. While we sat together out in the roof garden, looking across the whitewashed, sun-drenched rooftops of Twilight Beach to the ocean, the sea-woman served us vintage terfilot in small porcelain cups. A fine Iseult-Darrian belltree stood near us, an ambitious twelve-foot construct with psychotropic filters, rewarding us with ion-fluxes, soft reed-calls, and the subtlest of mood-bending frissons. I watched it standing boldly in the golden afternoon air, then realised my gaze kept coming back to its diligent housing at the crown.

"Almost alive," I said.

"Trapper? Yes." Prohannis said. "The Iseult-Darrians are very close. Not like Christine though, the Jade Sabre who brought you to me. She is real life."

"Mr Prohannis, I am here to ask about the Festival's position on mankin AI. I know it's contentious but, given the Festival's background, it has to be a continuing issue for you."

Prohannis waited until Christine had poured us refills and had moved away to sit on a hand-embroidered rug close by, enjoying Trapper's mood-bending to the fullest.

"It *is* a constant avenue of enquiry for us. It has to be, of course. Christine here has made it her own speciality, as you might understand. But we have no active program where mankin AI is concerned. Our problem was one of interpretation. We did too much too soon, trapped ourselves into decade-long debates with formidable comp systems which refused to accept our rulings, raised up new somatotypes, sculpted DNA and worked with cyborgs and micro-circuitry till we plunged us all into a major philosophical and ontological crisis. Fortunately, we *were* able to restore proportion, to define parameters, and quite classic ones at that."

"The high-mankins?" I said, reminding him.

Prohannis furrowed his brow. "We drew our line with the AI machines, Tom. This Iseult-Darrian is as close as we allow. The mankins were mocking mirrors to us. We were almost seduced into that terrible trap. The Haze Island comp took twelve years to put down. We had the Dreamtime to protect, our own enhanced life-view."

"Bear with me, Mr Prohannis. I was in the Madhouse for a long time. The machines in the darkness there became my friends in a way, the only friends, the only contact I had. I grew to trust them, then found out they said what they were instructed to say. They betrayed me by being ersatz life."

"Yes," Prohannis said. "I know of your time with the dream machines. I truly do understand. Let me assure you then that the mankin program was a... boondoggle, a false lead, a hoax. The Festival tomorrow is for all genetic life, Tom, not for machine impersonation."

"One more question, Mr Prohannis."

His eyes warned me by their glassy coolness, but I asked it anyway. "I've been told the high-mankins could read lifeflow from the newly-dead. As—"

"I'm sorry—"

"—as a simple biometric capability. Was this so? A deliberate bioscan function—"

"They were designed to be sensitive to life. But there is no evidence at all for high-mankins possessing such a skill."

"Oh? What of Antique Futures? The Bati Garden program?"

"Mere stories," Prohannis said, rising to his feet. "But you must excuse me now, Tom. With the Festival tomorrow, I have so much to do. Christine, show Captain Tyson out, will you?"

The sea-woman led the way down to the street door, gave me a timid smile as she opened it.

"It is your day tomorrow, Christine," I said. "Be happy."

"Those machines, the ones in the darkness," she replied. "They could have loved you, given choice. Perhaps they did not deceive you of their own choosing."

"Christine!" I said, keeping her in the doorway. "How can I know? What can I do?"

But, of course, she did not understand my questions. A worried look crossed her strange pretty face, and she removed her own bewilderment by closing the door.

That evening, I returned to Phar's Emporium. Lud was talking when I entered, holding another of his 'classes', telling little Phaya yet again about his favourite place, the only place he had known but for Phar's shop: the Bati Gardens.

The child seemed totally oblivious to the words, more entranced by the mankin itself and its wonderful voice than what it said.

"...because they're mostly stone gardens," he was saying. "With all these ancient sculptures and sand-paintings arranged about. I used to tend the lenses that fused the paintings for the tourists to see, but we had a few bushes there too, small and hardy, lucky to survive in the heat. And I knew every one, Phaya, every single one. One day I shall see a real garden and a real forest and—Hello, Tom!"

"Hello, Lud. Hello, Phaya?" The little girl laughed at me and clapped her hands, but it was plain she did not recognise me from the night before.

"You will see the forest at Catherine Park," I told the mankin. "The Stone is hidden by it now."

"Yes," Lud said. Then he waited.

"Lud...?" I began.

"Yes?"

"I've solved nothing. Tomorrow I will go as far as the Sea Folly, but I will not go into the Square or to the Stone."

"Thank you, Tom. I am not disappointed."

"I'm disappointed," I said. "But it's the point I've reached. I am sorry to fail you. I do it for Phar and Phaya."

"The glass is not half-empty, is it?" Lud said. "You are going to the Sea Folly with us." And gently he bent at the waist, reached down, and stroked Phaya's dark hair, crooning deeply, a prolonged soothing note that made the child croon back happily as she settled down in her makeshift bed.

"Where is Phar?"

"He has preparations to make for tomorrow. He will be able to talk later. But, Tom, I think you should go now. I think you should return here tomorrow at 0900 so we can walk together, the four of us."

"To the Sea Folly?"

"Yes. Further than I thought you might. Better than the end of Socket Lane."

"You'd rather I didn't stay now?"

Lud's eyes glowed above the fixed expressionless features. "Tom, you are already grieving for what you cannot do. I grieve to see such alarm, such confusion. What do you say at a next-to-final goodbye? Distractions are better. Remember, I caught you in a trap; I put you back in the loop. You know better. Leave me with Phaya now. Tonight I would like to savour the dear shadows, the world I know, to enjoy the chance to re-choose."

I seized on that. "You might not go tomorrow?"

"Who knows?" Lud said. "Everything is suddenly so dear. Goodnight!"

I went to the door, wending my way through the piles of junk, keenly aware that every turn, every carefully-arranged stack and carelessly cluttered corner was part of a universe, vivid and cherished—if not through conventional modes of vision, then at some other percept level across the range of Lud's damaged sensors.

As I passed the front counter to the door, I was aware too of the planisphere lying there beneath the dark glass. Without looking at it, I stepped out into the night, went straight to my hotel, and put myself into one of their somniums, not caring about the resemblance it had to the machines in the Madhouse, escaping the only way I knew how.

At 0900 on that crystal-clear morning, we set out from Phar's shop, the four of us: Phar and Phaya to either side of Lud, each holding one of his big hands, with me two paces behind to one side.

Phar had polished the robot during the night so that Lud shone, his elaborate curlicues making threads of dazzling gold against the dull silver-grey as the sunlight caught them. Lud moved slowly, matching his stride to that of Phaya's little legs so she could keep up.

We almost resembled a family group as we moved down Socket Lane: a child and her grandfather leading an awkward arthritic invalid, with me a slightly detached, possibly reluctant and embarrassed uncle off to the side, keeping them company.

As we turned into Julianna Boulevard, spectators started to gather. People came rushing out of shops and houses, running from the bazaars and up the steps from the beach. By the time we started into Catherine Parade, there were at least four hundred people following us. Phaya, far from shrinking back at all the attention, was squealing with delight. So many people, so much awe and excitement.

At the end of the Parade, I could see the Sea Folly with its wooden sign showing Aphrodite rising from the waves. I kept my eye on it, not looking at Lud but constantly aware of his heavy distinctive tread near mine, thinking of how the mermaid sign reminded me of Prohannis' Jade Sabre, Christine.

"What did the king do, Lud?" I said, with only thirty of Phaya's paces to go.

Lud continued walking, intent on reaching the Park and the Stone, but he answered.

"He stopped his chariot," Lud said, as if the story had never been interrupted, as if the evening continued about us now and not this bright fateful morning. "His arm was raised, holding a great spear ready to cast. He was in midcharge. But he stopped, and he stopped his army. He walked across to his son."

"And forgave him," I said, finishing it.

"Yes."

"And the son?"

"Killed his father with his sword," Lud said, with ten paces to go.

"What!"

"The king knew, but the son did not yet know what he truly knew until his father lay dead before him. We discover by going through it."

"Goodbye, Tom," Phar said then, and fleetingly clasped my arm with his free one.

And like the warrior son, caught by the momentum of events, by the force of things said and done, the relentless pressure of following through, thrown out of the way of controlled choice now, I found myself standing on the curb outside the Sea Folly, feeling cheated and trapped, with the great crowd surging on slowly but surely towards the Square.

I stood blinking in the morning light which danced off the whitewashed walls, then followed the great throng, bewildered still, unresolved and unprepared.

Then I heard cries and saw the crowd dispersing up ahead. There were armed warriors at the end of the street, sealing off the openings into the Square behind Lud, Phar and Phaya.

Kurdaitcha. I heard their commands, saw them through the townsfolk rushing back my way.

As the crowds thinned out, I saw the robed Ab'Os clearly, saw the heavy weapons, the portables and Bok lasers they had set up, the laser batons they carried.

It had taken only fifteen minutes for word to get around, for the Kurdaitcha to act.

I walked towards the beginning of the Square, trying to see if the robot had reached the little park at its centre.

Two robed Kurdaitcha stood near the corner, members of the Chitalice tribe. They saw me, muttered some words, then one came over to me, his laser baton activated.

"You were with the robot!" the man said, his baton raised.

"No," I said, as calmly as I could. "I was with the man and his child. There is a difference. They were with the robot. I honoured a claim of friendship."

"You are Tom Rynosseros?" the Kurdaitcha said.

"Yes."

"Why were you with the robot?"

"I told you. I was not with the robot."

The other Kurdaitcha came up then.

"You support the mankins?" he asked. "You were with them."

"Are you scanning me?" I asked in turn.

"Yes," the first Kurdaitcha said, showing me his monitor unit.

"I do not support the mankins. I oppose AI!"

"It reads clear," the first Ab'O said, consulting the display.

The second Kurdaitcha made a doubtful sound. "Very well. But leave here. Go home!"

"What about the man and the child?"

"He is with the robot and forfeit. The child is not. She will be safe."

"I am champion for the man," I said quickly.

The eyes of the Kurdaitcha narrowed with suspicion.

"Why?" one said.

"A dear friend who acted against advice," I told them. "I will stand for him."

"But not for the robot?"

"No. Not for the robot."

"We will parole him to you if we can save him."

"The man?"

"Of course, the man! Move on!"

I did not go to the Emporium; there was not enough time. I went into the Sea Folly and joined the crowd around the wall screen which showed the scene in the Square: Phar and Phaya walking hand in hand with Lud towards the small ragged forest at its centre—a copse of dusty neglected trees, made suddenly glorious by the sunlight streaming down between two adjacent buildings.

"It's only a matter of time," the broadcast commentator was saying. "The Kurdaitcha have set up powerful Bok lasers at the ends of the streets. It will be an energy death. They say they have instructions to spare the forest, if possible, and the Stone, but we can't help but feel they have other orders in the matter: to let the robot reach the Stone, and destroy it there before it can make invocation. They will have an excuse to be rid of the Soul Stone and the Park donated by Antique Futures, a perfect opportunity and a way of forestalling similar incidents in future. But wait! The Kurdaitcha are moving in!"

On the screen, we saw the robed figures striding purposefully to block the trio's path. There were voices, firm commands, squeals from little Phaya as an Ab'O seized her and lifted her easily off the road, soft muffled protests from Phar, who was dragged off by two warriors.

Lud did not stop to help them. He moved as fast as he could towards the golden glade ahead. When four Kurdaitcha tried to swing the mankin aside, Lud did not attempt to engage them, he simply continued on his way, stiff-legged, comical, as if blundering through their line. Desperately trying to reach the Stone, I knew.

The warriors raised their batons, received a command, and moved back to their companions at the mounted portables.

I stared at the screen, not knowing what I wanted to happen, but not this, not these heroics, this waste.

Waste! I recoiled from the term I had provided. Waste. Loss. And more.

I thought of the chattering machines in the darkness of the Madhouse, watching dreams, reading madness. They had watched me, contemplated my thoughts and images, invading the only life I had, reducing me to behaviour patterns, to data and schematics.

And what else? I wondered.

"Very still now," the commentator said. "There is a countdown. But wait! The robot is stopping. We have tapped into its oriete, courtesy of the Kurdaitcha scan facility set up here, and moiré trace shows the mankin has recognised that a forest has replaced the old park and the Stone. It probably did not know that. It is waiting.

"No!" I cried. "No!", realising how Lud saw that forest. As life. Life! Life to be savoured, cherished, saved. Life to be worshipped for all the things Lud feared he might not be.

Lud could not go into the forest. He would cause its death too. Lud was remembering the Bati Gardens.

"The lasers are waiting," the voice on the screen continued. "Countdown is 30 and falling. Moiré trace shows a net of green. The robot is watching sunlight on leaves. It seems to be examining that; we register all sorts of percept functions engaged, some impaired, the scanning crew tells us. This mankin is in poor shape. I don't believe it knew the trees were living things. It is doing a life scan. It will not enter the glade!"

"Of course it won't!" I cried.

I ran to the door, but there was no time. The commentator's voice stopped me.

"The lasers are powering up for a strike!"—the whine was clearly audible in the background—"The countdown is at 18. The robot is turning. There are tracers all over the thing, indicating strike points. But it will not go into the forest! For all its much-vaunted intelligence, the aspirations these high-mankins were meant to have to be human-like, it will not go to the Soul Stone, if that's even what it intended."

I was standing before the screen, tears rolling from my eyes. "Of course he won't, you idiot! Of course he won't!"

He won't, I heard myself say. He!

"Countdown is at 10. The lasers are ready. The mankin is just standing there. Wait! Wait! It is moving. The robot is running away from the trees!"

There was a tearing sound of laser fire.

"Lud!"

It was a lost day for me. But that evening I went back to Phar's, though, of course, the shop was shut and locked.

The old Ab'O was with the Kurdaitcha, probably little Phaya as well.

Lud had left Phar and Phaya to my care, had left me the part of this that I could carry out.

I seized on that thought as I stood before the locked door. There was something I could still do, and I was turning to be about it when I saw a tall robed figure in the lane, moving towards me out of the shadows.

Ab'O, I noted by his manner. And read more. Kurdaitcha.

"Tom Rynosseros?" the Ab'O said, drawing nearer, and I saw it was Prohannis. "You were with the mankin today."

"For a time, yes. Where is the old man and the child?"

"The child is safe."

"Where is the old man?"

"Phar is dead. He was forfeit."

"I spoke for him!" I cried in despair. "I told the assassins!"

"He transgressed too far."

"He walked his mankin." My voice broke on the words. "He walked with his old friend, that's all!"

"No," the Kurdaitcha said. "He did more."

"What, you bastard? What did he do?"

"He had the head of another mankin. He hid it where it could watch the first mankin's destruction. We detected it on scan. It was treason!"

I grabbed the Ab'O by the front of his robe, but he pulled free, and brought something out from under his djellaba.

"Is that it? What did it see? Life-flow?"

"This is not the head," the Ab'O said, but gently, not scorning me for thinking he would bring such a thing here. "This is from the shop. It is the old man's final wish, something he wanted you to have."

I took the parcel in numb hands.

"What did it see?" I called, as the Ab'O turned away. "What did the head see?"

But the Kurdaitcha did not stop. He moved down Socket Lane towards the sea.

I stood at the door of Phar's Emporium, clutching the parcel, and called after him: "What did it see?", cried it again and again into the night until the words no longer mattered.

The Man Who Lost Red

ERIC DID WHAT the medic said. He did go to the top of Carlieu. It was a good half hour's climb in the wind and the bright sunlight, and not once did he turn from climbing to discover the truth.

Only when he reached the top, sprawling breathless on the hard stones and tufts of grass at the summit, did he look back down at the town—at the green fields and blue-misted hills far off, at the sparkling blue river and the white houses with their grey roofs.

Grey roofs, yes! Grey!

Only then did Eric believe it was true, when he saw the roofs.

He had lost red.

He proved it by locating Mrs Spain's gardens, confirmed it by seeking out the dyeworks near St Benedict's. He found all the places where he had remembered the colour—a post box in the street, certain shop fronts in Daper Avenue, the old faded bus as it crossed the town. In swelling despair, he found their sullen greys.

His gaze became even more intense, searching the landscape, seizing, insinuating. But then Eric sank back in the wind. He stretched out on the hard ground and stared up at the easy spread of morning sky.

Barely two hours ago, down in the infirmary next to the Occlusion Centre where he had been treated, Eric had expected to be deceived. He was sure that would be the punishment for a first offence, contrary to what was said, a glimpse of what it could be like. Or, at the most, a temporary treatment that would wear off after a day or two and leave him shaken, grateful for another chance.

In spite of what he knew about the Seven, he still clung to this. Everyone who was treated did at first, though Eric knew this was not the iquiri way.

But, like any human, he had expected to be tricked all the same. The little white First Aid box with its grey cross, that could have been planted just to spite him, though spite was not their way either. The redless streets and sudden unreddened gardens could have been staged too. The paranoia ran deep.

He remembered laughing at the ridiculous cunning of such trickery, at the knowledge that the iquiri were highly skilled in the use of things like controlled spectrometry.

As he had rushed across the bridge and out of town, past Mrs Spain's changed gardens, still not believing, these were his two certainties, his dearest truths: the adjustment was real but temporary, or he was in the field of a spectrometric device of some sort.

Then he had climbed Carlieu, doggedly nursing his twin fictions, till he was at the top and the sky was a vast blue bowl and there was no doubting anymore.

He had lost it. One colour gone forever, picked clean from his mind, from his world. Switched off.

Red. Hearts and courage and clowns' smiles, the hot embroidery of war, six roses in ten. Everything from the tones of his favourite Bellini to the firelight-on-paddlewheel effect of the Mayor's bicycle reflectors as he pedalled through the town at night. Gone.

He sat on Carlieu, leaning up on his arms now, legs stuck out in front as he had fallen, and wept for the first time in years. He did it more as a release from tension and uncertainty, because it was not so real yet, more absurd than anything, and he remembered red well enough. He did it because what else do you do when you have gaped and laughed and are still faced with such an astonishing and simple discovery? Knowing, too, that the day would come when the memory of red would not be enough to overrule the greys, to give blood its hue or make a roof red again. Who would have thought that the roofs of Carlieu were red enough to lose?

That thought did it. Eric sat there, legs thrust out like a child's toy clown, and the despair came. Now he wept because he would never again see a red roof or blood or the last blush of sunset, just a gamut of browns and golds, a conspiracy of purples and yellows and hot burnt oranges edging towards their sly treachery of grey. Greys in every shade and depth and wicked taunting imposture. Grey for vermilion, grey for crimson, grey for fire, grey for blood. Grey for the lips of a woman and the cheeks of a child.

He knew then how well he had been punished. For a crime he no longer remembered.

It was two weeks before he returned to the Centre; two weeks in which he discovered colour again, and seeing, and went from despair to elation at no longer being a criminal.

Nights, he found, were easy. Candles and lamps were kind, gave mostly golds and warm yellows, rich alternatives. Eric's eyes sharpened to the nuances of any of the warm colours and he cultivated them. He could walk the darkened streets and sometimes forget what he lacked. A light through a red shade in a window or a diamond-pane of red stained glass was the stillest of grey-whites, like the lambent ghostliness of a television screen. If he moved quickly past such windows, he could never tell.

He avoided Carlieu's few major intersections. Once, in his second day, he played his game with the traffic lights at the end of Daper Avenue, watching the shift from green to amber to grey, timing the shift back to green again, then watching the amber for as long as he could before pressing his eyes shut.

This was his bravado stage, of course, and it lasted the two weeks. Eric took a room at Mrs Spain's and had several of his more sympathetic fellow tenants help him decorate it. A well-meaning old man named Claude had plans for making it a masterpiece of evasion, and Eric at first consented to this, partly for the company and partly to explore his new needs and tolerances.

But after one evening in this foolish, intensely-coloured bower, crowded by the rich curtains and bright walls, Eric moved his few belongings to a room on the other side of the building, a drab quiet room overlooking a lane and starved of light.

As for the days in Carlieu itself, he avoided certain streets altogether. He did not look at the old bus whenever he heard it coming, and kept away from the porch of St Benedict's where the dyeworks were. He never went to the back of the guest-house either;

the gardens were there. By habit, his eyes avoided the roofs.

Nor did he climb Carlieu again in daylight, though at night he would go there, night after night, to look down at the town. That was where he learnt that red is not the worst colour to lose, that blue is the worst, then yellow and green. Red was a highlight colour, Eric discovered, a hue for flourishes and intensities and vivid small doses. Or so he remembered it. Now it had a new dramatic role; now he knew it by so many shades of grey.

Day was the enemy. Eric played the early days with great care. He made his daily visits to the Clinic in the middle of the town so the medics could check for any signs of occlusion shock, each morning striding down the safer streets like a horse with blinders, head down, eyes fixed on the central square.

Then that began to change too. By his twelfth day, he was ready for his biggest test. He took the bus into Ansard, then made the tube connections that took him to Barracamba itself. He used up most of that week's pension to secure a compartment to himself, and when the carriage eased into its platform at Maize Street Station, Eric emerged pale but composed on to the bright windy streets of the capital.

Eric made himself use that day. He went down to the harbour and watched the Casaeri fishing-fleets; he stood by the fence at the spaceport and watched the shuttles going up, his eyes riding each hot fantail. He went to the Tandercote Gallery and saw his favourite Bellini (a copy) and Corben's "Bat Out of Hell" (the original)— seeing this as a sere grey place out of Brontë or Poe rather than the fiery Dantesque field that it was.

By mid-afternoon, the man who could not bear to watch the ends of people's cigarettes was sitting in the Public Smokery near Bosty Market, chatting with the longshoremen.

He returned to Carlieu that night exhausted but victorious. He left the bus in the square—it was no longer high courage to ride the bus—and walked back to Mrs Spain's, making himself take the road that ran beside the flower beds. Night was well-advanced on the town, and all this was easy, a mere gesture after what the day had been; but he did it anyway.

Then he went to bed and sank into a deep welcome sleep, believing he had won.

The next step was just as inevitable.

The following morning he walked back down to the square, to the old-style stone building set there in the cool morning light as if separate from the rest of the town. The single-storeyed sandstone structure with its high-pitched slate roof always reminded him of the old railway stations you came across now and then. The infirmary at the side where he went for his check-ups was a later addition, but built from the same lion-coloured stone as the rest. That was where he had been adjusted and it had its own door marked 'Clinic'.

Today Eric did not go there. Today he went to the door of the main building, the door with the blue iquiri rosette and the sign with the words 'Regional Occlusion Centre: Carlieu Facility'. Below it, a second sign was lettered with words that Eric had seen a thousand times but only now fully understood: 'Isolation is the ultimate deterrent'.

Once there had been some graffiti sprayed on the wall in black next to it, a desperate plea: 'Send the ikky buggers to Coventry!' The capital 'C' had made Eric look up the word for the first time. He had learned of a city, of a famous ride made by a naked woman named Godiva, and of the isolation of the infamous Peeping Tom by his fellows. Mixed up in the account, too, was how, in Cromwell's time, difficult prisoners were once sent to Coventry for a similar reason. Isolation.

The graffiti had lasted a day and had never appeared there again.

Eric read and re-read the sign that still did remain, smiling ruefully now that he had a little 'coventry' of his own, as the saying had it.

He looked around the square once, at the bright plumes of steam from the dyeworks behind St Benedict's, at the terrace of the Café Milo. The proprietor's son was serving a young grey-haired woman at one of the tables. That caught his eye.

Eric laughed, though his breath caught first as it often did when he was taken unawares. Then, before his thoughts could angle off further, he turned the old brass handle and stepped inside.

The main office of the Centre was as he remembered it from his previous visit: the walls decorated with travel posters and a Chol tapestry (ugly but an original); an iquiri jelly-clock beside the long front desk, the glycerine sluggish in the clear tubes; the same grey-haired receptionist, Mrs Mills, seated at her keyboard. As he entered, the woman stopped typing and looked up, saw who it was and smiled.

"Mr Andlan. Eric. It's good to see you. You've kept all your appointments."

"You expected me about now."

"Well, yes. I did," the woman said, and there was a warm, caring quality to her voice. Mrs Mills was an equate. Her empathy rating, like those of all humans who worked for the iquiri, was very high. Had she been standing close to him, no doubt she would have instinctively rested a hand on Eric's arm—and genuinely, feelingly so, without pretence or intrusion. As it was, she let her eyes do their healing best.

Eric looked about the large quiet room, fascinated by the oh-so-easy marriage of things iquiri with things human. He noticed the careful lack of greys, the medic's report on the desk beside the keyboard, and silently accepted the extreme finesse of this aging woman.

"You've been watching me?" he asked.

"Only now and then, Eric," she said. "Your movements in Barracamba yesterday. That was a big day. You did well."

Eric began to feel angry. In spite of everything, he had not expected surveillance like this.

"What if I walk out right now?"

"Then you walk out. Possibly you'll come back later. If not, then we can't help you."

"Will surveillance stop?" he snapped. Somehow it mattered.

"It already has. The directive was issued this morning."

"From Osiris?"

"No. From Sebek. A new iquiri facility on the Moon."

"They're spreading," Eric said. "We're supposed to be getting more rights and they build on the Moon."

"Self-government is close, Eric." Mrs Mills rose to none of the barbs. "The Custodianship will end soon."

"Could I see Doctor Rite, please?" he said then. "Or one of the medics?"

"I'm sorry. This station operates on a rotation basis. Doctor Rite was here to do an adjustment earlier this morning. Now the team is over in Ichos."

"Coventry grows!" Eric spoke the old adage, astonished at his own bitterness. He had not come here with bitter thoughts. They were brought on by the controlled calmness of everything, by the casual news of another occlusion in the town.

But the equates always drew this. It was why they were chosen.

"That's right, Eric," Mrs Mills said. "But it also grows less."

"Can you tell me what led to my treatment?"

There, he had said it. He had asked the question.

Mrs Mills shook her head. "No, I can't do that, Eric. They do not let us do that. We don't even keep records of such things here. It's part of our arrangement with the iquiri."

"But the iquiri know?"

"They do. Yes. The records go to them in return for their services. As Doctor Rite told you, the crime is determined by human law and the Compact; the adjustment according to the iquiri schedule. We don't know why you were treated. It's best that way."

Eric recalled the unreality of that other morning two weeks before, the small doctor talking to him, briefing him. That was before he knew the meaning of the sign on the door, the one below the rosette. Nothing Doctor Rite had said could encompass this.

Now, in the layered silence, Eric gazed past the grey-haired woman (an honest hard-won grey that) out through a window and across the square to the Café Milo, studied the few customers at the white metal tables, the grey-haired girl and two others, noted again the grey-haired girl.

"This is for you, Eric," Mrs Mills said, gently interrupting, as if knowing exactly where his reveries had to lead and when to cut them short. She handed him a long white envelope stamped in one corner with the blue iquiri rosette and addressed to 'Eric James Andlan, Adjustee J83902'.

He held it dumbly in his hands, staring at it and through it, trapped in this moment of terrible relapse. Was this occlusion shock, he wondered? Now, after all he had been through? Was this the loop of madness that would catch him?

The questions kept coming. Crime may have virtually disappeared, but what did become of the criminals? Were they able to live their lives in places like Carlieu, accepting their awful punishments, managing to conduct their lives chastened and changed? Could that be done?

It hardly seemed possible.

Eric found he needed to discover what became of the criminals, his fellows in this altered world—the ones with the coventries, with the bits switched off.

"That document," Mrs Mills (damn the woman!) began, "is from the iquiri offices in Barracamba, straight from Osiris. It explains the special circumstances of your case. Your offence, Eric, whatever it was, no doubt involved aspects of your previous lifestyle, notably your position in the design section of the shipyards at Kent-Molly. Doctor Rite could not easily erase knowledge of the infringement without tampering to some extent with your skills training as an aerospace engineer. Compensation details are in there. You will not return to Kent-Molly. You are to present yourself at Sea Platform on the first of next month. A complete re-orientation program has been logged for you. Your pension will continue until then, of course."

And when she saw how Eric was looking at her, she did reach across the counter and touch his arm, a dry-leaf, feather-soft touch, a comfort in spite of what he knew of her and still no intrusion.

"No, Eric. I do not know what your crime was either. Only your penalty. I do know that."

"So what did you change?"

"I beg your pardon? Oh, I see. The tapestry. I changed the tapestry."

"It's awful."

"It is, isn't it?" Mrs Mills agreed, smiling, looking over to the Chol piece.

"And will you put up the old one when I leave?"

"Just as soon as you leave!" the equate said.

They laughed, and though Eric felt the wave of panic ebb in him a little, the despair remained. All his victories, all his small painful triumphs, came to nothing in the face of it. Tears ran down his cheeks, fell on to the envelope.

Again the hand reached out, but Eric tore away, infuriated by his tears, not wanting to be touched, not wanting to see the mirror tears that he knew would be in the equate's eyes.

Clutching the envelope, he rushed out into the strong light of the square, careless of whatever newly brutal reds might lie in ambush, angrily challenging Carlieu to display all it had, daring the dyeworks to show their bravest vermilion and richest scarlet.

But the town took him calmly into its morning silence. The bus was not there; at the dyeworks it was a cool colour day, had been all that week. The awnings at the Café Milo were their familiar faded green and white. Only that girl at one of the tables had hair the shining metallic grey of coventried red.

She stood out like a target at that distance. His eye had perfected the skill, refined in Carlieu, tested on the raw streets of Barracamba. He could tell the red greys quickly now and the girl's was one. Her hair had to be a brilliant shade to cancel into grey like that, not copper, not auburn or golden brown.

Before he quite knew it, Eric was at the Café Milo, seated in one of the chairs and looking from the grey-haired girl back to the building he had left. He held the crumpled envelope, unthinkingly smoothing it out, reading the name and number again, noting the distinctive blue flower—the imprint of the iquiri.

Then he looked at the girl four tables away. She was a mirror-image of himself, one moment staring down into the empty coffee cup in front of her, then across to the Centre and the Clinic, then about the square. The action was unmistakable.

Eric got up and crossed to where she was sitting.

"Have you been adjusted today?" he said, blurting out the words.

The girl flinched, badly startled, and Eric was left looming there, feeling foolish and cruel.

"What?" she said, her clear attractive face still pinched with distraction. Then, hearing his words: "Yes."

"I've lost red," he told her and sank down into a chair.

She saw his envelope and gave a tight smile.

Eric realised then that she did not know yet, that she hadn't discovered what her coventry was. He saw that much in the distraction, in the clasped and twisting hands on her lap, in her moments of sudden concentration. She was touring her sensations, mentally ticking them off.

Eric saw how lucky he had been. He'd had the First Aid box with the grey cross, so comical and obvious and mercifully, mercifully, soon after his occlusion.

This girl did not have that comfort.

"We make poor companions, I've been told," he said. "I've had two weeks."

"I don't mind if you stay," she said. "I've been here all morning going through my senses, trying to find out. I'm pretty sure it's not visual or tactile, but it's too soon. I need an ocean. I need flowers. There are textures and sounds..."

He held his envelope before her darting eyes.

"Eric James Andlan," she read. "Oh—I'm Tey. Tey Manton. I'm—I was—a programmer from Branseller before this. Who knows what I am now."

She went on, sketching in her life for him between intense glances, sudden anglings of the head to listen, a tilt back to smell. In some ways, her story resembled his. Whatever her offence had been it had already ruined a career, a family's reputation, and the chance of a marriage. The facts emerged in their broken, disjointed way, always overshadowed by the more important task of isolating her penalty.

Without knowing it, Eric began helping her. He used their surroundings, the square, the café, the hills beyond the town. He bought pastries and entrées to test a range of tastes and smells—sweet, sour, tart, pungent, bitter, salty. He made her sing songs she knew, then add octaves and harmonies to one of his; had her think of animals, listen for the wind (and feel it and smell it) and children laughing in a house on the far side of the square. He made her touch surfaces: fabric, metal, wood, stone paving, skin, rough and smooth, all the trivial, unsuspected things. Tey would reach for the smallest pebble with a desperation he keenly understood.

They worked for hours at this, as the sun climbed from mid-morning into a golden afternoon. Each phase of their quest brought first the tension (would it be this?) then relief as they played on in the game that was not a game, trying not to miss the obvious.

Which, of course, they did.

One moment there was laughter, the next a taut silence as they explored a new touch, a different smell, sought out a new sound. Then relief and more laughter, an absurd counterpoint between them. Milo and his son joined the game from time to time, making suggestions, doing their jovial best.

Eric began to be optimistic. Whatever coventry Tey had been given did not seem to be a blatant one. Or rather, nothing too basic. Not like his, he thought, but mentally retracted that. Any coventry would be major and basic and totally precious. Losing the smell of ozone after a storm, the hum of telephone wires in the wind, the thrill of driving over a hill into a sudden dip, the immediate, total, immeasurable gift of smelling the first gardenia of a season, hearing cicadas on a hot afternoon, tasting salt.

He worked harder on her behalf, becoming a friend out of empathy rather than sympathy, an equate to her in fact. He laughed with her, concentrated when she did, suggested things to try, easily forgetting his own loss—that her hair was a blowing, flashing silver grey, that the roofs of the houses reaching up towards Carlieu were tramp's patches of grey against the smooth green curve of the hill.

But in their fourth hour together, the mystery was solved. It was astonishing for both of them how quickly it happened, and what an obvious and precious and cruel coventry it was.

There was a fountain at the south-east corner of the square close to where the café terrace ended and Dose Avenue began, a small bubbling fountain visited by many birds. Eric saw Tey glance at it (she had done so many times), concentrate on it—her eyes widening; saw the blankness of expression twist into silent tears.

He grabbed her hand, his own eyes sweeping from Tey to the fountain and back.

"What, Tey? What?"

She turned to him, panic gone, but despair everywhere in her eyes, in the tears streaming down her cheeks.

"Can you hear them?" she asked.

"The birds?" Eric said. "Yes. I can hear them."

And knew she couldn't.

He could find nothing to say. He sat holding Tey's hand, watching her trace the course of each bird that landed in the square, watching the small shapes that tumbled and ducked and flicked about the fountain. And sang. She looked up once as if to have him confirm that, yes, they were still singing and chirruping there.

Eric nodded, feeling leaden and angry. He noticed the greys more than ever now, even the safe ones: every roof, every fleck and mote, real and imagined, cherished red, memory red, fantasy red, the strands of Tey's blowing hair.

"What kind of justice is this?" he asked, not of Tey but of everything around him, of himself, the day, the universe.

And what had been a dimming, subsiding urge to know more and persevere, a tolerance and an acceptance, now became the only cause.

Because of Tey. Because he was seeing it, living it all again through her.

He went from sorrow to incredible fury, honest burning fury, while next to him Tey looked up, sensing his rage. He looked at her and his rage doubled.

The tears had stopped, but her eyes were grey from crying.

He lost Tey. She stayed with him that night, as a child, too grieved for love, wanting nothing but to be held, to lose lost birds in sleep. In the morning she was gone, back to Branseller, back to whatever fragments of her past life were left to her—the residue—so she could sort those pieces and discover what sense they made now.

For Eric, Carlieu became more of a limbo, more of a prison. He was glad to go to Sea Platform as a line-engineer, and then on to Bass Strait III. He worked the European and Oceanian spaceports for a time, earning himself the clutch of names that were to dog his new life in one form or another in the days to come. To most of his workmates he was known as Red Andlan or Red 'Anded or simply Red. A Swede in Naples christened him Eric the Redless after some ancient hero; an Oceanian engineer in Canberra came up with the unlikely name of Blue.

In the first three months he went to most of the ports on Earth, but never back to Kent-Molly or Carlieu. And wherever he went, Eric found he was biding his time. He never forgot his brief intense time with Tey; never forgot the tumbling songless birds he could hear, thank God, but she couldn't. He fell in love with her somewhere between Canberra and Amsterdam, not that he really noticed. It was all part of what drove him, what gave him his plan.

For Eric found he did have a plan. He was the adjustee who asked the questions, the engineer who wanted to know all about the iquiri. Time and time again, everywhere he went, he confirmed all he had ever heard about them, and about the Custodianship. That they had come to Earth on a cool September afternoon in 2014, appeared—the seven of them—at the General Assembly of the United Nations during a full session, just walked in through the great doors, down the aisle to the rostrum.

They looked like men, these invaders, well-made men; each impeccably dressed in a sober three-piece business suit with shirt and tie and neat black shoes. Each wore a ceramic mask fitted to his face and had hair brushed and shining and cut in close to the neck. They had moved calmly to the front of the massed delegates, turned and faced that awestruck crowd.

The middle one of the seven—Bofari Thames, as he came to be known, the one with the smooth plain mask of surging greys fixed in mid-roil—had spoken then in perfect English.

"We shall give you time to arrange adequate global coverage of what we have to say."

Guards had moved in; guards had vanished in sudden detonations of light. Yes, exactly that. Detonations and the flashes of light. A clap, an implosion for each man. The infamous flash-gate effect.

At the same time, three enormous oblate machines moved into orbit around the Earth, dead black craft picked with light. As a matter of course, satellites and weapons installations belonging to the different nations went into precise action, smoothly, routinely.

More detonations, more quick flashes. Each engaged facility was gone, flash-gated out of existence. For several seconds a receptor on the side of one of the ships then passing over Northern Africa glowed just perceptibly with the influx of energy then went dark.

When the cameras were set in place and running, another of the creatures—the one with the mask of cool pale blue, Barlu Octavian—stepped forward. In a full rich voice, he announced that a conquest of Earth had taken place, then stated the terms of the iquiri occupancy. The delegates watched in disbelief as the creature listed them.

There was to be enforced cosmopolitanism, denationalisation of Earth's peoples with large-scale re-locations; the formation of a World Council, with elected delegates approved by the Seven; and a careful resources control and development program. The planet was to be one. It was to be very much a rule of non-interference, though the iquiri with the pale blue mask—The Fair Countenance, he also called himself—would be present at all Council meetings, to assess decisions and motives and occasionally overrule. Zero population growth would be in effect for two human generations; efficient male contraception was made available.

Also, the iquiri reserved the right to punish all criminals according to the ancient iquiri schedule, using a system of penalties which usually meant an occlusion plus removal of all knowledge of the crime. The adjusted criminals were left to discover for themselves the full nature of their 'coventry'. That came to be the popular name for it, right from the start. A coventry. Being 'sent to Coventry' once meant being ignored, cut off and isolated from all about you. Now it meant an isolation of a different sort and, more than that, one stage in a potentially unending isolation from all reality.

All these things were made possible by iquiri technology.

There were other stipulations, of course, but they surfaced only when the Custodianship was in force, when the blue iquiri rosette began appearing on the doors of medical centres, libraries and the offices of public utilities. That small blue shape came to mean a great deal, everything from the most effective of warnings to an indication of an absolute and impartial caring—the sign of something necessary and temporary.

For that was the sense of it.

Even from the first intimidating days, the Occupation seemed somehow to be a transitional thing; it would not last. The great ships, now joined into an orbiting tripartite installation called Osiris-Anubis-Set after the ancient terrestrial gods whose functions they usurped—Judgement, Intercession and Destruction—would one day go, running out of system away from Sol to jump free of this place. That was the feeling.

Meanwhile, the iquiri nationals themselves represented the Greatest Enemy, the Greatest Friend, the Greatest Mystery humanity had yet faced. Set destroyed the few armies that were mobilised in those first anxious days, changed land-masses, built viable biospheres on the Moon and Mars. Anubis guided the world's economy, deployed skills, moved people, regulated resources, co-ordinated travel across the world. Osiris judged. With uncanny skill, all criminals were tracked down and sent to one of the occlusion centres. True, some were not found for years, but punishments—the coventries—were adjusted accordingly. Criminals began turning themselves in.

Then there were changes. Not all criminals were punished by occlusion. Some were fined, some set to working on public services for a fixed period though with pay and always the threat of occlusion should they shirk their assigned tasks.

Crime could not pay except as a gesture of rebellion, but when the memory of the act was taken away as well, such gestures were better made by public debate or petition to the World Council. Petitions, handled under iquiri supervision, that were always heard.

For the first time, bureaucracy worked with smoothness and precision. A faltering bureaucracy was counter-productive; it amounted to criminal negligence.

There were so many changes, so many huge projects, so much prosperity with the equalisation of resources. The factors that encouraged crime—the frustrations, the indolence, the disadvantage and opportunism—vanished. There were enough jobs and dangers and challenges, colonies on Mars and Luna, hazardous reclamations, sea-farming, new risk professions. There could never have been a world like it without the Outsider.

Eric relearned all this with new purpose, became sure of all that was known about the iquiri, so he could be informed, if possible impartial, totally fair, unprejudiced. Each new re-location brought him to it again, led to off-hours at the information systems, getting the latest data on the Seven. It brought the sobriquets, rarely original now, rarely a trouble.

Rarely.

One American in Oslo, noting Eric's zealous preoccupation, called him Captain Justice. It was there, the night after that joke had soured in a bar and Eric fought the loud-mouthed man to silence, that his letters began. He wrote to Tey care of the Carlieu Centre, knowing Mrs Mills would do her best to pass his letter on.

> *Tey,*
> *I thought of you today as I do most days. I want to hear from you. Are you managing? Are you well? Try to write to me at this address, or through Carlieu.*
> *Love, Eric.*
> *(Red Andlan)*

He wrote to her again a month later from Cos in the Aegean, then again from Port Michaelmas.

> *Six more months of this and I'll be back in Carlieu. Full circle. Can we meet, Tey?*
> *Eric (Andlan)*

Her first letter to answer his second caught up with him at the big top-security installation near Syrtis Major on the grey planet Mars (though this was Eric's joke—Mars was rarely red enough to bother him).

He was staying at the Major-Minor complex for just six weeks, and there, of all places, her letter reached him, her too short, regulation-sized letter.

> *Dear Eric,*
>
> *I've wondered about you too, many times. You'll be pleased to know that I haven't lost all birds—there are raptors I can hear caw and shriek, though no true songbirds. Not like at the fountain. As for the meeting, no, not yet. Too soon for me. And they wouldn't let us. I haven't done as well as you might think. Programming is finished for me. They won't let me go back to it. I've applied for that new diplomatic corps arm: Population Assimilation. I might become an equate. Did you know many of us do? Mrs Mills is probably one of us. Do keep writing, but let's not meet just yet.*
>
> *Love, Tey.*

Eric sat in his tiny M-M room, holding her letter, not sure what he had expected; not this guarded neutral note, not something as unfeeling as this.

But what should he have expected? What right did he have to expect something more?

Yet even as he resigned himself to the drab, orange-green, brown-green, grey-green tumble of the Martian plains and the silence, he started to recognise just how time and days and distance were wearing him down, turning him away from much of his resolve. It gave him a new determination.

He began to see how the whole year-long circuit from Sea Platform, around the world, off planet to Syrtis Major, was part of a deliberate process, a careful rehabilitation—his own trip to Barracamba on a larger scale—and that Tey was being kept busy in just the same way. He had expected her letter to goad him on, but it had come to him out of that same turmoil somewhere else.

They did meet once during that year as it turned out—two brief days when their duty paths crossed in Amsterdam, which only confirmed it all for Eric, that it was a planned thing. Tey was off to Amazon House again; he was back on Earth and down for Rengal's Gate for a three week stay at the Great Mill.

They met nervously, both of them aware that they weren't even lovers and not really friends. They had met on a morning months ago, shared their occlusions, shared a night together, closeness and distance both, and written letters ever since.

Now they had to back it up or let it pass.

So they began with a walk from the terminal where they met, and hadn't gone half a mile before they spoke of coventries. It was the sort of desperate, selfish, meticulous conversation that only adjustees could appreciate: hard questions, broken thrusting answers, obsessive monologues. Their body language showed them more, fortunately: that yes, they would be—were—lovers even before they could wonder about it; the way they turned in on each other as they walked, leant together as they sat over coffee, gripped each other's hands, assumed that the other would bear unquestioningly with their intense preoccupations.

"I've found that I haven't lost all reds, Tey," Eric said. "My colour vision coventries at about 60 angstroms, around the 606 nanometer mark. I lose at the brownish-yellow shades around Crayfish, Fraise and Madder Red, that whole area. I can see all the lower reds below those, the yellow and brown reds. I lose the very wide middle range, the best intensities, then it coventries out above the 495 nanometer wavelength, at the blue red tints between Flamingo and Cerise. They're the first blue reds I see. Then there are the purplish and greyish reds..."

"Precisely?" Tey asked.

"No. Never precisely," he said. "It's not that definite, not that regulated at all. It fluctuates. But I can name the hues, tones and intensities that frame it. I usually lose on a heavy shade and regain on a full tint."

Tey let him talk. He needed to do it more than she did. She could allow him the incredible unthinking selfishness; she knew that one met so few people who had been treated. When a coventry was known, there was more likely to be extreme self-consciousness and caring (and not so caring) jocularity than thoughtful, sober questions. As with blindness or a deformity, it was polite not to ask. Many adjustees avoided the subject of coventries also, pretending the deprivation did not exist. You could not small-talk about such things as the loss of 'soft' or the smell of sea-brine or the sound of a closing door. Most often, the coventried ones came to be cut off in the one area they needed to live the most.

So Tey understood. She let Eric talk about Mars and Port Michaelmas and Bass Strait III and Rengal's Gate, his knowledge of the subjects of the iquiri and colours that he kept coming back to, unable to leave them alone, not with her.

Because she had lost birds, she had given him back birds in a way; because he had lost red, he had given her every red there was—and, in a sense, colour itself.

But one thing threw her as they walked along once more; one thing broke her great control.

"I can read the greys, Tey!" he was telling her. "Read them and red them!" He laughed, excited to be sharing it. "I know the tones and intensities. I know what grey is Scarlet Red and Medici Crimson and Claret and Attic Rose. I even know the colour of your hair now. I know equivalents. It's a silver grey, a tint, but I know what it reds out at. I know!" And Tey began weeping. To know just how Eric would have laboured at that one task struck her to the heart; that he now used 'red' as a verb hit home like nothing else had.

"Eric..." she began.

But like a child at school, jabbering, excited, babbling out what his day—his year—had been like, he kept on.

"Did you know there was a colour called Lizard? You'll find it in the Mortlake tapestries of the eighteenth century. And Midnight? That's another name for Ming Blue or Mohammedan Blue. What about Ecru and Smalt and Oporto? Cardinal and Ormolu?"

"You're making them up! Stop it!"

"No, Tey! No! They're real, all of them! They exist! Scarab Blue, Satinwood, Kermes, Green Beetle, Gault Grey, Mummy Brown, and Flame. All real colours! I love the blues: Cyanine Blue, Florentine Blue, Lapis Lazuli—"

"Stop it, Eric! Please! Enough!"

She wailed the words and he stopped.

Tey looked at him, blinking back tears.

"Shall I talk about birds now?" she said, and the tears streamed down her cheeks. "Shall I tell you about the forty-seven types of bird I can hear, Eric? You would not love them very much; none them are very beautiful. But, of course, the buzzard sings like a nightingale for me these days. Shall I tell you what it's like to face Amazon House again without the birds?"

But now Eric was weeping too and Tey stopped.

Now they could be lovers. Now they could leave the streets and cafés and bars and go back to the small hotel near the canal. Now they could leave their obsessions. For as long as they could bear it.

He went back to Mars shortly after Rengal's Gate, spent another three months out on the dreary plains, breathing stale air and avoiding windows. He found that Mars was redder in places than he remembered.

He thought a lot about the motives for the coventries too—about the whole issue of occlusion, of the differences between imposed, unknowing and even willful de-sensitisation.

Some of his companions at M-M, he discovered, did not see Mars when they gazed out through the ports. They refused to see it, internalised it, made it just another inhospitable desert, so that the installation could have been in Mongolia or Antarctica for all the difference it made.

These men and women gambled and doped and filled their off-duty hours as if no gulf existed between the worlds, as if Mars did not take its chill plains and tiny frantic moons off to the far side of the Sun from Earth.

They terrestrialised almost anything that said Mars, calling the shallow riff leading away from the base Happy Valley, giving the surface vehicles their names: Easy Joe, Maisie J, Slow Wally Walker. Many of the crew were engaged in the long slow process of terraforming Mars, but they would not willingly see it until it wore more of an Earthly face.

One thing impressed Eric with the desperate edge of this more than anything.

In the main rec room of the M-M complex was a big, slightly convex window, double-layered, a huge thing and a luxury in any pressurised environment. When Scroff Hanley was rostered to Major-Minor for a brief stint, they persuaded him to paint a terrestrial landscape on this space, concealing the real Mars beyond with a false though splendidly detailed Earthscape, using the Marslight to bring it alive. This, with the plastic leaves stuck around the air vents, the newscasts relayed from home, the subliminal sound-tapes of birdsong, insects sawing, wavefalls and voices talking, did the very opposite for Eric. He felt Mars more keenly than ever, there beyond the scenic glass. He wanted to pick away at Hanley's glass-painting, to take a coin and scour just one line down the magnificent vista of valleys, sky and mountains. One line would be enough to force Mars back on them.

But how they would hate him for it.

That blind window fascinated Eric. He would suit up and walk the plain outside, trying to allay the fear, sometimes going up to the glass to run gloved hands over the back of the painting, making sudden spiders on the sky for those within.

Or would he visit the cells of those who, in imitation of Hanley, took paints to their own cabin ports? Only once did he make that mistake. He paid a morning visit to the only other adjustee at M-M, an aging geologist named Valerie Henty, who had painted a stained-glass Judgement scene on her window—the whole thing lit beautifully by the early morning sun.

The cabin had oppressed Eric. The impulse to deny Mars in this woman who had lost the sense of touch in the third finger of her left hand was disturbing, even frightening.

All the same, it was while visiting Valerie Henty that Eric learned of the most recent development in human-iquiri relations: the appearance of what the media were calling the Riddle System. She played Eric the tape of that particular newscast, and he heard of how the iquiri had now taken to asking some of the adjusted ones questions, sometimes answering questions in return.

A lot was being made of this; it betokened a new open-door policy from the Seven, even if the questions and answers often took the form of conundrums.

Eric was excited, revitalised by the news. It showed that things could happen—were happening. But, as with so many other things relating to the iquiri, he was unable to get further details from the M-M information systems. He had to file it away with the other things he wanted to ask about. He had to be patient again and wait.

In spite of everything, Eric used Mars well. It was Mars, more than anywhere else, that kept him aware of what an awful commonplace occlusion was, imposed—like his, but also the other voluntary kind he saw all about him. He found it was true, that people didn't really notice the streets they walked down, the views from windows, the door handles they reached for, the cups and tools and pieces of clothing they used. He saw the extent of the crisis it represented: the gradual elimination of the keenest edge of perception, the wearing down of the survival alertness, the awareness of subtleties and detail.

He understood how people threw a light-switch and expected to see light, how they pressed call buttons and expected to see elevator doors opening, not on an empty shaft, but on a lighted interior. That was the logic of it, the cause and effect. Throw a switch: light! Turn the ignition of a car: it started! The whole middle ground of wires and circuitry, the technology of function, eliminated except for an attentive few.

By extension, he observed how people 'neutralised' themselves, the lack of eye contact disguised by posture and gesture, the body language for discouraging approaches outside the safe, set forms. That was another side of it: lose touch, withdraw individual peculiarities by adopting conventions, bland out the input to self and the output from self. These things were all there at M-M.

No wonder the windows were painted over, Eric realised—the rec room one in particular. If you cannot make Mars tolerable and cannot switch it off, then make it safe from within, switch yourself off just a little. Coventry up the facts until you can live with them, handle them. Most of his companions on Mars, in the labs, out at the mines and observatories and testing stations, were self-occluded in some shared conspiracy of survival, shut off and coping.

That is what Mars showed him—between Scroff Hanley, Valerie Henty and the news from Earth.

And it was as if the iquiri knew. For when the lesson had been driven home, not obliterated but re-enforced every day, another letter came, brought to him in his cabin by a petty officer off a supply freighter. It was sealed with a blue flower.

Andlan, Eric James. J83902. Charge of Hand/Sebek 910.
Return to Carlieu, 1100 hours exactly, April 10/24. Mills.
JA492.

Eric was fascinated. Why the letter? Why not a screen transmission direct from Sebek or Osiris or whatever iquiri centre handled this sort of thing? The protocols of the Seven were often quaint like this, ultimately beyond knowing.

But there was no disputing the nature of the orders. His term at Major-Minor had ended. It was back to Earth, to Barracamba and then out to Carlieu. Home.

Almost a year to the day, Eric occupied a table at the Café Milo, sunning cold Mars out of his bones, watching the square come alive as morning advanced on the town.

The Occlusion Centre had not changed, nor the houses facing the square. Nothing in itself seemed different, not really, but of course everything had that quality of being totally altered at the same time.

As the hour of his appointment drew close, Eric noted that the Centre was becoming unusually busy. Several cars arrived, waited while people got out, and left. He could see shapes behind the windows, moving about inside.

He was glad when 1055 came, so he could cross to the building and satisfy his curiosity.

Again, it was like stepping through a slip in time. There was Mrs Mills at her keyboard, busily at work, though the ugly Chol-work had gone. A magnificent piece hung in its place—oranges, rusty browns, coventried reds everywhere.

At the very moment Mrs Mills looked up, three other staff members appeared from an inner office carrying a desk and some files, and the *déjà vu* was short-lived.

There was no mistaking the feeling in the air. Something important was going to happen.

The equate came out from behind the counter, smiling. They shook hands—a strange and intense thing to do, he found. Too formal. The male and two female assistants returned to the inner office then and once again, suddenly, there was the double time-frame, the sense that the year had not existed.

"You've earned yourself a great privilege, Eric," she said, before he could speak any of the courtesies that would make their handshake bearable, safely a formality. "Today, any time now, one of the iquiri will arrive to speak with you."

The scale of it escaped Eric. "An equate?" he asked, thinking of the top-ranking human officials from Barracamba, New York or Sestos.

"No! No, Eric! An iquiri! One of the Seven. They do it now, talk with humans they've adjusted."

"And they brought me back from Mars?" He was amazed.

"Yes. But sit down—over here—and I'll get you coffee."

Eric was glad for the chance to sit, though the coffee did not come at once. There was too much to do. The equate went off to scan some master continuity photographs, as if the room had to be arranged just so. It was eight minutes before one of the young women brought him a cup from the little urn they carried in from the Clinic next door. After another ten minutes, Mrs Mills surrendered her photographs to her staff and came to sit with him.

"They don't want us to give you too much advance warning, Eric. That's why I left you to yourself. Are you feeling better?"

Eric nodded, and she smiled and drank strong coffee with him.

"They're strange masters," she said. "They will excuse all sorts of lapses in the running of their centres—files not processed on the day, employees late back from lunch, the obvious things. But they will remark on a four-volume set of books not grouped together on the shelves, or a blind down too far to permit a view of the east face of Carlieu that was visible on a previous visit by one of them. It's become a game for us, spotting the alterations before they can and putting them right."

"Will it matter which one of them comes?" Eric asked, directing her back to this visit.

"It shouldn't. It never has," Mrs Mills replied. "The last iquiri to set foot in this office two months ago was The Bright Hand. That's Bromarti Warrender. He stayed twenty minutes and was utterly charming, but didn't once let on why he had come."

"These names . .?"

"What the reports say. Affectations. They chose them. The Masks are the real names. Do you know the Masks?"

Eric nodded. "I've learnt them."

"I thought you would. After today, you'll be seeing Derek Tartule from the World Council Department of Cohabitation Studies. He'll want to talk with you when you've spoken with your iquiri."

"The Riddle System?"

"You know about it? Good. Tartule monitors it all. A nice little fellow."

She left him then for a last-minute check.

At 1130, they heard the drop-ship approaching, the distinctive whine descending the scale as it got nearer and slowed for landing, the snuffling back of engines as it came down in the square.

The staff arranged themselves in a reception line just inside the door, with Mrs Mills at the open doorway ready to step out and greet their distinguished visitor.

Eric still sat on the long waiting-bench, but he could turn his head to look out at the landing ship through the window. The others standing by the door couldn't do that.

It was silent in the room. Only the dribbling of the iquiri jelly-clock marked the silence, the glycerine moving sluggishly in the tubes and tumblers, catching the light, the little air-bubbles riding round and round, down into the time-house at the bottom, ascending again to repeat the endless journey through the maze.

Eric's attention shifted from the clock back to the ship. He watched the craft settle in the square, saw the iquiri step from it. The visitor was attended by two human flashmen, as they were called, wearing their brown service coveralls marked with the blue flower at the shoulder. These companions walked halfway to the Centre, then stopped and turned to watch the square.

The iquiri came on alone; in his grey three-piece suit, his hair brushed and shining, this immaculate creature seemed nothing more than a tall elegant human.

A human male.

Masked.

There was no doubting which one it was when Eric saw that Mask.

The Sky Face.

Jeuven Samuels.

As the iquiri strode to the door, Eric studied the glorious porcelain visage, the pattern of full cumulus clouds in a bright spring sky; the regular, vaguely muliebrile features of the face depicted. He felt the extreme presence of the creature even at this distance.

"The Sky Face!" he heard Mrs Mills tell her staff. "It's The Sky Face."

There were murmurs of excitement at the news. Then the creature was at the door and had taken both of Mrs Mills's hands in his own.

"You are Beth," The Sky Face said, and the voice coming from the Mask was rich and full, the perfect voice for a ruler. "And this is Helga, Mara, and Tony. And over there, Eric. Good. I'm glad to meet you all."

He moved into the room, studying it, fixing every point of it with that sealed gaze.

"Carlieu is one of the good towns. I have been told about it. And you are alert to security."

"Pardon, Mr Samuels?" Beth Mills said, puzzled by the last words and forgetting herself.

"Jeuven. Please call me Jeuven, Beth. You have replaced the lock on the door of the inner office there."

"Why, yes," the equate said. "We have. We lost the key..."

"I believe the game goes to me then," he added, utterly charming.

There was a moment of absolute silence, then they all laughed. The Sky Face walked about the room, then approached Eric, who had risen to his feet when the creature entered.

"It is very good to meet you, Eric," he said, and shook hands.

Before Eric could form his words, the iquiri had turned back to the others.

"I don't have much time today, I'm afraid. But we will be meeting again. I will see your town and the bright new locks, and you can have your chance to test the iquiri eye for detail. Now Eric and I must talk. Excuse us, please."

Jeuven Samuels indicated the inner office. Eric led the way into the room and took the chair before the bare wooden desk, automatically expecting The Sky Face to take the chair across from him.

Jeuven Samuels did not. He stepped to the window, closed the blinds, and stood with his back to them, facing Eric, who wondered if he too should stand and made as if to rise.

"No. No. Do sit, please! I want you to be comfortable. There are some questions I would like to ask you."

"If you were to sit as well, Jeuven, I could relax more."

"Very well. And you call me Jeuven. Good. I prefer the first names always—Eric."

Eric smiled. He found that he was less tense than he had expected to be. He liked the creature. That much he knew for certain.

"Today," The Sky Face continued when he had seated himself at the desk, "I have only two questions to ask you—and I would like your fullest answers. At a future meeting, we can spend more time together. Tell me, please, what you fear most about us, our power or our anonymity, our lack of background? Answer quickly!"

"Your power!" Eric surprised himself by saying it, the speed of his reply.

"You did not hesitate, Eric. You are so certain?"

"I believe so, Jeuven. I fear your power. I prefer your anonymity."

"Do you really? But, yes. I understand you, I think. Power in the hands of the incorruptible, faceless few. You'd rather the powerful had no faces?"

"I think so. But only if—"

"Yes, I tricked you. I made you hesitate. Only if we are the Outsider. You find now that you really prefer the opposite. You ordinarily prefer to know the identities of those who have the power."

"Yes," Eric said. "But it's because you are different, I—"

Jeuven Samuels interrupted smoothly. "We get to my second question, Eric. We are the Invader. Do you think we would gain anything by being better known to you?"

"Without your Masks?"

The Sky Face paused for the barest moment.

"In a sense. Yes, that too. Do we lose or gain? Advise us on the position we should take."

Caught out once, Eric watched the iquiri shrewdly.

"You are asking this because you are in the process of revealing yourselves," he said. "I can't answer you yet."

The Sky Face stood.

"Of course," he said, reaching out to shake Eric's hand again. The touch was cool, very human. "We'll talk again soon. Beth will notify you."

And that was it. Jeuven Samuels walked out, spent a few moments with Beth Mills, and departed the Centre.

Eric vaguely heard the drop-ship lift and go. He closed his eyes and listened hard, straining to hear, but the small craft had gone and there was only the deep silence where it had been.

Minutes before Eric reached Mrs Spain's guest-house, the downstairs phone rang. It was from the University of Barracamba, from the secretary of the Department of Cohabitation Studies. Mrs Spain took the call, and relayed to Eric the message that Professor Emeritus Derek Tartule would like to meet with him at his earliest convenience, if possible that evening at 1900.

Eric was glad to keep the appointment. After the anticlimax of actually meeting his iquiri (for in terms of what it could have been, it was very much that), he needed to meet with the ones who lived the doings of the Seven every day of their lives—the equates, the Beth Mills, the Helgas, Maras and Tonys, and the Derek Tartules.

Eric arrived at the University well before time so he could wander the darkening avenues and shadowed quadrangles, taking his precise colour advantage of the hour and collecting his thoughts.

At the appointed time, he knocked on Derek Tartule's door, and let the vigorous little man sweep him into his cluttered office. Nothing in plain view pertained to the iquiri—no photographs, no promising titles on the bookshelves, no curiosities or replicas, not even the near-mandatory jelly-clock.

"Sit down! Sit down, Eric! And be welcome," Tartule said. "You had trouble finding me?"

Eric assured him otherwise, took the seat, and found it hard to restrain a smile at this intense little academic, this specialist on the iquiri with his thick, antique-style glasses and the explosions of grey hair behind each ear.

Professor Tartule sat forward at his desk, scrutinising Eric intently. It was unnerving, even comical, until Eric realised that in a sense his coventry had made him into an iquiri artifact, and that this was how Tartule was now seeing him.

"To think, you actually met one," Tartule said. "So many humans never will." His voice trembled with excitement.

"Jeuven Samuels."

"Oh, yes. I know, Eric. Beth told me. The Sky Face himself. There are only the Seven here, you know. Forgive me, but of course you know. The Masks mean a great deal. Your Jeuven Samuels is a good one. I've met him twice. I wondered when he'd participate in these question and answer sessions. I sometimes think it is he who heads the iquiri nationals here on Earth. He is so calm, so composed."

"Just the Seven?" Eric said, partly to get the old scholar back on the track, partly because, even now, it was still hard to accept that there were only that many.

"Seven." Tartule confirmed it with a vigorous nod. "Jeuven Samuels you've met. There is Barlu Octavian, The Fair Countenance: that's the cool eggshell blue. He sits in on the World Council sessions. He says little, though occasionally when the Council is not in session and the place is deserted he sings. No words, just a keening really. Very beautiful. I have tapes.

"Mack Sown is The Sand Garden. His Mask is usually buff-coloured, pitted, the only Mask not to have the smooth porcelain finish. It sometimes changes colour too, very slowly, from bisque to a deep Genoese gold. Beautiful to see. He supervises the big building projects around the Mediterranean and in Brazil."

"Amazon House?"

"Yes," Tartule said. "There too. He looks after it all. Bofari Thames is The Storm Face, that roiling grey Mask we see on television all the time. He's the most active. He could be their military specialist, a strategist, but it doesn't do to speculate too much. Jacob Glass is The Heart Face, a name not easily fathomed. His Mask is that brilliant rainforest green. Bromarti Warrender eludes me as well. His Mask is almost the Yin-Yang division, half-black, half-white. He calls himself The Bright Hand, make of that what you will. Then there is Jack Haunts, The Sea Face, another shifter. His Mask changes from indigo to sea-green. Marvellous to watch, just marvellous! We used to call him The Chameleon but he didn't like it."

"All males?" Eric said.

"We don't know that. The voices are regularised by the Masks. They sound masculine. The physiognomies, too, suggest they are males, but we don't know the iquiri physiotype. The Masks could be the iquiri for all we know; the bodies might be organic or robot carriers, though we believe they are not."

"It's a novel thought," Eric said, fascinated by the idea.

"We are never short of novel thoughts, Eric. Oh, no. Like: the iquiri as we see them are puppets, android extensions from the real iquiri who remain in orbit operating them. Or just one iquiri with seven extensions. Or a computer. We don't believe that, incidentally. Our instruments show localised vitality signs, separate encephalic activity. They may be deceiving us, but we think they are people. Their names for themselves, the Earthly apparel they have chosen to wear—these things strike us as eccentric and whimsical. The force behind our novel thoughts is simply a determination to stand back and be as objective as we can. We watch; we monitor the occlusions they choose to inflict. It's down to less than a thousand a day now, did you know that? Can you believe it? World crime figures: one thousand a day! The iquiri always seem to know when a crime has been committed. It makes me shudder to think of it, as if they are a race of mind-readers. They always locate the culprits."

"And you interview all these people? The thousand a day?"

Professor Tartule shook his head vigorously. "No! Impossible! We get all the figures sent to us naturally. Of what occlusions are dealt out, that is, not the crimes. In case there are patterns. When duplications occur and where, that sort of thing. The iquiri computers keep the details of the crimes."

"So I'm here because of Jeuven Samuels?" Eric said.

"Because he spoke with you, yes. You, Eric. He went to—where is it again, your town?—Carlieu, and spoke with you. Because he's indicated he will speak with you again. Please, what did he say?"

Eric described the meeting, explained the questions put to him by The Sky Face, tried to give him the exact words that were used.

"Does it tell you much?" he asked when he had finished.

Tartule nodded, bobbing his head happily.

"Two things occur to me. The obvious one is that you are a test case for them, a random sampling from whom they can learn the consequences of their justice, possibly even gain results to some experiment."

"I felt I was confirming something for him."

"I'm sure of it. The other possibility is that your crime was such that they wanted a first-hand dealing with the person who committed it."

Eric didn't care to face the implications of that just then. "Which do you think it is?"

Professor Tartule smiled suddenly, an absurd flash of teeth, like the function of a mechanical toy. He shrugged, bobbed, an odd dipping of the toy head.

"The former. I believe it is the former. There are fewer occlusions now, comparatively speaking."

Eric smiled too, but grimly, then peered out through the small leadlight panes to the lights in the quadrangle.

Tartule continued. "What this means for us, my group, the observers, is that we have a unique chance to try drawing the iquiri out a little. They permit it. For a year now, whenever an adjustee is visited, there have been subsequent conversations. One had five meetings with Mack Sown over a two-month period following his adjustment. Another met with Jack Haunts seven times; a third had three visits from Bofari Thames after losing the ability to feel wind."

"So you do feel I will see Jeuven Samuels again?" The thought, Eric found, was pleasing.

"That's the way it has been. And this is where you may do us and yourself a service. For a long time, these interviews were one-sided affairs; the iquiri asked their questions and presumably got and recorded what they hoped to learn. When we here at DCS realised this was going on—and it took a little time; none of it was publicised then—we tried to make it known generally that adjustees invited to have these meetings should contact us first, at the very least so we could record what was being said.

"Paul Litger was our first real success. He was both alert and very shrewd, a good observer. He's on our team now. Litger helped a pattern to emerge. He discovered, during his interviews, that he could get a question answered too. It was an undivulged privilege; nothing was said. Unlike yourself, Eric, Litger didn't lose the memory of his previous vocation. He had been an anthropologist; his training made what he asked a reasonable, self-directed request. He was able to manoeuvre Mack Sown into revealing all their names; a simple enough thing really, but a marvellous breakthrough. One day he posed the question; at the next meeting he was given a list—the chosen names matched with photographs and Mask-names. We'd only known a few before that.

"The iquiri don't lie as far as we can tell. They evade. When we got the list, we thought we had been given a key. We tried to find connections, significances, but there seemed to be none. But from the day Litger got his list, all iquiri will discuss the subject, answer to the names, just like that. It's as if we have to work for these disclosures though. They seem prepared to divulge a great deal, but only if we earn it."

"The Riddle System?"

"Yes."

Eric watched the old man closely. "What did Litger have to do?"

"Mack Sown asked him what the Great Consistency was. Just that."

"And the answer?" Eric was fascinated.

"You'll laugh," Tartule said. "Litger had no idea, so he became rather sardonic. After days of thinking about it, he said: 'We endure!', having assumed that the question meant the Great Consistency between us and them. The answer seemed to please The Sand Garden. At their next meeting he gave Paul the list. Litger tried to deal again. He asked Mack Sown what his crime had been. The iquiri gave him another riddle: 'What are the Three Traps?' Not one of Paul's answers would do. He was clever; he tried everything, but none of the answers satisfied Mack Sown. Eventually the meetings stopped."

"But now you have all the Masks and names?"

Tartule nodded. "Yes, we have those. But only those—their chosen names and their Mask-names. Very tantalising. The media picked up on the affair; they called it the Riddle System. Our second success was Michele Tyman. Some adjustees refused to have anything to do with us; others demanded exorbitant fees. But Michele we were able to persuade. As with Litger, the first question would be for us, the second for her, the next for us, and so on. It seemed a fair arrangement."

"What happened?" Eric asked.

"Michele saw Jack Haunts. He asked her what the Great Danger was. We mulled over that one for ages, couldn't get a consensus, finally left it up to Michele herself. She took three weeks over it, living with her coventry. Then one day she asked to meet with Jack Haunts. He came at once. Her answer: 'Not to know how and when you are isolated. How you are cut off!' He invited her to comment further. She said that desensitisation was the enemy of all intelligent life. They discussed the iquiri truism that isolation is the great deterrent. Finally, Jack Haunts consented to a question from her, and she posed our choice as agreed: 'Are you artificial creatures?' In spite of the life signs, we wanted that settled once and for all. We were testing their essential honesty, you see. We believed we knew the answer to this already, and we felt we could afford to gamble on Michele. We felt she would do even better than Paul for some reason."

Professor Tartule took a piece of paper from a folder.

"Let me read you the answer The Sea Face gave Michele: 'No, Michele. Your instruments have already told you. We are not artificial beings. We are not robots, androids, clones, cyborgs, remotes of any kind; neither ambulans nor extensors. We are people, as you. Our Masks contain a great deal of instrumentation: implants, important telemetric aids—you know this. But the Masks are not us.'

"They talked further. She answered his questions, as is usually the way at these meetings. They want to know everything about how the coventried ones feel and react. Michele knew she had another riddle to answer before she could get to ask her own question, but she decided to ask it anyway, not to test the system but just because she probably forgot the arrangement in her preoccupation and excitement. Jack Haunts answered her."

Eric felt a prickling at the back of his neck. "What did she ask?"

"A woman's question, Eric. Michele sat across from Jack Haunts and said: 'What do you fear?' The question surprised us all. Haunts—Jack Haunts—they dislike being called by their chosen surnames, both names, first or none. Forgive me, you know this! He did not speak for several minutes. He did not remind her of her breach of form; he answered her, told her this."

Tartule read again from the transcript. "'Michele, we too fear the Great Danger. We fear failure in our task as custodians; we fear loss of face.'"

Eric stared, dumbfounded, about to laugh at the absurdity of it.

Tartule anticipated him. "Go ahead, Eric. Laugh. Michele did. We all did. Those are the words he used. A masked creature speaks words like that. If we take it seriously, literally, they need their Masks to rule, to control Sebek and Osiris and Anubis and Set. Or maybe as life-support assists. We've considered that already, suspected it from the beginning. Take it sociologically: they are rigidly caste-conscious creatures, behaving according to the most exacting strictures and protocols, codes of conduct we cannot begin to understand. Their Masks, their dress and mannerisms, their magnificent urbanity, the males-only angle, the Riddle System they've recently fostered—all these things re-enforce the idea of caste and ritual behaviour.

"If we take it humourously, then a question out of turn prompts a comical answer. He was reprimanding her, you see. "Michele returned to playing the game by the rules. But she had to answer the same question put to Paul Litger: 'What are the Three Traps?' She came away, consulted with us, and we gave her our best answers, then she suggested her own. None satisfied The Sea Face."

"What were the answers? And Litger's?"

Derek Tartule shook his head. "I won't tell you, Eric. Just trust us that a consensus didn't help at all. Michele's answers, like Paul's, were probably closer to the half-whimsical, spontaneous-seeming nature of the Riddle System. You are the occluded ones. This game is meant for you. The answers from us just don't seem to be acceptable."

"You make me sound privileged," Eric said.

"From where I'm sitting now, you are very much that. A tiny minority of adjustees get interviewed, get the chance to swap questions like this. No World Council member or diplomat or research specialist does. Even if we committed crimes and got treated, we probably wouldn't be chosen. Yes, to me you are privileged. I envy you."

Eric realised the simple truth of the scientist's words, considered for the first time what a small price Tartule would think he had paid to be so eligible.

"So where do I take it up?"

"On two levels, Eric. We wonder about the game itself. Why this trend? Why have the iquiri recently started this, selecting certain occluded subjects?"

"You keep sidestepping that very well, Professor. We are criminals."

Tartule looked at him strangely. "Are you? Can you prove it?"

It was a ridiculous question, but Eric realised that, no, he couldn't prove it. "Are you suggesting I might not be? That the iquiri tampered with me for some other reason?"

"No," the little man said carefully. "But isn't that a possibility you ought to have considered anyway? You have no memory of an offence."

"But the iquiri do not lie!"

"We all lie to serve a purpose, Eric. By omission or commission, we all know when to lie. Parents lie to children about reality all the time, a most heinous and culpable offence since it does involve the way reality is perceived. But, then as now, lying can be seen as a sign of extreme care. It all has to do with the motive and ethic behind the lie, doesn't it?"

"Do they lie to us?" Eric asked.

"They evade, as I told you, and the Riddle System helps them do this. They manipulate situations, and there are questions they will not answer. Before the question and answer format was properly established with Litger, we had one subject who met with Bofari Thames. Only three meetings. Brian Trace had been a journalist and he kept at The Storm Face about where his race had come from and what they wanted, things like that. Too bold, too aggressively direct. We learned of this later. Bofari Thames ignored the questions, then discontinued the meetings. A wasted opportunity.

"This whole idea of a trade-off to get information isn't just a game. Oh, no. Seven aliens do not take over a world without reason. Where are their colonists, the demands on our resources? Why conquer and rule benignly what you don't plan to use? No, they are grooming us. They have not done one thing to harm our planetary society. They seem to want to improve it. They have qualified not removed self-determination. They have raised our consciousness to a global level in, what, twenty years? They've provided the Outsider we all knew was the only way to do that. So what is this Occupation, this Cohabitation: a lovely dream or a pending nightmare?"

Eric saw the scholar's deep concern. "There is an urgency for you?"

Tartule looked up. "Oh, yes. A personal urgency because I have worked with it from the start. A personal urgency because I am old. I would like to know. I believe—prefer to believe—in a noble motive behind what they do."

"So what should I ask them?"

"A simple question: what their Masks do. What the Masks really are for them. As I said, they are marvellously shielded things, far more than ornamental. We have the fragments given to Michele. We get general readings and deduce function, but no details. A direct question would help."

"Provided I get past their first question."

"Yes. Provided you do that."

Eric did, more easily than he would have dreamed. His second meeting with The Sky Face took place in Carlieu a week later. It followed the same pattern as before—the solitary drop-ship, the two human aides who remained outside to watch the square. This time, however, the formal reception was dispensed with, and Beth Mills let Eric usher Jeuven Samuels into the inner office by himself.

When they were seated opposite one another at the desk, Jeuven Samuels began by asking Eric about his reactions to the occlusion he suffered.

Before he answered, Eric switched on the small pocket recorder provided by the DCS and placed it in plain view as Tartule had suggested. Then he went on to detail the different stages of feeling he had experienced.

More questions followed, and Eric found it easier and easier to answer them. They were clearly phrased, and The Sky Face seemed so polite and interested.

What was Mars like?

What did he feel in Barracamba?

What was the red he missed most of all?

What occlusion would he hate more than any other?

Did he feel estranged from his non-coventried fellows?

Were the iquiri good for mankind?

Questions on so many issues, so many subjects. Not once did The Sky Face interrupt before Eric had finished an answer; not once did the iquiri ask to have anything rephrased or repeated or write anything down.

Eric knew the Mask was recording or relaying everything he said. It was disquieting to stare across at that brilliant field of sky knowing that it did such things, and several times Eric realised he had become lost in the cloud pattern before noticing the clear, blue, very human eyes gazing at him through the eye-slits.

One such lapse was Jeuven's cue.

The Sky Face leant forward a fraction, and Eric sensed that the game was about to begin.

"You visited Derek Tartule," Jeuven Samuels said. "No doubt you discussed iquiri riddles and our Masks. Why do you wish to know us so badly?"

This is it, Eric realised, and swallowed, feeling a moment of panic. "What we began to talk about the other day. You are powerful; you have the advantage. We fear the unknown you represent. At the same time, it fascinates us. You have not harmed us. You have become our greatest mystery."

The Sky Face nodded, and Eric wondered if his answer was adequate. He dared not wait any longer.

"Jeuven," he said. "What are your Masks to you?"

"What is a man?" The Sky Face countered at once.

"What? A man?" Eric said, and paused, thrown by the directness of it. The game had started.

His mind raced. Then he knew, something he had read years ago in his childhood. With incredible certainty, he found he had an answer.

"'A child gone sour in the cathedral vault of Time's huge house'."

The Sky Face inclined his head. "That sounds like a quotation, Eric. In a very mannered idiom. Still, it will do. Why is desensitisation the Great Enemy?"

Eric didn't even consider the injustice of a second question. The game was nothing like he had imagined it; he had to answer. "Because we have no choice."

"Very good. Too quick an answer to be anything but wise."

Eric had hoped to last long enough to ask why they posed questions like these, but he saw why. Like looking down some vast corridor of understanding, he knew the reason.

But before he could repeat his prepared question, Jeuven Samuels pressed him again, violating the rules of the game. There were no rules.

"What makes you think the loss of red was not the gift of everything else?"

"I am no longer sure of that, Jeuven. I am a tide on the turn there."

"Ask your question," The Sky Face said.

Eric stared, pleased with himself, thinking too quickly to feel any ego satisfaction from the victory. He found that he was richly, deeply involved now. The conversation with Jeuven Samuels had his complete attention.

"What are the Masks really? What do they mean to you?" When the words were said, Eric worried about the ambiguities, any loopholes he might have left.

The Sky Face accepted the two-part question however, exactly as Eric had meant it.

"My Mask is a sensorium, Eric. It filters your reality for me, interprets things. You have guessed that we are more alien than we appear. We need... scramblers, decoders. Our sensoria do this service; they are computer faces. But here we tell Derek Tartule's people no more than they have already assumed. In a way, it is a wasted question for you. So let me add more. It is time for more information.

"When we were just iquiri—the iquiri—we were the Outsider. Now we have names and identities we are personalities, people. Different people, but people. You see our traits. It is even conceivable that we shall become dear to you. Don't look surprised, Eric. You are already finding that you are very fond of me. You know that we are loyal to you."

"The motive?"

"That which you see."

Eric laughed. Always the evasion, the things nimbly fenced. Tartule's specialists would be alert for the subtleties and nuances of such remarks, but here, now, Eric was on his own. He would have to listen carefully.

Eric tried a new tack. "Professor Tartule has a query to make, Jeuven. Pertaining to the schedule."

"Yes?" Did the voice show a new level of interest?

"You made a copy available to Council and Archives, another to the DCS people. Both the iquiri original and the translation were authorised."

"Yes?"

"Tartule has discovered an error in the translation."

"Go on. Please." The voice betrayed nothing. He could have been saying 'At last!' or even 'So what?'

"Whenever the word *andaio* appears in the Charter, we take it to mean the adult iquiri. In translation, we have replaced the term with human adult. This raises a curious point for us..."

"A technicality?"

"That's right. We see *andaio* as an exclusive word. A race word for you, like iquiri is. It strictly relates to you according to the analogies established at Compact. We suggest *plaire* has to be the word for 'human' in your language, as least as you have revealed it to us. Your schedule should not apply to us without a codicil."

"How do you wish me to respond to this?"

That threw Eric. This damn game, he thought. The playing continues all the time, almost out of grasp. Then he realised the obvious, that The Sky Face—all of the iquiri—knew of the oversight, had deliberately left it there for just such an occasion. Tartule had armed him with the information, but Eric hated the thought of using it. This wasn't the way to proceed, bargaining like this, not over technicalities, not now. Eric had the grace to relinquish the claim.

"You could grant me the privilege of another question," he said, but humbly, showing that he knew he had demeaned them both by such quibbling.

The iquiri nodded once. The calm voice came from that airy Magritte countenance as steadily as before. "Very well, Eric. Ask your next careful question."

Eric sensed the importance of the moment. Not only was the game broken, but Jeuven Samuels was now ready to deal with a deliberate breach of the Charter—a breach his race had left behind to be found, wanting to be challenged on it. The obvious question was to ask why the iquiri had allowed this oversight to remain. But this could be asked another time, and there was a more important question.

"We are fascinated by your approach. The Riddle System."

"So you should be," Jeuven Samuels said. "Before you make it a question, I shall tell you something, Eric. As we see it, a race, like a person, earns its spurs by the questions it asks. It takes courage to ask questions, such real courage. And now we only ever answer the questions of those we punish. The rest of the time, we say what we want. Now we choose from among the deprived ones."

"The reasons?"

"You have guessed your own, Eric. Say them!"

"You make us observe you," Eric said. "You slow down the process of discovering more about you. You stall for time so that people really do see you."

"So that people notice us. Yes." The iquiri's voice was more resonant than Eric had ever heard it. Was it his imagination, or had the voice changed, taken on new emotion? "Were we to answer one question a year, the world would wait for that question like nothing else."

Eric saw that it was true. "Ten questions speed you up. One question slows you down."

"Exactly. Also, when you get only silences or evasions, you impute to us the motives you wish us to have."

For Eric, that was even more intriguing. "You benefit from projection?"

"We certainly do. Always. Because we are powerful enough to rule you, to destroy you too, you will not choose to see the worst motives. Naturally you want us to be wise overseers of your destiny. The Riddle System, as we together call it, serves all our purposes. We draw attention to the questions you ask us. Everything becomes important, re-sensitised. But go on! Why do we answer your questions at all?"

Eric had already considered this. "There is something you want us to know about you. At last, the time has come for it, but you wish to set up the revelation properly. That's it. You're framing it, setting it up. No doubt you've fed us clues we haven't recognised yet, told us more than we suspect. Like the oversight in the Charter, and why your revelations are only made to adjusted criminals." And then there was the afterthought. "Or to people you've selected who may not be criminals, but whom you think occlusion will affect in a special way."

The Mask inclined slightly at that, but Jeuven Samuels ignored the terrible accusation. "It accords with the schedule," he said, "that only adjustees are chosen."

"I don't believe that's it, Jeuven! Why do you choose us, I wonder? What does the criminal of a society have that equips him for your needs?"

"You may be missing the point, Eric. But I pass on these questions anyway. I take them as rhetorical."

"Too direct?" Eric said, pressing the point.

"At the moment, yes. But more. It is not our way."

"The schedule?"

"The schedule. We must play the game."

"Sphinx!" Eric snapped, angry at the evasion, at this iquiri's return to distance and form on the verge of yielding so much.

"As you say," The Sky Face said. "I play the sphinx."

"Jeuven, please! Why do you choose us? Was I a criminal or not?"

"What are the Three Traps?"

The words stopped him short. Here was the warning, the end-game question, the one neither Paul nor Michele had answered correctly or adequately or personally enough. Eric realised that if he answered now and failed, that would be it. He may never see Jeuven Samuels again. Two meetings only. He would score even more poorly than Brian Trace.

"I must have time to think," he said.

"Of course. But remember, Eric. I would not ask anyone that question unless they had lived the answer."

A function of the sensorium must have summoned Beth Mills, for the equate suddenly appeared at the door.

"I will go," Jeuven Samuels said, standing. "Beth will call our central office when you have your answer. We shall meet then."

Eric rose to his feet also, numbed by the suddenness, the anticlimax of the situation. He watched out the window as the iquiri crossed the square to the drop-ship. He saw the craft lift and slip off into the east, then sat at the desk again, trembling to think of how close he had been to losing this contact, this precious contact. He sat, with not a coveted, coventried red in sight, and thought of traps he had lived.

Three.

A letter came from Tey that afternoon. She had been brought back from Amazon House to Geneva to meet with Barlu Octavian.

Eric marvelled at the news. The only other adjustee he knew well and she had been chosen for the interviews too. Now that he had been given the statistics by Tartule, it seemed amazing.

And yet it was a good choice. Tartule would have more from the iquiri yet, knowing Tey.

Eric desperately wanted to contact her, to let her know that he was seeing The Sky Face, that again they were together in a sense, pacing one another. But after four attempts to get the necessary information out of the Geneva com-comp, he gave up. He phoned the University instead.

Derek Tartule admitted that he knew of Tey's summons, was in fact waiting for the first meeting to take place so he could arrange a briefing through the DCS agent at the Geneva office.

Eric felt a surge of annoyance that the Professor had not told him of Tey's induction, then realised it was no doubt a requirement forced on him by the Seven. When he asked the little man if he felt the iquiri were deliberately keeping him apart from Tey, Tartule agreed that they might be held incommunicado as part of a plan, and that the coincidence of the Geneva interviews did seem to indicate an accelerated interest of some kind.

Tartule's voice trembled with excitement. "It looks promising, Eric: more meetings, fewer major occlusions, The Riddle System, increased selectivity—the iquiri do seem to be assessing the temper of the times. It is leading somewhere, surely. If the question sessions are as controlled as they appear, you must be kept from Tey, for both your sakes, to maintain your sense of isolation, your sureness of intuition, to preserve the one-to-one relationship you have with The Sky Face. Read me Tey's letter. Please!"

After the barest hesitation, a vestige of his earlier annoyance, Eric did so.

> *My Eric,*
>
> *Guess what has happened? I am off to Geneva to meet Barlu Octavian, The Fair Countenance, the one who sings. The equate here at Amazon House tells me I'll be contacted by a Professor Tartule at the University of Barracamba. Next door to you. I'll ask him to get word to you of how I do. I haven't forgotten Amsterdam.*
>
> *Your Loving Tey.*
>
> *PS: I have a songbird after all, the real thing, a hybrid they've made here called a Crown Spectre. It took me five months to find it.*

"Soon now, Eric," Tartule said.

"I believe so too," Eric told him. He bid the Professor goodbye and rang off.

Eric decided to force his own hand. He arranged the date of the third meeting for a week's time, then took leave from the job at Ichos he had never properly started. He gave himself that week to decide on the Three Traps—three that, according to Jeuven Samuels, were to come from what he had lived.

With two days to go, he went in to Barracamba once again, covering more or less the same route he had taken a year before. Eric surfaced at Maize Street, went down to the harbour, then out to the spaceport. The Tandercote Gallery was closed, so he took the slidewalk through Bosty Market to the Smokery again, kept on going, street by street, and found himself at last on the sea-wall at Travnes.

He sat on the rough stones in the bright windy morning, watching the waves fall on his left and the trams swinging around on his right before beginning their long slow climb back up into the city, laden with tourists. Gulls swung in like brittle toys on unseen threads, shrieking, and swung out again. Children laughed and played on the beach below; the trams clanged their ancient bells, completed their turns and were off.

It was the richest focus of life Eric could remember, so full and busy and varied, nothing like the quiet square at Carlieu, or the chill Martian plains or the heaving swells of Sea Platform and Bass Strait III.

He sat there three hours and got his Traps. As simply as that, hardly trying. He sat there another hour and tested them, going past the clever glib answers, proving their honesty by relating them to Tey and himself and the iquiri.

Then he got something more. Out of the strong sea wind and the sunlight and the children playing on the sand, he realised something far more significant than the nature of Three Traps. And the enormity—the simplicity—of what he knew struck him to the heart, so straightforward and amazing it was.

All the way back from Travnes to Carlieu, by tram, slidewalk, tube and the old bus, he turned his discovery over in his mind. He fell into exhausted sleep in his room at Mrs Spain's knowing the Three Traps, and certain now of what it was the iquiri wanted humans to know.

The meeting was almost identical to the two before it: the same time of day, the same chairs in the office, the same morning quiet; nothing like being on the sea-wall at Travnes.

But now there was no evasion, and no preliminaries either.

"You have an answer, Eric?" Jeuven Samuels began, when they were seated and the recorder was going. "What are the Three Traps?"

Eric looked across at The Sky Face, took a deep breath to steady his voice.

"First and least," he said. "There's the Trap you do not know you are in. That's the cunning Trap and the most common, and often the individual is to blame. Mars showed me that, but it's everywhere on Earth."

Jeuven Samuels said nothing.

Eric studied the Mask a moment, then continued.

"Then there's the Trap you are betrayed into. That's the worst, for invariably it means treachery, deceit by someone else. If I have lived this one, Jeuven, then maybe it is that you have deceived me and I am not a criminal at all."

The Sky Face seemed to nod. Seemed to. Eric couldn't be sure, though his eyes never left the Mask.

"So what is the last, Eric? Have you kept the best or worst till last?"

"The best, Jeuven. The Third Trap is the best, the most endurable. It is the Trap you do not care you are in."

The Sky Face considered that for a minute.

"I like them, Eric. I like your Traps. Do you have something to ask me now?"

"No," Eric said.

If it were possible for the impassive sky to show surprise, then that one word had done it. Nothing in Jeuven Samuel's expression could show it, but the stillness, the sudden hushed waiting of the creature, told Eric that this was not expected.

"You surprise me, Eric," The Sky Face said finally.

"I expect I do, Jeuven. I'm glad I do."

"You have broken the game."

"Nothing new. The game doesn't exist. You depart from it when it suits you. It only has the illusion of rules anyway. You use it to prepare us."

The Mask watched him. "Why don't you ask me the question you raised last time?" came the steady voice, genuinely intrigued and showing it now in curious inflections. "Why don't you ask me one of Derek's questions? He longs for answers."

"Because, first, you will tell us what you want us to know when, and only when, you are ready. And second, because I've guessed who and what you are." There, he had said it. "No proof. I just know. Everything is secondary to that at the moment."

There was a flash of eyelight behind the sky. "Oh?"

"I know what your Masks are for you and what you are behind your Masks."

Another flicker of light, the movement of intent eyes.

There was a charged feeling between them now, more than the quiet of the hour: the absolute imminence of knowledge.

Eric knew that, all over the world, the scattered iquiri were listening in, the great iquiri computers were recording. He knew too what was crucially important, that the Seven did want to be known for what they were.

"So?" The Sky Face said.

Eric watched the iquiri, his eyes never leaving that soft spread of spring sky. This was it.

"You are totally occluded," he said. "Every sense gone. Your Masks—the sensoria—tie you in to phenomenal reality. Without them—"

"We lose face!" Jeuven Samuels said, completing the horribly ironic joke, explaining it. "The greatest thing we fear."

Eric actually laughed, a single jarring bray of surprise. To think: he hadn't suspected that, the inconceivable loss of it. It shook him, so cruelly obvious now.

"What else, Eric?" The Sky Face said. "What else do you know?" The eyes inside the sky never left his.

"You are the criminals of your race. Your sentence is to serve and care. For this they give you back—"

"Everything, Eric! Oh, everything! Life! Our respite from Coventry. Can you imagine it? We get back wind and sunset and feeling. The sounds of cataracts and furnaces and laughter. The smell of roses and semen and hot oil; the sharp smell of railroad tracks in the rain and grass in hot sunshine. Catspaws and cloud-shadow; everything there is, everything! There at the end of the corridor of our Masks, filtered through a veil, Maya, but there! Plato's shadow on the cave wall. Framed and distant, but there!"

And the fists clenched, or rather drew into a clench, slowly, then as slowly relaxed out again. Jeuven Samuels was once more in total control.

The silence continued for a time in that closed room, with the sounds from the square half-heard, the rumbling of drays, the ordinary sounds of day. They underscored the heaviest, fullest silence Eric had ever known, with realisation funnelling down on him, every thought triggering another, all of them leading back to the inescapable tragedy of it.

Then the Mask spoke. "Do you want red back?"

Eric was startled by the question. There was only one answer. "No," he said, and was surprised to discover it was true.

"Why not?"

Eric faltered over his reply, his thoughts not yet clear. He was afraid he wouldn't know why, though of course he did. That realisation was there too.

"I want to... remember... what it's like. I can't afford not to remember."

"A small price, Mr Ambassador."

"Pardon?"

The voice came softly. "You are an envoy to us, a go-between."

"I can reveal this?" Eric said. "What you've told me?"

"What you've told me," The Sky Face reminded him. "What you've guessed. Yes, go and tell them. The outcome will be interesting. You will make us the perfect custodians; perhaps you will ask us not to leave you. We keep a tidy house. Perhaps you will go forth into space knowing that your housekeepers are doing their job, grateful for their chance to do it."

Eric got up to leave. He moved towards the door, pausing only for a final question.

The Sky Face answered him before he could say it.

"No. We do not know our crimes either, Eric. But it doesn't matter, does it? It is your third Trap. The chance to be what we are for you makes it so."

Nothing could surprise Eric after that, so finding Tey waiting for him in the square, back from Geneva, here where everything had started for them, simply made him smile.

"Did your answers satisfy him?" Tey asked, her silver hair blowing in the morning breeze.

Eric took her hand and they started walking towards Carlieu the hill.

"They love us, Tey," he said, feeling exhilarated. "They really do. And we must care for them." He wondered suddenly about her own time with Barlu Octavian. "What did you ask The Fair Countenance?"

Tey smiled. "I asked him why the iquiri had brought us together, me with my red hair and all."

"What did Barlu Octavian say?"

She laughed. "He said that now I had asked him a hard question, and that he would need time to think of an answer."

"Sphinxes!" Eric said. "Damn sphinxes!"

And they walked on across the square, this man without red and the woman who had lost birds, both silently grateful that, in a world of cruelties and such clever traps, neither of them—and none of the Seven—had suffered the greatest coventry of them all, the ultimate isolation, the loss of all that had grown between them, all that surrounded them and held them even now. The love.

The Only Bird in Her Name

THAT SUMMER THERE were fourteen of them hunting the Forgetty, fourteen hard men with fierce eyes, minds like traps, and no compassion.

The bounty hunters met at the Astronomers' Bar and made their plans for finding the creature, or sat near the members of the Bird Club on the terrace of the Gaza Hotel discussing past hunts and this final attempt.

That was where I met Tom Rynosseros, an honorary member of the Bird Club and a sort of bounty hunter himself. He was here to locate the Forgetty too, though his task was to stop the killing, to save it if he could.

I was covering the hunt, a new assignment and an important one. Even Sam didn't know how excited I felt. He just knew, with his veteran editor's intuition, that I was good at quest stories, that they suited my personality and fed the sort of mind I had. Many journalists had tried, but I had been the one to locate Sunset Joe, the mad old charvi captain who buried treasure in the desert out near Maas, then sold his baffling maps to unknowing young sailors; to give them quests, he said, to put even more risk, danger and reward into the world.

Landing the Forgetty story on this, the last hunt, was something else entirely. I was the second female reporter *Caravanserai* had taken on; but, for all Sam's fondness, I had never made it past page two. Now I had my first real chance. The thought of being with Tom Rynosseros only made it more special.

The Bird Club and Tom were all on the terrace when I arrived, wearing their elegant Edwardian finery, carrying the polished brass binoculars that they never seemed to use. I smiled at the distinctive way these folk had of combining an exclusive *Kaffee-klatsch* with an often serious scientific salon. In the midst of it all stood the gleaming samovar, their focal point, as absurd and yet as studiedly quaint as the binoculars, the dark evening jackets of the men, the narrow gowns of the women. Wherever the samovar stood, there the Bird Club was in session.

I approached the group, showed my ident and introduced myself.

Tom stood and shook my hand.

"Beth Leossa-Tojian. From *Caravansesrai*," he said, then introduced the Bird Club members: Graeme Fowler, the President, Nathan Hawkless, John Wren, Joanne Henderson, Aubrey Quayle, Sally Nightingale, Jeremy Eagleton, and the newest member, Anton Ankil, the eccentric young geneticist who had bred a new species, the Ank, to gain membership.

"How did you qualify, Tom?" I asked.

"The position's honorary, Beth," he said, smiling. "They allow me the Dodo."

The other members smiled. John Wren, drawing me some coffee from the modified samovar, gave a mock-flourish with one hand.

I almost fell for it.

"But there's no Dodo in—oh, I see."

The others laughed, because I had been so earnest and so completely gulled by what was such an old joke for them.

"I swear to get even," I said, and between sips of coffee began outlining my assignment. The atmosphere on the terrace changed at once. They listened with complete attention, all traces of the their former mirth gone from their faces. This was serious business for them.

Before I had finished, six more bounty hunters appeared from the loggia and joined the three who were sitting several tables away. Their leader saw Tom and came over. I recognised the man from previous hunts, a tall African named Misla.

"Hello, Captain Tom," the hunter said. "So far from *Rynosseros*. All because of us. You will stop us, do you think?"

"If I can, Misla. If it comes to that."

"We are fourteen this time."

"I intend to be careful."

I felt the private nature of the contest between the two men. Misla had led most of the hunts in past years, had helped exterminate most of the Forgetties left in Australia. Tom had thwarted him twice, but only twice.

As Misla and Tom talked, I watched the other hunters in the African's group. They were all here on a technicality, because of a loophole in both States and Nation law. New legislation had been drafted and ratified to protect the last of the Forgetty race, but could not come into effect for two days. An interim injunction had stopped the issuing of licences within Australia, but fourteen had been sold through a scalper's office at Old Java Beach.

These hunters—Islanders and Niuginians mostly—were the last of them, with the cool desperation of that knowledge, moved by a quiet urgency and the promise of huge rewards. They were here to hunt in person, with no hi-tech weapons, but they had been given unlimited computer access before reaching Twilight Beach. They knew as much as anyone about the Forgetties, with the possible exception of the Bird Club. And they were the best, these hunters. Misla had made sure that the licences had gone to the best.

There were three Treece clones who had more than ten kills to their credit, and Paulo who had made five. I knew several of the others, too, and some who weren't with Misla now. All deadly men.

Here in the bright sunlight on the terrace in front of the Gaza, it hardly seemed possible that these groups were in such opposition, that they would put their lives at risk like this.

Or rather, that Tom would. He was here without his crew because the tribes had accepted that the Bird Club was earnestly concerned with protecting this tangental species, and had allowed them one field agent, though only one. It seemed neither fair nor realistic, but that was how it had to be. The hunt would take place on tribal land.

When Misla and his band had departed to make their final preparations, the Bird Club adjourned to the Astronomers' Bar, four of the men hoisting the samovar on its portable stand and carrying it with them. Tom stayed behind, looking at me in his oddly penetrating way as if he wanted to say something but had thought better of it.

I bridled a little, thinking for a moment that it was because I was female, but that wasn't it. He seemed to be considering whether or not to share confidences with me.

I gave him a look that I hoped made me seem trustworthy, and waited. I knew very little about Tom, just facts acquired from the popular stories, but he fascinated me, more than I cared to show openly. This was the man who had spent some subjective years in the Madhouse, probably on a 50:3 sentence for an unknown crime; who had survived it and won *Rynosseros* in the ship-lotteries at Cyrimiri. He was not tall as the stories have it, and around thirty, though he's well kept and looks younger. In many ways, his appearance is unremarkable, but his eyes are everything. They show that the stories can be true, that he is a sensitive accepted by the Clever Men, that he is one of the few National captains to be granted a Colour and an all-lander mandate from the Princes, allowed to sail "all Roads, all States from coast to coast" as the Ab'O tribes say it. Afervarro's *Songwing* was the first charvolant to win that honour, and there have been only six other ships since then.

Here was one such Captain—holding such an honour for some undisclosed service to the tribes.

I felt a definite thrill of excitement, but also of concern and uncertainty to be alone with him. I did not wish to consider my reasons then, and that annoyed me slightly. It was a confusion I put down to nerves and the unique nature of what I was about to share with this sand-ship captain—the Blue Captain—and representative of the famous Bird Club.

I found I was pleased when he suggested we discuss my part in the hunt as the media observer requested by the Club's President. Sam had been concerned that Tom would have objections there. But I sensed none, and felt rather an easy acceptance as he took my arm and led me down the Promenade, though with every step I wondered what he knew, and how he planned to locate and protect the Forgetty.

"Will they know more than you do, Tom?" I asked.

"Possibly, Beth, but not likely. They'll know kill-sites and hunt-patterns from all the past hunts, and have estimates on how this present creature will behave. I have much the same information. This one conforms to the Bale standard. We know it's a true shape-changer, though a comparatively slow one, that like all Forgetties it mimics only humans as the most fitting mask for its intelligence. We know it's definitely not androphagic, contrary to what Misla says, that it doesn't kill even when cornered. We know its bite causes loss of memory—"

I was taking notes as we walked. "Is that recent memory or all memory as Munce claims?"

"Recent memory, yes. And it is not immune to its own bite. Our Anton Ankil discovered that several years ago."

I shuddered. In bright sunlight, surrounded by the sound of belltrees and the ocean, there was the old fear to be mentioned again "It's easy to think of the vampyre legends."

"Vampyres and werewolves," Tom said. "Misla's arguments ten years ago. That's where the misconceptions about the Forgetty begin. The biting. How well have you been briefed, Beth?"

"I've talked with Rossibo and Munce. I know the Bale standards—all the variants. I've scanned the report your Bird Club did."

Tom nodded "Then you know there's no biting at all." We were near a derelict belltree, stripped long ago, its naked nine-foot shaft thrumming in the wind. He gazed at it as he spoke. "There's an ancillary tooth—a dew tooth—folded in against the lower jaw. The Forgetty presses its open mouth against the—victim's neck, so the tooth pierces the skin, and secretes the lethophoric. Then there's the stupor and the amnesia. But it's not biting."

"That's what Munce told me, yes. I've heard, too, that the Ab'Os are calling it the Philosopher Beast."

Tom laughed. "Yes. The Aurelius. That's the Bird Club's doing, a deliberate tactic to upgrade the creature's status and a way of describing how the Ab'Os have finally started to see the creature. 'Andromorph Aurelius. The Philosopher Beast. The Beast of Lethe, or Forgetty. This quasi-human dweller of the coastal deserts, first identified by—'"

"Graeme Fowler. Twelve years ago, right? Thanks, Sam told me. Is it so enlightened? Munce fears it's just a mutation, that most of its intelligence is mimicry as well."

"That too is Misla's argument because there's no apparent purpose for the creature, no clear ecological niche for it. Mutations don't always have an obvious place in the natural order; that's the nature of mutation."

"Then what could be its purpose? What use is a humanoid mimic that is a lethophore? Is it just a highly specialised mutation?"

"You think it's human, don't you, Beth?"

"Of course I do. Calling it an andromorph simply conceals the fact that it's another tangental. I think we've accelerated a sub-type."

"Haldane genetics?" Tom asked. "A failed tribal experiment?"

I looked across the low balustrade at the waves falling and the seagrass tossing in the wind. Near us, the belltree thrummed. "Not even failed. But you're testing me. The Bird Club already considers it to be viable and worthy of protection. And you aren't convinced that I'm not working with Misla, are you? That's why we're out here. You do what you need to, Tom, but you do believe it's viable, with a very real place in the natural order. That's where you base your whole defence, isn't it?"

Tom ignored my comment about Misla.

"Our problem, Beth, is that we simply have not been able to converse with a Beast and study its motivations."

"I find that odd. I'd say your group is committed to stopping further research, not encouraging it."

"That's because of the means researchers want to use. Once you grant its intelligence, then you grant it its desire for reclusiveness as well. We feel that when the hunts are ended, the Forgetties will reveal themselves on their terms. That option has not existed before."

I laughed. "Well done. Good honest self-determination. And you said 'Forgetties'. You believe there are more than just this one."

"We need to. We don't approach this as scientists, more as allies. We really do want the Beasts to trust us when they are ready."

"It occurs to me that you all have an excellent reason to conceal what you know. As part of this tolerance and patience. And maybe worse."

"Worse?"

"Yes. How would you know if you'd encountered a Beast? You may have already had your encounters and dialogues, been bitten and simply forgotten. Isn't that possible? The mnemonic residue might be this unscientific caring the group displays."

Tom smiled at me, looking like some displaced Edwardian time-traveller in the harsh desert light. "We often laugh about that, Beth. Protective déjà-vu! Now and then we bare our necks to one another, looking for the signs. No, if the Forgetties are viable, true tangentals and not some short-term mutation, they deserve to live. We draw our line there. And they have never needed to infiltrate our ranks. We are already their friends. Our members know one another too well anyway. The little memory games and passwords we use make a sustained impersonation impossible."

"I was just curious.

"I know. And you're not with Misla."

"Thank you," I said, and we turned and walked back to Twilight Beach.

Tom took me to The Traitor's Face. We drank tautine and watched the ocean, then started discussing the hunt. He made me realise just how crucial an accredited observer was in what was soon to happen. This was Misla's last trophy hunt for a Forgetty, the Bird Club's last great defence.

I relaxed more and more, found that I was letting my attraction for him show easily now. The earlier self-consciousness, the concern about being seen as some infatuated neophyte, had passed. I could see, too, that the feelings went both ways, that Tom was enjoying this chance to be away from the Gaza where the hunters were gathering. He seemed pleased that I was here and would be with him in the desert.

"What made you sure of me?" I asked.

Tom evaded the question gently, making light of it.

"There's a bird in your name," he said, and though I begged to know which one, he would not tell me.

To the north of Twilight Beach are the Restoration towns, a handful of small Mayan, Phoenician and Minoan communities strung out like beads on a necklace along the coast. They are mournfully sad places, these quiet, neglected temple precincts more desolate than Uxmal or the Puuc, and these white Mediterranean settlements facing the sea.

The people there are impoverished, inbred and almost xenophobic, though they can sometimes be seen carrying the labrys or sailing sand-ships with staring eyes painted at the bows, or worshipping their re-kindled deities atop pyramid citadels more like failed ziggurats than truly steep-sided Mayan monuments.

These places are where the Dreamtime has failed, where well-meaning Ab'O mystics seeking contact with the power vectors Chac and Astarte, Tanit and the Great Snake Mother, lost their controlling hand in that quest and became used instead of user. No longer inspired by their own wisdoms, rejected by the States and even the other Ab'O coastal tribes, these outcast tainted folk have embraced the acculturisation brought out of the haldane trance, and have slowly become sea-peoples like some of their adopted ancestors.

Visiting these museum towns has always been a melancholy but compelling thing for me. The people know what the have lost and what they now must be. I did not relish the thought of going among them again.

But, as Tom and the hunters knew, the Forgetty's town-room had been located in the Mayan Quarter of Twilight Beach, with a Tanit altar and other clear signs that the creature had its secret place, its omphalos, near the Mayan-Phoenician–Minoan town of Tyla. That discovery had brought the hunters in again and had led to this final hunt.

Tyla is officially a closed town. Nevertheless, the inhabitants make their livelihoods from what little tourism there is, and bar all charvis from the moorings but their own.

To go there, the curious sightseer must take passage on one of the strange Tylan ships, and travel the sacbeobs through the arid coastal desert. These holy roads are pitted and poorly maintained and sometimes prey to brigands. But to see Tyla and the rest of the Restored towns, the exorbitant fare is paid and the two-hour journey made.

The hunters knew of the arrangement and liked it even less than we did, but since the rules of the outcasts are enforced by the States, there is no other way. Tom and I and Misla's unrelenting band all booked passage on the *Ahuacan*, the only Tylan vessel out of Twilight Beach that day. At noon we boarded her, the kites went up, and the sand-ship left the moorings.

We rode in a tense silence, Tom and I down on the commons watching the dark shrouded Tylans, hardly recognisable as Ab'Os, tend the cable-boss; Misla and his companions up on the poop attempting conversation with the captain.

The holy road ran through terminator dunes mostly, with the ocean to one side and seagrass flanking our course. Belltrees marked the kilometre distances, regularly at first but then more and more infrequently, until there were only fitful winds from the sea, seagrass, dust and silence.

At mid-afternoon, we came to the towns.

First there was Itlos, a handful of white buildings perched above a short span of beach, a gleaming white town built around a stone breakwater, with shipyards and three seagoing sun-ships under repair.

Then came Maas, a neo-Mayan settlement and one of the largest, with a pyramid citadel, a royal storage labyrinth in the Minoan fashion, and a determined priesthood. Near Maas there were checkpoints on the Road where other sacbeobs crossed ours on their radial course into the desert. The Tylan captain explained who we were as he paid the corn-levy. The Maatians muttered cleansing prayers and sent us on our way.

Tyla was next, less successful than Maas or Itlos, and less defined in its acculturalisation. It rose on long low beach terraces above the ocean, a hundred white buildings set about narrow streets and many small squares, like nothing Mayan or Phoenician, more Cretan or Greek if anything.

We disembarked at the quay and found accommodation, again with Misla's group, at the Phalan Gade, the only outlander hotel in the town. There we learned of our latest misfortune. Though nothing about the town showed it, there was a festival to Tanit in progress. No outlanders could leave the hotel after sunset; no-one could cross the town perimeter until the evening of the next day.

Misla's eyes were like pieces of dark steel as the Ab'O woman at the reception desk gave us the news. He glanced at the water clock on the desk and grunted some words to his men.

"Tomorrow then," he said to Tom and me in suppressed fury. Then he waited.

Tom leant in close and asked me to activate my camera.

"Let Misla see we're recording this," he said.

The African glared when he noticed the red telltale, grunted another order, and stalked away. His men followed without so much as a backward glance.

When they had gone, Tom signed the register for us, then asked if any messages had arrived for him.

The Tylan woman, with poor grace, produced a crumpled white envelope from a drawer and passed it across. Tom slipped it into a pocket of his fatigues. Then we left our bags in the woman's keeping and went out to walk the streets.

Tom had no doubts that Misla would know of the likelihood of some contact with the Forgetty. Depending on what hi-tech assistance the mercenary had on call, shielded and hidden, he may have tried for a quick operation, despite the festival, regardless of reprisals from the Tylans or the tribes. But any thought of taking the letter by force and striking out for the omphalos now had been stopped. The African needed his public image unsullied for a while longer. My camera had prevented an incident at the Phalan Gade.

But now we were away from the hotel, beyond scrutiny. Tom led us from the windy sun-dazzled terraces overlooking the sea, through quiet narrow streets, under strips and squares of blue sky, into a maze of blank white walls and shuttered windows. We could have been in any hot white town in Northern Africa or the Near East, though here we were surrounded by a silence that was more than the hush of the hot afternoon or the siesta. Many of the houses were deserted, and now and then we gazed through an open doorway to other open doorways beyond, and peered through those in turn into quiet courtyards and silent colonnades.

Eventually, in a tiny square at the junction of several crooked streets, we stopped. I looked up at the white walls converging on their patch of vivid blue, saw that next to me in this startling duality of light and shadow Tom was doing the same.

"You feel it, Tom?"

"Yes. The life of the indrawn breath."

"The waiting is real, isn't it? Things will happen only when we have gone away. No wonder the Forgetties come to Tyla and the other Restoration towns. I wonder how many occupy these houses, passing as Tylans?"

"You still believe there is more than one, Beth?"

"Yes. I realise I do. Possibly because I cannot accept the reality of there ever being a last one. What does the Beast say?"

I watched him take out the envelope, inscribed with his name in a faded neat script, and remove the letter from it. Tom looked about him once, then opened it out. We read it together in silence.

Captain Tom,

Thank you for coming. Thank the Bird Club. For this service to me I shall never take your face or that of those you love. I shall be direct and honest in our dealings.

The hunters will guess I am among the chultunes at the Stone Door. Help me if you can, but do not risk your life That is all I ask.

Tom put the letter away and we walked through twenty more squares like the one where we'd stopped, pausing only to savour the quiet or call one another's attention to the slightest touch of a sea breeze that had found its way through the crooked streets to us. There was no music, no belltrees, no voices, just the occasional breath of wind and the silence.

We were glad to get back to the Phalan Gade and be shown to our adjoining rooms. I watched Tom burn the letter in the small votive fire below the bas-relief of Tanit that was near the window. I noted the tension in him as he did it.

The letter helped him little, I realised, though he was glad to know exactly where the omphalos was, and that there was goodwill at least from the Forgetty in this sorry enterprise.

Misla had maps. He already knew that the omphalos was near fresh water, and that on the outskirts of Tyla were twelve stone reservoirs, stone-lined cisterns set into the earth and tapping bores, or designed for catching the run-off from coastal rainfall and fed by stone conduits. These chultunes were protected by natural rock formations, and the secret place would be somewhere close at hand.

Searching there was the obvious course for Misla. The letter confirmed it. Tom explained how the Forgetty would normally pass itself off as a Tylan to visit the town's markets, or as an outland visitor to use the excursion ships travelling to and from Twilight Beach. The lethophore would be adept at such masquerades, he said, but never before had it had so many hunters eager for its life. Misla's men were alert for mimicry and obviously had pain-tests and passwords to safeguard their group against infiltration. The Beast would not try that.

Paradoxically, the bounty hunters were safer from the creature in Tyla, where an unusually stringent security was in force for the Tanit curfew, than in Twilight Beach. By the happenings of chance, Tom explained, the Forgetty would be forced to remain out in the chultunes for the duration of the festival. It could not leave Tyla overland; the Tanit priesthood would have its Maatian counterparts alert for that. The same holy day that had delayed the bounty hunters was working against the Beast as well. It was at its most vulnerable.

"Misla will move at sunset?" I asked him.

"Yes. As Soon as the festival ends."

"I'm going to follow the hunt, Tom. All of it."

"I want you there, Beth. I'll have to assume the Forgetty will not do anything. It may just wait to die. If hi-tech is used, I'll especially need a witness and media contact. What worries me is that you—"

"Can I fight if they try to kill me? Will that invite tribal payback?"

Tom smiled. "The moment a weapon is raised in your direction, you can fight. Let's hope the weapons they use make it possible. But the important thing, Beth, is to get the facts out so this becomes an unforgotten incident. Are you trained?"

The question made me smile. I thought of Sam, my editor, and what passed for weapons training at *Caravanserai*. "I'm a writer, Tom. I've had in-house training, that's all."

"It won't come to that," Tom said, but I saw the concern he put quickly from his eyes. "Misla will keep the rules. And please understand, Beth," he continued, and I could tell that his words were to answer my unasked question, "I'm not as reckless as I sound. I'll oppose Misla only to slow him down, to use up the time he has. The Tanit festival helps me there. I knew about it but Misla did not. I am hoping he will do something foolish that will give me other things I can use. But tomorrow evening at the chultunes I will fight only till I know I cannot win any longer, then I will stop. I am a philosopher beast too, you see."

But I sensed otherwise. I feared that Tom might not have time to discover if the omphalos were occupied or deserted, that he might fight until he was killed, that a vengeful Misla might not let him disengage.

I felt an ache and a sudden despair.

"Will we need two rooms, Dodo?" I said, and surprised him.

"Not if I were choosing," he said, laughing.

"Nor I," I said, and decided for us.

Later, in the silence of midnight, in silent Tyla, he turned to me. His eyes glinted, watching.

"Dodo?" I asked.

"You're the only one ever to use that as an endearment with me, Beth."

"Oh?"

"I've been told French parents still use it with their children when they sing them to sleep. *Mon petit, Dodo.*"

"I've heard that too. You've made that bird very important to me, Tom. Which bird is mine?"

"Not yet."

I waited, then leant in close. "I do hope you will know when to stop fighting tomorrow." And I held him till he slept, worrying for him and thinking about the contest that was coming, thinking of so many things that held me back from sleep, and fearing what would soon happen. Tom had spoken of tribal vigilance, of surveillance by the States, but what he didn't say was that in the Restoration towns the rules of the tribes were far-off things, depending on the whims of the sea-people, and very difficult to enforce.

The truth was brought home more clearly the next morning when First Treece was found dead in his room. Killed not by the Forgetty, though the Philosopher Beast was blamed in the stories that Misla quickly put out, but indirectly by the sea-people themselves.

Apparently the Treece, against all code regulations, had an implant giving him access to an orbiting Japano comsat, and during the night had made a preliminary infra-red scan of the chultunes area, no doubt at Misla's instruction. The Ab'O Princes, with satellites and monitors of their own, did not act on the infringement. It was the nearby Maatians, with no greater technology than a custodian transmitter and grudgingly rented comsat time, who detected the test-runs Treece was making and sent down a hot-signal to flash-burn the bounty hunter's brain.

Misla was furious, both that a Treece had been killed and that people would know his team had broken the code. He could not be sure if the Maatians would tell the Princes or not, but he decided to brave it out in the time he had. The implant wasn't mentioned. He had his own men remove the body from the hotel, and hinted that the Forgetty had been involved. He claimed hunter discretion over the details.

The Tylans didn't believe it; they didn't even seem to care. But the small group of tourists and trainee archaeologists going back to Twilight Beach accepted the story readily enough. It made their trip to Tyla that much more interesting. Misla calculated he would be out of Australia with the bounty before the Princes learned of the breach.

Tom was far less concerned than I thought he would be.

"What did you expect, Beth? Of course laws will be broken. This is the last hunt, the final chance. And the tribes don't learn everything. Certainly the Tylans won't tell them, though I imagine enquiries will reveal why the Maatians requested a hot-signal. Misla doesn't care if he's banned for several years. He can wait it out, then buy his way back into tribal favour. The difference is, the Forgetties won't be worth any bounty when he returns. What matters most now is that Misla *has* been caught out on a breach of rules."

"Does that help? You said he'll suppress that story."

"Only for the authorities, Beth. The National officials. The Ab'Os will be far more willing to tolerate payback from me now. To restore balance. I need to get a letter to Graeme Fowler on today's ship. It's a risk, but the Bird Club may decide it can show its teeth."

"Archaeopteryx!"

"I'm sorry?" Tom looked surprised, even startled by what I'd said.

"The Bird Club will show its teeth. Birds. Teeth. Forget it."

Tom smiled. "I'm slow. Archaeopteryx, of course. The 'dawn bird'. I won't underestimate you again, Beth."

The rest of the day went quietly for all of us. Some of Misla's hunters roamed the streets, others went as far as the road leading out into the hills but no further. Tylan priests, their dark robes showing the white ominously innocent child's doll outline of Tanit, stood there barring the way. Their ceremonial staves were barely disguised laser batons.

But at sunset, when the streets of Tyla were deep in shadow and the temple gong was sounding out the end of the Tanit festival, Misla and his band set off for the chultunes.

Tom and I watched them go, two lines moving along the narrow road that led into the hills. We waited twenty minutes then followed, hoping to use the growing shadows to escape Misla's notice. But the African had enough hunters to post lookouts and see which direction we took. Despite feints and back-tracking, by the time the moon had risen, we were facing one another at Stone Door.

The cistern itself was hidden in a wind-break of natural stone towers. They reared up against the lustrous evening sky like so many black daggers. Stars appeared, reflecting back at us from the cool dark water, and soon the moon was adding its light to the silent place where we stood, lifting above the largest of the stone blades to throw a richer lamp onto the water.

Unlike a Forgetty's town-room, where it lives as a tangential human, the omphalos is the meditation place that gives the Philosopher Beast its name. It is often unadorned, usually empty of all possessions, and it is easy to miss—but easy to find too when a general location is known.

This secret site was no more than a shallow cleft formed by a rockfall years ago, made deeper by some rocks piled at the opening. We had barely got there with enough time to guard the only approach. Tom had not yet examined the cave to see if it was occupied.

"An interesting dilemma, Captain Tom," Misla called as his men formed up about him. "You dared not show us which chultune it was, yet you could not afford to keep away. Do not be hard on yourself, Captain. There were clear tracks that would have led us here."

Tom said nothing. I moved back towards the cave mouth, then edged up from it to some rocks so I was looking down at the group assembling in front of Tom. I could not fight, but I was determined to watch for treachery.

I was fortunate. With the brilliant moonlight, I could see everything. Tom stood at the edge of the chultune, on the narrow sandy approach around its paved rim. The hunters could not even send missiles into the omphalos without gaining more ground first.

Misla gave orders. His crooked smile flashed amid the sudden, richer flash of drawn swords. He was looking beyond Tom to the opening of the cave.

"Let us by, Captain Tom," Misla said. "You need not die for this. The creature is ours."

Tom stood his ground, his kitana drawn, the bright blade resting on his shoulder. In his other hand he held his narrow-bladed sticker.

"This might be the last of them, Misla," Tom said. "Just this once, do a really brave thing. Turn and go. Let the creature be."

Misla laughed. Second Treece unhooked his atl-atl and fitted an arrow to it. The others began to advance.

Tom dropped into his fighting stance, blades before him, crossed and touching.

The mercenaries came on. Tom and Misla met in a flashing exchange of blades, evenly matched it seemed to me then. A hunter rushed past, eager to reach the cave before his chief. I barely saw how Tom's blade darted from the shapes between the two men to strike the Islander down, but the hunter spouted blood and fell. Then I realised that Misla, not Tom, had done it. Misla meant to be first; he had given clear instructions.

The swordplay continued, a frantic rush in the moonlight and dust.

Now I saw how it really was. Tom was not going to defeat this tall African. Misla was stronger, the more skilful opponent. He drove Tom around the edge of the cistern, further and further back towards the cave.

My heart pounded. My hands were clenched at my sides; I felt my fingernails stinging my palms. In my mind, the word "Archaeopteryx" kept returning, kept surprising me by being there, with the importance of the link it gave me to Tom, and the sudden understanding of all that was happening.

I could not interfere. I could not. And yet I could not stand there, not for any reason he had given or that I could find.

Tom was alone but for me. That's what I saw then. Tom alone, with Misla striking, striking, blades turning and weaving, binding up the dark air between them.

Tom stumbled, made the act into a desperate roll to the side. He regained his feet, but had to lose more ground. Misla advanced quickly and Tom stumbled again under a sudden rush of blows. He fell.

I seized a stone, my hand did, my mind not even deciding, and threw it hard. It fell short, but it caught Misla's eye for an instant. It used Misla's own trained reflexes against him.

Tom scrambled to his feet, swords crossed, breathing quickly.

Misla smiled "Treece!" he called out.

Misla's new lieutenant raised his atl-atl to make a cast. The arrow flashed towards the chultune, struck the path at Tom's foot; a warning, acknowledging that rules had been broken.

Tom brought up his swords, ready to deflect the next arrow if he could.

Second Treece loaded again, but before he could throw, he cried out and fell, a spear through his chest.

Tom and Misla backed off from one another and looked up. We all did. We saw the huge dark shape against the blue evening sky, watched as the balloon settled above the stone towers and men dropped down ropes from the gondola. We heard their swords leave scabbards.

The balloon lifted; other dark shapes lined the sides of the basket and sent arrows down at the waiting hunters.

Misla shouted orders. His mercenaries rounded on the newcomers, but the dark shapes kept their distance. Arrows came from the balloon, most of them poorly aimed, but three of Misla's men were struck all the same and fell back.

The dark shapes advanced. I could see the shining naked bodies, the strange masks they wore, the silhouettes of beaks and long staves ending in talons No Edwardian dress now, none of the elegance.

The Bird Club had come.

"Very well," Misla said, rounding on Tom. He cried out another command and Third Treece sheathed his swords, stood back and pulled off his own right arm. From the prosthetic sheath he drew three laser batons, threw them in a practised move to his nearby companions.

"Burn that thing down!" Misla cried, and attacked Tom once more.

But as if by precise reckoning, every transgression matched by a response, there were sudden detonations and flashes of energy. Misla's hi-tech warriors fell before they had even aimed their weapons, smoking holes in their skulls.

The Tylan priests put their batons away, and vanished as quickly as they had appeared on the rocks about us.

Misla renewed his efforts. His swords danced in the moonlight, blooding Tom repeatedly, though Tom dealt glancing blows that brought shiny streaks to the African's arms and dark patches to his uniform. The two men slid and lunged in the dust, Tom being driven ever backward, around the edge of the chultune towards the cave.

The rest of the fighters stood watching: the shining, beaked men from that greatest of infringements: the balloon, the eight remaining mercenaries, the silent Tylan priests of Tanit who had emerged from hiding once again and now stood with starlight glinting on their staves of power.

Further and further towards the Cave Tom retreated, back into the shadows of the last ten metres. Misla was grinning in triumph.

Then there was a slide of rocks, and a heavy splash from the dark waters of the chultune, followed by silence.

Yet again the two swordsmen parted, staggering back into the moonlight, breathing hard and looking down into the cool darkness.

A member of the Bird Club spoke. "Your Philosopher Beast has taken the philosopher's way out."

Misla stared at the settling water, his hard eyes flashing, then pushed past Tom and searched the shallow cave beyond. It was empty, with only a scuffed patch of earth beside the stones to show where something had gone over the side.

"That finishes it, Misla!" Tom said. "That cistern is deep, but you just may find the body. You have until midnight."

The African swore, then spoke in dialect to his men. They set to work, even as the Tylan priests ordered the balloon abandoned, then burned it from the sky.

And though the hunters dredged Stone Door until midnight, they found only stones for their pains.

The next morning, we returned to Twilight Beach on the *Elissa*, the mercenaries, the Bird Club, and Tom and I, riding the Road south in a silence of varied parts: exhaustion, bewilderment, fury and relief.

The Tylans had relayed the tribes' decision as we boarded. The Club was to disband as an official and privileged body because of the enormity of its crime in resorting to the balloon, its great secret. Not even payback could justify such a breach of Ab'O law, though it helped lessen the penalty.

The members took it well. No more hunters would be coming; anyone who broke both tribal and Nation law would be hunted forever.

In his room at the Gaza, Tom and I made love well into the afternoon, gently, carefully, and with much laughter because of his wounds. We talked now and then of the hunt, and he asked me what I thought had happened.

"Did it take its own life, Beth? Was our Beast that determined to end the strife?"

"No, Tom. You have told me again and again that the species is viable, inclined to life. I think the cave was empty, that a rockslide had been arranged. That's what we heard. Misla would have thought of it too but so much had happened."

"Yes," Tom said, and there was a touch of sadness in his voice.

I turned to him, seized his shoulders.

"Well, Sir Dodo. Now my bird. What have you chosen for me?"

"I think you know already, Beth. It is something special naturally, something provocative, with the implications of the phoenix. The first bird."

"Archaeopteryx?"

"That's it. The 'eos' in Leossa—the Greek 'dawn'. A creature in transition. A precursor. The phoenix is always regarded as the bird of change, but archaeopteryx existed. The pragmatist's phoenix." He paused. "You think it was a rockfall?"

"Yes," I said, sure now that he knew the truth. "A decoy."

"You're so certain, Beth. There was no-one near the cave but Misla, you and me.

"You were so nearly extinct, my Dodo."

"So were you, Beth."

Tom held me to him and we kissed long and deeply. I was absolutely, totally aware of him, of his tongue in my mouth, of his arm under my back pulling me to him, of where my breasts touched him, of the hardness of him in my body.

Our mouths parted, then I dropped my head and let him cradle it against his chest and neck.

The impulse came, strong and sure, but I fought it, remembering yet again the precious ancient bird he had found for me, and something he had said long ago, in another remembering, of the part that choice played in being human.

I saw him the next morning on the terrace of the Gaza. I watched him talking with the other members of the Bird Club around the samovar, carefully keeping myself hidden behind the sanche palms, wondering why I had not taken his memory this time either and what he thought, knowing it all. It is good that he knows, that someone knows.

I watched him discussing matters on this vivid morning, then returned to my other dark place, my secret room in the backstreets of the Mayan Quarter. There I found a letter propped up against the edge of the small Tanit altar. I sat on the bed and read it, not at all surprised that he had found me.

> *Dear Beth*
>
> *Having you in my life again, one more time, this dangerous time, makes me know all over again what human is. Come back to me now, just as you are. I cannot promise what will happen, but you need not go through all this again, especially now with Misla gone. We can make a place for all of your kind—finish properly what we have begun. We need you to help us. Think of what you do now, Beth. Please think of what you do.*
>
> *Love,*
> *Tom.*

I burned the letter in the votive flame, cancelling out that sharp exquisite hurt at least in part, the hurt that he did understand but could never completely know. Then I arranged the brief mnemonic display to remind me that I was a sometime itinerant journalist between Twilight Beach and Tyla. So there would be a next time. I recited the trigger word several times then, in case I needed to know it all, to have something more than chance that might lead me back to Tom.

"Archaeopteryx. Archaeopteryx. Archaeopteryx."

When that was done, I sat on my bed, fretting, aching with need for him. Yes, Forgetties are philosopher beasts indeed. You learn it again every time. You give, you take, you lower your head to your arm, slowly, purposefully. There is the tooth, the slightest prick is all it takes. The last words you cry are a broken whisper, a sigh of love *"Dodo, mon petit, Dodo!"*, then you give yourself over to Lethe and all the sweet blessings of forgetfulness.

The Last Elephant

WE WERE NEARLY over the coast of eastern Africa when the Chief finally figured out who I was. He gave a cry that carried the length of the gondola and made the other passengers and the air stewards all turn to see.

"Hey, you're Terence Harm, right?"

"Right, Chief," I said. I'd made him suffer all the way in from Madagascar, so I deserved this. Not once had I given in to the facial contortions and forehead furrowings that were unspoken questions from him. In fact, I'd been enjoying his antics, wondering when he'd break. I should have known the coast of Africa would do it.

"Bet I can guess why you're here, boyo!" he cried, pleased with himself. Everything was falling into place now.

"Oh?" I said, really not wanting this but smiling anyway.

"Sure," he said. "You're the celebrant. I never thought you'd be travelling alone. That's what threw me. You're the one who covered the ceremony for the Last Whale at Davenport."

"You read about that, did you, Chief?"

"Sure!" he cried, taking the empty seat beside me. "It was beautiful, what you said there. My nation got all the broadcasts, by satellite. We all saw it."

"They used to have whale watches there every year," I told him. After all, this was his country. He could be part of Borona security for all I knew.

"That's what I heard too. You're going down to Borona for the Festival, right?"

This was becoming ridiculous.

"Exactly right."

"You're going to see the Last Elephant."

"Right again."

"And decide what can be done. You've got to keep checking up on those Animals, eh?"

"Right."

He sat back, either genuinely impressed or African sly. "Wish I had that much clout," he said. "We had an elephant in Johannesburg when I was growing up, but the Keepers couldn't keep it alive. They lost it. It died. It was too old, too worn out. I'll never forget it."

I heard his words, sensing there was something more behind them. My suspicions were growing.

"I know all about that elephant," I told him, my voice more serious now. "I won't forget it either."

The Chief looked at me with enormous respect, or with feigned enormous respect. Now I did have a feeling about him. He was dissembling.

"No, I don't suppose you will," he said, standing up. "Not you."

He seemed to be thinking about the Johannesburg elephant then, or the Borona elephant or both, as our dirigible swung in over the newest of the African coastal states.

I looked at my watch. We'd be docking in twenty minutes. Last orders for drinks were being taken; passengers were crowding the ports and big observation windows to see Africa sweeping by underneath. Or rather looking at Africa, then at me, Africa and me.

When I sought him out again, I saw that the Chief was talking with a strikingly beautiful black woman. She had obviously been up front during the flight, and now she nodded and returned to speak to the flight crew.

I knew for certain then that my Chief was with Borona security, something governmental. Damn!

He knew that I knew, and when he came back over he didn't even bother to tell me he was.

"Excuse me, Mr Harm, please," he said in a very different tone of voice. "But why is it that you have booked passage on a commercial flight and under another name?"

"Do you have an answer for me, Chief?" I asked him.

The African looked discomfited slightly.

"Mr Harm, please. I am responsible for—"

"I'm sorry. I get a lot of hem-of-the-garment touching, that's all. Look at these people."

He did so and nodded.

"I understand, of course. But the commissioned flight from Rotterdam?"

"A decoy," I explained. "For the press and the crowds. We do it sometimes. The private flights are never truly private, you must realise. There are always the officials who want to chat, and the flight personnel and the security agents themselves."

"I see," he said, only slightly abashed, though the look on his face told me I'd messed up his security arrangements completely.

"You have a great land, Chief," I said, turning the conversation and looking out across Africa.

"Please, Mr Harm. Not Chief. Radu. I was Keeper Radu."

Now I was surprised and impressed. More than security, as I'd thought. A Keeper. And, more correctly, an ex-Keeper.

"Why are you here, Mr Radu?"

"I was on Madagascar," he said. "An agent thought he recognised you, so Bela and I came—"

"I don't mean that, Radu. I mean why is an ex-Keeper here?"

"I am not for this elephant, Mr Harm. Caza has his own Keepers. I belonged to the Johannesburg elephant. You will understand that we were given jobs like these when we failed to keep our elephant alive. You will understand that we like to be close."

I reached out to the man, not knowing his taboos, not knowing his feelings on this. I reached out as celebrant and touched his arm, and thought of what one does after one's life has been given over to being with the Animals.

"I know better than you think, Radu, what your grief is like."

He nodded with gratitude, with extreme dignity, granting that I did. I may have tricked him by being on this flight, but how well he had tricked me, posing as a local chieftain, even though I had suspected it at the last. This man had an empathy rating at least as high as my own; he had several degrees, training in a dozen disciplines, a lifetime of reverent dedication—all the skills of his custodianship of elephants.

There was no changing that. He belonged to the Animals, and would for all his life.

That he had lost his touch, that he had failed in his task of keeping his ailing beast alive, now seemed a small thing. I had known many men and women like Radu. Such people cared now for the Davenport Whale (one of the best and—bless us—a long, long way from extinction) and the Swansea Dog and the miraculous Great Panda at Beijing which had surprised us all and outlived so many more viable species. Most of these Keepers, too, would learn what it was like to lose an Animal some day.

"I think you can understand too, Radu, why we celebrants like taking the normal flights like this. We can be anonymous for a while. In a way, we can step outside our single-minded attention to the Animals."

A trace of the former Chief came back in his great bright smile. Radu wasn't one for dwelling on the past—or rather, for showing that he did. He sat with me for the remainder of the flight, which wasn't long. Now that the flight crew knew I was aboard, they had decided to cut short the usual scenic approach and head straight for the docking towers at Borona.

But it gave us enough time to discuss techniques for looking after the Animals we still had. Though he had seen the Davenport ceremony as it was televised and broadcast world-wide, I gave him my impressions, and he in turn gave me an idea of how the Borona celebration would be.

These occasions had become standardised by now, but I liked Radu, my Chief with a dead elephant on his conscience, and he enjoyed the talk, the chance to get close to it all again.

And though he was a security man now, holding this honorarium post from the State, he probably didn't realise how well briefed we celebrants were.

The ceremony surrounding the Last Elephant would hardly resemble the one at Davenport. There it had been the long ritual drive up from Morro Bay following the whale; here it would be a short half-mile procession from the Animal Door to the celebrant's podium and back. In past years it had been a longer walk out to the edge of the sanctuary, almost to the city, but no more.

Most of the population of Borona would be gathered for the Festival, as close as they could get to the actual route. Dignitaries from all over Africa, representatives from all the nations, tourists and pilgrims from just about anywhere you could name would be present. The ceremony would be televised, recorded and widely documented by the press, naturally, but being there! To see the elephant actually moving down the street to the place of celebration. There was nothing like it.

Caza was such an old elephant, a proud bull. The people of Borona had kept him alive for almost two hundred years, using every technique science and human care could give them. But like the Tortoise of Bin-Chow, Caza was failing. Radu knew this—all the world knew it.

Which is why the Festival had been advanced three years and the podium moved even closer to the Animal Door.

Which is why I was here.

And why so many of my smiles were false.

The docking towers at Borona are beautiful to see. The designers went totemic in their approach, and I would never have thought that things so large and functional could take it so well. There are eighteen of the things standing out in the Borona field, like some brotherhood of tribal gods clutching brightly coloured whales in their fists, seven of them satisfied, the others still reaching for heaven.

Our dirigible sidled in to nudge the eighth, the docking crews brought us in, and we took the elevator down to the landing stage itself.

Radu had an escort of thirty tribesmen waiting. I turned on my 'No Comment' blazer and asked Radu and Bela—his wife, I had discovered—to stay close. Radu met this request eagerly, more excited than I would have expected until I saw Bela's looks of unguarded happiness and realised how welcome this loss of control was. Though cherished, the ex-Keepers obviously became pariahs more quickly than I would have dreamed—good servants who had broken trust; to be respected, to be commemorated, but outsiders all the same.

Now, for this brief time, close to the celebrant, Radu could re-live the role he had forfeited, be close to the skills and thoughts and rich ambience that had been so much of his training.

We moved along, our native guard flanking us and looking splendid in their colours and synthetic skins.

Though it is always a difficult thing to arrange and control, the celebrant is meant to be seen in public, preferably walking, clearly visible among the people.

It is too easy for us to be seen as religious men and women, powerfully reverent, almost messianic figures. We resist these associations, but to an extent we adopt the mystique because it's easier and wanted and cannot be avoided anyway. The truth is we are most often quietly serious people, with little of the showman about us. Our intuition quotient is always exceptionally high. In the matter of Animals, we know in a second what the biologists and medics will arrive at after long hours of analysis and deliberation. Computers cannot match us. We began as independent watchers, part psychologist, part social scientist, part diplomat, and we are—in these later years, with so many Animals failing—judges, the ones who deem that an Animal should be allowed to die. To counter this darker side, we have had to foster the sanctity mystique more and more. Otherwise no one would listen to us or trust us, and the Animals would languish on in pain, living lives that are mockeries, the blindness of love having obscured all compassion.

So we took our walk, flanked by Radu's countrymen with their spears and authentic feathers. All around us the crowds had formed and were already chanting. As we moved towards the Borona Hyatt along the Way of the Elephant, we could hear broken fragments of Caza's Song.

Hey there, Brother, big forest wanderer,
Hey there, Brother, give us time to be like you.

I watched Radu, to my left near Bela, but he showed no signs of distraction. He was a Chief in his own right, and in charge of security and an ex-Keeper re-born for a time. He was sharing the walk more closely than any would guess.

Though Bela knew. Bela understood.

We passed through the crowds, the throngs of people adorned with their elephant tokens and other Animal fetishes, many of them masked and many holding aloft bright poles set with Caza's sign.

Even those who didn't recognise me outright saw Radu and knew he was involved with the Festival and so made the connection. We had a great following by the time we reached the foyer of the Hyatt, and the air was ringing with Caza's song, beautifully counterpointed by a melody from a group of whale people from Monterey and Twofold Bay.

The hotel's own guards had to come out as re-enforcements and help cordon off the spectators so we could get inside easily. We rode up to the penthouse suite (no avoiding that) in a comfortable silence, and I invited Radu and Bela to stay for a simple *cha* ceremony.

I could see how grateful Radu was, and was already sensing that he wanted to ask something—something that had to do with the Johannesburg elephant, Korshippa, and the Caza Festival.

It was not as if I had caught him about to ask a question or a favour, nothing as obvious as that. He just... lingered... and glanced out of the windows and wrestled silently with himself while Bela spoke softly of how life was for them in Borona.

I prepared the *cha* and laid out the kimonos for the three of us—host's right—and wondered what troubled my Chief.

Then, at the last minute, Bela asked to be excused, saying there were special comp clearances I might need and that she'd get them. A fiction, of course, and a way for Radu and me to be alone.

I accepted the grace of her excuse and saw her out. Then Radu and I knelt and took *cha* together. After the right space of time, and because he hadn't won the fight with himself, I asked what task he had been given in maintaining the rare Animal.

As I'd thought, he had been an apprentice Soul. With his smile and his quick vital ways, he had to be that, or the Heart, or the specialist for the Great Mind.

Radu seemed glad to talk, relieved to do so. He told me how he had trained under Tiff, the Great Master himself and Korshippa's Soul, and that following Tiff's death had been only seven months in the job when Korshippa had languished and died.

A sympathy death.

It happened often these days. The Animals did not long outlive their Souls, their closest companions. The Belgian Horse, the Great Ape of Sarawak, all died when their dearly loved Souls had died. The head apprentice was sometimes able to imbue the beast with the right feelings and sustain it and encourage it, depending on how well those apprentices had been trained and imbued themselves. But usually the creatures died in extreme sympathy for their lost friends. Even the generically wildest, the most feral, had become so human-dependent in the last hundred years, as if sensing this reliance. It was all part of the tragedy.

Without Radu telling me, I already knew that Caza's loss of vitality was probably a reflection of a faltering Soul: the old man, Modat. But I would not mention this, not to Radu, not to anyone.

By the time we had finished the *cha* ceremony and the kimonos were folded and laid on the bed, Radu knew he'd have to leave. His inner struggle had been continuing all through the pouring and drinking and polite question and answer.

Now I wondered whether his question would surface.

It did.

As Radu turned to go, he hesitated a last time, then faced me.

"Excuse me, Terence, but is there any special dispensation to be given here?"

Which was a way of saying: Are you here to see if Caza needs to be put down? To see if at long last our elephant is beyond human care, simply too old and too ailing to be forced to live on for human selfishness?

Radu had broken form and he showed the strain of it. He had used his unique position here to refer openly to that other task of the celebrant: to be judge and in a sense executioner to the Animals. As I say, it is a measure of the acute global sensitivity of the times that our name has not come to be used in any opprobrious way. The world knows, too, that we love the Animals, that we have far more detachment than Keepers could ever have, working as they do every day with the few treasured creatures we have left.

The doubters had only to recall the times a hundred years back when the owning of Animals by individuals and households was common and permitted, and how eventually this could only be afforded by the wealthy; how shares and sponsorships and rotation became the way of it; how the Closed Zoos appeared and the black market flourished. How the clonings and breeding programs failed and the species were squeezed out of existence regardless.

And how could I say to Radu that things did not look good for Caza? That this was why I was here and not Chingi or Palleas or a consensus. (How that would alarm them—a group of celebrants!)

There is no ego-pleasure at being called the best of my profession, reckoned as it is on empathy factors and what we call instinctivity. I didn't ask to come to Caza's Festival, but how could I refuse?

I did not answer Radu's question, partly because he would be furious with himself afterwards if I did, and partly because I realised suddenly that this was not what Radu had been originally going to ask.

He was concealing a more desperate question; that was what I sensed. Perhaps he knew I had discovered it.

Radu stood in the doorway, taking my silent reprimand, grateful for the smile that told him I understood.

"Thank Bela," I said.

Radu nodded.

"I'll be here tomorrow at eight, Terence." And then: "Let me know if there is anything I can do." Then he went off to the elevator.

He had found a way to ask his desperate question after all.

I smiled and sat alone in my room at last, looking out over Borona, thinking of the morning and what could be done. As always, I knew that there was—had to be—a point at which the interests of the Keepers ran contrary to those of the celebrants. Theirs was more of a priesthood than ours; it had to be loyal to itself first. They kept secrets, were expert in all the ways of hiding the vital facts of Caza and his Soul, Modat.

But reports had come through all the same—that Caza was probably going to die at last. Soon now. They could no longer conceal it and had done the honourable and fair thing. They had advanced the Festival date.

I did something then I had not done in years, not since the loss of our last wonderful Kangaroo. I opened the Primer left by the management for its guests, and turned to the pages on Celebration. There were the words of Ted Hughes, A. A. Milne and Rudyard Kipling, Herman Melville and Antoine Saint Exupery. In the section on Exercises, there were the unforgettable and prophetic words from Lien-Tsin:

Imagine your Animal. Imagine its shape, its smell, the steam of its breath, the way it moves to hunt, sleep and mate. Part by part, make the Animal real. Then, when you think you are ready, imagine it gone. If you weep, your task is done. If you do not, you must start again.

Fireworks burst all about me, close to my balcony. In the streets below, the Festival had already begun. The music, the songs, the excitement, came through the warm air; the sounds of many people awake and aware and full of expectation.

To them, there could be no thought that this might be the last Festival.

I looked at Lien-Tsin's words and imagined Caza gone, wanting to cry. But though I stood there a long time, the tears would not come.

Radu's question-that-was-not-a-question did not let them come.

On the morning of the Festival, I met with Caza's Keepers, both those of the actual Animal and of its Shadow—those lesser Hearts, Minds and Souls, all the apprentices presently being trained by Modat.

They sat waiting for me in the hotel auditorium, nearly sixty of them, all looking at me with the same eager desperation I had glimpsed for a moment in Radu's eyes the day before.

Would Caza live?

We did not discuss that, of course. That could not be an issue. It is never discussed, never. They were gathered here for the very opposite reason—to hear me enthuse and praise and give thanks: in short, to celebrate Caza with them. Nothing I said or did cued them otherwise.

But the question remained in every mind, even in Modat's, who was absent—shut away in the Animal Room all night with his charge, being the Great Soul to his precious beast, communing, getting ready for the procession at noon. I would speak with Modat only after the procession had ended, when I had made my evaluation.

No subliminals were used at this meeting, none of the hypnogogics. This, too, was decided upon my discretion. Often these aids help relax the Keepers for the certain trauma of taking their beast out in public, but today I wanted the intensity untouched.

Outside it was a different story. Outside, the day was Elephant. From the high poles, the subsonics and olfactories blasted out the sounds and musks of the Animal, synthesised, enhanced, all over the crowds. The slopes along Caza's Way were jammed with people;

the media-blimps were in place, tethered or roaming down their cables, rehearsing the half-mile route. Chartered dirigibles moved back and forth overhead.

The door of the Animal Room was still firmly closed. The white flag would go up when Caza was about to appear, but now the pole was empty.

I went to the podium at the far end of Caza's Way and joined Radu. He stood next to Bela in full tribal regalia, holding his Keeper's staff with its crest of Korshippa. His eyes met mine, asking, asking both of his questions, and getting an answer to neither.

I squeezed his left forearm.

"I need to see him first," I said, breaking form that much.

"The people will never know!"

"We would know," I said. "And the people would know eventually."

"No!" But it was a plea from him.

"You know better, Radu. If we turn up the supports and they notice, they will never trust the Animals again. They will know if Caza is ailing, and should know why he is to be put down."

I felt a chill of foreboding then. If Radu was expressing so much doubt, things could not be good for Caza, even worse than I had been informed. In a sense, I had been using Radu this way. As an ex-Keeper, it was natural for him to stay as close as he could to another Animal like his own; he became the ideal barometer, a way of reading this brother-beast, a reflector, too, of Modat's own fears and doubts.

For the first time, standing there above the seething crowds, I wished it had been consensus after all, that Chingi and Palleas and Gromelli were all with me, that it wouldn't be up to me alone.

I calmed myself, noticing the media ships. The other celebrants *were* with me. How could it be otherwise?

I looked across at Radu and Bela. They were gazing straight ahead, down the processional way to the Door and the empty flagpole. Many of the cameras were on us, and they had composed themselves accordingly.

I noticed many details at that moment, and noted for the first time the gentle curve of Bela's belly, that she was pregnant.

And out of synchronicity, inspiration, whatever, the idea came to me—an answer for Radu as well, though a great cry went up and obscured it for the instant.

The flag was rising on its pole, cutting out in the breeze.

The door to the Animal Room was lifting too, slowly, ponderously. And slowly, ponderously, ancient Caza was moving out.

The crowds roared in a frenzy of adoration, a mixture of incredible joy and pride, and the chorus of his song, guided by the chorists through the speakers, took form, predominated now.

Hey there, Brother Elephant, Brother Elephant,
Brother Elephant, Brother!
Hey there, Brother Elephant, Brother Elephant,
Brother Elephant, Brother!

Over and over the words came, the wash of emotion threatening to obliterate everything, but not the thought that had come to me.

I looked once at Bela's belly under her robe and it came back. I turned to my Chief.

"Radu, what would you want to have most in all the world? Tell me! Now!"

Radu blinked at me. After the barest hesitation (in which wife, child, all of his dreams must have rushed across his mind) he answered.

"Korshippa!"

"Can you be Korshippa's Soul? Now?"

Radu stared at me.

"No... Yes... But, Terence—"

"Caza is dying! Can you?"

"I'm not eligible. It's been too long. Bela is pregnant."

"None of that matters now. Caza is dying. We must try."

"How? How, Terence?"

"Go down there. Go to Modat."

"He has apprentices—"

"Do it, Radu. Before it's too late!"

The black man leapt from the podium, trusting me. He ran down through the guards in their bright native dress, ran on down the avenue towards the seven Africans who were Caza, the man-elephant Caza.

He was a wild figure, racing towards the stately procession, startling guards who began to raise their weapons till they saw it was their own Chief. Their eyelines raced on to locate a threat, a reason for his haste, but found none.

There was only Caza, the seven parts of Caza, moving towards them between the rows of spectators: six younger African men and women grouped around the old man, Modat, fiercely determined, each of them, to keep their part of the Animal intact, but failing from within, from the Soul, and fighting that.

And Radu was there, was inside the formation of seven, and had taken Modat's hand.

The Souls walked together.

All around them, the chanting of the vast crowd had fallen into a hush, a charged silence. Even the chorists had stopped singing.

What did this mean in terms of Caza? What had Radu done?

But they soon saw. They saw it when the Zulu prince who was Caza's Great Mind stood even straighter, even prouder; how Kefta, Caza's Heart, became suddenly radiant, not just intently reverent; when they saw how Eyes and Voice took on an added presence. The whole man-beast was different.

Somehow, as they all watched, those many thousands, the definition of Caza became an incredible, almost palpable thing, an inarguable fact, stronger than it had ever been.

The Animal was there, undeniably there, stretched taut between the frame of... eight.

Caza-Korshippa.

And all about me now the chanting had resumed, swelling up into the bright air. The frenzy of celebration fed, yes, by the subliminals, the elephant calls and hypnogogics too, but free of those things—held more now by the simple enormous yearning.

The great gamble—the grafting—was done. I stood, tears streaming down my cheeks, and sang with all the rest of that desperate, joyful, fervent humanity, the first verse of Caza's Song, and let the eight people—and the last elephant we have—carry me along.

Hey there, Brother, big forest wanderer,
Hey there, Brother, give us time to be like you.
We atone the day, we sent you away,
Now we be elephant,
We be you.

Spinners

IN THE DESERT outside Wani, at a place called Bullen Meddi, are the remains of Sat's Carnival: gaming arcades and galleries half-submerged on the shore of the sand-sea, a sun-faded merry-go-round, the gantry and broken frame of a ferris wheel, pavilions that are mostly struts and solitary walls with ragged awnings and sagging roofs, and an ornamental gate in poor repair, its twin Luna Park towers leaning in the sand, supporting the traditional wild-eyed Laughing Clown.

No one goes there. At night the winds sigh about the struts and uprights and set the gantry to creaking, slamming loose sheets of tin, flapping the scraps of canvas. Sometimes, when the westerlies are blowing, min-min lights dance along the horizon and an eerie keening can be heard in the broken arc of the ferris, the saddest of all the wind voices at Bullen Meddi.

By day there is the heat and the silence, the sand-sea ashimmer under a blazing sun, mirages dancing in the haze at the edge of the sky. The merry-go-round horses bake and blister, the ferris curves into the hot bright air, and the arcades and pavilions form a crosswork of dusty streets like the quiet avenues of an ancient funerary town.

It has the sadness of all carnivals, and more, as I was to discover.

Cas took me there. We stood together on the slope above the sand-sea, shrouded in our djellabas, eyes shut away behind dark glasses.

"Well?" she said, as if I had never seen it before.

"Well, what?" I answered. "Nothing's changed."

"No, Tom? Look again."

Cas Arana ran Twilight Beach's most respected repertory company. She was in her forties, beautiful, and ten years beyond her prime as a truly unique dramatic stylist. Success came now as a poet, a playwright and an entrepreneur. There was always the sense of the theatrical in her affairs—always—and I was surprised there was no audience other than the two of us. I found that curious. Why had she brought me here?

I studied the quiet shapes below us on the desert shore: the antique gate with its absurd Deco spires and laughing face (two crippled kings bearing the head of an idiot giant), the leaning puzzle of the ferris, the sagging lonely galleries, the merry-go-round resting on the sand like a sculpted dish.

"What, Cas?" I asked, seeing nothing out of place.

Then I did, from the corner of my eye, and lost it as quickly, a glimpse of movement—not canvas stirring in heated air, not sunlight off tin.

"Midway," she said. "Along from the first set of dunes there. This side of the Grand Doranza and the hoosy house."

"Right." I placed it, identifying the shape. "A belltree!"

"And?"

There was movement again, at the top of the tall post.

"A spinner! Is it?"

"It is," Cas said, and began to move down the slope.

"So?" I matched her stride. "Someone's put up a relic."

"Not a relic, Tom. And not just one."

It was true. Now that we were closer, lower down, I could see two more of the ceremonial wind-posts set about the old fairground, one on the perimeter close to us and one beyond the ferris on the sand-banks nearer the baking shore. The finned blades set atop the diligent canisters moved ever so slightly, the new metal fittings catching the light, responding to the smallest whispers of moving air, each vagrant breath, thermals off heated tin, irregular gradients of hot air rolling in across the empty sand-sea to fall upon Bullen Meddi.

"Someone has been busy," I said, excited by the thought that these could be functioning belltrees. And so new?

"There's more," Cas said. "That someone is restoring the merry-go-round as well. You'll find jacks and fill on the other side."

Now it was Cas who had to keep up with me, though I barely knew I was hurrying. We approached the carnival from the southeast, avoiding the sun-blinded gate, heading for the closest windpost.

It was an eighteen-footer, taller than most Ab'O road-posts. I had nearly reached it when the force of that discovery struck me.

Not Ab'O constructs, not tribal at all.

I felt a stab of fear, an old fear, familiar and not unexpected. And with it, unstoppable, came the memories of the Madhouse, of the cunning dream machines, the lying AI, the only friends I'd had. I made myself concentrate on the post.

There were sensor vanes halfway up, and again near the top, just below the diligent canister with its free-moving crown of blades. There was what seemed to be a bounty-box and dim-recall rods worked into the housing at the base.

But it was not Ab'O. There were none of the carved and painted totemic divisions—just strange, black-stencilled ideograms on the weather-worn metal trunk, patterns of lines like compressed zodiacs.

"Real," I said, marvelling. "But not tribal. Spinners haven't been seen in Australia for a hundred years. Not like this. Not new."

"And sentient," Cas said, delivering her ultimate surprise.

I stared at her, but her shaded eyes told me nothing. "Sentient? Really?"

She nodded. "All talkers."

"Dialect?"

"Some words in the old languages. But National mainly. No Ab'O put these up. These are rogues."

Again fear gripped me, more than just the fear of what the tribes could do to those connected with illicit constructs. Instinctively, I fled from the Madhouse memory, out into the quiet landscape with the far-off gentle hills, the shimmering sand-sea.

So few things got through from those days, those subjective years in the Madhouse gloom. But those things, those images— Why now? Why here?

In a glance, I took in Sat's indulgence, the sad array scattered about me, the quiet streets, indistinct and shifting in the morning heat, more like the avenues of a plundered mastaba town in the lee of Khufu's Pyramid than those of a carnival. I could almost imagine

Khafre's Sphinx out there, serenely regarding the vast distances, all this silence.

But there was just the gate, the great face locked in its instant of demented glee, crazy eyes tilted at the sun. Whatever serenity was to be had in this lonely place seemed to come from these newcomers, the spinner posts themselves. Regardless of what they meant for me, they did represent the possibility of change and renewal; their presence somehow held the melancholy in check.

"All right, Cas. The rest of it please."

"The rest?" And she smiled. "You're interested in belltrees—in the whole Ab'O belltree program. I knew you'd want to see these."

"Cas, the rest. How did you learn of them? You don't make a habit of touring desert sites for novelty venues, do you?"

Cas Arana stood watching the sand drifts at the edge of the fairground. She seemed to be considering something.

"I'm not supposed to tell you anything until you meet their maker. He'll be about somewhere. His workshop is that building there. Why not ask the tree?"

"The tree?"

"Go on. Ask it where Quint is."

"Quint? The old clockmaker from Twilight Beach? But he—"

"Disappeared, yes. Came to Bullen Meddi six months ago. Grew tired of restoring old full-face clocks and scribbling poetry. My cousin found him two days ago while researching a story for *Caravanserai*—a retrospective on Constantin Sat and his eccentricities. He found Quint here working on his spinner posts.

"Clockmakers go mad, you know, especially the poetic ones. I imagine they work too close to the process of measuring time. They get filled up with the desperation of hours, the relentless transition from one instant to the next. They never seem to be free of that intense awareness."

I looked at Cas, intrigued, wondering if her oddly rhapsodic tone was mocking.

"And?"

"I came out here to speak with him. To see if there was material for a play, for a performance. Clockmakers often escape to deserts. Many time-conscious, time-saturated people do. And carnivals *are* timeless, a ruined carnival in a desert many times more so. Ghost-towns for hyperchronics, the time-afflicted. Ask the tree."

I looked up at the tall post standing quietly in the heat, its bright fluted crown turning very slowly in the late morning air. Around noon the breezes on the sand-sea would start changing. By sunset the spinners would be moving steadily, recharging the accumulators, working away into the night.

"All right." I said. "Tree, where is Quint?"

I waited but there was no answer.

"No one's home," I said to Cas, and my apprehensions faded a little. Cas smiled. "They didn't work for me either. But you feel like you're being watched, yes?"

I did when I thought about it, but that was part of the atmosphere of the place.

We moved down the midway towards the building where Cas told me Quint had his workshop. The wide door was open, but the sunlight ended in roiling, eye-twisting shadow—a plastic dust-curtain had been fitted to the surrounding timbers. Beyond that, in the shadow-light, a work-bench was visible, covered with circuitry and tools. Off to the side, on three saw-horses, another post rested, almost finished. This one had a different spinner cap. Instead of the usual bladed cylinder crown fitted down over the shaft head, it had a large bladed pinwheel fitted vertically to its front in the manner of the traditional windmill.

"That goes up tonight." Cas said.

I studied the long metal post with its sensor spines and its trunk not yet decorated with ideograms. "I suppose if you're going to break tribal law you should try for a modicum of secrecy."

Cas smiled. "True. But the tribes are hardly going to do a sat-scan of this forsaken spot, are they? Come on. Quint will be over at the carousel."

We moved on from the workshop, down one of the hot, quiet avenues leading to the sand-shore.

"The tribes mustn't learn of this, Cas," I said as we walked, reminding her of the obvious danger, worried that, true to her media-conscious and entrepreneurial nature, she might have ideas for publicising this. I just didn't know Cas well enough to be sure.

Without giving an answer she pointed. "There he is."

A tanned, white-haired figure crouched on the beach beside a circle of bright wooden horses. Brass poles pierced them, gleaming; glass eyes glistened before flashing mirror panels and polished wood.

The decorated awning threw much of the interior into shadow all the same; it was like looking through a cool verandah at the bright desert beyond.

"I'm back!" Cas called, and the old man looked round. "With Tom Tyson."

Quint stood, wiped his hands on his fatigues, and smiled.

I had seen him months ago in his shop on the South Esplanade, a bent-over and compressed package of a man, scrawny, diminutive, a comfortable stereotype of the aged craftsman. Now he was something else, no longer compressed, no longer doubled-over. He was tanned instead of pallid; now his eyes shone with all sorts of mad lights.

"What do you think?" he asked, fixing me with those eyes.

"Quint, I hardly know you," was all I could think to say, the simple truth.

"I knew they'd find me," he said. "But I'm about done. The carousel's working again. I've just finished raising it."

I looked from the clockmaker back to this new and different timepiece, set with brilliants, vivid with brightwork, as if to solve the unlikely equation of man and place. Quint here. A workshop. Spinner posts, for heaven's sake. The expertise needed, the sheer effort involved!

"Why, Quint?"

"Hah!" the old man said. He turned back to the bright wheel on the beach. "I'm baiting a trap."

"For what?"

"Hah!" he said again, and looked for Cas. She had wandered off towards the wreck of the Grand Doranza, was studying the ruined concession.

"She will bring others," I said.

"She's most welcome. We open today, this afternoon. Not much to see until tomorrow though. Then we'll have the fortune-telling posts and the carousel. Another month or two and the whole place would have been ready. Sat's Carnival, working again. Still, it's meant to be like this. Daystar said."

"Daystar?"

"The spinner out by the hoosy house. It said last week that someone would find me soon."

"Visitors must attract Ab'O attention. Your belltrees—"

"Tom," he said, clutching my arm. "I know. Highly illegal. But it's all right. Cas can bring her visitors. I'm ready for that."

"Why me?" I said. "Why did you ask for me?"

"Who better than you, Tom? You're interested in Artificial Intelligence. You've made a study of belltrees. My spinners are quite your thing."

"Quint..." I began, wanting to tell him just how ambivalent my reaction to AI was, but he drew me over to the merry-go-round.

"Truth is I doubt I can manage it on my own. My back is troubling me. I need help with the lifting. Khoumy, Ankh and Daystar I managed myself, though it wasn't easy. I fear Tiresias is too much for me alone. Help me tonight. We can bring it out, the two of us. And I need to steady the carousel more."

"Listen, Quint. If I'd known why Cas was bringing me here I'd never have come. You'll be exposed. The tribes tend to watch me."

The old man shrugged and grinned. "Too late. Help me now, eh? It doesn't matter. Help me finish here. Help me bring out Tiresias."

I watched Cas tossing stones at a sagging wall of tin. Freed of her promise she seemed eager to get back to Twilight Beach, no doubt to tell her friends.

"She'll be back," I said. "We're on the National side here. Bullen Meddi marks the border. She'll bring others. Ab'Os will come."

The light in his eyes never wavered. "Tom, it's all right. Please help."

I tried to consider it, tried to be objective and see where this could lead. It made no sense, Quint's endangering his life this way, but then it *was* probably already too late. A routine surveillance already made by a Clever Man given the task of keeping an eye on Tom Rynosseros would be all it needed.

"Cas," I called. "Go back without me. I'm staying."

"And tell them!" Quint shouted. "Tell them they can come! But the official opening is tomorrow."

Cas smiled and waved, called out something I couldn't catch, and began walking up the long slope to where her four-seater skiff was moored. She was an experienced sailor; though the winds were poor, photonic kites would put her back in Twilight Beach within the hour. And back again an hour after that, knowing her, knowing her coterie's appetite for the latest sensations.

"I told her you would stay," Quint said, leading me back down the midway towards his shed. "I made her promise to find you even before I told her what these wind-posts meant. She didn't concern herself about them as you do."

"She'll bring others this afternoon."

Quint nodded. "There's nothing to see until tomorrow. I'll be working on Tiresias till sundown. You can finish packing the fill here, take some power cells out to the gate, then help me with the response testing."

"If I can. Just show me what to do."

At 1400, in the heat of the blazing afternoon, the visitors came. Two passenger charvis moored beyond the hills and fifty or more Nationals came straggling down the slope to Bullen Meddi—Cas sweeping along in front, splendid in new white sand-robes, attended by producers and tame (and not so tame) critics, followed by members of her company and others eager for an afternoon's diversion at Sat's Carnival.

Most of them had seen it before. There had been the Taylor readings, and the San-Topuri fire-sculptures on the desert sea, but those events were nearly a decade old—the carnival had long since lost its novelty. This was something new. The newcomers chattered excitedly despite the heat. They paused by the spinners, Daystar and Khoumy, trying to raise answers without success, then, barely disappointed, trusting in surprises to come, strolled down the midway towards the carousel.

We came out from behind the dust-screen and went to meet them.

"We must give them something," Quint said. "Or they'll be peeking here and there, getting up to mischief."

I accepted his explanation, not bothering to remind him of his earlier resolve to stay out of sight. Without speaking we walked to where the crowd waited.

I was surprised and disappointed to see how brash and insensitive this manifestation of the public Cas Arana seemed to be. She rushed forward, seized Quint by the arms and waltzed him around, owning him before the others.

"Our ringmaster! Our own biotect!" she cried. "Everyone, here he is! Master of the Revels! Maker of belltrees!"

"Please," Quint said, gently disengaging his hands from hers, looking down. "I simply needed to be alone."

"Nonsense!" Cas said. "There's more. There's more, Tom, everyone! We all remember the play *Merinda*. How the Ab'O girl loved the young National. Now it can be told! Guess who wrote it, who financed the production we did?"

"Not Quint!" someone cried in delight.

"Dominic Quint!" Cas announced triumphantly. "Our carnival master here! Merinda goes to be with her David. The Kurdaitcha avengers come for her. The lovers flee on to the desert and are not seen again. Quint's one play, this legend! All his savings went into the Todthaus season."

And she smiled at me, radiantly, as if to say: 'Now do you see what goes on here? A surprise for you too, Tom!'

I could scarcely believe she was doing it, creating such drama, such inevitable publicity—exposing this former artisan, failed playwright, maker of illicit spinner posts, this man captivated by his love for the Merinda myth, embroiled now too with me, the sand-ship captain from the Ab'O Madhouse, someone the Ab'Os watched.

"Cas!" I cried.

"No, Tom!" Quint said. "It is all right. We had our arrangement. Please, Ms Arana. Take your friends. Show them." And he turned away. When I went to follow he made a sharp gesture. "No, Tom. Stay here. Keep an eye on them for a while."

So I stayed, wandering among the guests, listening to snatches of conversation, amazed at the excitement, at the earnest theorising. Some were guarded in what they said, deliberately uncommitted; others affected indifference, even a sneering detachment. But whatever the overt expressions, I sensed that more than anything they wanted this to matter. Even the coolly aloof ones on this burning afternoon showed a determination to have that: something meaningful, something important in their lives.

And yet I sensed the opposite of this as well: a paradoxical and ferocious determination to challenge anything short of what convinced them was the real thing.

One discussion caught my attention, two men in expensive sand-robes talking by the door of the derelict hoosy house.

"These have the later type of cap," one of them, a bearded man I knew only as Seth, was saying. "A free-moving bladed cylinder fitted down over the shaft head. The earlier spinners had the vertical windmill arrangement, but you know why that was changed."

"No, I don't," his friend said. "Tell me."

Seth indicated the patch on the other's scrap-jacket, visible through the front of his djellaba: a clutch of narrow ochre triangles converging on a central point. "The National sign," he said. "The Sun of Nation. What do you think that is?"

"Not a spinner!"

"Of course it is. A stylised windmill, a bladed sun. Fitting symbol for the land, don't you think? Of the hostile interior and how it was tamed?"

Seth's companion shook his head. "I don't believe it. It's just a stylised sun motif."

"Exactly!" Seth insisted. "A bladed sun! Interesting, eh?"

I continued around behind the group, glad that despite Cas's use of my name, few seemed to recognise me as anything more than Quint's assistant. Perhaps she had kept part of the developing story even from them.

Raised voices drew my attention: another animated discussion, this time from a group standing by the Grand Doranza.

"It's where the cry 'Come in, Spinner!' originated," a man was saying.

And there was Seth's friend, again playing the role of sceptic.

"Nonsense!" he cried. "That came from the game of two-up!"

"Yes," the other man answered. "It did. But the antecedents for that game go back a long way, to well before the Chinese massacre at Beechworth. The coins tossed were *I Ching* fortune-telling coins brought to Australia by the Chinese goldseekers in the 19th century."

"The Chinese used yarrow stalks originally, not coins."

"Yes. Well, the idea for divination posts started way back then too..."

I moved away. Something in this determination to find answers reminded me of what I so often did, how I openly considered my Madhouse past in order to know I did so, could be so objective and reasonable. A way of hiding a deeper truth, of hiding from it. It seemed like that now—proper, healthy speculation but with a secret purpose. For there *was* more to it, a different side, the other thing these people were doing. Faced with a mystery, they wished to contain it, neutralise it, even destroy it to ease the curiosity, the not-knowing, the possibility of a something-more that eluded easy and comfortable understanding. They had to be safe again, no less than I.

Was the bladed Sun of Nation truly a spinner? What a joke! And did the *I Ching* have a part to play? I thought of the ideograms on the shafts, wanting to ask Quint about them and realising again that this did put me with the rest.

Cas saw me skirting the crowd. She excused herself and came over. "So worried, Tom?"

"You amaze me, Cas! You've ensured his death, don't you see?"

"Tom! He desperately wants *Merinda* performed again. We discussed it months ago, before he came to Bullen Meddi. My cousin never found him; Quint contacted me, sent a letter suggesting another Todthaus season. I came out at once. We reached an agreement: *Merinda* performed with this present development, whatever happens, as a prelude. Tom, he had no money—"

"No money! Cas, he's building belltrees, for heaven's sake! How has he financed that? He's more in control of this than you know."

"Well, the arrangement stands. We do *Merinda* this summer, provided the carnival opens. He's kept his word."

I could think of nothing more to say. Three months, a year from now, Cas would apologise, invite me to one of her dinners, spend hours trying to convince me that, after all, it was life being lived, nothing more.

"What part do you think the spinners play?" she asked then, as if I were another of her guests and this was the natural question to ask.

I did not answer her. I left her with her companions and headed for the carousel—to complete shoring up the table.

Some time later Cas and her friends departed, though Quint and I never knew exactly when. I was sequestered with the old man most of the time, running checks on Tiresias, deliberately losing myself in the exhaustive procedures, not wanting to think about working on the AI I feared so much. Whenever he did the response testing, I tried to be elsewhere in the workshop, or out on an errand. But sometimes I couldn't help watching the blurred figure inside the makeshift booth of clear plastic sheets, studying him as he bent over the crown with his light and his tuning instruments. When at last he left the dust-booth for the tea I made us, I had my chance to discuss what Cas had revealed.

"I never knew about your connection with the *Merinda* production," I told him. "I liked it."

Quint nodded. "I always wanted to be the storyteller, Tom. The maker. Merinda was a gifted storyteller, like Scheherazade was. She knew seven old languages, all their legends. But the greatest story is her own. You saw it. I followed the story exactly. Her champion, the young sailor, David, was a National who came with his four companions, rescued the Ab'O girl from the Kurdaitcha and fled with her into the desert. The companions acted as decoys; all but one was slain—the survivor who some say later told their story. In my play I took a small liberty there. I made the survivor the narrating chorus."

"I remember that. But is what Cas said true? Are you revising the legend, planning another season? One story in another?"

Quint smiled and looked back at the spinner post, its bladed crown like a rare flower shut away inside a makeshift glasshouse. "Who knows?" he said. "That would be Cas's wish. This way is better. All my money is gone on this."

He stood. "Tom, the stencils are over there. You can spray ideograms on the lower half. One of each." Then he returned to the dust-booth and presently resumed his testing.

The moon was high over Bullen Meddi when we brought out his final belltree. Moonlight washed the carnival streets, giving the buildings and ruined concessions the dramatic shadows of a penumbral noon.

We had said nothing more about *Merinda* or Cas's remarks. We simply accepted the reality of the task at hand.

The tree was heavier than I expected. I took the lower end of the trunk, Quint managed the end with the upper shaft and diligent housing, the bladed wheel turning as we stumbled along. He steered us between the deserted buildings, up the midway, down a side-street full of ink-black shadow, around a corner towards the merry-go-round on the beach. There everything was bathed in the moon's warming glow, bright and still except for the spinner cap on the one other post I could see: Daystar. It turned freely in the breeze.

Finally we reached the spot Quint had prepared. He guided the footing into its hole; I hauled on the pulley rope slung across the tube-steel tripod hoist and lifted the tree to its upright position.

It took surprisingly little time. We packed the base with sand and quick-drying algen foam and mounded more foamed sand up to the collar of the bounty-box analogue. Then Quint tripped the recessed activator with a hooked pole he had left nearby for the purpose.

At first nothing happened; the spinner disk was still. These were no longer function tests. The diligent was exploring sensation, probably selecting modes. Then the vertical wheel began to turn, its blades flashing with moonlight.

It was alive. I left Quint to watch that happen—troubled as I always was by AI—and began dismantling the hoist.

"Look at it, Tom!" he cried beyond my shoulder. "Djuringa!"

I reacted at the word.

Djuringa. All that is sacred in Ab'O lore: the hills, the wind, the stones, the Dreamtime heroes, the haldanes, the land itself.

Careful, Quint, I wanted to cry. Careful. That's tribal land out there. A ship will come. Clever Men or Kurdaitcha. Don't go too far. Don't be too daring.

But Quint crouched before Tiresias, crooning softly to himself, watching the blades spin, flashing and hypnotic, waiting. I was an intruder here. This was his place, his precious spot. I wanted to leave him with it.

When he showed no signs of ending his vigil, I took up the hoist poles, the tools and foam canister and began carrying them back to his workshop. As I stumbled along, balancing my load, I again felt the sense of disquiet that went beyond my apprehension over tribal detection. Perhaps it was the wind getting in behind the tin and loose boards, creating a hundred tiny half-heard sounds; perhaps it was the contrasts of light, the intense pools of darkness that I found about me and always feared because of the Madhouse gloom I remembered so well. Looking down a side-street, there would be that darkness, then moonlight, then darkness again, laid out in a strip mosaic, with moonlit desert beyond. Always the vivid contrasts. Beside me loomed a vacant interior, also chillingly dark, but there beyond it the ferris gleamed in a long vivid curve, and the

Deco spires of the gate held aloft their moonstruck face so it blazed like a shield, clown-eyes crammed with light.

I hunched up my load and continued walking, thinking of the job at hand so that my fears subsided in physical effort. Subsided, not faded entirely. For something remained, some quality in this moon-bleached, forsaken carnival that played on my old AI fears and gave the quiet and sadness its edge of uncertainty and unease.

I placed my load behind the dust-screen, then, to avoid the streets, walked off the midway altogether, meaning to trace my way back to Quint along the open fairground perimeter. I would be in moonlight all the way.

How it happened I couldn't say. Loose sand slid under my boots; I reached down to steady myself on a shifting slope, scrambled to regain my footing and looked up again, to yelp in fright at something blocking my way. My cry echoed across the fairground, faded to nothing in the silvery dunes beyond.

Khoumy stood like a silver knife on the sand.

I could feel my heart pounding; I heard the soft whirring of the spinner cap.

I laughed, trying to regain composure, fighting the panic, the rush of anger it surfaced as.

It lived, Cas had said, Quint had assured me. Would it answer? Could it?

"Hello, tree—Khoumy," I said.

The post stood in near-silence, the spinner whirring away, feeding the accumulators. A minute passed, with just the steady mindless sound. My mistrust grew, my restlessness. It was the old paradox again: disbelief and the need to believe.

"Fake!" I cried at last. "Imposter!" Then, wanting it to be true, needing the release. "It's a hoax! Quint playing tricks!"

The blades turned; the tree said nothing.

I remembered the trigger Quint had used.

"Djuringa!" I cried.

And the word echoed.

"Djuringa."

Not an echo. Too close for that. Khoumy had answered.

"Why has Quint made you?" I asked.

Again the voice came, measured, artificial, but not unpleasant to the ear.

"I wasn't told," Khoumy said. "I was the first, the prototype. I'm very fragile and primitive."

No, I thought. *Not life. It couldn't be.*

"You're following a program!"

"No," it replied. "I don't think so. I do bioscan. I can tell you all about Father's medical profile. Or ask about stars. I can report on them all, the constellations, the angles of declivity. I watch stars. I love them. I can tell you—"

"A program!"

"No! I don't believe—"

"You don't know!" I said, driven by remembered fears, helpless before them.

"I'm not very sophisticated, but I believe I am alive. I do. I can—"

"But you don't know. It's just programming. Quint's a one-shot playwright, a clockmaker, not a biotect. He couldn't have the skill."

"Please! Ask Father. Or one of the others. You confuse me. You sadden me..."

"All coded in," I told it. "That too."

"No. I don't feel—"

"Consider it, Khoumy!" I cried, amazed to hear my voice snapping the words, amazed at the vehemence, the cruelty in what I said, but giving in to it all the same. I had to know. "I am Quint's assistant. Consider that possibility now!"

The tree did not answer. It shone; its crown spun, collecting the life of the wind. But it no longer spoke.

"Khoumy?"

There was no reply, no sound at all it seemed but the spinner cap whirring in the winds coming in to Bullen Meddi, sliding in under the cold bright stars.

"Djuringa!" I called. "Djuringa!"

But all I got was the thrumming of the breeze about the shaft, the whirring of the cap and, distinct again, the occasional creakings and soughings from the carnival streets behind me. Then, a plangent note from the bell-chamber, so very sad, followed by the soft chiming of the dim-recall rods in Khoumy's base, the ghost of its own life.

I stood stunned by the confusion of emotions: alarm, guilt, absolute despair. What had I done? Why?

I fled. I rushed into the shadowed fairground streets, oblivious now to the patches of darkness, needing to find Quint.

But when I reached the beach and saw him still kneeling before Tiresias, I could not bring myself to confess what I had done. The words died on my lips, not just from shame, but because somehow Quint looked even more lost and wayward than I felt I did in my confusion and distress.

The sight of him there, the knowledge of his need, buried the terrible news.

"What should we do now?" I asked instead, grateful for the reprieve, wanting to hear a voice, any voice, but his most of all.

Quint rose to his feet. "Help me with the carousel," he said.

Did the words hold accusation? No. He was simply disoriented from being alone with his thoughts. "Help me test it."

I was glad to, so relieved to hear him chattering about what he had done to fix it, the re-wiring involved, the complete overhaul he had given the old motor and music-box.

While he made his final electrical adjustments, I set to polishing the already-gleaming brass poles, encouraging him with questions.

Perhaps Khoumy would recover, I told myself as I worked. Or all it would take would be some minor routine adjustments during one of Quint's service rounds. Yes, that would do it. The tree hadn't been sophisticated enough to kill like that.

Or, the thought came immediately, not sophisticated enough to withstand such an attack as mine.

I kept polishing, hiding the self-contempt, the undefined rage, hiding from voices in another, crueller darkness, until Quint came over to discuss tomorrow's performance.

"We must act as custodians and guides, Tom," he said resolutely. "We must direct people to the different trees, distribute the numbers, suggest questions they can ask. Tiresias is my pride and joy. He can talk their philosophies with the best of them. Daystar and Ankh are not as spirited; poor personality definition—I was too eager there, too unskilled. But they can manage. We must protect Khoumy, my poor firstborn. Very fragile that one. Very limited. But stars, Tom: it can tell you all about stars."

I worked on the poles, rubbing them, fiercely polishing the smooth metal, trying not to think of the post out on the perimeter.

From 2000 to 2100, I helped string coloured lights over the ornamental gate and the gantry of the ferris while Quint gave directions.

At 2100, he ran the carousel for half an hour while we stood on the beach and watched. The lights shone, warm and golden, the horses leapt and plunged in the moonlight, the music rang along the shore and brought a strange new life to the old buildings—and an added loneliness as well. The spinners gave back an eerie keening and chiming from their dim-recall rods. For a time the sound of the wind was hidden, concealed under this joyful, less timeless music.

Quint left me and went to finish coupling the festival lights to the power cells. I knew that was done when the already moon-bright gate and ferris tower lit up with a sudden prickle of small coloured points.

So I rode the carousel, happy to be under the dazzling mantle of lights and mirrors, one moment curving out over the empty sand-sea, the next swinging in to the quiet streets. I rode half-blinded by the lights flashing in my eyes, reflecting from the brightwork and gleaming poles.

As I swung out on the desert arc, I thought I saw a single lamp showing, as if a ship waited out there. As I swung in on the carnival leg there was a glimpse of a white figure hurrying across the midway.

I gripped the pole intently, straining to see, but on my next pass both images were gone—ship and figure—probably after-images formed by the dazzle of mirror-light against the darkness, ghosts at the inside of my eyes.

"Tom, she's been here!"

Quint's words came to me above the sound of the calliope, shouted through the dry air. I saw him on successive turns as he came running down the midway, each turn bringing him closer, like a figure seen through the shutter of a magic lantern, a time-wounded magician trapped into instalments, blinks of imminence.

"Who? For heaven's sake, who?" I cried, dismounting, waiting for him, reluctant to jump free of the pedestal in case tools or wedges had been left about.

The old man reached the controls and cut the power. The music stopped and the platform glided to a halt.

"Who?" I said again, jumping down.

"I don't know her name. She's been with Khoumy. Tampered with it. It won't answer me."

I went to comment, but my own images stopped me.

"I saw a light out there," was all I said. "And a white figure back on the midway."

"You did? You did!"

"I thought it was you. I wasn't sure. The light was too bright here."

"Tom, we must search! I said I was baiting a trap. There are phantoms here. We must find out!"

"No, Quint," I said, again wanting to confess my crime against him, needing his understanding, desperately needing his forgiveness, but not wanting to ruin his excitement, not now. "Probably an Ab'O drawn by the calliope. Or Cas wanting to provoke you. Teasing. She'd do it!"

"No!" Quint was adamant. "She wouldn't do that. I told her what I was after."

"What *are* you after?" I asked. *Merinda?* I almost said, but stopped myself.

"No, Tom, no! Just help me check Ankh and Daystar. She may have disturbed them as well."

We hurried along the beach to where Ankh stood, washed in moonlight.

"Djuringa!" Quint called before we reached it.

"Djuringa," Ankh answered, spinner cap whirring against the stars. "Hello, Father."

"Someone has been with Khoumy. Do you know who?"

"No, Father." The voice came down to us from the diligent. "I know only that Khoumy will not answer me now."

"But living? Living? What do you read?"

"Unliving. That's what I read, Father. Or the signal is too faint for me to tell."

I went to speak, but the old man pressed on.

"Have you seen a light out on the desert? A ship? Or someone other than Tom or me moving through the fairground?" Quint's excitement made him stumble on the words.

"No, Father. Nothing like that."

"Could you have been tampered with and not know it?"

"Yes. I probably would not be able to tell."

Quint turned to me. "I'll check Daystar. You ask Tiresias. Watch from there. See if the light returns."

"But Ankh says—"

"He may be occluded. It can be done."

By the tribes—Quint had no need to say it. By Ab'O hi-tech interference from over the desert waste, or from out of the sky, from an orbiting comsat given that precise task.

The old man hurried away and I went back to where Tiresias stood near the carousel.

"Djuringa!" I called, and waited below the spinning blades.

There was no password response.

"You harmed Khoumy!" the belltree said, startling me with the accusation.

"I didn't mean to," I said.

"Yes, you did," it accused, but without rancour, merely saying what it knew. "You were testing it for life. In your own way, that's what you were doing."

I moved in closer, fearing our voices would carry. "You didn't tell Quint."

"It would not help Father now. His task is nearly done."

Such a compassionate, life-seeming answer. Such a good strong voice—the tree sounded and looked so powerful, its wheel moving briskly, drawing the eye into its disk of fractured moonlight, blades paring the wind.

"Was there a ship?"

"Yes," Tiresias said.

"A figure in the streets?"

"Yes."

"Who? Do you know?"

"Look out there!" the spinner said.

I turned and scanned the desert. To my left the carousel sat untended on the beach, blazing like a Tsar's precious crown. To the right the low dunes folded and re-folded until they levelled out completely. Far out on the windswept waste a light shone. I watched it flash once, twice, go dark, come again, then vanish altogether.

"A signal! A code!" I said. "For whom, Tiresias? You?"

Was this tree a traitor? I wondered. Suborned, acting willingly for interests other than Quint's? Or was it under some compulsion? I doubted everything now. A belltree would not need such a primitive visual signal, merely an override beamed to its function centres. Was the beacon for someone human?

Like Khoumy before it, Tiresias would not or could not answer.

"Tiresias, who is out there?"

"*Muki winorbin*," it replied in dialect, an expression even Nationals knew, from one of the old languages.

"Ghosts? That was no min-min light. Who?"

But driven to silence or choosing it, Tiresias did not say.

I ran to find Quint. He was nowhere near the carousel that I could see, so I went back along the beach to Ankh, stopping long enough to say the password and ask it the same question I had put to Tiresias.

"Ankh, who is out there?"

"*Wandang*," it said, the same answer in a different dialect.

Ghosts. Again, ghosts. Merinda the storyteller coming to get her old champion, another storyteller, the man who had told her story as best he could.

I believed otherwise, but when I had looked for him at the deserted workshop and reached the midway again I immediately doubted myself; there before me was a tableau—figures waiting, frozen where they stood but for the wind picking at their garments.

Quint stood in the middle of the main avenue. At the far end, close to the ornamental gate, was a solitary white-clad form, a cowled female shape, her robes stirring in the moonwind. At the other end of the midway, near the carousel and Tiresias where I had been but a few moments ago, were three figures, all dark: two men and a tall slender woman between them, backlit by the carousel so that it seemed min-min lights danced in their hair.

"Quint!" I cried, but said no more. There was moonlight glinting off metal; the figures with the dark woman carried weapons.

Ab'Os, I knew. Tribal people from the ship I had seen.

"Merinda?" Quint called, his voice full of desperation and hope.

From the white figure near the gate came "Here, Quint! I am here! Come now!"

And from the dark woman by the carousel: "No, Quint! Here!"

The tableau dissolved. While the old man stood undecided, the Ab'O men came forward and led him quietly back to where the dark woman waited. Then, with not another word spoken, the small group turned and walked down on to the desert sea, the distinctive shape of the clockmaker in their midst. By moonlight their silver forms and accompanying dark shadows dwindled into the gloom, merged with the desert.

The white figure came running towards me, flinging her sand-cape open.

"Cas?" I said, knowing it had to be.

"It seems I wasn't the only one to have the idea," she said. "I was trying to help." She looked to where Quint had been taken. "What will they do to him?"

"He's broken their law. I don't know. Khoumy could have told us; he had bioscan function, Quint said."

We stood on the deserted midway, and even by moonlight Cas could see my look of reproach.

"I wanted to save him, Tom. Grant me more than what you saw today when I was with the others. That was all part of it. He wanted to be found—to expand the Merinda legend, to make it his. He gave me my script. Only tonight did I improvise, dare depart from it. I didn't know what was coming but I had to try."

"One of his own trees betrayed him," I said, realising as I spoke the words that it had to be true.

"What!"

"Yes. Can you see it, Cas? He made life, then one of his own creations, his greatest, Tiresias, inquisitive, seeking information, learnt of its forbidden nature. One of the first discoveries it made. It sought confirmation; it wanted to know more. It called in the tribes. Kurdaitcha!"

Suddenly three detonations shook the fairground; three brilliant balls of fire lit the air as the diligents of Tiresias, Ankh and Daystar exploded, scattering incandescent fragments across the midway, bright flickering sparks which slowly settled and died.

There would be no performance after all, no re-opening of Sat's Carnival with fortune-telling posts and carousel rides.

"The ghosts were busy tonight," I said.

"But they left one intact," Cas replied. "Out on the perimeter."

"Khoumy is moribund. It would not have registered on their scan. I killed it."

But as we walked up the slope towards her skiff, leaving behind us the burning candles of the spinner posts, the mad gate and ferris tower decked out in their small sad web of party lights, the merry-go-round on the beach untended, to glow by day and night until the cells failed, we heard a voice calling across the quiet sandhills of Bullen Meddi.

"I have decided," it cried, the words clear and distinct. "I am alive!"

Cas looked at me, eyebrows raised in an unasked question. "Tell no one," I said, cherishing those few simple words from Khoumy.

"Only if you come to the opening night of *Merinda*," she said.

"Done," I said, not looking back. "Done."

A Deadly Edge Their Red

Beaks Pass Along

Hearts have as many fashions as the world has shapes.
— Ovid

HERE, TIMON (that's what I've decided to call you), is the account you wanted, just as it happened, the conversations set down exactly as I recorded them on my dag.

It started as a three-way in Joab's with plenty of passengers, and it was the afternoon of Day 362.

For the record, I should have known better, in spite of my highly-developed print's curiosity about these things. It was too much of a coincidence, you see, even in a city this large.

You *never* discuss life and death around a Hoproi. Never! You especially don't do it with a Darzie listening in, and you never do it with a closing-down Salman sitting across from you in its hand-carved wheel-chair, calmly sipping on Easy-End, slowly embalming itself before your very eyes.

As I say, I should have known better. I'll just keep telling myself that I was too young; that it was Day 362 after all, my almost full year of true consciousness in our lovely mixed-up world. But the truth is that being a print I probably decided not to notice certain things at the time.

A coincidence like that is quite an event, let me tell you, hence the passengers. The rest of Joab's customers, at least forty of them, were lined up around us, and growing in number as the word got around. Everyone who came into the bar grabbed a drink and joined the crowd at the big corner table.

People would talk about it for months, years: off-worlders talking like that. A three-way with a Human; a true-life interface adventure right there in a humble dockside tavern.

And I was responsible, whichever way you look at it. But I had the perfect excuse, didn't I?

I am a clogue, you see, Timon: a twenty-five-year-old lookalike fresh out of a rent-tent in a Salman hordat; a rogue clone brought to life when both my template, Rael Green, and my A-mate bought it a year ago in a series duel. My template, Rael, had known money in his time, and had invested in the next-best thing to immortality. Three clones, three robust prints, all laid down in hordat, to be held at male clonal prime-time: age twenty-five.

Unfortunately, in what has to be the worst piece of luck I know of, my A-mate had come to consciousness three weeks after Rael's death and, before getting a full orientation, had been killed as well. Fortunately for me and my clone brother, his death fulfilled the obligation of the Hatch vs. Green duel series and I was vitalised a free agent.

My C-mate—or so I'd thought—had been still packed away in his tent at the time, waiting his turn, dreaming those strange brown dreams that clones never remember on waking, though the memory of the sepia-toned pre-life stays with them forever.

Then came the bad news.

I was the C-mate. My remaining identikin was supposed to have been temporised first. Somebody at the hordat had made a terrible mistake. I came out thinking myself the B, went through the briefing, took over the identity-codes of my template and founder, Rael Green.

Three hours later, my true B-mate was brought into the world by some slave-delay check in the hordat's computer systems and there were two of us.

I automatically forfeited the identity of Rael, of course, and had a choice: back to the womb till my B-mate bought it, or be rogued. It was no choice, as I saw it. I became a clogue, the first one in eight years (the hordats are usually very careful about this sort of thing) and called myself Hollis.

Everyone watched to see what sort of clogue-and-daggery I got up to.

(Have you got that, Timon? Along with this account I'll be keying in some speed data transmissions to give background. Like so:

daggery or dag: Etymology uncertain, possibly from datagatherer. The compact shoulder computers devised originally as portable quick retrieval systems for clones and off-worlders unable to afford a full in-house acclimatisation.

Right, you see how it is for we less well-off prints. Anyway...)

Most people expected me to take out a contract on my B-mate, though in truth I wished my identikin well and still do. I knew the rules and he was still me after a fashion. A lot of my friends thought I was dangerously wrong-headed about this, but I didn't care.

Then I discovered I had a talent for songsmithing, a talent which our template had used to get himself a reputation as a sometime raconteur and confidence trickster. I wrote songs: songs about space and life, about the Occupation and the interface, and that's really what brought this on. The three-way I'm referring to.

"Say the verse again, Hollis," Smart Alec said, rumbling thunder down in himself. Hoproi don't use chairs. They park their great three-metre vertical barrel torsos on the cut-off sections of wooden barrels, with their four trunks tucked up like coiled whips against their brown-grey bodies. There are single eyes set in the cartilaginous girdle between each of the trunks, sensory fibres and an eating orifice set at the top of the barrel. Monstrous is the word, but they're too funny for that, and they love beer. Hoproi.

I repeated the words, even then feeling a growing apprehension, a suspicion that perhaps this wasn't the right theme to be discussing around an ET triune this way.

"Have you seen the birds of prey?
Have you seen the kites that lean upon the day?

Making whirlwinds in the peace we all hold dear,
Giving signs and sounds to make it disappear.

"Hear them answering that this is not a song,
It's a deadly edge their red beaks pass along.
Hear them answering!
Hear them answering!"

The bar was quiet when I had finished.

"Do you believe that?" Smart Alec asked, huge on his wooden tub, dominating the room with his massive form.

The Salman sipped at its Easy-End, tipping the glass into the peak of its visor-like face. The Darzie, shut into an already fading localisation, spending his last hours of access in Human company, looked at me and smiled. I liked the Darzie, though this one hadn't spoken yet. They smile pretty much as we do.

"For if you believe it," Smart Alec continued before I could answer. "It would seem to me that we are much closer in our understanding of the vital margin than I would have thought."

"I have only recently come to term," I told them. "Being a clogue, I have to gain knowledge quickly, particularly about the things that seem important for survival for one in my condition and with my gifts. Think of what it's like! I wake, without memories, as a young adult. I learn my world is occupied by many alien peoples, co-ruled by three races who are themselves custodians for absentee landlords. Therefore I hasten to know the three as best I can: three vastly different races chosen by the Nobodoi to administer a race like ours. I ponder the qualities needed for that. I go further and look for common factors, asking 'What do these people have in common that permits a viable alignment with Humanity, a valid congruence?' This is a difficult question, but I find it is partly a common awareness of death as a limit to consciousness. The Hoproi, the Darzie and, it seems, the Matta all share this."

Then I acknowledged T'lenbenbo the Salman, seated in its special wheel-chair. "Not the Salmans, however."

The leatherman stopped drinking, inclined the dried casque of its head.

"While travelling near (your word) Aurigae," it hissed and clicked in very good Antique, "I met a worm from another starfaring race, incredibly long-lived. It called itself an Ol, and was eager to know about the world to which the Nobodoi were sending us. It had been (your word) dead for eight thousand Sol-3 years. Its body had been fitted into a tomb-ship which it powered by an effort of will beyond anything I have ever known. It was dead, as we all say, built into its ship, but its final act of self was to ferry its own corpse to the tomb-field of its race halfway across this galaxy... at sub-light speed. At my (your word) death, my offspring will contact this ship and tell of my passing into humber. Our talk here now will be mentioned. Who knows? This dead Ol scholar may have some answers. It has had... millennia... to ponder all the deaths there are."

Everyone marvelled at T'lenbenbo's words, as much at the fact that the closing-down Salman was saying this as because of its tale of the Ol. Nor had the creature finished speaking.

"We from Salmi who must come to settle our small share of your Earth, know something of this afterlife such as the Ol experiences. Life and death (your words) are not adequate terms. For us, there are no (your idiom) blacks and whites. We see into the grey of the Shoulder—the Shelf before the Deep. Each of us is custodian of the aftertime, shepherd of the tree. The way you live your life teaches; the way you leave your life teaches. The transition, the slow withdrawal, permits the crucial insights, allows the finer understanding of both stations.

"I, for one, choose Easy-End. It is a careful choice for me. I shall become a humber and serve as a—yes, corpseman (your word)—so that my offspring can return to Salmi. It is a small price. In life I am vulnerable. In (your word) death I am invincible, for then I cannot die. The Ol understands this."

No one spoke for a moment. The Salman ethos was by its nature beyond the grasp of any of us. The thought of selling one's life—or rather one's death—to the highest bidder, to live out the days, possibly weeks, of a dwindling sub-conscious half-life as a golem or whatever you would call the humber state, was beyond comprehension.

Even those of us around Joab's taproom with our expensive conditionings and empathee-totes could not grasp the idea of that grim voluntary transit onto what they called the Shoulder-and-the-Shelf.

But those same conditionings still made us genial companions, and the Salman seemed interested and willing to share—a good sort from anyone's point of view. No phobes stay around a solace-house like Joab's for long. All the passengers were enjoying this: a Salman becoming a mummy—a humber—before their very eyes, and telling stories of the universe from which Humanity had been generally debarred; a senior Hoproi war-tech, supposedly in from wandering the streets looking for excitement, who had remained at Joab's, fascinated with a Human clogue's song about death; a Darzie prime just back from some important service for his race and still localised into a Human-biased worldview for another hour or so, killing time before reverting back into far-look.

And a clogue.

All speaking Antique too. Little wonder there were reporters here.

The towering Hoproi war-master burped ridiculously over his beer and leant forward. He was having great fun, discussing the subject around which his whole race had developed its amazing civilisation. The Hoproi lived for war, thrived on it, shared every nuance of it through a dozen captive races of their own—peoples kept as symbiotes to give vicarious pleasure to these monstrous masters. As jovial and good-natured as they were, the Hoproi were to be feared. After all, the absentee Nobodoi conquerors of Earth had chosen this race to conduct a ruthless on-surface conquest of the remaining national blocs—assisted expertly by the Matt technologists and the Darzie administrative and ordinance specialists. One million prime-age Humans were at present in active field service to the Hoproi, surgically and psychologically modified to act as *choi* soldiers: voluntary or enforced symbiotes. Another two million across a patchwork, post-Wormwood, xenoformed Earth served as mercenary soldiers, not connected with Hoproi directly but following the Code recognised by the choi troops themselves.

(I don't know how much of this you want, Timon, but since you may not know the Hoproi:

choi: literally 'successful conversion': a Hoproi term of very ancient origin. Traditionally it means 'fighting star', 'fighting wheel', 'wheel companions', 'optimum arrangement' etc. The Hoproi, by surgically adapting some of the more sophisticated lifeforms, can physically link themselves to subjects. Four warriors, each connected to the Hoproi by the fixing of a modified trunk horn into a synthetic socket at the base of the spine, form a fighting-star and what is customarily known as choi. The host can then enjoy the sensations and reactions of these choi-mates vicariously, especially during combat. This is a refinement of an ancient carnivorous feeding-process, wherein the fixing of the trunk horns meant a subject's death, the Hoproi enjoying the final moments of agony and anguish. As the Hoproi gravitated to a more omnivorous feeding-cycle, this brutal and amazing practice became more an intellectual thing, a powerful tropism for the race but no longer part of an immediate survival mechanism.

I think you understand 'xenoforming' well enough, but here's what I get on my dag:

xenoforming: a refinement of terraforming. Antique expression coined during the immediate post-Wormwood period. It refers not to the stabilisation of whole worlds for single-species occupancy (as undertaken by the Bridge Races for the Nobodoi), but to the creation of ley corridors and regional enclaves (with flora, fauna, weather control, etc) for a number of cohabiting species. It can involve gargantuan projects such as the land-bridges and the leys themselves and the great waste of the Wormwood Impact covering most of the Australian continent, or simply cosmetic alterations: pigmented deserts, mild stasis-chains or a-tree forests. It goes without saying that xenoforming presupposes compatibility in certain areas. One often wonders what amazing races missed coming to Earth merely because of excess humidity, or one or two rare gases, or a random bacterium in our atmosphere.)

"This is exhilarating, Hollis!" Smart Alec boomed. "We got quite a pow-wow going here, I tell you."

I grinned and made a mental note of the odd term he had used. Despite what Aspen Dirk had once said about making Hoproi friends, I could probably use one, though exactly how I had no idea.

"How 'bout you, Darzie?" Smart Alec went on. "How do you view the vital exchange?"

The Darzie inclined his head, anticipating far-look. His hot-glass armour was off, looking brittle now with an oily-blue sheen to its plates. He tapped a bony finger at his chest blazon.

"I am Lucq-Sverre," he said. "We have talked before, am I not correct, Smart Alec? Each time you ask, we avoid. My people find service in your leavings. We continue to fill in gaps you create with order and the safe web of Encosium. Now I am localised, so I answer. Death for us is so simple. We derive from a hive ancestry; we cherish what is corporate. We find little pleasure in discorporation and disfunction, since our bliss is to belong to the ongoing whole. But we know the priorities. We smile at you, at your zeal. We love your madness."

Smart Alec roared with laughter, unsnapped one of his four trunks so that the horn at its tip flickered in the light from the ceiling lamps before recoiling. At the same time he gave a piercing whistle from up near his sensory fibres.

At the sound, two armoured choi burst into the solace-house, jerrykins drawn, stars ready. In one horrifying, practised movement that no conditioning could ever make normal, the two Humans were beside their master and two of the trunks had snaked out to bury horned tips in the spinal sockets at the base of each warrior's back. Now they were physically joined to their host; Smart Alec was drawing on Human emotions as well.

The bar was in an uproar. Patrons had dived for cover, scrambling under benches, tables, down behind the bar with Joab's cursing sons.

I was still seated, too numb to do anything but gape. Unlike most of the passengers, I had not known what the whistle meant. Lack of experience again.

The Darzie also remained, hot-glass still switched off, and naturally the Salman hadn't moved either—but then both knew no Hoproi would harm them.

Smart Alec was tipping back and forth, rocking dangerously on his tub, filling the room with great gusts of laughter.

"You see! You see!" he roared. "I bring you all into a confrontation with the vital margin. No charge! I explore that exhilaration. Wheeeeeeeeee!"

Then the trunks snapped back, freeing his Human extensions to go remote once more. Both warriors, cruel and faceless in their armour, sheathed their weapons and moved back out into the street, forever prepared.

"Humans are different," I told the big creature across from me. "We use a fear of death to enrich our living as you do, but our evolution has not freed us to the extent yours has. Both our races contemplate the threshold, but since we don't know what awaits, ours draws back and turns to more accessible life pursuits, while yours cavorts at that final doorway—"

"Hey, I like that, Hollis!" Smart Alec said. "We cavort at the door. Anyone comes, we give him a push!"

I resigned myself to my position then and gave up. My words, my images out-of-song, were at best clumsy attempts to capture what I wanted to say, and yet to this Hoproi they somehow rang with the truth of the ages. I was getting in deeper and deeper. Even my slack-witted failure to go for cover when Smart Alec whistled in his choi-mates had been interpreted as a special courage.

"We get back to your song," the dusty-grey creature said. "What are these birds? Are they death symbols?"

"Yes," I said. "We have many traditions of birds signifying death or heralding death's coming. It's a complex origin partly to do with scavenger birds feeding off cadavers, carrion eaters, and also an association with night and blackness, with night birds and their calls."

"Ah, yes," the Darzie interrupted quietly, losing his localisation with every passing moment but still holding back, enjoying enough of this conversation not to leave yet. "Humans are so emotionally sensitive to light and sound. Like the Salmans. The wind is a death symbol too, I take it?"

Smart Alec was impatient with Lucq-Sverre's interruption.

"Yes. Yes. But why do you produce this song, Hollis? Why did you think to sing it here?"

Damn, I thought. *They're really locked into this, all of them.* T'lenbenbo was still sipping its fortifying and debilitating poison, Lucq-Sverre was smiling ever so slightly, and the passengers were sandwiched in every which way so as not to miss a word. I could hear several cameras running, a soft but distinct whirring audible in the hush.

Dominating the scene was my Hoproi friend, a member of a warrior people who had refined warfare to a precise artform, whose word for war literally meant 'vital dalliance'. I loved the paradox of that.

"When I first left the hordat," I said, trying again, "I had several choices. Go Code, perhaps even work a choi with your people, Alec—"

"That's Smart Alec, Hollis."

"Sorry. Smart Alec. Or become a privateer or an entertainer. I found I was good with words and music, then noticed that around me was a world rife with contrasts and contradictions. So many non-Human peoples coexisting, their ideas foreign and unique to one another. Issues like life and death, ontology, belief, all with new parameters. Philosophers, scholars, poets and fools working at discovering these, trying to sift absolutes out of diverse worldviews and so many inscrutable drives and imperatives.

"In my first two months, I learned how twenty-seven thousand Humans pay a million dollars annually for prime conditionings in this city alone, just to have a comprehensive range of referents encoded, or RNA injections, or profile totes so they can relate. That really hit home. For the first time I understood how a conquest can go two ways; that the vanquished have a real advantage. I wondered at why the Nobodoi brought you all here to begin with. What is *their* plan? It isn't yours. Or yours, T'lenbenbo. Or mine. We mustn't impute motives. I wonder this especially when I see that the concept of 'conquest' is a different thing for a Salman, a Darzie and a Hoproi. What does it mean for a Nobodoi overlord?"

"You say overlord twice there, Hollis," Smart Alec pointed out. "Nobodoi means overlord."

"Fine. But you see my point. We do not know the purpose for our races coming together in this combination."

"Hoproi take orders from Nobodoi. We understand them."

"But from your ideological and genetic bias, Smart Alec. We look for what we know. No natural selection I know of produces a natural cosmopolitan."

"Maybe you have it there," Lucq-Sverre said quietly, intrigued by the notion. "The very fact that we can all use Antique now suggests an intended congruence."

Smart Alec wasn't convinced. "Occupation compatibility," he said. "We have done it many times, finding which combinations expedite the program."

"And leaving those combinations behind afterwards," Lucq-Sverre said. "To adapt. To create new combinations. I see Hollis's point."

"But we cannot interbreed!" Smart Alec roared, understanding the Darzie's line of thought.

"Perhaps not," Lucq-Sverre continued. "But there *are* other considerations. Hollis could be right. Whatever else happens here, we are being conditioned, acclimatised. What do the masters want from this interaction? Presuming they will Return for us."

"Exactly," I said, wanting to stop this before Smart Alec did. "But now we Humanise their motivations. Darzify them, and so on. We are back to square one."

"So speak of vital margin!" Smart Alec boomed. "How does that relate?"

I craned my neck up at the Hoproi's eye girdle.

"I guess I realised how death was no longer the comparatively simple event we Humans—apart from our many metaphysical treatments—had thought it. We don't think about it much, but the reason that Humans find the Darzie so accessible is because we have similar fears about death. This thing that a Human and even a Darzie fears most as the final mystery, becomes for you Hoproi a source of exaltation and absolute preoccupation, probably what should be expected from a long-lived race like yours. From what I've gathered, the Matta live on in a sort of half-life state through the goldwire they secrete, woven into houses, clothing, furniture and machinery. For a Salman, it is a stepping-down from one sort of corporeal life to another more rudimentary golem-state, where consciousness is voluntarily surrendered to a non-conscious, life-in-death condition."

I saw I had their complete attention and continued.

"When I studied the Salman biologues—and correct me here, T'lenbenbo—I learned how the Salman anthrotype evolved under the sort of harsh desert conditions where long periods of non-sentient function was preferable to a more vulnerable, stress and insanity-prone conscious state. Let's say a Salman is buried deep underground during a sandstorm, with no hope of escape or rescue. It automatically lets itself die as a personality, immediately fertilises itself and finally gives birth, then becomes a durable reflex machine existing only to protect the offspring. Our best Human experts in sensory deprivation and trance states can deny the personality for long periods of time, but they cannot function irreversibly as zombies. Free the Salman parent from the responsibility of its young, and it becomes a humber and ready for service. Your civilisation, T'lenbenbo, is built on the most intricate distinction, right there in the vital margin. No wonder this Ol valued your contact. We all value confirmation."

Smart Alec made humphing sounds of pleasure.

"That is why we like you Sallys so much," he said. "Though you make lousy choi!"

"I don't wonder," I continued. "They don't fear death enough to fight for life."

"Right, Hollis. Humans best there. Always want to live, you betcha! Code never better."

"That's why I write about death, I suppose. To remind Humans, and any thinking, interested creature for that matter, that it is only a relative absolute, applicable *only* to us. Our view of it: parochial, Human-limited. Who holds an overview of all the deaths there are—Nobodoi?"

Smart Alec made a thoughtful rumble, then humphed with pleasure again. "This is the stuff!" he bellowed. "Impasse!"

I smiled and nodded. "Yes, impasse. But I continue to explore what continues to fascinate me. There is so much that is new now, so much that has been complicated. It's an exciting time. Because I am a print and a clogue and always at risk anyway, I also find exhilaration in these confrontations with death."

"Bravo, Hollis! Bravo! Just what I want to hear," Smart Alec said. Then: "What's wrong, Lucky?"

For Lucq-Sverre had stood. Our audience folded back to give him room.

"I will go now," he said. "It begins to tell, and I must make the enclave before I lose my bias altogether. Goodbye. I have enjoyed this."

The creature moved away, headed out of Joab's into the late afternoon light and was gone.

Almost at the same moment, Joab's eldest son, Ero, came over to remind T'lenbenbo that its sunset-watch was due to start in fifteen minutes. The Salman nodded slowly to Smart Alec and me and let the boy guide its wheel-chair to the elevator on the far side of the bar.

That left the Hoproi and me. Many of the passengers decided the truly unique part of the confab was over and began to leave.

I was glad of that, the release of pressure, the freedom from having to perform. Everything was suddenly different. Those that remained were more interested in the topic of our conversation than the novelty of it. Only one was visibly a journalist, and I knew her from an interview she had done with me a month or so earlier. Her name was Tamari, and she had recordings of many of my songs, had in fact been responsible for my sudden reputation. Though her recorder was going now, her interest in this was probably more personal than professional. We liked one another a lot, and it was nice to look up and see her face. I hadn't seen her arrive.

Now Smart Alec tipped forward, an ominous sight for those not convinced of the power of those four stabilising legs.

"You good fellow, Hollis. How 'bout I give you an adventure in the vital margin no Human has had before?"

I regarded him shrewdly. He was doing me no favours here. This was for his own pleasure, I had to remember that. Fun, for a Hoproi, meant life and death games.

"Tell me about it," I said guardedly, not wishing to appear too interested.

"Do you know the Qualagi?" the Hoproi said, almost confidentially though in that same resonant bass voice.

"What? The barge people? No, not really. Only the colour-codings for their barges. They're off-limits to us. Non-accessible."

"Right. They are here because they are being rewarded by the Nobodoi for services elsewhere, on other worlds. But do you know why they get a no-go?"

I shook my head, remembered there might be mode problems and made it verbal. "No, tell me."

"They are born dead!"

I said nothing. Tamari and I exchanged glances, then watched Smart Alec. He was being awfully free with race-private information, the sort of data which had to have a security rating.

The facts sank in. This had to be intentional, a prearranged provocation. Tamari met my gaze again. Her eyes told me she agreed with me.

It had been no coincidental three-way, I realised. There had to have been a clearance for this or Tamari's recorder wouldn't be permitted, or my daggery, not to mention the passengers. Lucq-Sverre and T'lenbenbo could be in on it too, part of some Hoproi—experiment wasn't the word—spectacle? confrontation? refinement?

I realised that because of my peculiar handicap, my full intrinsic maturity with less than a year's life-experience, I had been selected for Humanity's first official contact with a new Lesser Race. Perhaps I was part of a program that would clear the Qualagi barge folk as Accessible. It bore thinking about.

"Born dead?" I queried, as I was meant to, checking my dag to see I was getting it all.

"It's true," Smart Alec said. "So listen closely, Hollis. I shall tell you wondrous things about Qualagi." And his voice changed, became more precise. He was reciting. "Take the most basic stage of the Qualagi lifeform—the four-captain. It is expelled from the parent's womb-sac but remains joined by a heavy umbilicus, relying on its parent's heart and bloodstream. Though it walks and acts, a fully-made organism, the brain is not yet activated, okay? Not yet an autonomous creature, you get me? Just a mobile extension of the parent, capable of feeding and grooming its mothersire, of steering the barge while the parent rests below, and so on. Able to carry out no independent action. It is effectively no more than an organic servo-mechanism, grown by the Qualagi adult to serve its own needs. Quite handy, too, having an extra cluster of senses to attend you. The four-captain is limited only by the health of the parent and the length of its umbilicus, which becomes hardened and callused and quite durable with time. You following this, Hollis?"

I nodded, quickly checking my dag telltale again. It was hard to know which was more fascinating: what Smart Alec was saying or the way he now spoke. These were rote-learned patterns he was recalling, the syntax nearly perfect, so my dag recording would be clear. It confirmed my suspicion that all this was planned.

"We Hoproi," Smart Alec continued, "see an affinity here with choi, of course, with the connecting trunks, though it is absolutely different. The Salmans, too, recognise an affinity, an interesting parallel, but this too is so different as to be out-of-mind, a superficial resemblance, the Salman cycle in reverse.

"There are as many as several four-captains at a time, and they are totally dependent on their parent for survival, to the extent that a parent might decide to keep its young forever at the four-captain stage, rejecting them only when they are injured or ailing. A mothersire may even decide to waste the offspring before they can grow further, draining off their vitality along the same umbilici that give them life. A starving mothersire or the adult choosing to go solitary will feed off its own four-captains without a second thought. They are ancillary parts of itself still, you see. I have seen Qualagi mothersires wearing the withered umbilici and shrivelled corpses of their own wasted young wound about their bodies, as signs of rank. The meaning is deep here, Hollis, and the two-captains and the one-captains who practise this will not speak of it. You understand?"

"Yes. Yes," I said, fascinated in spite of myself. "There are things here even you do not know about yet. Go on."

"In time, if the mothersire so decides, the signal is given for the mind of the dormant four to awaken: at first into a rudimentary, hind-brain consciousness, still very much vestigial, but soon gaining and displaying its own personality. This is the three-captain: the Conscious Servant or, if things do not go well, the Heart Pirate."

"Why that?"

"You will learn," Smart Alec said. "Occasionally the transition to this independent three-captain state is not smooth. There is severe trauma at losing its parent's consciousness before it has fully gained its own. Given the precise and critical nature of the process going on, I'm not surprised it doesn't happen more often than it does. When the transition is not smooth, the traumatised offspring goes into an *amok* condition in which it will attempt to destroy its parent. Quite a powerful reflex, that. Poetic justice too, hey?"

"This is fascinating," Tamari said, the first words I had heard her speak during the whole meeting. I smiled, welcoming her involvement, but Smart Alec humphed with annoyance, his trunks tightening against his side. His recital was requiring great concentration; he was impatient to get it done.

"Poetic justice indeed," I said, to put him back on track, and Tamari seemed to understand what I was doing.

"There are greater wonders among the Qualagi!" Smart Alec went on. "They are superb mentalists from birth as a three. Even the Darzie mind-riders avoid them. By an evolutionary process unlike that of any species I know, the promoted offspring—now a three-captain and dawning sentient—must grow its own heart!"

The number of passengers had grown again the moment Smart Alec mentioned the Qualagi barge-folk. Nowhere else on Earth, never once since the Nobodoi had brushed Wormwood against the

Australian land-mass so many years ago and brought down their three powerful Bridge Races, had the ways of the Qualagi been revealed to Humans. They had been as reclusive and mysterious a people as the Salmans, the Amazi, and even a major race like the Matta. The little knowledge Humankind had of them came from dock-front rumours and tavern-talk, and from the experiences of those who had dared approach the barges and escaped with their sanity and their lives.

Now, a rogue-clone minstrel, a mere print, and sixty or more passengers, were being told the answers to the questions most often asked by curious and baffled Human xenologists.

I understood the subtle trap being sprung here.

The more I heard, the more difficult it would be to refuse this Hoproi's invitation to indulge in his adventure. With this generalised confidence-sharing here in the taproom of Joab's solace-house came commitment. My attempt to generalise it further by acknowledging Tamari had been ignored. Smart Alec had made my position clear: all this was for my benefit.

"How does it do that?" I asked. "How can a creature grow its own heart?"

Smart Alec knew he had me. He tipped even further forward, Human-conspiratorial in intention but an alarming sight for anyone sitting beneath his vast bulk. Their mass was deceptive. I had new respect for Hoproi agility.

"By some amazing evolutionary imperative even we cannot fathom," he boomed. "The Qualagi has an organ completely separate from its body: a cartilaginous pod ejected from the three-captain's breast-sac, kept secret and hidden, probably on its barge, and made to function by the power of the Qualagi's mind. Reciprocally, this remote heart sustains the vital functions of the Qualagi's body."

"But that's impossible, surely!" I said, forgetting what severe qualifications those words had undergone since the Occupation. "No remote heart could work. What about nutrients, simple functional requirements like cell regeneration and the circulatory process? It can't be a heart! It—"

"Patience!" Smart Alec boomed. "You misunderstand concepts! Don't be such a local-yokel, Hollis. We talk here of a heart not simply as a pump mechanism but as a stabilising vitality agent for an organism. Your chest-pump is not your centre of vitality really. Grasp the concept!"

"I do! I do!"

"Good. Then again consider the Qualagi. It is a mentalist. It has two hearts to pump its blood. But that is not its vitality centre, no more than it is for T'lenbenbo, our Salman friend upstairs, who will soon function by an effort of will in its mummified state of humber. This Qualagi heart, nurtured internally and ejected the moment a four-captain is freed from the umbilicus and permitted to change to a three, is a vitality amplifier—"

"So it's an auxiliary organ?" I said, then shook my head again. "But a functioning organ?"

"Used to be, Hollis! There was a time when the Qualagi could do without it; they had a balance. But let us not debate. Who knows? It may be no more than a placebo artifact, or like a reflecting mirror; part of some metabolic process no longer needed for its original purpose, like your appendix; redundant, but come to represent a symbol of self.

"But all that matters really is that the creature grew it itself—it obviously *believes* it's more! Over the years, as the Qualagi refined their mental talents, they came to regard this organ as vital, to rely on it more and more as a means of boosting the force of their mind-commands. They should have evolved away from it with their development of technology, but instead abandoned higher developments in technology and went the other way. They refined the ability around it and because of it!"

I understood the point Smart Alec was making. "So now they're uniquely vulnerable?"

"In a sense, Hollis. All we know is that the Qualagi's personality, its vitality, is now properly maintained only as long as this 'heart' can function, receiving mental instructions, bringing equilibrium to all functions of the body. Without it, there is trauma and considerable strain on the semi-atrophied in-body systems. A strong Qualagi can certainly survive the loss of its remote heart, but its function as a mentalist would be severely impaired, and it would be quite likely insane."

"A mixed blessing if ever there was one," I said, resisting the urge to smile at the word-patterns this creature was required to utter.

Smart Alec humphed in agreement.

"Yes, a delicate and absurd evolution, almost beyond parallel in my experience. Except that the Qualagi are no terminal species doomed to extinction, though they might have been. Possibly this remote heart is a direct result of the four-captain first belonging to its mothersire, an extension of that personality altogether and not autonomous as a personality itself. When the signal is given that animates the Qualagi into a three, its first autonomous act is to eject the special organ that makes possible the full range of its personal growth, a sublime act of self. That heart, like its dormant brain, was probably there from its birth as a four-captain. But now it is activated as the brain becomes conscious—two parts of the earlier primitive ambulatory form that didn't quite belong to the parent, that represented a kernel of this new self. It has a beautiful logic to it."

It was silent in Joab's when the Hoproi had finished speaking, and I tried to use that time well. I was still grasping the concept of 'heart' as Smart Alec used it, recalling the ancient notion from long before Wormwood, from before our Earth's industrial age, that the heart was in fact the centre of self. That had changed well before the twentieth century, and the stage had been reached where the Human brain was seen as a personality centre in a mobile life-support system. This gave rise to all manner of interesting speculations: was a fully conscious Human brain, sustained in a mechanical life-support system, with full memory and full sensory input, still a Human being? Humanity had been getting itself off the horns of that dilemma when the Nobodoi arrived.

But again I took Smart Alec's point. He was speaking of a creature which grew and then thrust into the world the unique organ that would enable it to extend its personality into a full new phase of self-extension.

"But how did such a lifeform originally evolve?" I asked. "The survival value of such an arrangement has to be minimal—the creature forever dependent upon the safekeeping of a vital organ that is not within the body."

"I agree!" Smart Alec boomed, returning to the spiel with gusto; my question anticipated and prepared for. "But remember it was not always that way. The Qualagi could function without it once. And look at it differently, Hollis. Look how vulnerable you and I are, carrying all our vital organs, all our centres of self, around with us, under one roof so to speak. For simple truth, there may be environments which this arrangement does not suit. We do not know the Qualagi homeworld. And to answer your earlier objection: perhaps the heart does not *live*, does *not* get nourished. Perhaps, like the goldwire of the Matta, it is an organic artifact, but with a half-life ability."

"No, Smart Alec! It doesn't—"

"Yes, Hollis! Like the Salman. Like the Ol. But that cannot be the issue. The remote organ exists, and it has a job to do. That is the science here, the fact. One day we shall know how it can be. What matters is that the organ is the individuality focus for the new individual while still an adjunct of its parent, a place where self can grow. Later, as a full two-captain, that detached aspect of self is crucial for the transformation into that splendid rarity: a one!"

"What is a two and a one?" Tamari asked, and I made sure I did not repeat her question, though I very much wanted to.

Smart Alec's expression was, of course, unreadable. With all-points vision, he could not miss who had asked the question. As before, however, he addressed me.

"The two-captain is the Qualagi as full mentalist: able to use its heart to carry out a host of telepathic and telekinetic feats. At this stage in its steady movement away from non-being towards optimum selfness as a one, it is always conscious of its remote heart. It can use it as a sensor to warn of danger or intrusion, and it can even be entrusted to a friend making a short journey—the range of mental viability can be that extensive. Most of the time, though, it is used to guard the barge. Sometimes, when the Qualagi is badly injured, the personality can actually—what is the word?—consolidate itself in the remote heart until the dying host can be repaired or revived, in much the same way as our Salman's spacefaring Ol seems to have had its identity imprinted on the slave-mechanisms of its mortuary ship. Yes, a place of consolidation."

"And then what happens?" I said.

Smart Alec humphed jubilantly, but only once. He was getting close to the end of the rote and was becoming excited. "It is at this stage of a two that the Qualagi usually leaves the barge of its mothersire and considers building a barge of its own. Once it is independent this way, it will probably produce offspring: four-captain extensions to serve it, three captains to succeed it, other twos to spread its genetic prowess. If it is truly fortunate, it may become a one-captain to..."

Smart Alec hesitated so I could rise to the bait.

"A one-captain to what?" I said.

"Ah," said Smart Alec. "That is the adventure!"

"What? Learning what one-captains do?"

"Yes, Hollis. That is the adventure! You will be the first Human to know directly, at first-hand, what the ultimate refinement is these Qualagi aspire to."

"But others have discovered it indirectly?" I said.

"Yes! Yes!" he humphed. "So be inquisitive! Parade along the vital margin! Go knowing where careless folk have gone in ignorance."

It was time for a 'What's in it for me' comment of some sort, but there seemed little point in doing that. Smart Alec would go no further. He had made me an offer. If I refused, he would make it again somewhere else. Perhaps even to Tamari or one of the others who had heard all this, though I suspected not. They had a reason for choosing a songsmith who had displayed such an interest in the central issue of their ethos as a race.

"What am I to do?" I said, wondering how Aspen Dirk would react to my decision.

Smart Alec twitched one of his trunks, a sign of excitement and pleasure.

"This goes so well, Hollis! You will visit a Qualagi barge, of course. You will call on a one-captain."

"Do I go armed?"

"That is up to you, amigo. I should think so. I shall equip you with anything you desire, within reason."

"A confile?"

"If you wish. A confile, stars, occlusion weapons, a shattergun if you can carry it. We got good stuff!"

"Hmm. When do I go on this adventure?"

Smart Alec's trunks twitched and flicked in excitement.

"Why not tonight? Go and ready yourself. Meet my choi back here in one hour. They will equip and direct you."

That was how the confab ended, with me accepting Smart Alec's offer. Without another word, the Hoproi rose from his tub and moved heavily towards the door. I heard him greeting his choi out in the street.

Then, realising that people would stay around asking questions, I moved across to Tamari.

"Tam, let's go upstairs and watch the sunset."

She smiled and nodded, clicked off her recorder, and led the way to the elevator.

(And for you, Timon:

sunset-watch: There is a brief moment in the average sunset at the latitude of ancient Cymny when the light and colours most closely resemble the skies of the Salman homeworld, Salmi. All across the old city, the photophilic Salmans will take themselves to lonely rooftops to watch dusk fall over the estuary and mudflats of the Brae. At the moment of approximation, a single sustained mournful note will escape from the mouths of all these watchers. Such are the variables that it becomes difficult to predict the exact moment when this 'song' will begin. It is an unforgettable experience to wait with these leathermen and hear this melancholy sunset cry, as from one echoing voice.)

Joab's solace-house opened on to a small square about half a kilometre from the harbour. It was a six-storey building of liver-red brick, well-appointed on its façade and in its taproom, guest chambers and lower floors, dwindling noticeably in quality the higher up and further back one went.

The flat roof area was dusty and rarely used. Occasionally, Salmans came there for their sunset-watches, to contemplate humber as T'lenbenbo was doing, and perhaps (our word) die.

I came there now with Tamari, my mind racing, feeling both distracted and exhilarated. I was impressed anew with the wonder of all this, recalling historical parallels for this present condition of planetary coexistence. One kept nagging at me.

The ancient Assyrians had conquered their enemies by a twofold method: first by adopting an unrelenting military ruthlessness that often made genocide seem their intention, and secondly by following a strict program of relocating entire peoples away from their homelands, often transplanting them in quite hostile terrain where the very fight for survival kept them dispirited and submissive.

When the three Bridge Races and the myriad Lesser Races set up their enclaves across the Earth, custodians of a subject Humanity for their absent masters, they had suffered this ancient program in reverse. As conquerors, it was *they* who were relocated, whole communities far away from their homes, for long years at a time or forever. The Hoproi and the Matta had adapted easily enough it seemed, all things considered, but the Darzie needed exacting treatments—their localisations—to keep them from far-look, and the Salmans pathetically watched Earth's sunsets for a fleeting glimpse of a condition of light which stirred race memories of a world many of them had never even seen.

I had often wondered about the aching disappointment caused by an overcast evening for a creature like T'lenbenbo, just as I had once watched the Purple-and-Blacks and the Elsewheres outside the great Darzie Arsenal at Dayasse, shut away in far-look, their haunted eyes forever locked on to an impossibly distant Daza'o, and sensed a little of what it must be like to be so cut off. So desperately alone.

Such things came to me now as Tamari and I went to the balustrade near where the closing-down Salman sat propped up in its special chair. No one else was on the roof; Ero had left the Salman alone.

"It's me," I said. "Hollis Green. And Tamari. May we wait with you?"

The leatherman's head moved slightly, giving approval. The Salmans were not at all embarrassed being seen at this time.

"How near?" I asked.

"Soon now," it said in a dry whisper, quite faint. "How did your provocation end?"

"My provocation? Oh... well enough. I'm to meet a one-captain later this evening."

"*Pulchroi*," T'lenbenbo said softly out into the dying day. I saw Tamari react at the Hoproi word.

"*Pulchroi?*" I said, reaching for my dag for a translation; then thought better of it and waited. There would be time later.

We watched T'lenbenbo. The Salman sat unmoving, but the peak of its near-featureless casque trembled slightly in the breeze off the river. The Brae was already brilliant quicksilver as old Sol slid down the sky. I could hear dogs barking and the sound of light traffic in some of the narrow streets below. Cymny is an old city, pre-Wormwood, renamed, famous for its romance and the arts. Here it seemed to spread out before us across the Brae, justifying every word ever written about it. Under different circumstances I would have been stirred to song, to compose music.

But not now. It would soon be time. The sky was darkening; the clouds were streaked with orange and red over a golden yellow, edging to bronze.

"A Hoproi word," T'lenbenbo murmured suddenly. "It means..." The Salman hesitated.

"Vitality engineer," Tamari said, then cautioned me to silence with a hand on my arm.

It was time.

From over the rooftops came a distant keening, taken up on nearby buildings, swelling to become a forlorn drawn-out hooting.

Next to us, T'lenbenbo tensed. In the middle of its face, the inverted V of its peak—the hood of skin protecting its sensory centre—stiffened. Then, oblivious to Tamari and myself, it began its song, the same low keening at first, swelling to a full note of anguish and loss, joining the others.

Presently it ended, as sunset advanced and the brilliantly-lit clouds darkened gradually beyond the stage to which the leathermen were so acutely sensitive.

Ero, as stolidly businesslike as ever, appeared on the rooftop the moment the song had finished. He went to move the Salman, but stopped and turned to us.

"He's done it!" the lad said. "He's a humber!"

"Take T'lenbenbo down," I told him. "Call the hordat."

The boy did as I said, leaving me with Tamari. We stood together, leaning on the balustrade, watching the last traces of colour seep from the sky.

Through that fading twilight I could make out the dark silhouettes of at least half a dozen Qualagi barges moored near the Salman quarter: low black shapes with long deckhouses, some with masts and fine traceries of rigging. A few already showed lights in differing colours and combinations, signifying that various captains were aboard.

(Again, Timon, for you:

The Qualagi use a simple colour-coding to show the crewing status of a barge: a pale-green light signifies the presence of a four-captain; a pale-pink means a three; a dark-blue represents a two; a pale-blue stands for a one-captain. The most frequent crewing combinations are: (a) 3 pale-greens and 1 dark-blue (3 four-captains serving a two); (b) 2 pale-greens, 1 pale-pink, 1 dark-blue (2 fours, 1 three, serving a two); (c) 3 pale-greens and 1 pale-blue (3 fours serving a one-captain); (d) 1 pale-blue (a one-captain solitary).)

"Vitality engineers, Tam. What do you make of that?"

"Sounds ominous, doesn't it?" she said, with obvious misgivings. "I've heard the expression a few times. In dock argot it breaks down to life-eaters."

"I like that even less. One can imagine what it means plainly enough."

"So don't go," she said. "You don't have to. A Hoproi's game is never worth it."

She was right, of course, but I would go just the same. Smart Alec had chosen well, had come to Joab's not by accident or from mere curiosity about a gifted clogue, but as the result of a carefully conducted program of selection and surveillance. I was sure of it now.

He had known that clones had a preoccupation with death and what it meant, that as a prematurely temporised C-mate I was always aware that somewhere my B-mate was operating as Rael Green. Since we were both temporised, the Rael Green persona now had two operatives for that name and its possessions, separated only by a technicality. The mistake which had caused me to be temporised before my identikin had at the same instant elevated us, potentially at least, to the position of bitter enemies. I could only hope that Rael had seen Tam's interview, that he believed I wished him well and would never employ assassins so I could be *the* Rael Green. We had never met; we had never even spoken, but I trusted that much.

I had survived almost a year as Hollis, making my reputation as a songsmith and hoping I seemed completely uninterested in usurping his status. Rael had made no attempts to eliminate me; perhaps he would never try. Then again, thinking himself under constant threat, he might take that precaution. Just as I sometimes wondered if his lack of interest might be to catch me off-guard, so too my reputation and lack of interest might look to him, in a moment of paranoia, as a careful deception, Tam's interview with me a deliberate ploy. Even a C-mate like myself, who had elected to become a clogue and forfeit all claims whatsoever, posed a curious threat—and so lived constantly in fear of the assassin, forever on Smart Alec's vital margin.

Yes, they had researched my case well. I was predisposed to the Hoproi's quest, had been since temporisation, probably would be all my life.

Tamari knew all this too and so said no more about it.

"Want company?" she asked.

"No," I said, squeezing her hand. Our relationship, always casual, was polarising towards something stronger. We both knew it, but both pretended it wasn't true—a lovely moment in any relationship but now a sensible expedient.

"I'm good with weapons," she said.

"No, Tam. They want me to go alone. Even if I set out with a dozen Code soldiers, I guarantee I'd still step onto that barge alone. There'd be accidents, distractions, all sorts of last minute developments."

Tamari nodded, knowing I was right in this, then glanced at her watch.

"Let's go down," she said. "It's nearly time, and you have to change."

The two choi soldiers who had been with Smart Alec earlier now waited at the bar, a large field-kit open in front of them. They wore the armour of Nefarious Waylayers, and both gave chest-salutes with gauntleted fists as I joined them. I'd gone to my room before coming down, partly to review the Qualagi material, but mainly to change into a blacksuit. Apart from the daggery clipped to my shoulder, it was plain, unadorned.

"*Haitee!*" they said in unison.

"*Haitee-teve!*" I replied in Hoproi.

That pleased them.

"I'm Chris; this is Heber," one said. "We're here to arm you and give you safe conduct."

It took them the next thirteen minutes to do my kit properly, adjusting the harness, reckoning the tolerances on the power-pac. They spread the silver net of a confile over my shoulders, placing its contact sphere above my right wrist, adjusted it, gave me two stars at the hip and offered me a choice of jerrykins. Never having mastered the long-bladed inert killing-swords favoured by most Humans in the service of Hoproi, the Code mercenaries and Aviators, I chose a shorter body-sword—good, I hoped, for close fighting in the cramped confines of a Qualagi deck-house. Unlike the longer jerrykins, the body-sword is a powered-option weapon. I adjusted the handle setting for left hand at two-fifths and packed it away in its insulated sheath.

There were several monitoring motes—one fixed over my heart, another on my forehead—by which Smart Alec and his friends could follow my progress and reactions; then a smooth, metallic-looking egg on a black cord which Chris informed me was protection against any non-regulation energy weapons used by my one-captain host. I arranged my confile over it.

Tamari stayed nearby, smiling at each stage of my transformation.

"A real hero-type," she said, as I stood shimmering in my confile, my daggery chattering softly as it adjusted to the unfamiliar power-flow from the energy cells and accumulators.

"*Taibee*!" I said, thanking Chris and Heber for the care they had taken. They nodded, gave me a Code finger-sign for luck.

"Now we go," Chris said. Heber finished packing the equipment I had not wanted onto his own well-loaded harness, and we moved to the door.

"Goodbye, Tam," I said and kissed her. I knew she would be here at Joab's when—if—I returned.

The narrow streets leading down to the waterfront were cool and dark at this hour. Occasional street-lamps glowed at the small intersections; one or two power-wagons and an omno passed us by.

Chris and Heber walked to either side of me in simple two-for-one deployment, their harness—not fastened down for combat stealth—tinkling and clinking with every stride. Choi armour had a designed noise factor, a psychological deterrent. The few Humans we met reacted to it immediately. They stopped to watch us pass, three figures augmented, 'with the edge' as the popular term had it.

Ten minutes later we stood at the beginning of a laneway leading by the Salman quarter down to the harbour, the towering brick walls of hordats and dark residential blocks flanking it closely on either side. Far down the lane, between two large wharves, I could see a Qualagi mooring, made out at least one barge hard up against the stones of the sea-wall: a darkened shape with one light showing at the end of the deck-house, probably close to where the gangway would be.

"That is the *Beam*," Chris said. "Her one-captain is Masq. Are you ready?"

"Yes."

Chris nodded and made the finger-sign.

"*Haitee*!" he said, and Heber next to him echoed it softly.

"*Haitee-teve*!" I replied, as before, then watched as they walked off in the opposite direction, back towards Joab's.

I was alone in the street. Reaching down, I adjusted my confile, regulating the power-flow a little as I'd been shown, checked my weapons, my motes and the shield-egg on my chest to see that they were all in place. In the silence, I could hear the barest hum of the confile; noted the familiar pinpoint of the ready light on my dag. I made sure it was on automatic scan and store, and started off towards the harbour.

The laneway was not deserted as I'd first thought. Before I was six metres in, two youths holding cudgels emerged from the shadows and blocked my way. Then they saw my battle kit glinting in the dim light.

"Evenin'," one said, swinging his cudgel back into the shadows in a smooth and comical motion. "You a patrol?"

"Just out for a stroll," I answered, controlling a grin. It was a relief to have this encounter; I felt the tension ease.

"You're all done up, ain't ya?" the other youth said. "A real orgy!"

(Timon: *orgy* or *augy*—from augmented.)

I didn't answer that, just made sure I could see both of them, watching for others.

I glanced down. My dag told me the lane was otherwise deserted. I checked the contact sphere at my wrist, learning to use it. The confile confirmed what my dag gave. Nothing above or concealed in front or behind.

"Nothin' down there but a sapper," the first youth said. "What d'you want with a sapper? You an assassin, mister?"

I smiled at the thought. "No," I said. "What's a sapper?"

"A sapper?" The youth looked puzzled by my ignorance. I had lost a little of his respect. "One of the barge weirds."

"Why that name?" I pressed.

"They're pulchas, aren't they?"

"*Pulchroi?*"

"Yeah. Pulchas. We don't see 'em, o'course, but we hear stories and lose friends now and then."

"Go on."

"Sorry, orgy. This area's a no-go for us."

I flipped my confile up a notch, twisted the palm of my left hand. In a flash, the body-sword was there, buzzing ominously.

"Hey, whoa, mister!" the youth bawled. "We ain't done nothin'."

I held the sword in clear view. They knew I could send it at them, even if they ran in different directions, and have it back in my hand before they were flat on the stones.

"Walk with me," I said. "Tell me about sappers."

"What! The lugs?"

"Lugs, pulchas, whatever you call them. What about these friends you've lost?"

The youths trudged resentfully down the lane, wanting to run for it, afraid to do anything of the kind.

"Aw, you know," one said. "Over the years there's always been someone takin' a dare. *Beam*'s been down there since I was a kid. Use t'run three greens and a dark-blue. Now she's only got the pale-blue. That means a sapper 'n we don't go near old *Beam* no more. Y'go crazy if you do."

"Or go missin'," the other said. "Dark-blues are dangerous enough." He became talkative too now, easing his tension with words. "Back when she was three greens 'n a dark-blue, we use' to dare one 'nother to rap on the deck plates an' the skylights. I did it meself, twice. But friends'd go missin'."

"Like Charlie and Dek," his friend said.

"Yeah. Ya gotta be careful 'round the barges. Sometimes there's fours jus' waitin' for ya to come aboard. Sharkey tripped over one's cord and nearly copped a harpoon in his ear."

"What about the ones who disappeared?" I asked them.

The first youth indicated his friend. "Crow's dad was out fishin' once and hooked the remains of Cholly. We could tell 'im by 'is tattoo. Cholly took a dare one night down on the point: a dark-blue, two pinks and a green."

"Yeah," Crow said. "So we keep clear now. 'Specially of pale-blues like the *Beam*. Off limits!"

"So vanish!" I said, and they were gone, running back up the lane, their footsteps ringing dully on the stones.

I was close to the end of the lane now. Before me was a lonely intersection, with the sea-wall and a single street-lamp already wearing its soft halo of mist. I could hear the gentle lapping of the waves against the stones, could smell tar and brine and the faint Salman smells from the massed hordats of the quarter behind me. Heavy fog was rolling up the estuary, and the *Beam* was a black shape close by, a long two-storey barge with a solitary pale-blue light set above a narrow gangway.

That light was no courtesy light; it told simply that a one-captain was aboard. I imagined this Masq seated somewhere below-deck. Since it was a solitary, there would be no four-captains, no attendant threes. Or rather, shouldn't be. Though custom required that lights show the muster, the very nature of being a one-captain suggested an arrogance that might lead it not to reveal the crew-status of its barge. This was reckless on my part, imputing Human motives to such a creature, but I had to remind myself that they were relatively Human-accessible after all, even to be on Earth in the first place. It seemed a sound precaution.

But, the thought came, what if it *were* deceiving me? I knew so little of Qualagi, next to nothing. Books and Human-accessible records either did not exist or were not permitted. Perhaps if I survived the night all that would change but, standing there safely out of the street-lamp's wan glow, twenty metres from the benighted *Beam*, I realised fully for the first time that I wasn't *meant* to survive.

I was here simply to bear Smart Alec's monitor motes into this taboo place, to be the point-of-view vehicle for a rare experience and a dramatic exit.

It was all so simple. What's more, I'd known it all along really, but back at Joab's it was not the main point. It hadn't been real there. Recklessly, Humanly, I had made the simple assumption that because Smart Alec liked me he would not wish me harm, when the opposite was true. It was *because* he liked me so much that he wanted me to have this exquisite experience. He had done me a service.

I checked my gear one more time. The confile resisted energy fields; it would conceal me from sensors and any kind of homeotropic device. Along with the smooth egg around my neck, it would protect me against energy weapons. So Chris and Heber had assured me.

But there was something about being this well-armed that disturbed me. I felt overdressed somehow, so impervious to attack that I knew I had to be vulnerable in some way. Smart Alec would want it like that, I knew. I was meant to feel secure in my person, even while expecting the avenue of attack to be mental. They wanted a full range of reactions, and what better way to get extremes than to have an overconfident orgy who suddenly discovers that all his safeguards are not enough!

Ideas began to connect. The confile was a worry if Masq had one too. They would cancel out and it would simply hinder movement to wear one. Also, there were confile functions that could interfere with the guidance-system of a body-sword, leaving it non-powered and inert. That was no problem; I could use an inert sword well enough. If I had the opportunity.

Again, I reviewed the scant facts. The Qualagi were mentalists. When I put that with the ominous term 'sapper' used by the waterfront toughs, I began to understand the shape of my danger— more clearly here by the lonely sea-wall, mere metres from the barge, than ever I could have in the taproom at Joab's.

Sapper. Vitality-engineer. Life-eater. Lugs and pulchas!

The implications had always been clear. My weapons would be useless simply because this Masq would tell me that I did not want to use them. It would mentate a command and I would obey. The proto-Qualagi, climbing towards sentience in the backwaters and fens of their homeworld, must have refined this skill as an early defence against predators.

In the shadows of the laneway, I muttered these observations to my dag, reflecting grimly that at least posterity was being well served this night.

Now was the moment to abandon the mission and return to Joab's.

But I was no longer alone in the lane.

Behind me, standing in the shadows and partly back-lit, was a dark shape, shorter than a man, with a wet shrouded appearance in the gloom.

At first I thought it might be one of the young toughs come back to see what I was up to. Then I caught the smell.

Qualagi!

It was the smell one sometimes noticed when passing a locked and shuttered barge in the full light of day, but much stronger now. Musty, chemical, vaguely piscine.

A three-captain! A Conscious Servant, dawning sentient and in service to its mothersire, already able to send powerful mental commands.

It stood in the lane, not moving.

A sense of prickling horror crept over me. I sweated with it and knew I was right.

For I did not wish to use my sword! I *wanted* to go aboard the *Beam*. At the moment when I wished to withdraw, I found myself walking across to the barge with the single light.

The light-code *had* lied. The one-captain was not alone. It had threes, probably fours, waiting for me.

Perspiration ran down my forehead, dropped on to my cheeks. My mind raced, but my limbs and musculature felt easy enough. I found I had lost all desire to resist, to retaliate.

My one calming thought, somewhere there in my mind: a one-captain like Masq would probably not wish help beyond this initial inducement. Perhaps it was monitoring me even now, without need of motes, adjusting to my reactions. The three-captain was simply insurance—possibly on loan from another barge, if Masq were truly a solitary.

Or perhaps it had not been there at all! A phantom mentated into my perceptions—smell and all—by the lone Qualagi on the barge. I had not checked my dag.

At the foot of the gangway, another thought occurred to me—was gone in a flash, blanked out.

My feet were on the gangway. I could feel the gentle lift and fall of the barge. All around, fog was rolling in, thick under the pylons and balconies of the wharves, thick in the streets tracing the sea-wall. The street-lamp with its dim halo seemed suddenly far off.

I trod on what felt like a thick cable and recoiled in horror, thinking it to be a four-captain's horny umbilicus. But no, it was an ordinary hawser stretched across the deck.

I kept my mind working, searching for the dampened thought, for any connections I might have missed.

There had to be an arrangement, a deal of some sort. Smart Alec was gaining so much from this encounter in the vicarious fashion of the Hoproi war-techs. What was Masq getting in return? Apart from me, one more Human to mentate to death, devitalise. I had a picture of Masq sitting below, waiting, its wasted young wrapped about its body.

Again a thought flashed through my mind. Again it slipped by, vanished, suppressed.

All I had was the conviction that it was there, something terribly important, a key insight I had already had that was being selectively dampened. My subconscious had integrated a discovery but couldn't get it through.

How long had the dampening been going on? I wondered. Since first entering the lane? My confile had said the laneway was empty; perhaps Masq and its borrowed three-captain were interfering with sensory input and deductive thinking even then.

I needed an interference, I realised, then felt the conviction that I didn't—but not my conviction. Distractedly, with supreme detachment, I observed this fact, cherished it.

I double-thought then, that reflexive quick-think practised and sometimes perfected by phobe Humans in this world newly-stocked with mentalists, mind-riders, and hive-telepaths. It was a form of saturation lateral thinking, giving too much data, long involved patterns of rehearsed thoughts, guided by mnemonics and subconscious association triggers. This flood of data often reached a speed and intricacy to baffle and delay even a seasoned telepath, especially one with a non-Human worldview. You only needed an excellent enough reason to develop it.

As a C-mate, I had been oriented by RNA shots and telepathee-totes. Like most prints, predisposed to pan-cultural survival, I had refined quick-think in my first weeks of temporisation. We had called it 'junk-think' or 'scrambling'.

I used it now, building on Masq's command not to resist. I thought openly that I would discard my confile, that it was a nuisance, hampering me. I didn't need it.

The thought received no dampening. My unseen Qualagi host welcomed it.

Standing near the door to the deck-house, I gathered the net together in both hands at my shoulders, raised it about my ears as if to remove it, then pressed it close, muffling my head. At the same time, my thumb sent the setting to maximum.

It worked. Just as confiles always interfered with monitor readings, giving erroneous signals and confusing the Q-K scanners, this net set up a brief interference to outside mentalist activity.

And the thought was there!

No redundancy factor existed in Hoproi combat equipment, no duplication. The Hoproi were experts. If there were something a confile couldn't do defensively for its wearer, you didn't add a separate unit. You improved the original so it remained a single convenient whole. Back-up units suggested that a confile could fail. The only embellishment would be implants, and they too would be knocked out by whatever took out the battle-net.

The egg was redundant. It was a bogus, a fake.

In the instant, I knew it!

In the next instant, just before the one-captain overrode the Q-K interference, I knew what it was, and saw too the extent of Smart Alec's scheme. The elabourate combat equipment had been a way of getting the egg on board the *Beam*.

As the confile fell back down over my body, my first act was to seize the egg on its cord and scrape the blade of my sword across it. There was a sudden thumping below-deck, a sudden relaxation of mental pressure that I hadn't known was there, crowding my mind.

At the same time, I kicked open the door of the deck-house and stepped inside, gambling there were no four-captain extensibles waiting in the shadows, no threes bearing swords or hooks.

My eyes were adequately night-sighted by now. The cabin was empty, the Qualagi scent strong. I saw steps leading down into the hull and took them, all the while letting my blade scrape across the egg in my hand.

In the undercabin, which seemed to stretch the *Beam*'s entire length, there was a pallid blue light, phosphorescence on the hull itself. It gave me my first startling glimpse of a one-captain.

Masq was seated on a pallet against the curve of the hull, a heavy, shrouded, wet-looking shape swathed in the dried bodies of its four-captains and shimmering in a confile net of its own. Squeezed into a face cowled with wetly-glistening cartilage were two bulging eye-lenses, large, blue-black. Beneath them, a gullet opened like the broad spout of an old-style coffee-pot—comical really and even more horrifying because of it. The spout worked in and out in distraught snufflings. Masq was in distress.

Then it came: an awful sagging feeling in my gut, a nausea and a terrible lethargy, a heavy throbbing at the base of my skull. Suddenly leaden, my arms and legs seemed impossible to move. I wanted to slump to the ground where I stood. I was dying.

"More easy than you dreamed," the thought came, from Masq. "Let it happen."

My sword and the egg were frightfully heavy, unbearably so. I heard the sword drop, but clung to the egg, desperately clung to it.

"You have returned it to me," came the thought, or voice—I could not tell. "The Great Lord kept his word. Masq the sea-hag does too."

And the *pulchroi*, the vitality-engineer, the sapper, proceeded to drain my life away, performing an act I had only begun to suspect at the last. That knowledge had been suppressed from the moment I left Joab's, perhaps even earlier, by a three-captain following close behind, possibly by the awesome Masq itself, reaching out with its mind to control my reality, using the very egg which Smart Alec had hidden close by precisely for that purpose.

Affecting everyone, I realised. Lucq-Sverre, Tamari, all of us. Smart Alec and Masq working together, crafting the three-way, the long detailed discussion; Smart Alec persuading from without, Masq working quietly from within, coaxing, suggesting, gently coercing.

Now the truth of what the one-captains did filled my universe. There seemed to be nothing else. Raised from witless golem appendages, from an almost insuperable birth trauma, becoming vulnerable threes and then twos, these creatures had a vast desire to dominate, to gain identity through the vitality of others, to feed off identity and self wherever they found it. A ghoulish life-mode, throwing the death-switches of the careless and the unwary, pirating the life-force, building more four-captains to launch on the tortuous road to life, or to wear as grim bandoliers, tokens of status.

Through a haze of pain, I realised I lay curled up on the damp floor at the foot of the stairs, dying and angry. Angry with myself, with this shrouded one-captain Masq, most of all with whatever Hoproi were monitoring this, courtesy of Smart Alec.

I felt cheated, betrayed and, more than anything, stupid.

But my hand was near my head, and I was able to put the Qualagi's heart to my teeth and bite it hard, with all the remaining force I could manage.

Masq started up on its pallet, its body galvanised and shaking. Again, the frantic snufflings began.

I gnawed at the egg, desperately, like an animal. Flakes of it came off in my mouth, bitter and probably poisonous, tasting both animal and vegetable. I tried to work the pieces to the front and out with my tongue, but couldn't afford the time. I just kept gnawing, eating the Qualagi's heart.

Masq was driven to desperate measures, probably unprecedented measures for a one. It moved free of its pallet on thick sluggish legs, uttering little yelps of panic, a steady rhythm of wet snufflings now.

Our confiles were working; we could not use stars or powered weapons unless there were the right distractions—a total distraction, like the one now facing Masq.

I saw the heavy creature seize a sword-hook from an armour-lay and come tottering towards me.

I bit harder, in a frenzy.

The egg gave. My teeth sank into a sour pithy core. And I stopped dying, just like that.

I lay exhausted, retching, my throat burning with alien poisons, but alive.

Masq was almost upon me, staggering now, shrieking, distressed to the point of insanity.

Total distraction.

I worked my sword-hand in a single violent spasm of command. Too violent. My body-sword leapt from the deck, slapped my palm so hard that fingers were broken, but it leapt into Masq's chest to do its quick programmed Z-dance of evisceration, and was out again, back in my palm.

I cried out as it hit, dropping it. More fingers broken. The setting had slipped up to five-fifths, non-Human tolerances.

But I had won. In the shock of heart-loss, Masq had not used its confile to block my sword. I lay there, sobbing and giggling, hysterical with relief, while Masq gurgled and died a few feet away, its hot alien blood bubbling on the boards.

Chris and Heber were at the head of the laneway when I got there, probably alerted by Smart Alec when the motes signalled the outcome.

I grew annoyed when I saw them, feeling in some vague way that they should pay too for their part in this.

But they greeted me well. Chris immediately set about splint-locking and bandaging my broken hand, while Heber gave me a vitaliser from their field-kit. Then, together, they helped me back to Joab's, giving small reassurances now and then as I hung between them in an exhausted stupor. At Joab's, even as I crossed that brightly-lit threshold, home safe, I promptly lost consciousness.

Tamari nursed me for two days while I lay unconscious, till an assignment took her off to Wenna, deep in the Impact.

I was sorry to miss her, but I knew I'd see her again soon, both for the exclusive I had to give her and for something more.

Joab himself brought me word that Smart Alec had gone to space for an indefinite period; no one knew where.

I smiled at that. The big warmonger wanted me to cool down a bit before our next confab. He feared revenge.

True, that had been among my waking thoughts. He had followed his own ethos; I would follow mine. But my conditionings and totes and several long sessions with my dag, going over Hoproi imperatives, worked away at this. I had known about Hoproi. Even with Masq coercing me from afar, I had only myself to blame.

And I had my rewards. My life, for one, and you, Timon, as well as the confile, stars and body-sword, all kept as payment for services rendered. Tamari had been quick to lock these away, knowing their worth, before Chris and Heber could take them back. No doubt they had expected to pick them up from Masq.

Though the two choi had made strong protest, four Darzie Purple-and-Blacks in full hot-glass armour had miraculously appeared to keep the peace on the premises till I recovered. The choi, unable to make an executive decision while their master was off-planet, had sullenly departed.

I owed Tamari and Joab for that call to Lucq-Sverre. I was now the best-armed clogue this side of Wenna, and I wondered how my identikin, Rael, would greet the news. A confile and the story of my adventure on the *Beam* would up the price on any contract. Rael would either panic or be extremely civil when we met.

But I wasn't worrying. That was for the future, and I loved the uncertainty. Most people never know the shape of their danger.

The great surprise, Timon, was the communication from you, from your tomb-ship out there in the deeps. T'lenbenbo said you were interested in the nature of life and death. Let me tell you that I have become something of a specialist.

I felt that, at the very least, I owed Smart Alec a song. I had Ero bring me my instrument and my dag, and set about composing the most jaunty ballad I could manage under the circumstances: a song about death, Human death.

But even before I finished it, a message arrived from Smart Alec, brief and no surprise at all.

> *Hey, Hollis,*
>
> *All is forgiven, yes? Rael's contract finito! Had his chance; he warned off for good. You my special friend, amigo.*
>
> *Now the best part. I have located the mortuary ship of the Ol our Salman friend mentioned. We've got things to discuss, Hollis. This whole new ballgame. The Ol wants to meet you. Oh, boy! Have I got an adventure for you!*
>
> *Smart Alec.*

I smiled when I read it, and wondered what Tam would say. Timon, it seems I'll be bringing you this account myself.

Some folks just can't keep out of that vital margin!

Privateers' Moon

USUALLY THE HOUSE sang. It was built to make music out of the seven winds that found it on its desert rise. Vents in the walls, cunning terraces, cleverly-angled embrasures in the canted terrazo facings drew them in; three spiral core-shafts tuned them into vortices and descants, threw them across galleries, flung them around precise cornices and carefully filigreed escarpments so that more than anything the house resembled the ancient breathing caves of the Nullarbor.

Which many said was Cheimarrhos' intention, that his great granite and limestone pylon was nothing less than an inverted network of caves set in the sky, chimnies and vaults and inclines in a structure such as Sumer must have seen, or Ur of the Chaldees, or Teoteochan of the Toltecs.

Paul Cheimarrhos called his house Balin, and on the day he finally showed me the roof-field there was a stillness on the red sand beyond the large deep-set windows, a lull I could not help but take personally, knowing Paul as I did, as an omen of some sort, as if my presence had caused it to be.

And, accordingly, as if unable to bear that terrible quiet, the middle-aged, incredibly vital Three-line tycoon talked about winds. Obliquely but inevitably. As we walked along the polished limestone corridor of Gallery 52, Paul rounded on me yet again, fixed me with his piercing blue gaze.

"When was the last time, Tom?"

"Only the once, Paul, three years ago. You used to come out to the coasts. I was here for the Anderlee hearings, but never got this far up. There were too many of us."

"The Anderlee thing, yes. I'm sorry." The polite show of regret quickly vanished from his eyes. He was too excited. "Then this makes up for it. Today is unusual, Tom. We usually get one of the four. The brinraga reaches this far north, and leftovers from the angry red-sky larrikin. I tune them down to gentle house-guests, mere palimpsests. Balin can do it. I'm so glad you're here."

We reached a corner window and looked out on the desert once more, but on a new vista entirely, stretching red and empty to the horizon.

"We even get spill-off from the sanalatti at this latitude, can you believe it? The experts say it's impossible but I know better. It's why Tyrren and I chose this spot, this exact place. I know the Soul when I feel it. Those scatterlings are unmistakable."

We stood looking out on the empty desert and I couldn't help but wonder how he did view my presence. Portentously, no doubt—the visitor who had arrived on the first windless day in four months.

"Are you familiar with the name Memnon?" he asked.

Knowing Paul Cheimarrhos' interest in antiquities and the ancient Mediterranean civilizations, I welcomed the change of subject.

"One of Alexander's generals?"

But of course Paul had been talking winds. He laughed, throwing back his thick mane of silver hair so it shifted like a magnesium shower along the shoulders of his cobalt house-robe.

"You are thinking of the general who led the Persian Greeks at Granicus. No, I mean the Colossi of Memnon, Tom. Two seated statues of Amenophis III on the Nile banks near Thebes. Some still believe they were designed so the sunrise and sunset winds made them sing..."

"Sing?"

"A plaintive hooting song, yes. But that was an accident, nothing more than a freak thing. Others claim the Great Pyramid sang before it was sealed, that the engineering equations covered that. Some say Djoser's pyramid at Saqqara did the same, that Architect Imhotep was master of the micro-zephyrs, expert in a whole secret art of hierocantrics. These tales are apocryphal. Balin exists and does all this. David Tyrren worked with me on it."

I made a sound of acknowledgement to show him I knew what pretty well anyone did, that the great architect had worked on the house, pylon, monument—though I knew that Paul had done all the initial layouts himself. It was his own design, despite the careful elaboration that had made the design a reality.

We were walking again because that filled the silences, turning up into Gallery 55-B, working our way to the final upper levels, to the elaborate totemic roof-field at the pylon's crest where the wind-banks stood and the rows of strange acroteria were laid out like memorial pieces in a graveyard in the sky.

I needed to see that field, to find out if Paul Cheimarrhos had in fact done what David Tyrren suspected, and had—after much agonizing—revealed to Council at long last. It seemed I was in time.

Gallery 55-B was blind, no windows there to show the desert and sky in its twin infinite registers of red and blue, just cool limestone and granite—part of a wind-race when the vents and conduits were aligned and operating.

The whole truncated pyramid of Balin was a wind-trap, a man-made mesa over three hundred metres high, full of cave-chambers—every one part of some cunning, precisely-reckoned equation—and with a 'cemetery' field on its flattened crest. With its canted sides, its cavetto cornice and taurus moulding, it did look very much like the pylon of some great ancient temple gate never completed, never given its companion pylon or connecting wall, with no temple precinct at its back.

We turned into the wide transverse apron of Gallery 60, and there it was, laid out before us under the hot blue sky: the summit field set all over with shimmering, totem-like acroteria, tall blank ceramic and stone pillars, some elaborately painted, others bone-white and glaring in the sunlight, pierced with fibrile openings, set with airfoils and sonic wires.

It was exhilarating to see it all at last, and deeply disturbing—for at the very centre was a shallow basin, like a radar dish thirty metres across, and at the middle of that, so I believed, so Tyrren had confirmed, Paul Cheimarrhos' great act of sacrilege.

The twenty-six wooden burial poles were ancient, without doubt the undeclared cache stolen from the Vatican collection decades ago, smuggled back into Australia in ones and twos, hidden in black market havens, finally incorporated into Balin, perhaps the ultimate purpose of the place, though I quickly put that fancy aside. It was hardly likely—the idea was a measure of my own reaction to being here at last, to seeing the forbidden relics set up so boldly on this vast open deck.

Each post had its special ceramic cap, making it safe from orbital surveillance. Tribal comsats scanning the site saw nothing more than a shallow dish set with one more group of aerodynamic wind-posts. The angle of curvature of that depression had to make oblique scanning impossible as well.

Paul stepped down on to the flat roof-field, looking for all the world like some notable out of antiquity with his blue robe and silver hair, a Chaldean prince or an Akkadian merchant atop a ziggurat in ancient Ur or Sumer. Or again—allowing my fancies free rein, trying for the composure I needed—some of the acroteria, the totemic signs carved on them, took me half a world away—from Mesopotamia to Meso-America, and I imagined I was an Aztec priest in jaguar headdress and cloak of human skin stepping out to officiate at a ceremony to Chac Mool. Balin invited such notions.

I was hurrying ahead now, heart pounding, so that Paul was following me, making no attempt at all to keep me from the depression at the centre. He did want me to see it.

Only when I remembered what hung in the sky high above us did I slow my pace, force myself to look less eager, more the casual visitor overwhelmed by this magnificent display.

Slowly, more slowly, I completed a gradual arc towards my real goal, giving Paul time to catch up. Then, together again, our footsteps ringing on the limestone flagging, we made our way to the very edge of the dish and looked down at the cluster of poles at the centre.

"Every now and then," I said, quietly in the vast expanse of air and light, "a National does something like this. Luna Geary. Tony Wessex. Dominic Quint. If we're lucky, Council learns of it before the tribes do. And I hope we're lucky this time, Paul, though I doubt it."

"The tribes who made those poles died out long ago, Tom. Bloodlines lost, only revenant DNA trace, languages forgotten. This is as fitting a place for them as any."

"How we see it isn't important, you know that. It's what they think. Every act like this—even suspected acts, rumoured acts—harm Nation."

"The tribes can't blame Nation for what I do. It's like privateering in the sixteenth century, the sea-captains operating on a special brief from the Crown. Drake, Hawkins and Frobisher were not legal agents of Elizabeth Tudor but they acted for her."

"A handy rationalisation, Paul. They held letters of marque. They *were* legal agents."

"No, Tom!" One hand cut the air, a dramatic sudden gesture, a measure of the force of his feelings. "It is exactly what I say. It's like Iran-Contra once was and the Special Operations Division of the CIA—"

"Secret agenda. Deceiving the populace."

"No! No!" Again the hand cut the air. "We are both privateers, Tom. Me with Balin, you on *Rynosseros*, keeping back details from all but a trusted few—"

"And having them kept back from me."

He took the reproach calmly.

"Who told you? Tyrren?"

"No. We asked for the plans. There's been a tribal satellite tethered above Balin for a month. That's what really brought me here."

"Ah, yes. My Star above Bethlehem."

"A very deadly star. It can't be simple reconnaissance. Not coincidence. I'd say a warning."

"Tom, I've had those poles for twenty years—"

"They're from the Vatican catalogue. The ones they didn't give back. Part of a *cause célèbre*."

Paul Cheimarrhos said nothing for a moment. His clear blue eyes flashed in the sunlight.

"You're well informed."

"You know I work with Council."

"Exactly what I mean! A privateer!"

"All right, a privateer myself. I didn't bring *Rynosseros*, but my coming here will have been monitored. That roadstop you specified, seven k's out—"

"Sabro."

"Sabro, yes. There were tribesmen there. No questions were asked; the continent-crosser dropped me; it was a routine transit stop. But I made no attempt to conceal my identity either. That would've alerted them. It's why I wrote instead of using tech. The invitation had to come from you."

"I'm glad to have you."

"Despite the omen of no wind?"

Cheimarrhos laughed. "Despite that omen, yes!"

We were silent for a moment, each of us alone with our thoughts, gazing down into the dish at the small forest of shapes clustered there. The glare from the hollow and the surrounding field made it easy to shut my eyes, to escape the ancient painted posts masked from the sky by their insulated caps. Paul's voice startled me when he spoke.

"Tom, I will tell you something you will not know. What Three-line is, or was. Thirty years ago I invented a device which could measure haldane force around individual Clever Men, show which ones could access the most powerful vectors."

I couldn't believe what I was hearing.

"Council knows about this?"

"No. Secrecy was a condition. I tell you only because of our guest upstairs."

I resisted the urge to look up. This was incredible.

"The tribes couldn't allow such a device to be used," Paul continued, "especially by non-Ab'Os. They bought the Three-line patent, demanded it, the plans and prototypes, made sure it remained a lost invention. They gave me this concession, on tribal land because the winds fell here, with enough funds and tech support to build Balin and establish a fortune in service companies.

"Those gave me a certain limited political power, as you know, which I've finally managed to pass on to my sister. Some of those companies help me acquire antiquities for my collection. The tribes permit them to operate. Ironically they made it possible for me to get these Vatican posts."

"But you've kept them," I said, my thoughts racing, wanting more than anything to ask more about the device. "You haven't given them back."

"As I say, Tom, the bloodlines no longer exist. Or if they do, only as revenant imposters. Who makes the claim? Who truly can? I do nothing more than collectors of antiquities and *objets d'art* have always done. For my pleasure I accumulate and keep safe objects which even their makers and inheritors might damage or ruin. It's the paradox of antiquarians and special collections everywhere." He looked into the sky. "My own Star now. I've been watching it. I have an antique Meade LX6 over there. It does the job."

"A laser strike at any moment, Paul. Balin might not survive it."

"What do they see, Tom? Nothing."

"There's more," I said. "Earlier this month, authorities in Rome finally confirmed that a special collection of burial posts—part of a personal gift to the Popes—was stolen in the years after Balin was built. An antiques smuggler was named; he named someone once attached to Three-line who has since disappeared. Nothing definite, all very tenuous, but your Star suggests how they're seeing it."

Paul surveyed the silent glade before us. "I've had them twenty years. I'm for this land, Tom, for all this. I'm the right sort of collector—"

"How they're seeing it, I said. You didn't even try to trade for such relics."

Paul laughed. "Oh, I made enquiries. But why haven't they confronted me? Sent in a search team, demanded entry, interrogated my staff? Why no formal investigation?"

I hesitated. He seemed perfectly serious; as if the obvious answer had not occurred to him? It made me cautious.

"You tell me, Paul, assuming you can trust your staff here, assuming they're not serving outside interests. I can only guess that it's part of the deal you made—what?—thirty years ago? This Three-line device you created would seem by its nature to weigh in as something between a holy artefact, something pertaining to the Dreamtime, and a National crisis. I'd say they made a deal with you at the level of their belief systems. Gave oaths, never expecting this. Now they have a dilemma requiring careful deliberation."

Paul turned away from the small forest of posts.

I followed him back across the roof-field, not wanting to ask my next question under the naked sky. Gain-monitors could never reach down so far, but scan could, and how did we seem, I wondered? Like conspirators? Very much Paul's privateers?

"One more thing," I said as we reached the open gallery that would lead us back into Balin's great mass. My heart was pounding as I said the words. "Did you hold back any Three-line knowledge? Plans? A duplicate prototype?"

"Of course not," Paul said, and was as closed to me then as a new moon, as the invisible satellite was—his Star, that sinister moonlet locked and turning with the world, geo-tethered by its micro-filament to the parent facility over the equator.

Paul Cheimarrhos smiled. "So serious, Tom. Come. We must not be late for lunch. Sarete is Three-line now. She might never forgive us."

"Paul, I have to know. The device—"

"Later. Come now."

There were six of us for lunch, and the others were already seated at the long cedar table before a breathtaking view of the western desert: Sarete Cheimarrhos, Paul's reputedly formidable sister, her dark-skinned Islander assistant, Naesé; to her left one of Paul's actor friends, the renowned John Newmarket, looking splendid in the Edwardian finery that was his Todthaus trademark, and next to him, white-suited, so urbane, the economist, James Aganture, agent for one of Three-line's longstanding European clients.

Sarete had been overseas during my visit to Balin three years before. I had heard a great deal about this celebrated woman; even Tyrren had issued several cautions. Now here she was rising to greet me.

If the flamboyant and expansive Paul could be likened to a messianic Beethoven cast in silver and blue, then his calm and elegant sister, with her black gown, long dark hair and sombre, appraising gaze, was something from the shadowed spaces of the El Greco that hung on the room's northern wall. She was ten years younger than her brother by all accounts, but the smooth untanned skin gave her a timelessness, a twenty year range of possibilities at least.

There was a smile, a generous one, but it never reached the eyes, and in the instant I knew that this pale, severely pretty woman intended me to see this duality of response. I was Paul's guest, the luncheon no doubt his idea. Just as Balin was completely his domain, the administration of the Three-line holdings was hers, and this had to be taking precious time out of a very busy day.

Rather than feeling affronted, I was glad of the hard honesty. There were probably enough lies in this great house already.

"Captain Tyson," she said as we shook hands. "I believe you and John know one another." I nodded and smiled at the actor. An answering smile softened those famous gaunt cheeks. "This is James Aganture, one of our European consultants." Aganture and I exchanged smiles as well. "And this is Naesé, my secretary."

A fitting assistant for her employer, I decided, an Islander woman, quite dark, middle-aged, with small eyes and small fleeting smile. Naesé rose, gave a slight bow of the head. I did the same.

We took our places. I was seated next to James Aganture at Sarete's right, opposite John Newmarket and Naesé. Paul spoke a word to Anquan, the major-domo, and joined us, immediately taking charge of the dinner conversation by asking James Aganture to bring us up to date on the situation in Europe.

The svelte, white-suited European did that until the food arrived, when the business of eating gave me an opportunity to study Sarete and the others, though I found it harder to do that than I expected. Thoughts of what Paul had said about his invention kept crossing my mind, and I was glad when the meal was over at last and I could adjourn to my quarters for siesta.

Around 1500 there was wind.

I was drawn from sleep by the deep swelling song, went to the windows and looked out, used house tech to bring different vistas to the wall-screen, one cycling after the other, every angle but where the posts stood.

It was thrilling to see and hear—the outward signs of Balin coming alive. The pennants and long windsock drogues at the corners of the roof-field stirred on their poles, the helium- filled outrider kites floating high above the house started shifting in the sky, inditing their signatures on the bright air. Spinner caps turned, the most sensitive of the sonic acroteria began to sound. Like some great ship advancing through time, trailing cloud-wrack and windsong, Balin was on its way again.

Tolerances were adjusted: within ten minutes the field was thrumming and whistling, within twenty howling and keening. From further down the great sloping mass came a deep moaning that meant one or more of the induction vents were cycling open, the spiral cores engaged, that power-cells were regenerating and airflow was being guided through the mighty house. There were corridors now where my casual passage from one room to another would vary pitch and tone, add a subtle difference to the house-song. This was Paul's great legacy. This!

I must have stood there for fifteen, twenty minutes, reading the land, studying how this structure stood upon it, considering what micro-climates might exist in its shadow. Then the phone chimed, drawing me back, and it was Naesé's face in the glass.

"Forgive the interruption, Captain. Sensors showed tech use in your quarters—we assumed you were awake. If it's convenient, my mistress would appreciate your calling on her in, say, fifteen minutes?"

The request did not surprise me.

"Certainly," I said. "I'll be ready."

On Balin's sloping west wall was a small open place like a col or cirque on the side of a mountain, and in the sun-trap made there was a walled garden, little more than some lawn and a grove of dusty orange trees.

A house-servant, Cristofer, led me there, opened the low bronze door and let me out into the tiny grove. The westering sun warmed the spot; the sloping planes of the wall-face came together above me in a gradual point, with stone wind-masks spinning on their pins in the vents.

The wind had strengthened, I noticed. The pressure systems over the desert had shifted—it was probably the brinraga which struck the parapet of the garden, stirring the fruit trees, whistling up the granite face to the vents above, where extruded murtains randomized the flow, altering its direction, tailoring it to the house-song.

Tyrren had built well. The massif of Balin sang but the garden was a pocket of calm, not only a sun-trap and a wind-haven, but also a place sheltered from the vast music forming all around us.

Sarete was sitting on a white wooden bench amid the trees, wearing a gown of dark green polysar and speaking softly into a comlink at her wrist. Though Three-line's Chief Executive, she apparently did much of her work from Balin, away from the coasts, privileged with the com tech that required. I marvelled at such easy luxuries. Near her, on another bench and using a lap-scan, sat Naesé.

Both women looked up when I approached, but Naesé turned her attention back to the scan display almost immediately. Sarete gave a polite smile and switched off the link.

"Thank you for coming. Paul considers you his so I won't keep you long."

I went to make some appropriate remark, but thought better of it. This audience was wholly on her terms; she had reminded me as much.

"We could not discuss it at lunch, but tell me frankly, Captain, what does that comsat mean?"

"They're geo-tethered, as you know. The logistics of moving them, aligning them—"

"Costs."

"Yes. They use them that way all the time, but it means filing deployments, getting clearances, logging variations. It's a busy sky."

"So I've discovered. It tells us how seriously they regard this."

"It does. It may be a routine shift, simple reconnaissance, coincidence—"

"Council sees it as a warning."

"Strong probability."

"Because David talked."

"No, Sarete. Tyrren told us nothing, simply confirmed what was already available through channels."

"Ah, channels. And do you think there is an agent in our midst?"

After Paul's empassioned evasions, again I found this directness refreshing.

"Can you doubt it? I would have thought infiltration preceded a tech commitment like this." And I glanced briefly upwards. "Given what Balin is, I would assume infiltration occurred a long time ago. This is unique."

"Agreed."

"How large is your staff?"

"Here? Seven including Naesé. All trusted. All here a long time. Some rarely go above. We keep house secrets, Captain."

"Your guests?"

"Possible. Unlikely. They will not see the...relics either. But what can that station do? I've been given general configuration data but I'd like you to tell me."

So you can make a decision, I realised. Make policy for Three-line.

"We read lenses deployed. It's probably *irijinti*. Given twenty minutes it could effectively demolish Balin."

"Which took eight years to build. Twenty minutes."

"Depending on intensity and duration. They sometimes move deployed like that—"

"Target the roof-field?"

"Easily. To a square metre, possibly less. But hardly their intention." I glanced at the Islander woman sitting quietly among the trees. "They'd want to commandeer the...relics."

"Naesé knows everything, Captain. Should I leave?"

It was such an unexpected question that I hesitated.

"You understand that I'm still making up my mind about all this?"

— 287 —

"Of course."

"All right. Then as Three-line you should. But only if it's a regular routine to do so. Anything could seem provocative now. Do you leave Balin often?"

"Occasionally. You like Paul, don't you? You're like him."

'Like' and 'like', both words revealing more about Sarete and her relationship with her brother than she perhaps intended.

"We understand something in common, something difficult, probably irreconcilable in our affairs."

"Ah, your role as privateers."

"Paul's word, Sarete. I suppose it suits."

"What would yours be? Patriot? National? Romantic?"

"Privateer will do."

"You have no satellite over your head."

"I do now. And for all I know I may have one for every Ab'O Prince I've ever dealt with as Blue."

Naesé looked up suddenly, made a hand-sign. Sarete raised a hand to excuse herself for a moment.

"Yes?"

"Foreman has entered the Manada."

"Excellent. Send on that." And to me: "Your advice?"

"In what capacity?" I said it to remind her of the levels that separated us, wanting the distinctions to matter. There were different values at work here; Naesé's interruption, this allocation of time, had shown me that.

"As a State of Nation man?"

"Persuade him to give the poles back. Or leave here immediately."

"As the Blue Captain?"

"The same."

"As Paul's friend?"

"Sarete—"

"As his friend?"

"I'm still deciding, but I'd say stay. Risk it."

"Really?"

"If Balin is struck and the reason is given as sacred relics, there are many who will not believe. The tribes are seen as ruthless aggressors, hostile to Three-line, to Nation, to all non-Ab'Os, displeased with past concessions because of a device Paul invented long ago—"

"Nation knows about the device?" It was the first time I had seen surprise on Sarete's face. The eyes first widened, then narrowed. Her mouth drew into a line. Alarm, disappointment, annoyance, I couldn't tell.

"No. Paul told me before lunch."

Sarete nodded. Her head lifted a fraction. She glanced out at an errant drogue—orange, red and bright blue—cutting the wind forty metres away. I could not be sure, but I believed she did it to conceal something contained in her gaze—or perhaps missing from it. More than ever she resembled the El Greco madonna above the cedar table.

"What will you do?" she asked finally. "As yourself?"

I smiled, watching the kite as well, seeing it as some complex bird-equation worked out upon the registers of air, left to find resolution, to create its own fragment of meaning. It occurred to me, absurdly, very fondly, that Paul would probably have names for his kites. This was his house, his ultimate statement. Everything belonged, made for the homeostasis Paul Cheimarrhos needed, externalized in kite and corridor and wind-chase. In the burial poles in that shallow dish.

No wonder he had been glad to relinquish the operation of Three-line. Dreamer, idealist, monomaniac, he wanted none of it. Who knew what wonders, what pieces of self, Balin's vaults and chambers contained? This was more than a vast schema of the Nullarbor's Breathing Caves, those hundreds of miles of underground conduits, chambers, tortuous chimneys. This was a living extension of the man, every corridor, each framed vista and spinning wind-mask. Seeing it any other way just didn't begin to give the truth.

He had to continue, remain just what he was. He had no choice.

The kite, set upon its wall of air, mindlessly navigating, brought that in, gave that answer. Just as he had set it there, given it that brave and futile task, serving, being, till it was finally destroyed and replaced, he had put Balin upon the land, raised it up for its time. His statement. His stand.

I watched the woman whose lift of head, whose gaze had led me out to the kite, realizing, imagining what she too had been through, the years of dealing with this reality of Paul's.

She had seemed hard and alien before. Now she seemed trapped and committed, caught at the moment of deciding. Caught in the choices of others. As I was. As Paul might yet be.

"I will remain here till that satellite moves away," I said. "If my presence can deter them, provide another reason for not striking, then good. Do you mind having one more house-guest, Sarete?"

"It's not my place—"

"I'm asking you anyway."

"Not at all, Captain. It was good of you to see me."

Again the safe courtesy, the illusion of my having gifted her and not the reverse. She was alien again in that moment, and I found myself hating it, hating what she represented, this seeming lack of connection, the cool pragmatism, the failure to read or simply accept one set of equations because she had equations of her own.

I left the garden but did not return to my quarters. Instead I climbed the escarpment, gallery by gallery, to a viewing lounge close to the summit. There I stood amid the low ochre-coloured furniture, safe behind the thick glass, watching the sturdy outrider kites hanging in the sky and the long streamers of dust and cloud which boiled off this stone massif and converged at the horizon as lines in an endlessly moving yet strangely constant perspective.

The house-song was clear but at a comfortable remove—like an orchestra tuning somewhere else. I began to see the great structure as something to be maintained in that other sense, and wondered which of the staff members—Anquan? Cristofer? Deric?—might abseil down these vast faces, clearing wind-wrack from the vents, carrying out service checks, replacing fixtures, tuning the structure in fact.

I recalled the meeting in the garden. Could Sarete not see the virtue in this vital reality? It was an eternal act of defiance, this great demense, a continuing statement of identity, personal for Paul, but for Nation too, a crucial affirmation.

Or was that just my bias?

I tracked clouds to the horizon and considered equations, found myself coming back to the new integer, probably the ultimate issue in all this.

What a device Paul must have created to be allowed such a thing as Balin.

I sensed someone at my back, turned to find the calm figure of James Aganture standing near me, the cultured, white-suited gentleman from our luncheon. Like me, he was gazing out at the desert, deep-set brown eyes filled with admiration.

"Amazing, isn't it? It just goes on forever."

"Yes."

He moved in beside me, stood watching the sweep of the land, the boiling ribbons of red dust streaming past, gloriously capped now with low cloud, trimmed with gold by the afternoon sun.

"You lose a sense of such scale in Europe," he said. "It might be said that here you lack density, weight of identity, but that surely is changing. We stand upon a great symbol. Another waits above. It is a testing of symbols really."

During lunch I had imagined what conversations I might have with someone like James Aganture, had wondered what talk there could be with that avenging moon fixed in our sky, steadier by far than those trembling outriders at the ends of their cables. That he had almost read my thoughts startled me.

I nearly smiled as he worked his way into what he wished to say, Sarete's question, no doubt Paul's. My own.

"Will it strike?" he said.

"Will it strike?" I answered him.

"Pardon me?"

"I ask you the same question, James. And I wonder why you remain when the risk is so great."

Aganture's well-shaped mouth turned down, his dark eyes widened. "A visit planned weeks ago. I did not know until I arrived."

"Of course. So will you leave soon?"

Aganture did not answer. He waited a few moments, bringing his long hands together before him, then came to it again. This time he was even more direct.

"What will Council do, Captain?"

"Excuse me, James, but I'm still not sure what you mean."

"I know you are here as a representative of Nation," he said. "I know about the posts. It is why I was sent."

"Sent? By whom?"

"The Vatican, Captain Tyson. I am Monsignior James Aganture, the instrument of the Cardinals Elect and the Holy See."

"Hm. Your interest here, Monsignior Aganture?"

"Please. It is James. And it is merely a visit to negotiate for full restoration of the posts."

"How did you learn of them?"

The man smiled. "Our own investigators. There are those who saw to the actual handling who could later be bought. Thieves prosper in this. Once they had disposed of the merchandise, theystill had information to sell. Once we had the principal's name—"

"Cheimarrhos would be an expensive name, I imagine?"

"Expensive enough. We had made reasonable guesses. Balin is world-famous. Our host is known for his collecting. And he is hardly subtle. Once he even enquired about direct sale; he is on public record as a 'liberator' and 'protector' of relics."

"Does Paul know?"

"Not yet, Captain. I have not lied, simply withheld. I am a senior operative for a legitimate corporation dealing with Three-line in other areas. It was easy to come here. My first loyalty, however, is to Mother Church. I thought it best I learn of Council's intentions before declaring myself. And, yes, we know about the satellite. It will settle eveything, ne?"

I met the churchman's gaze. "I hold Blue. I have full executive authority where Council is concerned in matters like this."

"I suspected as much. Will you order him to return the posts?"

"Order him? First you ask what will Council do, as if it can do anything, and now this."

"Captain, please. You will understand, I hope, when I say that you are not altogether the best choice here, ne? You are Paul's friend, you are a champion of National interests. Is it not provocative to have sent you?"

I fought down my anger. "Sent, Monsignior?"

Aganture frowned, clenched his hands again, though elegantly, without force.

"But...forgive me, Captain. I naturally assumed that was how it was. I know you can travel where you will—"

"James, go and declare yourself. Make your official representations and get away from here. That is a very deadly star."

James Aganture nodded, studied the striations of dust and cloud beyond the glass, the sharp and startling perspectives of the sky.

"Yes. But this is as delicate as it is urgent."

"You are here as a businessman as well as a friend."

"Exactly. We mean to buy them back if we can. Make them a gift to the tribes."

"Ah, I see. All good business, Monsignior Aganture. Curry favour for the Church."

"Captain, it really is not that simple."

"Of course. It isn't for Council either. They can't help themselves. I like to think I am here for simpler reasons."

"I see that now, of course. May I ask what they are?"

"Paul is an old friend. At a distance, it is easy to take positions, have the luxury of serving ideologies and some greater good. I came to make up my mind. I needed to know."

"Yes. I'm glad we've had the opportunity to speak. And please—"

"Your identity is safe for the moment."

"Thank you, Captain. You must understand that I cannot afford to jeopardize my organization's trade dealings with Three-line. It is difficult to know what to do for all of us."

"Keeping options open just in case."

"Very awkward, yes."

"You have spoken to his sister?"

But I saw at once that he had, that this was Sarete's answer too, and more of her questions. James Aganture was here at the invitation of Sarete Cheimarrhos, I was suddenly sure of it. I left him no time to answer.

"You ask for confidentiality. You impose upon my duty to my friend. I now ask you to tell him who you are. I give you until, let us say, dinner this evening, Monsignior, yes?"

"Yes. Yes, Captain."

And I left him, found my way down to my quarters on Level 42, welcoming the option of silence and opaqued windows, needing the time to consider what really had to be done, thinking of the Three-line device and wondering what my real reasons now were.

At sunset we saw the view that made Balin renowned across the world—the Inferno, great boiling lines of cloud plunging towards the horizon, meeting in the pit of the sun, drawn like great rivers, like tattered banners, cohorts, cables of molten gold laid upon the sky, the angles of a mad geometer hauled and hurtled into the blazing, settling point like a rehearsal for the end of days.

Even Sarete and Naesé were there for it. We sat and stood about the lounge and could not find enough words for conversation, no moment when the few comments made did not do more than force silence again.

There was only the sky, the whole world drawn to that single ravenous point. And finally, as if in scorn, the sun closed its mighty eye in one slow blink, denying the clouds their lustre, turning them to lead where they sailed, streamed, panicked in the sky: you are too late, too late, little brothers, I turn my gaze from you all.

We subsided where we sat or stood, muscles loosened, sighs sounded above the rolling, healing frenzy of the house-song. John Newmarket tugged at his collar; James Aganture slowly shook his stately head. Naesé sat with what seemed like a rapt expression on her face, considering the changed world beyond the glass. Sarete saw me give a deeper unsounded sigh, allowed the faintest trace of a smile to touch her pale lips.

Paul turned to us all, stood with his back to the glass.

"The world has many great identifying winds, enabling winds, precise expressions of the pneuma. The simoom, the sirocco, the kham-sin, the monsoons and the santanas. Pieces of the patchwork.

"I accept the reality; I accepted the challenge as Imhotep did. Here is the codex that lets us read what it tells us: not understand, never understand, but know. Just take in and know. The wind moves upon the land. It completes an equation in the soul, resolves itself through only those devices nature has raised up, precisely designed, to read what such things mean. Us. *We* are the world's way of apprehending itself. We complete all that out there. Our affirmations, our emotions, are the lock for that great key. This house reminds us."

I smiled. Paul had uttered similar words at the Anderlee gathering three years ago. I was an easy convert; I used my own ship to affirm such truths in myself, such a rich and simple knowing.

"Tomorrow," he said, "there will be towers of cumulus and laze-lions all day, nothing like this. This is justice, Tom, for Fate having served up a windless man, trying to build some new Tarot here. So you never add this to your legend! *Comprendez?*"

"I do, Paul," I said, laughing. "I'll hobble you with eclipses and minor comets from now on. Nothing less!"

"Apology accepted, gracious man. And you, James?" Paul was exalted, magnanimous; it was a pointed gaze, laden with irony and fond reprimand that he gave the clergyman. James Aganture had no doubt confessed.

"We have riches, an embarrassment of all that humanity has wrought. Cloisters, scriptoria, great art collections, antiquities, centuries of sophistry and clever talk, the doctrines and arguments. Now I find the simplicity of my God here. I remember that my eyes are the windows of the first and last cathedral I shall ever know."

"Accepted. And you, Honest John? You've seen it before. Anything to add?"

I was interested to see that lean, spirited John Newmarket also looked abashed.

"I lost words for this ten years ago, Paul," the actor said in his rich full voice. "This must endure at all costs."

Which reminded us all and stole the edges from Paul's smile for a moment, though just a moment. Our host was not to be discouraged.

"Tonight we hold a starwatch in honour of our uninvited guest. We dress warmly. We go above. We find our personal monkey-moon and regale it, drag it up close, count its legs, tell our fortunes on its parts. I'll name every wind that troubles us. Yes?"

There was general assent, but I caught quick unguarded glances from Newmarket and Aganture towards Paul's sister, then found myself at the end of Naesé's own coolly appraising gaze.

"Dinner is at 1900," Sarete announced, and led the way out of the lounge.

Paul held back, like some captain reluctant to leave the bridge of his ship, and I held back as well, not surprised when his expansive mood fell away like the gold of the departed sun.

"Do you know what Aganture is, Tom?" he said when we were alone.

"A churchman."

"He told you!" Surprise and suspicion sat in Paul's eyes for a brief, flickering instant. "Well, he hinted at trade cutbacks. Direct dealings with the tribes. Circumventing Three-line altogether. All veiled, of course, the spineless fool!"

"What will you do?"

"About Aganture?"

"About your Star?"

"They'll do it, you think?"

I shrugged, not mentioning the device, determined to keep away from that topic for the moment. "You said it yourself earlier today. The bloodlines are gone. They may not care about the poles at all.

What you are becoming is a very useful example. If they strike at you, it's a warning to everyone else. They may need a precedent."

"Do you know who Newmarket represents?"

The question surprised me. "Newmarket?"

"A Tosi-Go subsidiary, a Three-line rival. A mercenary actor, Tom. *My* friend. Leave the posts where they are but sell them to Tosi-Go so the tribes dare not act. Not why he visited, oh no. Just happened to have been approached; thought he'd mention it like a caring friend."

"So what will you do?"

"No offers, Tom? Nothing from Council?"

They were bitter words, from a man who was trying hard to reconcile different realities. Forcing himself. Again.

"Nothing. I told Aganture. I cannot be who I am and come here without representing Council, but I do not follow their specific wishes."

"And what are their specific wishes, do you think?"

"I imagine to see you continue. To see Paul Cheimarrhos and Balin and Three-line survive."

"In that order? Well, two of those I heartily agree with, though I'm not sure I believe you. I'm no longer Three-line. It's an alien thing."

"You know what I mean. Council can't order you. They want you to remain as a symbol. That's your great worth to Nation. The posts matter because they put you and Balin at risk. That's how I think they'd see it anyway."

"Hm, well thank them for that. That much I can accept."

I discovered it was what I wanted, Paul believing that I was here for reasons of my own, out of friendship and personal esteem, for reasons ultimately as elusive and mysterious as his own. Learning of the Three-line invention had complicated the issue; I found myself needing to ask about it, realized how partisan I now felt, would be the moment I asked the questions that had tormented me all afternoon.

"What would you advise?" Paul said.

"What I told Sarete earlier. I'd stay."

"Good. The poles?"

"Hardly the issue."

"No?"

Perhaps I could ask about it. Paul had mentioned the device to me. Knowing my background, of my time in the Madhouse, he had brought it up. But again I hesitated, knowing that the moment I did ask, I was no better than Newmarket or Aganture.

"It's what I was leading up to earlier when you showed me the posts. It's the Three-line holding itself that concerns them. Not the company—this great house of yours. The concession was given a long time ago and it's become too celebrated, too newsworthy, too steady a slight. I would think getting you to admit to having the poles will be used as counter-propaganda to discredit you in National and International eyes, making you appear as someone plundering, stealing away art treasures for his own material gain. Pirate rather than privateer, Paul, the critical difference. Just one more exploiter and opportunist. I believe the satellite is meant to force your hand."

"They won't strike?"

"They'd possibly destroy what they're overtly trying to save, if that matters. It seems an unnecessarily dramatic thing, using a comsat."

Paul nodded, finally asked the inevitable question.

"Why haven't they mounted a land assault or at least done a search? Sent Kurdaitcha in?"

"Because they already have."

"What? Who?"

"Your guess. I told Sarete this afternoon. I would assume it was done long before they moved that station."

"But who?" Paul was genuinely amazed; it obviously had not occurred to him at all. Again I could see that the dream was being spoiled. "Our staff has been here since Balin was built. Cristofer and Deric came in from other Three-line holdings—"

"Exactly how I would have done it. Planted someone when Balin was being built. Before then, if I could."

"Kurdaitcha?" Paul was making himself accept another way of thinking, a hated spoiling pragmatism.

"To keep an eye on Three-line initially, yes. To make sure no new inventions came along. To keep an eye on acquisitions."

"So what happens when I don't frighten?"

"A land strike, I'd say. They must already have verification that the poles are here, so it depends on how willing they are to sacrifice a handful of relics. If they can't neutralize what Balin represents by embarrassing you, they could use the posts as an excuse to destroy it anyway. A regrettable casualty. But whatever this is, Paul, it's the final stages of some carefully planned action."

"Yet...you came."

"One Coloured Captain may suggest all the Captains are involved. And the other Captains will come if you ask. It may stay their hand. You're a symbol, Paul, just as we are. Not Balin, *you*. There can be other Balins, other ways of doing this. It's you we can't replace. And that's my comment, Paul, not Council's, not the Captains'."

"Yes. Yes. Thank you, Tom."

We watched the streaming, shadowing chains of cloud racing for the edge of the world. The words of my handful of desperate questions were right there, held back, barely held. It might have been the sight of Paul that stopped me. His hands were fists at his sides. He sighed.

"Tom, I have changed my will. In view of circumstances. Regarding Balin. Will you be notary to it, take the signed original back to Council?"

"Paul—"

"Whichever way it goes, Tom, I want it officially lodged. Yes?"

"I'll be glad to take it."

"And see the terms are carried out?"

The fists, the tension across his shoulders, were more vivid than words, than any other persuasion.

"Yes. If I can. Yes."

"I'll give it to you before dinner. Before we go above. Come to me in my quarters at 1840."

"At 1840."

And he left me standing there with my questions, with sudden relief and self-reproach, and before me the rushing, frenzied, cloud-wrack chasing the sun, lean, iron-grey conquistadores seeking gold but succeeding only in building night in the far hidden places of the sky.

After showering and changing, by the time I knocked on his door at precisely 1840, I had put my curiosity aside, determined to wait, trusting that he would reveal more later.

When the door slid back, I entered and found Paul sitting on a divan by the windows, the last of the day a tattered ruin of light behind him in the western sky. He was examining a Canopic jar, one of a set of four 18th Dynasty pieces resting on a low table to one side, replacing the jackal-head stopper. He set it down as I approached, took an envelope from inside his black and gold house-robe, and handed it to me as I sat down.

"A formality, Tom. I've involved Council. It's fair they know my position."

I put it in a pocket of my sandsman's fatigues and went to tell him again that it was a pleasure, but Paul spoke first.

"Tom, why were you in the Madhouse?"

I tensed immediately, feeling the barest edge of panic, residual reflex fear. It never failed to surprise me. This was the question no-one asked, that was only rarely answered if ever, that now permitted my questions to him. Paul asking it mattered. I didn't give any of the usual replies.

"I don't remember. They would not tell me."

"They?"

"Tartalen. He was in charge. One day I'll return. I'll ask."

He kept at it. "You should."

"Why, Paul?"

"There is a mystery about you. You're a National and a sensitive. The field is strong—"

"The other Captains—"

"No. I've met them. They've all been here at one time or another. You're different."

"Paul!"

There was a knock at the door.

"Dinner and starwatch," he said. "This will be Sarete."

"Paul!"

"Gain monitors, Tom. We may have an audience. Later."

We went to the door, found Sarete and John Newmarket waiting there.

"We go to study our demon," Sarete said, pleasantly enough. "The others will be waiting."

"On to the feast!" Paul said, and together we headed along the corridor, the house adding our variables to its ongoing song.

Dinner was an easy affair, first Paul then John Newmarket telling stories, James Aganture giving his views on the future of Mother Church in view of new tech embargoes recently imposed.

Finally the dishes were cleared away, and the six of us started our climb to the summit. In the Gallery of Record, Cristofer and

Deric gave us jackets; warmly dressed, we stepped out onto the dark windy field.

It sang under the moonless sky. Under our feet, the house moaned deeply to itself. We crossed the plateau, the acroteria looming beside us like funerary totems, bleached bones keening in the cold brinraga. We made our way through the restless shapes, keeping well clear of the central depression, heading for the northwestern corner where Anquan had set up the old Meade telescope, its short thick barrel pointed at the sky directly overhead.

"The refreshments, please," Sarete told the old major-domo, raising her voice above the rush of wind so she could be heard, and Anquan went off with Cristofer to get the evening's collation.

Paul sat on the low stool before the telescope and used the eye-piece, made some quick adjustments.

"I have him," he said, his voice strong above the air-flow. "Very wicked-looking deployed like that. They really do know how to use psychology. Who's first? James?"

The churchman moved to the stool, settled himself and peered through the eye-piece. Paul stood beside him, looking straight up, silver hair streaming in the wind.

"See it?" he asked loudly so we could all hear. "The red lights are mainly tactical—'barrican stars' to frighten us. Tom will confirm it. They're supposed to light up like that just before a strike."

"Really?" Aganture said, moving clear of the stool. "Is that true, Captain?"

"Yes," I said, studying the small group as best I could, dark shapes, blowing shapes, wanting to ask Paul about his comments earlier, concerned that we may have been overheard and interrupted deliberately, deeply worried by what that might mean.

"Your turn, John," Paul said, and the actor took his place at the telescope.

"It does look angry," was all he said.

Paul laughed. "It wants us to think that. It's trying to be hot and raging up there, but in reality it's a very cool thing, very calm."

Newmarket rose and moved away. "I've seen enough. Captain?"

"Sarete?" I said.

"No, thank you."

"Naesé?"

"No, Captain. Thank you."

I positioned myself on the stool, and after a split-second of auto-focus saw the *irijinti*, saw it again in actual fact, since I'd seen the displays Council had at Twilight Beach, began matching its configuration with other comsats I had seen up close this way, started when Paul whispered at my ear.

"The Canopic jar," he said. "is a second prototype. Get it away from here. Say a gift!"

The wind sang about us. Possibly no-one heard.

I made myself stay calm, my heart racing as I peered up at the evil red lights.

It explained everything. Not the posts. Not Balin. Not just those things. Far more serious, much greater danger. Paul had broken faith.

The jar, a duplicate. *He had used it to read me!*

"Paul—?"

"Finished already?" he said, speaking for the others to hear.

I rose from the stool. "Let me get my configuration lists. I still say *irijinti*, but I want to type it. I can almost make out its markings." My voice sounded steady above the wind.

"I'll try for a better fix," Paul said, calmly enough, taking his place at the eye-piece once more.

I hurried from the field, entered the Gallery, ran down the ramps towards our chambers. My footsteps echoed on the polished stone, set a desperate percussion into the air-flow.

The palm-lock to Paul's rooms had been keyed to me, no surprise at all; the door swept aside at my touch. I crossed the softly lit interior, immediately went to the four jars on the low table: monkey-head, falcon-head, human-head, jackal—seized the jackal-head, removed the ceramic cap, saw the dull black tech that gave it its extra weight, the recessed contacts and displays.

What had it shown? What?

"I will take that, Captain."

I turned at once. Naesé stood in the doorway, a laser baton in her hand.

"I'm sorry. This is a gift to me from Paul. Ask him."

She raised the baton, aimed it at my heart.

"Captain, I am Kurdaitcha in the final moments of a very long, very old mission."

"You—"

"Colour, Hero status, mean nothing compared to my brief, do you understand? Without that jar and the contents of the envelope in your pocket, I will be sung. I dare not fail. Save your life."

"The envelope contains Paul's will."

"No. His will was lodged with Nation long ago. What you have contains blueprints for what you hold in your hands. Look and see."

I placed the jar on the divan, brought out the envelope and opened it, saw words and schematics.

"Yes?" Naesé said. "They are mine. Paul's life might still be yours if you hurry."

I threw the plans onto the divan and ran for the door. She let me pass but called after me. "Captain! Wait!"

I ignored her, running for the ramps, needing to get Paul from the roof, away from the telescope and the field and the line of sight of that deadly watcher, aware that it already had all the commands it needed.

I saw the result of those commands as I leapt out upon the field, a thread, a wire, the tiniest filament of dazzling light connecting Balin for just an instant to its attendant moon, then the tearing scream of its brief and deadly anger above the keening windsong.

I did not need to go out to where the telescope had stood. There would be time later. I waited by the door as the three figures came to me across the windy field, Sarete in the lead, head raised, cool and detached, resolved as ever, yes, leading them, John Newmarket and James Aganture to either side, eyes downcast, ashamed.

As I watched them approach, their faces lit from the doorway, I heard Naesé at my back, panting lightly from her run. She did not have the jar or the plans; she no longer held her weapon.

"Your mistress has done well," I said.

"She has saved Three-line and Balin," Naesé replied. "She made a difficult choice. An only choice."

"What did Paul read, Naesé?"

"What do you mean?"

"With the contents of the jar?"

"That you are a sensitive. That's all."

"Nothing else?"

"Nothing else."

"I don't believe you."

"I know."

Sarete and her companions reached us, stopped before the doorway. Her words might have come from Naesé, from a script of exculpation they had jointly devised.

"He knew the consequences, Captain. He made a choice, without considering anyone, never consulting others. Something had to be done. I made a choice too."

More words than I would have expected. Still James Aganture and John Newmarket looked in different directions at the night. Only Sarete and Naesé met my gaze.

"It wasn't the posts," I said, so nothing was hidden. "There was a second Three-line device. A duplicate."

Aganture and Newmarket both looked at Sarete.

"Nonsense," she said calmly.

"Naesé has—"

"Nonsense, Captain. There was never a duplicate."

She knew. Of course she knew. Naesé did not say a word.

"I see. Privateering."

"What, this?" Sarete asked.

"All this."

"I suppose so. Not your kind, but yes."

"Not my kind, no. Never my kind."

I went out onto the field then, went to the where the old Meade telescope had stood, came back with the lines of blood painted on my cheeks.

Sarete grimaced with distaste when she saw them. "Captain, is that really necessary?"

"Tell her, Naesé."

The Kurdaitcha frowned. "He is Blue, Sarete. He has made vendetta against this house."

"You're joking. I am this house now."

"No, Sarete," I said. "I think you will find that Paul has bequeathed it to Nation. Years ago. Naesé can check."

"Ridiculous! That can be negated."

"Naesé," I said, drawing rage and loss into that small hard word.

"You don't understand, Sarete. Those signs. In front of witnesses, he has sworn vendetta. He can strike at anything to do with Three-line, at any ships coming here. Through him, Council can. You must leave here. All of you."

"This is not the end of this," Sarete said.

"No," I was able to say. "It is not."

On the desert near Sabro, there is a mighty house, a vast pylon set against the sky. Though left to Nation as a final bequest from the man who caused it to be, it is deserted now, neither National nor tribal, a monument at the interface. The great vents stand open; the structure howls and sings and braids the winds into endless tapestries, strange proclamations of desire. At the crest is a field and a shallow empty dish thirty metres across.

Once a year, seven ships go to that great house, the only ones who can since it is reached by crossing tribal land. The crews climb aloft and reach that field. While the crew-members do small acts of maintenance, the Captains sit in the depression and talk.

Sometimes there is a ritual of watching sunset, sometimes a starwatch. Kites are set upon the air, new pennants added to the dream.

At such times, coincidentally, no satellite ever crosses that sky. The comsats studiedly avoid the place as if contemptuous of something all too futile.

The Captains smile in the windy darkness or in the flowing riot of the dying sun. More than anyone, they know the worth of dreams.

They know it is never that.

Time of the Star

THE ANCIENT NAME for Airships is Eyreships, but most people never know this. They look at you oddly when you say it, and even more so when you tell them that the spelling for Lake Air, the ancient salt lake, is Lake Eyre. E-Y-R-E. It means nothing.

For a start, they confuse the infrequent Desert Sea of legend with the great man-made Inland Sea further to the north near the burning heart of Australia. Finally, when you've explained it carefully and they understand you at last, they will say something like: "Oh yes, Lake Air. The place where the Ab'O fleets fight. Where the wrecks are." But it's the word 'Air' they'll remember. Air and the ships.

This much you can discover from a postcard in the souvenir kiosks at Twilight Beach. Those busy little shops always have artists' impressions of the ships abandoned in the Air, or dramatic, so-called imagined scenes of the great, open-plan, vendetta fleets coming together over some matter of tribal honour.

Whenever I see these garish portrayals, or hear tourists talk of the dead salt lake in the south, I think of the times I have stood on the silent desolate beaches at Madiganna and Cresa and studied the wrecks way out in the salt, yearning to go out among them—and the one time I did go onto the lake and met a small part of my destiny during the Time of the Star.

It began with a postcard in a sense. A postcard and a comet.

Comet Halley had returned to the inner planets and was heading for perihelion, and in that period when it was in the sky, certain

Ab'O laws were in abeyance, some breaches of custom could be overlooked, traditions challenged and changed.

I was in Armfeld's in Twilight Beach, browsing through the comet material, enjoying an all-too-rare layover and some idle hours. I had picked out a postcard to examine from the Ab'O merchandise, an imagined scene from a famous battle held on the Air a year before, the collision of two great sand-ships in which the Ajaro Prince lost his life.

I was marvelling at the chance of a Prince dying that way, exposed and vulnerable as they so rarely are.

The ceremonial fleets which meet out on the dry salt-lake are allowed full use of holoform projections—ghost-ships for ancestors who have died on the Air—so the armadas are usually vast affairs, awesome spectacles of colour and display but with little substance. There might be as few as twenty core-ships to a side, and those scattered wide of each other so as not to foul their sailing canopies. But as they come together, projectors operating, a hundred ghost-ships might crowd the interstices, rolling along in front, kites filling the sky, making it a difficult and lengthy business to engage and destroy the enemy.

It is easy to see how the legends begin, of Anu and Coorina, of Bindakara, of how the Emmened fleet once fought all day, cutting back and forth through the phantom ships of the Wagiri seeking core-ships, only to find at end of day that there were no Wagiri core-ships at all, that the ghosts faded to leave an empty salt-plain littered with ancient hulks and detritus.

There are many such stories, with no one to prove what is myth or rumour or told from ignorance. All media and tourists are barred from the ritual fighting ground, and only a small number of Nationals have seen the battles there and come back with their stories of the great punitive formations. Now and then illicit photographs appear, or what resemble fairly-detailed satellite scan enhancements, but trafficking in such contraband images is a dangerous business. Still, as I studied the card, it was hard to look at the artist's representation and not see the photograph on which it was based. I could sense the captured moment beneath the linework and air-brushing.

"I nearly killed the men who took that picture," a voice said softly, very close to me.

"It is not a photograph," I replied, automatically, immediately doubting my words when I saw the tall fine-looking young Ab'O behind me. He wore a plain djellaba over soft fatigues, and ornate double swords thrust in his belt in the Japanese way.

"You know it is, Captain Tom," he said. "You of all people should recognise the Ajaro Airship *Baiame*. That is too close to what I saw to be an artist's rendering."

"You saw?"

The young man nodded. "I was on *Semmeret*. I saw my father and brother die, and I saw the Airmen pirate ship that slipped in to film the incident in between looting the wrecks."

I spoke my next words quietly. "Then you are—"

"Yes."

I replaced the postcard in the rack and walked with him out on to the street.

"But, Lord, how—?"

"I am John to you, Captain. John Stone Grey."

"How can you be here, John?"

"The comet. It is the Time of the Star. A Prince can dare such things."

"Your enemies would be glad to find you alone this way."

"No doubt. But there are reasons, and I will not be buried alive in Fire-on-Stone under all those traditions and never see my world. I have urgent business to discuss." The Ab'O raised the hood of his robe, hiding his handsome features, then made sure his swords were concealed.

I led him down to the sand-ship moorings, through the First Gate and on to the Sand Quay. Like most of the big coastal towns, depending on one's moods, needs and perceptions, Twilight Beach can seem large or small. Now it was too small to conceal this quiet young man, this most vulnerable and incredible of things, an Ab'O Prince without his entourage, without his Elders and Clever Men and his Unseen Spears.

We boarded *Rynosseros*. Rob Shannon was instructing our newest crewmember, an eighteen-year-old Ab'O youth, an oddly fair-skinned outcast named Buso who had joined us earlier in the week during this layover. Rob looked up from splicing cables with him and nodded.

"Mission," I told him, and made the finger-sign that said: "Watch the Quay. Be ready."

Then I saw that John Stone Grey was studying the Ab'O youth who knelt alongside Shannon.

"You have an Ab'O in your crew?"

"An outcast. He has no tribe."

John Stone Grey stared at the lad, probably six or seven years younger than himself, his expression unreadable.

"You fear a spy?" I asked him.

"No," he said. "I do not approve of an Ab'O who becomes an outcast."

We went below, and in the aft-cabin John Stone Grey sat at the chart table and seemed to relax at last. He covered his face with his fine brown hands, then removed them to regard me sitting across from him.

"My father and brother died in the Air a year ago," he said. "The Chaness are—at last reckoning—three times more powerful than the Ajaro. Several Princes had a betrothal claim on the Chaness princess, Chian, but ours is the oldest, the first, and had to be honoured or disputed. The Chaness Prince wanted his daughter to wed the Madupan Prince's son. We challenged the right. The dispute was taken into the Air and we lost."

"So the Madupan won Chian?"

"No. They should have. But it was more than the death of our Prince and my brother when *Baiame* and *Ptah* collided. Those ships were both flagships and each named for the god of creation in one of its different guises. A year's grace was made because of it, a year before Chian could be given over and before I could assume the title. During that year no new ships could be built. The battle would be resumed with exactly the same vessel count. That year expired four days ago, but now it is the Time of the Star and Chian chose me—a new Prince—as her consort."

"What does this mean, John? I don't know the full law on this."

"Many of the Elders did not either," the young Ab'O said. "But still they met and made a ruling. Stalemate. The Chaness and the Ajaro must fight again with exactly the ships left from last time, as if the year did not exist."

"So why are you here? I am a State of Nation captain."

"Yes, and one of the few captains who can sail his vessel anywhere near Lake Air without the Chaness and Madupan satellites destroying him outright. Chian's choice, claiming Star immunity, came while

I was away from Fire-on-Stone. I did not expect it, did not dream it could be possible, that she would be so headstrong as to defy her tribe. I had only a small group of Clever Men and Unseen Spears with me and I was out of my State. The Chaness and Madupan sent warriors and mind-fighters at once to stop my return."

"What of your entourage?"

"We used the shadow-warrior."

"A duplicate?"

"No. Not a duplicate. I am a younger son, the Anonymous Son. I am allowed a clone surrogate to take my place in the Japano shadow-warrior tradition. I have not had time to prepare one yet. But it doesn't matter. As the Anonymous Son I was never seen at the tribal fires. I did not become a known face during the year of waiting. I still have that advantage and another. I had a vat-grown andromorph conditioned to be me, to fool a monitor should such a device be used. He was with me and led my escort while I hid and then came here to Twilight Beach to wait for you. The deception worked. My enemies were halfway to Wani before my entourage was caught and destroyed."

"How did you learn of it?"

John Stone Grey touched his temple. "By implant. A signal sent the moment the shadow-warrior died."

"What do you wish me to do?"

"I have one companion, Captain Tom, a powerful Clever Man named Iain Summondamas, my last bodyguard and friend. He has been away from my side only twice: once as a temporary envoy to the Chaness for several months, once a year ago when he participated in the battle on the Air. The re-staging of this battle is in three days' time. I wish you to take the two of us to Lake Air and bring me to my fleet. It will be waiting there. We have only eighteen core-ships against the Chaness fifty-seven. I must be there to lead the Ajaro, to affirm that I am the Faced Prince, or I forfeit. Chian goes to the Madupan. The comet means nothing."

I studied the glittering dark eyes, the lean handsome face, the hands composed on the chart table.

"They will suspect immediately what we are doing."

"Yes," the Ab'O said. "They will. But only when we are near the Air. We are just another ship till then. Then it is too late. Your mandate is valid, the Roads are open to you and safe. The tribal satellites and our own ancient Ajaro facility know to watch. No Chaness or Madupan would dare strike at us. Once I am on your ship, on an official Road, under your protection, I am safe."

"Except for pirates and privateers. With carefully insulated hulls."

"That is true. That is the risk. But only when we are near the Air. When we have made it plain that our destination is that place and not some other."

I laughed.

"What is it?" the Ab'O said.

"To think that probably the only way the Chaness and Madupan can stop you is to use the very pirates who loot the Airships and photograph the battles."

"The Eagle Cleland Buchanan?"'

"He's the one."

John Stone Grey smiled. "I am an eagle too. My totem is the hammon-eagle. Buchanan will not stop us. Well?"

"I'll take the Ajaro Prince to the Air."

The Ab'O nodded. "I will not forget this."

"When will your Prince arrive?" I said.

The dark eyes widened. "What do you mean?"

"You are Iain Summondamas," I said.

The Ab'O smiled. "Of course I am, Captain Tom. And the Prince arrived several days ago. He is the young outcast we saw on deck splicing cables with your crewman."

I did not warm to the real John Stone Grey as quickly as I had the false one, though the Ajaro Prince was an intense and dedicated young man and promised to make the Ajaro a good Prince. If he lived.

As we ran towards Adelaide on the Aranda-Aidalay Road, the *Rynosseros* doing 80 k's under twenty kites, I stood with him on the forward deck, watching the wide gibber plain that flanked the Road on all sides, from time to time gazing at the slender figure beside me.

It was easy to tell from his remarks that he was the Anonymous Son, the younger son kept hidden at the tribal capital, with only the year that had lapsed in the company of Summondamas and the other Clever Men to ready him for what was soon to happen.

On some matters, he was still too innocent and uninformed, and there were moments when I forgot about his sheltered life, when his impatient questions became tiresome. Iain Summondamas tried to be there to spare me such moments, but John Stone Grey sometimes insisted, and angrily, that the Clever Man leave us alone together.

"My crime is being young *and* inexperienced, Captain," the Prince said on one occasion when Iain had left us. "What Iain forgets is that I must measure myself against as many strangers as I can. You, your crewmen, anyone we meet. He must not always be a filter to the world I see."

"That makes good sense, John. But Iain is the last of your bodyguard. Naturally he feels—"

"He is my only bodyguard," John Stone Grey said. "The others came to me when *Baiame* went into the salt. As Anonymous Son I had one andromorph and one Clever Man—Iain. The Ajaro are not a great tribe now. We must win or we will become extinct like the Wagiri."

"Chian chose you. That will force a great alliance with the Chaness."

"If we win at Air," the Prince said. "And Chian chose Iain Summondamas. Three years ago when he was Ajaro envoy to the Chaness for a time, they were close. She accepts me completely because he is my dear friend. Iain says this is not true, but I know better."

"Complex."

"What life is. Cleopatra, Helen of Sparta, Guinevere; men's love of women makes history. People dare things for power, wealth, ideas, all manner of reasons, but they sometimes do extraordinary things just for another person."

I watched the gibber flats, studied the kites, and brought my thoughts back to our journey. Even as we ran along the Aranda-Aidalay, I knew that in the south arrangements were being made with Buchanan and perhaps other renegade sandsmen to be ready for any ship changing course for the Roads leading near the Air.

With the Prince aboard, we had dispensation for constant comsat scans of the deserts we crossed. Several times during an hour, one of the crew—Rim or Strengi—would key in the Ajaro code and data would appear, telling us of any traffic in the region. We knew of the three Chitalice charvolants which passed us at 1042 on the second day a full hour before we met the vessels as they headed north.

It was reassuring that the tribal charvis barely bothered to acknowledge us, just a single banderole from the poop of the closest ship.

Iain Summondamas came on deck when the newcomers had gone. John Stone Grey followed.

"They knew a Clever Man was on board," Iain said, explaining the flag. "I sensed theirs—two. I wonder what they know."

"What can it matter?" I said. "We've carried Clever Men before. Even royalty. A registered ship carrying a Clever Man to his tribe is nothing to cause concern."

"Perhaps, Captain Tom. I cannot stop being my Prince's protector. He is all I have."

More and more clearly now, despite the bickering, I saw how strong the bond was between the young Prince and his adviser, bodyguard, weapons-master. And it was a two-way thing, a constant learning for them both.

When a look of concern crossed Iain Summondamas's face, I saw John rest a hand on his Clever Man's shoulder.

"We will be in time, Iain. It is our destiny." Then he faced me. "Captain, tell me of Lake Air."

"Lord, we have spoken of it—" Summondamas said.

But the youth cut him short. "Iain, I know what *you* have told me."

The Clever Man nodded and moved away, to stand by Shannon and Scarbo who were tending the controls.

"The ancient name for Air is Eyre," I began, "E-Y-R-E", then realised that, as Anonymous Son limited by the year of grace, John had never been to the fighting ground, that it was Iain who had seen *Baiame* die. I went on to tell him what many people did not know, that the vast salt lake was almost twenty metres below sea level in some places, and was even now the 'dead heart' of Australia that Professor Gregory had once spoken of, not the burning gibber and sand deserts further north. I could not tell what was new to him and what was known, but plainly my telling of it was as important as what I said.

One thing did fascinate him: when I spoke of how the 10,000 square kilometres of burning salt was the ancient flood plain for the river systems of the Diamantina, the Warburton and the Cooper, and told him how once all the inland rivers had sought to end there. Only twice in living memory had the Air flooded, and many suspected that the more recent Ab'O terraforming projects had interfered with the drainage systems and the great artesian table that fed the area. Now the Inland Sea to the north took most of the run-off from the northern and eastern rains, and the Air remained a terrible waste, almost totally empty of life.

John told me things in turn. He had seen recordings taken during the Air battles conducted by his tribe; he had the scans from his old Ajaro satellite of other actions on the lake. He knew the wrecks sunken into the salt, scattered across the immense fighting ground. He even recited the names of all the Ajaro charvolants which had been found amid the mirror-ships and rammed, left crippled and abandoned to the lake.

He said their names as he would a litany, and as he spoke them I turned to see Iain Summondamas watching his dutiful Prince, his eyes glittering with quiet pride and other hidden emotions, his own lips ghosting the words being said exactly as he had taught them. Too young himself to have done much fighting for his State, kept at the tribal capital by the side of a younger son except for his brief time among the Chaness and on the Air, he was thrust now into the affairs of the world: a chase, a vital mission, a pending battle to determine the future of one small world.

I understood more and more what was happening here: the completion of a forced growth, the dramatic changes, the levels of fulfilment being met and satisfied in both men.

At 1125, we turned off the Road and headed into the south-west towards the ancient course of the Cooper. The winds made it difficult for kites, so with John's consent we took the luxury of running on solar power. Scarbo put our silvered inflatables in the sky, four long wide sun-snares that kept the accumulators humming.

At noon, the pirates came.

We were on an old battle road, running between claypans and long steep sandhills red with ferric oxides and scoured by endless winds. We had scan going, and Strengi read an intermittent signal, the sort of indistinct reading that can mean anything from a freak power flux to regional interference to insulated vessels in hiding.

"Broken signal!" he cried, and we acted at once. In two minutes, Scarbo had the sun-snares down and had sent up death-lamps. Rim, Iain, John and I uncovered the deck lenses and harpoons.

"You know tribal policy, Iain," I said as we adjusted the deadly glass frames. "Will Buchanan's men use hi-tech?"

Iain shook his head. "No! Laser gives too clear a trace to the satellites. They dare not risk it. The Chaness could not allow it either. They would be incriminated and made to forfeit."

But no more discussion was possible. The Airmen pirates were suddenly there, two sixty-foot vessels in sand-ochre camouflage coming at us from either side down long open wadis. They had been waiting, primed and ready, but needed to gather speed, so we were past them before they reached the battle trail. All the same, they scored hits with their lamps, lenses and ballistics, and we were smoking at the bow and trailing a land-anchor hanging by its cable from an Airmen harpoon lodged near our stern. Once the anchor's barbs caught on an outcropping, Rynosseros would be lost—capsized or badly crippled.

But fortunately, for a time, the battle trail was straight and reasonably smooth, and Shannon steered a careful central course, though the Airmen did not mean to let that happen for long. With no other kites aloft than their twisting, flashing death-lamps, the low armoured and powered ships gathered speed and started closing. Behind us, the anchor dragged, bouncing and sending dust curling up. That at least was in our favour, for it concealed our position and gave Iain and Rim time to cut at the cable.

Above us, one of our death-lamps exploded, a direct hit, and another drag-line harpoon glanced off the starboard edge of our travel platform, then bounced back.

The Airmen were careless to have risked such a shot in the dust haze, for one of the raider ships ran across that deflected land-anchor and damaged itself. Strengi reported one of our pursuers dropping back. Meanwhile, Rim and Iain sawed at the cable.

While they worked, John Stone Grey, still dressed in the fatigues of Buso the deck-boy, came to me on the poop.

"Can we pull that anchor in?" he asked. "Ease the cable tension?"

"A major gamble, John," I said.

"They will not get it free in time. Your ship."

Gamble against gamble. I considered the Airmen strategy: a stretch of flats to get harpoons in then rocks to catch their anchors afterwards.

"Tell them!" I said.

The youth ran to Iain and spoke. The Clever Man glanced up at his Prince, then immediately changed actions. Rim fed the harpoon line through an open two-hand winch while Iain guided it.

The anchor came towards us as the line shortened.

Both men worked in a frantic double-handed motion about their cranks while John Stone Grey guided the line. Scarbo gave assistance too once tension was off the harpoon shaft, working it back and forth so that if it pulled free it would tear out less of our hull. Though the spring-barbed head had opened on impact and would still cause us great damage, it might pull free rather than turn and capsize the ship.

Shannon steered; I managed the lenses on the poop and sent flashes of burning light back at the unseen Airmen ships.

"Rocks on scan!" Shannon cried, loudly so Iain and the others could hear. "Five k's."

Now we would know. Iain and Rim winched furiously; John Stone Grey fed in the cable and hacked at it with Iain's short-sword; Scarbo pulled at the shaft. The anchor was four metres out, sending up a great cloud of dust which boiled along the battle trail and hid our attackers, though all our death-lamps had gone now and there were two more burn points where the light metal plating was buckled and the paint blistered.

There were shouts at the winch. The anchor was clear of the desert, ours to use as a weapon once the line was free. Scarbo immediately returned to the cable-boss, fitted two more lamps and our old Javanese fighting-kite. Iain and Rim hoisted the anchor up to where they could aim it, while John still worked at the cable.

I felt the uneven terrain under our wheels and sighed with relief.

"One ship only!" Strengi called up from scan. "They've definitely lost one."

We could see that was so with the anchor no longer raising its hull of dust: one Airmen raider still closing, its companion somewhere far behind amid red dunes, no doubt with a crippled travel platform.

I fired a small hot-pot harpoon back at the pirate vessel. It went wide, and the Airmen captain increased speed, obviously wanting to get in range of another land-anchor shot or their own hot-pots before we could prime and fire again.

"Now!" John cried, as the cable gave way, and the captured anchor went over the side.

Through the dust from our wheels, and the sun's relentless glare, the Buchanan crew may not have seen our retrieval of that iron claw earlier. Now they saw it coming back at them, and there was a choice of seconds: to go over it or swerve aside.

The raider swerved, but the battle trail had narrowed and the ground was broken and uneven with sand-drifts. As the craft began to topple, the captain applied more power, but it was too late—the Airmen craft disappeared into the sandhills. We barely heard its death roll above the roar of our own wheels.

"Scan clear!" Strengi called, and we relaxed at last, dividing up into our different watches as *Rynosseros* ran on through the harsh terrain.

The Chaness had tried subterfuge and failed. Now there was only the lake.

We approached the Air on its eastern side, along the graded battle circuit beside what had once been the Cooper. We ran between sandhills, below salmon-pink sandridges and knolls flashing with gypsum. Now and then we crossed remainders of the ancient Cooper watercourse, wide flat gullies, some green with lignum and samphire amid the white sand-crests, showing where an Ab'O bore had been sunk in the old way, others ragged with saltbush and nitrebush and strange clumps of never-fail.

Halfway through the afternoon, the sandhills cleared at last to reveal the immense glaring expanse of the lake itself, stretching to the horizon. There was no chance of seeing the Airships in this searing haze, with the sun a lid of burning mercury above a chrome land.

I brought up my old National map, a yellowing laminated facsimile, and placed it with the new map Summondamas had provided.

To the south, hazy in all this space and light, lay the vast sweep of the Madigan Gulf, and other landmarks with their ancient National names—Sulphur Peninsula, Pittosporum Head, Artemia Point, Jackboot Bay.

I turned the deck-scan fully on macro, trying to find any trace of those magical places. Such names had replaced far more ancient, prehistoric tribal names, I realised, just as those on Summondamas's chart had banished ours almost from memory.

Beside me, John Stone Grey surveyed those same distances unaided. "It is a place of lies," he said, and I wasn't sure how to take his words.

On the poop's port side, Iain Summondamas was using the other scan to examine the land ahead. Before I could ask John what he meant, the Clever Man stood back and pointed to a beach of sand and salt seven or eight kilometres away around the flat shoreline, where the road started to dissolve in the odd suffused light of a mirage. "There!" Summondamas said. "Go there!"

Scarbo had the helm and silently obeyed, shifting our course from the main road so we ran along another battle trail on the edge of the Air, travelling north to the Ajaro rendezvous.

A hot dry wind blew in off the lake, sent sand hissing in sudden plumes from the domed white sandhills and shifting sandridges on the shore.

We dared not trust our vision. Shannon and I used the scans, while Scarbo wore his desert glasses and steered us between the crests of fuming sand.

It was indeed a place of apocalypse. Bad enough when it filled with water in those rare times. Now, but for the bores and sinks, the condensation posts and the lonely clanking tribal windmills I had not seen but knew would be out there, it was a bone land.

I watched that beach for ten minutes, mesmerised by the wall of image-ridden light just beyond it, the ever-receding mirage.

Then there was a movement at my elbow. I looked up, and for a moment thought it was Iain Summondamas—the figure had that indefinable presence—but saw instead John Stone Grey. The lake was changing him. How could I have taken this light-skinned Ab'O for an outcast deck-boy? That identity had gone. Now John wore fighting leathers under his djellaba, and the twin swords were thrust into his belt. I dared not say it but he resembled Iain in so many ways, ways that were dear to them both and unspoken.

"You have been here before?" he said.

"Yes, John. A few times. Once I was allowed to witness mind-war on the Sulphur Peninsula. Big corroboree. Many Clever Men, many dragons. No media could attend, but they wanted National accreditation for the outcome. I came by tribal ship then."

Iain Summondamas had come up on deck also.

"Neo-Dieri?" he asked.

"Yes," I said. "The outcome made it possible to raise the new tribe. The Neo-Dieri."

"They are false men," Iain said.

"They did not ask to be cloned," I reminded him. "The Ulla are responsible. They found the Dieri mummy and gave the dead tissue.

They won the right to proceed, to restore that people."

Iain turned his dark eyes on me.

"They do not bring ships to the Air. The Neo-Dieri are not allowed ships yet."

"Worse than Nationals," I said, trying to make my point obliquely.

"Worse than most Nationals, yes," the Clever Man said.

I tried to change the subject. "The Neo-Dieri care for the lake, Iain. They sink bores and grow things. Sometimes the birds even come. The hammon-eagles," I added pointedly. "The kings of the sky."

Iain stared at me. He might have said "Vat-bred creatures!" were not that new strain his Prince's sign. He returned instead to the main point. "They are the corruption of an ancient people."

There was silence for a moment, then John Stone Grey spoke. "When the Neo-Dieri come, Iain, we will give them honour."

"They will have honour," Iain said. "Spoken honour is easy."

We discovered that the Ajaro fleet was already in position 20 k's or more out on the lake to the north. Only one ship waited at the rendezvous, standing quietly on the salt a hundred metres from shore. This was *Kuddimudra,* the one hundred-and-forty-foot Ajaro flagship, an eccentric painted and armoured charvolant with a stern coloured with dramatic orange flashes. Through half-closed eyes or at a distance, that stern did indeed resemble the tail of a hammon-eagle, though the vessel was named for the ancient water-demon of the Air, a different beast entirely.

Waiting on the shore across from the big charvi were the Neo-Dieri: four very dark, shorter-than-average Ab'Os wearing long desert robes. They stood near their modest camp—two wurlies, a battered condensation tower and four camels. John Stone Grey and Iain climbed down to the hard pan and went to greet them formally. They talked awhile out of our hearing, then John returned.

"It is hard for Iain," the young Prince said. "Sometimes he forgets. He tries to be an Elder for me, the father I did not often see. I have left him to make the arrangements with the Neo-Dieri. Can we see the Airship wrecks together?"

"I think we can," I said. "The light is less harsh now."

We left *Rynosseros* and walked several metres out upon the glaring surface of the Air, listening to the silence. The incredible emptiness made us lower our voices, brought awe, almost a reverence, welling up inside us when we did speak. I raised my pocket glass and peered down the hot metal tube at the horizon. At first there was nothing to mar the desolation, just the endless waste of white salt meeting a hot sky so pale a blue as to be an uncertain stained white itself.

I moved the glass from north to south, adjusted the magnification and tried again. Now what had been half-imagined darker motes dancing in the lake's searing shimmer resolved into the hulks of long-dead ships lifting out of the salt, curving lunate sections of hull, long skeletal prows thrusting into the sky, rusted broken stern assemblies. The sun and the wind had reduced them to ciphers and strange totems, had taken all meaning from them. At night the winds would race across the dead lake bed and whistle and thrum about the wrecks, lifting the loose deck plates, slamming them back and forth, soughing and crying through fused and shattered ports, whispering down the empty passageways, bringing salt and sand and a fleeting ghostly semblance of life.

In those rare years when the lake still filled itself from artesian springs and coastal rainfall, the wrecks would sit in a vast sheet of shallow water that glistened with a startling difference under the burning desert sun and moved to the ruffling breezes. Then the wrecks would be lonely twisted reefs painted with faded war-signs, crusted with verdigris and salt, and would for a time resemble sea-going vessels, the detritus of Salamis, Actium or Lepanto, shapes and forms from other places and other ages brought here to this ancient salt-sea, discarded from time.

I handed the glass to John but continued to stare out at where the wrecks were. Saying they reminded me of primeval land and sea animals, whales, dinosaurs, was not true. There was that other comparison, more recent, which always came first whenever I saw the postcard renderings.

"Aircraft," I said. "They're like aircraft."

"I know this," John said, hearing the term his way.

"No. No. Aircraft. Old hi-tech flying machines. I once saw pictures of a bomber aircraft buried in the desert. Big tail vanes like on some of those hulks out there. But with wings."

"I know," John added. "For the sky. Heavier than air, right? Like the shuttles." He sounded accepting but I knew it was an enormous conceptual leap.

"That's right. They are still used in parts of the world. In the great museum collections or as craft of State."

John swung the glass along the horizon.

"There are hundreds of them," he said, marvelling. Though he had seen pictures and recordings and knew the statistics, he was seeing them for the first time in reality.

"You're looking at lifetimes of tribal wars settled out there," I said. "Thousands of men, hundreds of ships. Great open-plan fleets, the new ones navigating around the wrecks of the old, leaving more wrecks behind."

John handed me the glass. "It is some joke, Tom."

"Yes," I said. "I think of aircraft, and here they are in this dry lake, fighting in the Air."

We laughed, then stood in silence. I had time to study John Stone Grey, to consider him as I did the lake, as part of this world.

There was something about the youth that impressed me, that stirred my admiration, a recognition of the worth in what is new and young and untried.

"Most people lack any sense of destiny," he said and caught me watching him. "But not you. Why?"

I began speaking of my time in the Madhouse and how it had changed me. I told him how I had made an oath when I was incarcerated there, coming to self-awareness and objective time-consciousness; of how I vowed quietly, in spoken words, there in my dark place that linked me to all times, all places and possibilities, that I would live as Alexander the Great was said to have lived, for the moment, for the instant couched in the promise of forever; that I would take risks, be reckless when it felt good and vital; that I would never be afraid to feel. I explained how it was an easy promise to make then, with all of my life coming back to me like that; but it wasn't simply the sort of pledge the reprieved man makes, a temporary provisional thing, short-lived and insubstantial.

I knew I would dare things, do things, strive at least, and knew that this would equip me to deal with not just the Ab'Os but all men. It was a divine moment, the sort we all have but often cannot fully grasp; a moment when the psyche is balanced and eloquent to itself, when it sees and knows what cannot be said. Having unlocked the door of my madness, I had such an instant. I knew how it had to be.

John Stone Grey listened, not speaking, not challenging, but seeming to accept that I believed what I said, measuring me as he did anyone he met. He thanked me afterwards and gave me an inquiring look.

"Do you think I am a man of destiny also?" he said.

"I have no doubt of it, John."

"How do you know?"

"Heart knows," I said, which he accepted as he had the rest.

Iain Summondamas had come out on to the lake and was standing a little apart, talking softly with the Neo-Dieri headman, Si Akara, and his three tribesmen. Now the young Prince turned to him.

"Iain?"

The Clever Man turned at once. "Yes?"

"Tomorrow you must stay with *Rynosseros*. You must wait until this action is done."

"No, Prince! I must—"

"Iain! Si Akara and Tom Rynosseros are listening. I have good reasons. You will stay with *Rynosseros*. Please accept this."

Iain did, but it caused him anguish. I watched the salt, not wishing to add to his shame, and only turned back when John and Iain, Si Akara and his men had gone.

At 0600 the next morning, *Kuddimudra* lofted twenty-four display kites and moved out on to the Air. We watched her grow smaller until nothing was visible without glass or scan.

Three hours later, in the sharp morning light, the Chaness fleet came. At first there was just a strange edge to the silence, so that we peered out among the wrecks, feeling rather than hearing something across the salt. Then, through scan, low against the horizon, appeared a dark line, a jagged crust between brilliant white and blue, widening, thickening, starting to move forward through the scattered, lonely ship-reefs.

A great fleet under full ceremonial display, advancing to the sound of drums and bullroarers. More than a hundred ships, possibly two hundred, with nearly sixty core-ships; a great array travelling close together—more closely than charvolants normally dared. It was how the Spanish Armada must have looked, or the converging galleys at Actium, only here the sky was filled with kites insulated against mirrorflash, riding lines coated with powdered glass or with tantalum alloy edges. The air thrummed and throbbed with their approach.

Then, from the north, came the Ajaro fleet, smaller, much smaller, and with a great many replicant ships considering the eighteen core-ships the Ajaro had.

It was a dreamlike scene. In the glare and the hot dry wind, the ships began to lose their sharpness as the lake surface heated and the air shimmered. It was already 55° Celsius.

Si Akara came aboard and climbed to the poop carrying two letters. One he handed to Iain Summondamas, the other he gave to me.

"Do not open," Si Akara told me. "Open later, when this is done." He turned to Iain. "You open this when it is clear in your heart how this business goes, you understand? Only then."

Iain nodded, and the Neo-Dieri went back to where his tribesmen stood with their camels on the hard salt-pan. Iain studied the sealed letter, then put it inside his djellaba. He gripped the rail, put his face into the hood of the macro-scan and watched the ships out on the lake. I did the same, slipping my letter into my own desert robes for later.

The fleets were very close now. Kites were changing, a fascinating thing to see. Most of the brightly-coloured topkites and parafoils were pulled down. Drab battle-kites took their place, and sparkling death-lamps gorging on deadly sunlight, flashing and spinning across the approaching lines.

On our scans, we started to see some of the ghost-ships for the enantiomorphs they were, which made the sight even more dreamlike and unreal. Now and then a charvolant would approach a wreck buried in the salt and pass through it, dissolving around the hulk and resolving again on the other side as substantial as before. I could not help but get a sense of intersecting realities, of two worlds merging, as if the wrecks scattered across the salt waste were the future remains of today's battle or, conversely, the ghosts of those dead and broken charvolants were re-enacting their final moments yet again, restless in death.

The Chaness and Ajaro ships met. Even where we stood, the air throbbed with sound, with the drone of bullroarers and war-didjeridoos, the constant boom boom boom of the damning-drums, with the chanting of warriors and the deeper roar of so many wheels travelling on salt-pan and sand-flat.

And then, as if in a dream, like so much heat-born mirage on this ancient sea of illusion, the fleets passed through each other.

"First pass," Iain Summondamas said. "Nothing."

Which was not quite true. On the lake surface behind the parting lines of ships were tangles of kites and cables from the hidden core-ships, snared out of the hot sky by long boom-gaffs and spring-powered boomerang snares fired at random into the canopies of the enemy.

But it was an easy pass, as Iain said, and as good as nothing. This early in the engagement, kites and cables could be replaced, new snares and booms set.

The fleets cleared one another by several kilometres, slowly turned and began moving together again, gathering speed.

Near me, Iain did not move from the macro-scan. He knew the configurations of the Ajaro ships well, could probably tell which of the twenty or more flagships replicated out there was the real *Kuddimudra* with his Prince aboard.

The second pass was slow and deadly. Before the ships met, harpoons and hot-pots arced out from the advancing armadas, death-lamps flashed concentrated light into the overlapping canopies. When a burn point on a hull showed fire, or a kite went up in flame, the gunnery crews plotted carefully the likely position of their target ship amidst the myriad random and instantaneous replications that occurred.

It was a complex business. So many ships were attacking at the same time, causing damage and trying to monitor the replications of their own successful hits in the endless search for core-ships. Distribution patterns were the first priority but any worthwhile captain knew what a distraction that could be. They posted spotters and samplers, but for the most part took their chances with any vessel that came at them. Weapon strikes first, if possible, then ramming.

No ships died on that exchange either, but both fleets took smoking hulls with them and the ground between was littered with burning kites, dumped fragments of smouldering superstructure, and bodies.

Another pass followed, and another, and with each one the captains gained a better idea of the enemy's disposition, the pattern of ship details being reproduced. It did not take the Chaness long to know how thinly-spaced the Ajaro ships were.

As the day wore on, we watched the next six passes, saw four Ajaro core-ships rammed and left burning, saw how sections of the

Ajaro fleet winked out, leaving large gaps that made safe travelling spaces for the Chaness on the next pass.

The Ajaro were fighting fiercely. Eleven Chaness were either burning on the salt or trailing their formations. It meant approaches came less frequently as the Chaness used the recoveries and turns to re-position their ships. The damaged vessels simply missed a pass to tend to their wounds; the Chaness formation tightened, which they could easily afford to do. The Chaness fleet may have looked smaller than when it first appeared, but it was still many times larger than the moving patchwork of the Ajaro.

I was awed by the spectacle. Here was what I had seen in the postcards and simulations, the reality of so many charvis working together, not allowed to use their com and comp systems or scanning equipment, their stored power or hi-tech armament, just the mirror-ship projectors; forced by their own tribal rulings to rely on code weaponry and the constant burning winds of the Air.

On the other side of the sky, looking down on this waste painted in ochre, red, gamboge, mustard and chrome, were the unseen tribal satellites, monitoring the silent com frequencies to see no one transgressed, reading energy levels and recording every phase of the operations.

There were four more passes that day, and we watched each one of them till our eyes ached. The Ajaro fleet remained an open lattice, the mirror-ships duplicating every hurt suffered by the vessel giving them their existence, the core-ships trying to protect the hidden ship of their Prince by not gathering too closely about him. The lake was dotted with burning hulls and broken travel platforms, some ships toppled on their sides, others standing upright, burning or crippled.

At sunset, the fighting stopped. Si Akara and the other Neo-Dieri watchers around the shore lit bonfires of canegrass to tell the fleets that they must disengage for the day.

The ships did so, gladly, returning in the deep silence of growing dusk to their ends of the lake, moving as dreamlike as ever, phantom silhouettes against the westering sun.

It was 40°C and cooling, and around us the land was changing. The dunes along the shore glowed furnace red, antique gold and salmon pink, flashing with flecks of lime and gypsum. In the strong wind, the sandhills fumed at their crests like newly-born volcanoes.

Canegrass and spinifex along the ridges soughed and rustled, and the sun sank like a vast red dish through a chameleon sky, one moment burnt copper, then a stained smoky lavender, and finally, before evening fell altogether, a deep and mournful grey, the colour of wounded angels.

Iain left the scan only when the visibility had gone. He stood away from it, his hair stirring in the wind from the west, and seemed half in trance, staring at the darkness.

"Iain?" I said, knowing better than to interrupt but too concerned for him to stay silent.

The eyes turned to me. "I was not with him," he said.

"Then you have obeyed your Prince well. You have given him his chance."

The Clever Man stared at me. Then he walked away, climbed down to the salt-shore and went to sit with the Neo-Dieri. It was an irony that he should take solace there with those dark revenant folk, but our best silences were still questions and theirs were easy with ancient understanding. I heard voices talking over the soft grumbling of the camels, then the chanting started as the beacon fires burned low. During the night, the hot wind continued to blow out of the west, to set the lanterns creaking and the lines thrumming and bringing salt and sand and little sleep.

The next morning made the darkness of the night seem an illusion, another lie, a promise which had been broken. Again there was the salt-sea shimmering in the clear relentless sunlight, the strong dry winds, a world resolved into a fierce duality, the startling twin registers of blue sky and blinding white salt-flat. The landscape hurt the eyes, even through our glasses. At 0950 it was already 50°C.

Iain Summondamas was back from the Neo-Dieri camp, and stood on deck in fighting-leathers and djellaba, plainly a replenished man, his swords and an ancient Dieri war-boomerang thrust in his belt, a great honour. A peace of sorts had been made, and it was easy to speak to him as if nothing had happened.

At 1000 the ships came with drums and pulsing bullroarers, the Chaness in a vast concentration, the Ajaro in a carefully-spaced grid, hoping to divide their enemy and see replication patterns. Again the first pass was a cautious thing, a tentative sounding-out of ghosts and distributions. No strikes were made.

On the second pass, an Ajaro ship was hit with a hot-pot, and instantly across the Ajaro formation twenty mirror-ships wore the same plumes of smoke.

Death-lamps flashing, some Chaness ships closed in on where the hot-pot had landed, and soon they had crippled the core-ship which was left burning on its travel platform. Moments later, the vessel exploded and took its ghosts out with it. Across the salt came the racket of snaphaunce fire that meant close deck-fighting, a steady prickle of sound almost lost in the roar of the wheels and the damning-drums.

Then, with the suddenness of dream, it seemed that half the Ajaro ships were burning. Billows of heavy black smoke folded out from them, which told us that John Stone Grey had semaphored for smokescreens. It was a sound gamble for a smaller fleet to take against a larger, though it meant there would be no more co-ordinated moves until the smoke cleared and the semaphores could be read again. Now the ghosts were useless, hidden in the pall that rolled across the waste.

For several hours we watched the dark smoke haze, using the scans to see which vessels came and went out of the billows. I shared my instrument with Shannon, Scarbo and Rim, and Strengi too when he came on deck, leaving Iain alone with the other scan.

All of us on *Rynosseros* had studied the accounts of smokescreen warfare; we could guess what would be happening on the lake. Tactics had changed. For a start, the Chaness had accepted the Ajaro's strategy and were adding smoke of their own, having no doubt decided that they need only manoeuvre as a moving barricade, close together, to catch the Ajaro core-ships or at least foul their kites and cables.

We saw only the black cloud now, deepening and swelling forth, distending and being replenished as the winds of the lake drew it into streamers and eddies. Under that mantle, the desperate contest continued. With visibility reduced to fifty metres in places, it had become a much slower affair. Now the passes did not happen at all. The ships remained in the boiling cathedrals of smoke they had erected for themselves, so many fuming chalices waiting for encounters, ready now for prolonged deck-fighting as much as fire and ballistic strikes and ramming. We waited to see what was resolved, feeling excluded and helpless, in a separate world.

Then, near the end of the day, Iain cried out and staggered away from the macro-scan to stand steadying himself at the rail.

"Iain!" I cried. "What is it?"

"Mind-war!" he said. "I felt it. A ship came close to *Kuddimudra*. With many Clever Men. As they passed, they went into trance and killed four of my Prince's Clever Men. They know his ship."

"Are you sure? Could it—"

"The ship that did this is called *Kurdimurka*."

"I don't understand."

"It is chance! 'Kuddimudra' and 'Kurdimurka' refer to the same mythic water creature—the ancient serpent of the Air. It is the same matter the tribes ruled on before. If that ship takes my Prince, there can be his death but no victory. The contest must be fought again a year from now, with fewer ships and fewer men. All we do here will have been in vain."

Without saying more, we went to our scans, though nothing could be seen but the palls of smoke along the horizon.

"Where is John's ship now?" I asked him.

"The extreme left of the Ajaro line," Iain said, not needing his eyes to know such things.

"And is *Kurdimurka* going after her?"

"They are going to try! Their Clever Men are searching down the mind-lines for Ajaro shapes."

I exchanged glances with Shannon and Rim who stood by the scan awaiting their turns.

"Open your Prince's letter, Iain," I said.

The Clever Man brought his head from the hood and looked across at me. "No!"

"You know how this is going to go," I told him. "If the similarly named ships collide, you will lose both your Prince and the victory. Those ships must be kept apart! Open the letter!"

The Ab'O hesitated, then reached into his desert robes and pulled forth the document. He tore it open and read.

"No!" he cried. "No!"

I reached for the paper and he let me take it. Then, while Iain moved to the rail, I looked at what the young Ajaro Prince had written.

Iain,

This is my final command to you. At the moment you read this, you are Prince of the Ajaro.

Remember that everything I now do is to confirm this

fact. It is the Time of the Star and all things can be dared.
Chian must be yours.
    John Stone Grey

There were tears in Iain's eyes, and anger and bewilderment. "What can be done?" he asked. Then, as if deciding, he shouted down to the tribesmen crouching on the shore. "Bilili! Bring camels!"

Bilili, the Neo-Dieri jackman, came running, Si Akara with him.

"I want camels!" Iain said when the revenant Ab'Os were on deck.

"No, Summondamas," the Neo-Dieri headman said. "No camels on the Air. It is law!"

Iain turned to face me. "Captain Tom?"

"Iain, we can't! No ships can be added!"

"You read it," he said. "I am Prince of the Ajaro! It is the Time of the Star. All things can be dared!"

"The satellites!" I reminded him.

Iain snatched the letter from me and thrust it at Si Akara. "Read!" he said. "Go to com and call the satellites for us! Tell them! Time of the Star. Tell them!"

Si Akara read the letter and muttered to Bilili in dialect. Then Shannon led both men below to our comlink.

Iain turned back to me. "Go, Tom! Go now!"

"The Neo-Dieri!" I said.

"Go! They are true men, you say? Then they are tribal people. Let them get honour. Go! Go!"

It was madness, but I went to the controls, brought life to the circuits. Scarbo hurried to the cable-boss. On the commons, Strengi and Rim began hooking on kites.

"Use power!" Iain cried. "Kites and power! This is now the flagship. But we must be in the battle. Go! Go!"

Rynosseros moved forward, down the salt-pan on to the lake itself. The big wheels ground the sand and salt crystals, gaining speed.

I had never feared for my ship so much. I expected a strike at any moment, a quick decisive death from the comsats in orbit, the Chaness and Madupan especially, but from any of the units appointed to watch the Air.

When the strikes did not come, I added more power from the cells. Our canopy strained out above, the photonic parafoils drinking in the hot light, the death-lamps building their charges. Scarbo put up five colourful top-kites so we would not appear as a pirate to those watching above.

Rynosseros gathered speed, running at 90 k's, then 100. On the commons, Shannon, Strengi and Rim were bringing out weapons: the harpoons and hot-pots and big deck lenses. Scarbo tended the cables, jockeying the kites for greatest pull.

Si Akara was on deck too, yammering in dialect at Iain Summondamas, demanding to know what was happening, while Bilili remained below at com, sending our message to all who would listen.

"Si Akara," I heard Iain tell the Neo-Dieri. "You are pariah people. Do you accept that? Here is your chance to be a tribe. The Ajaro are nearly gone. The Ajaro-Dieri may be here on *Rynosseros*. Here!"

Si Akara was as uncertain as we all were, as no doubt the arbitrators of the Air contests were at this moment. But it was an appeal that worked, that spoke to the pride and secret hopes of the revenant headman.

"We will talk later," Si Akara said, which was as much of an affirmation as Iain Summondamas needed.

We ran across the lake on a surface smoother and harder than any Road we had ever used before. Ahead, the smoke seemed to be thinning before the hot winds, but it was an illusion. The ships manoeuvring in those swirls and eddies were adding to the billows at the level where it was still the most effective tactic, creating a storm-light to fight in.

On the quarterdeck of *Rynosseros*, Iain Summondamas went into trance, questing for concentrations of enemy Clever Men he could engage in mind-war, or use to locate *Kuddimudra* and the Chaness *Kurdimurka* before it was too late, before similarly named flagships engaged and the contest was voided. The rest of us used the time to don fighting leathers and prepare our personal weapons.

Ten kilometres remained. Iain came back to us and saw we were suited and ready. He went to speak but hesitated, then flung aside his djellaba to reveal fully his suit of lights underneath, the small mirrors sewn to the leather catching the fierce sunlight so that he was a blinding figure to look upon.

At three kilometres, we were already in the pall of roiling smoke, and our display kites were hauled down ready for battle. The lowering sun had become a sharp-edged coppery shield, as one sometimes sees it during a sandstorm, suspended a handspan above the horizon.

We could see the first of the ships, hazy shapes, ghost-ships—or perhaps the core-ships themselves, we could not tell which. It was a navigator's nightmare—constant half-seen forms, startling in their sudden arrivals and departures, making us edgy, ready to fire at anything.

We had no damning-drums to warn of our position, to signal our allies among the Ajaro, no horns, didjeridoos or bullroarers. We ran along in increasing gloom to the last known position of the Chaness *Kurdimurka,* trusting to Iain's reading of the whereabouts of enemy Clever Men to lead us to the Chaness Prince, to save John Stone Grey if we could.

Drums sounded ahead. In the boiling funereal haze, we saw a charvi approaching—two, three, a small formation of Chaness ships. As they saw us, the drums stopped, to deprive us of an accurate bearing.

"No Clever Men aboard!" Iain cried, which meant there was probably only one true ship, but which meant too that we had to trust our own judgement.

Scarbo made that decision, confirming my own. "The one on the left is it!" he cried, and at that instant three hot-pot harpoons left our guns, trailing snare lines. There were two hits, one went wide. The Chaness ship flared into flame at the bow and on the starboard edge of its travelling stage—our good fortune for it hampered both steering and gunners. The damning-drums started again, a summoning rhythm: enemy strike, Ajaro core-ship engaged, come to us Chaness.

We veered away at once, not having enough fighting men to engage in deck-war using spears and snaphaunce fire, and not wishing to get caught up with other Chaness ships.

I knew yet again how mortal *Rynosseros* was, how completely vulnerable, and how untried in fleet fighting we were.

The burning ship tried to use its flames to stop us but, with drive cables afire, it manoeuvred too late. I ran *Rynosseros* through one of the holoforms, an uncanny thing, then corrected our course for *Kurdimurka.*

Iain had readings, more mind-war a kilometre ahead. I steered blindly, with the pall hanging across the sky, fed by a furnace-red sunset now, and Iain Summondamas, the new Ajaro Prince, half in trance, murmuring directions in my ear. Mind-war was ritual war, but in this blind fighting it had a new vital role: to let Clever Men track other Clever Men, and the greatest concentrations were naturally attending the Princes. So *Kurdimurka* was hunting *Kuddimudra*; so we were seeking them both, by the mind-fields of their own searching Clever Men.

Another ship crossed our bow, an Ajaro sixty-footer, *Jusu*, trailing smokescreen at the stern. The small ship saw our colours and the command pennon and changed course to follow *Rynosseros*. At the same time, Iain flashed into trance and told her Clever Man captain who we were. *Jusu's* damning-drums started up and on the poop, clear of the cables, crewmen swung their bullroarers in droning accompaniment, calling ships: Ajaro come to us, Prince formation here.

Now the gamble started in earnest, for there might be conflicting signals, two flagships calling, dividing the Ajaro fleet, though I doubted the problem would arise. John Stone Grey, paradoxically hampered by his ritual entourage of Clever Men, would have stopped calling. The brave youth would be gambling that Iain had read the formations, read the Chaness Clever Men, and knew of *Kurdimurka's* quest for the Ajaro flagship. There were technical breaches here that possibly the Star could not excuse, but there was so little to lose and so much to be gained.

Another ship darted past, a low insulated hull painted in sand-ochre camouflage, slipping by us under six photonic parafoils.

"Pirate!" I cried, but the vessel vanished down a smoke tunnel of its own making, drawing coils and wisps after it like hungry hands.

Buchanan's men again, after more photographs, more provocative and contraband footage for the souvenir kiosks and archives of the coastal cities, for the curiosity-seekers of the world. The Eagle's men may have assisted the Chaness for a time, but now we had reached the Air, they were back to their usual operations, capitalising on what had to be a sensational development: the presence of a National ship in all this. Comp estimates were seven chances in ten of that raider making it off the lake back to Buchanan's eyrie, four in ten at that speed of colliding with an ancient wreck or another core-vessel, but that was a considered risk. Many Buchanan pirates had become wealthy men.

"*Kurdimurka* ahead!" Iain Summondamas cried.

Before us, shapes were moving in the gloom. Iain went into trance, gave a mind-command for *Jusu* to rush ahead, the least he could do for *Rynosseros* and her crew. Then he turned to us.

"The Chaness know what we have done," he said.

"How? Clever Men?"

"Who can say? A powerful Clever Man read it. Buchanan may have told."

"What of *Kuddimudra* and John Stone Grey?"

"We are too late. His ship is down."

"Survivors?"

"I cannot tell. I believe all the Clever Men with him are dead from mind-war. *Jusu* will lead us there, but it is very late now. *Kurdimurka* has gone. I get no readings. All the Chaness ships have gone. Tomorrow will be the end of it."

When we found the broken and smouldering hulk of *Kuddimudra*, the sun had dropped below the line. The smoke haze had vanished before the dry desert wind and the sky had lost the last of its soft rose and lavender twilight. The horizon was rimmed with the deepest verdigris where the copper sun had set.

Kuddimudra had collided with an ancient Airship wreck, not at great speed but with enough force to snap the drive lines, sheer the main pins and cripple the leading wheels. The hundred-and-forty-foot Ajaro ship had toppled across the ancient hulk and wedged there, and the Chaness flagship and its escort vessels had simply halted and sent hot-pots then warriors across.

There were three Ajaro survivors, all crewmen, and one of them told us how the Ajaro Clever Men had faced their enemies, greatly outnumbered, and died in savage mind-war. Then most of *Kuddimudra's* complement, John Stone Grey included, had fallen to Chaness swords and spears, a sad and futile end to the day.

But instead of a voided war, another year of grace, a re-engagement, and one more chance for the Chaness to put an end to the Ajaro tribe forever for their impudence, the battle would continue tomorrow. For better or worse, we had that much.

Jusu's damning-drums began once more, a forlorn sound, and led the remaining Ajaro ships to us. Slowly, moving carefully, the survivors came kiting in the darkness on a refreshingly-cool change of winds, steering by starlight and moonlight, manoeuvring in around *Rynosseros* and *Jusu* and the wreck of *Kuddimudra.*

In all, there were only five tribal ships left, and one of these, *Emu*, was crippled and would not be repaired in time for battle. Still, Iain gave her captain honour and did not order his vessel from the lake.

For an hour the exhausted crews of the ships helped to move the Ajaro dead and wounded on to *Emu.* Then we trudged across the salt in the relief of the cool wind for a meeting on the canted but largely intact commons of *Kuddimudra.* The captains and their weary crews gathered on the sloping deck, watching the lanterns swinging and creaking in the wind, waiting for Iain Summondamas to tell them what was to happen now.

The young Clever Man climbed to the damaged quarterdeck and introduced himself, for most of the veteran sandsmen had never been to the tribal fires and seen the Anonymous Son's bodyguard, this man John Stone Grey had committed them to honouring.

Iain began softly, but as he explained how he had become Prince, how the similarly named flagships had almost voided the whole engagement, his voice took on a greater and greater presence.

"Tomorrow we will win!" he said finally, and left a silence.

"Tomorrow finishes it!" one shipmaster said. "Unless we are cunning and greatly fortunate."

"You are Pina," Iain said, identifying the man, name-claiming him before them all.

"Yes."

"Then if what you say is what you believe, Pina, you can do no worse than trust me as John Stone Grey did."

"John Stone Grey is dead," Pina said.

"And gave us a day. And an unvoided war, do you understand? Tomorrow is his."

"Who are these others?" an old Clever Man asked.

"You are Bel." Iain said, and name-claimed him too. "Tom Rynosseros and his crew you know, as I've explained. The others down on the lake there, waiting for us, are Si Akara and his jackman, Bilili, from the Neo-Dieri. Our friends and brothers."

There was muttering and many hard looks. Several tribesmen peered through the darkness at the figures on the cooling lake.

Si Akara and Bilili did not seem to care. While Iain outlined his plan for bonding the tribes, the Neo-Dieri were studying the lake surface, Si Akara crouched on his haunches running a handful of salt crystals through his fingers.

Iain came to the end of his proposal. "I ask for a ruling on this," he said, and discussion began.

This was tribal business so I went down to where the Neo-Dieri communed with the lake. Si Akara looked up.

"Do you trust us older Ab'Os, Captain Tom?" he said, his dark eyes catching the lamplight from ruined *Kuddimudra,* the barest hint of a frown visible on the weathered face.

"This is your land twice over," I said. "I trust you."

Si Akara squeezed salt through his fingers. "The Ajaro must go from here. Twenty kilometres. There!" He pointed in the direction of the Neo-Dieri camp, where we had entered the lake.

"Why?"

"Nothing is lost if we do it," he said. "We will still be on the lake. Trust."

"In the morning. These men are tired."

Si Akara stood. "Too late. Now!"

"Tell Iain Summondamas."

Si Akara shook his head once. "The Ajaro will not accept it from a Prince who is still unproven. They will not accept it from dead men made hot again."

"Me?"

"*Rynosseros* is the flagship until Iain orders you from the lake, which he will do soon now to save you from tomorrow's battle. You made this possible, this chance, as much as the boy did. You must persuade him."

"There is so much to lose."

"Trust," Si Akara said, and gave me what was left of his handful of salt. The lumps and flakes felt moist, oddly frangible to the touch, and spoke their silent message clearly enough.

I went to Iain Summondamas. The captains and Clever Men were still deciding on the Neo-Dieri brotherhood, talking as if this was the tribal home-fire and there was a future for the Ajaro beyond the setting of tomorrow's sun.

In a low voice, I told the young Prince what Si Akara had said. He hesitated less time than I had.

"Enough!" he cried, and drew his sword, an echoing, superbly-deft action, so that all eyes locked on him at once. "I have ruled. It is done. We go to the shoreline and we launch our attack from there. Follow *Rynosseros*. Pina, sit down! Any man who disputes this may fight me, here, now, warriors with sword, Clever Men with mind-war. I am your Prince or I am not."

Everyone stared at the figure on the quarterdeck of *Kuddimudra*, where so recently John Stone Grey had fought and died. Iain's suit of lights shone through the front of his djellaba. His sword was a mirror curve of reflected lamplight.

The simplicity of the fierce ultimatum was inspiring. Iain had owned his Princehood. I looked to where Si Akara was standing with Bilili and saw the Neo-Dieri headman nodding with what I took to be approval.

Iain strode across the canted deck, through the assembled warriors and Clever Men. "We move in ten minutes," he said. "Follow my drums!" Then he went back to *Rynosseros*, taking with him four drummers and seven of the remaining Clever Men.

At the end of the allotted time, the drums and bullroarers began, and the small Ajaro fleet moved away from *Kuddimudra*. The twenty kilometres to the eastern shore took several hours due to the pace of the damaged hospital ship, and because of the dark wrecks which loomed like flattened twisted skulls, silent death totems, in the searchlights striking out from the atropaic eyes in *Rynosseros'* bow.

The salt under our wheels told the same story as Si Akara's handful earlier. The lake surface was more powdery than it had been. Our wheels made grooves rimmed with flashing, crumbling salt crystals.

What the Chaness would be thinking, what the comsats understood, we could not know, but they were reading six charvolants moving in convoy under non-photonic parafoils, driving across the Air with searchlights ablaze and drums pounding.

With five kilometres to go, there was water under our wheels at last, the beginnings of the flooding that had nearly spelt our doom.

Iain remained with the body of John Stone Grey during our journey across the salt, chanting softly at times, paying his final respects. But when our searchlights picked out clumps of spinifex and hummocks of canegrass on the sandridges, he abandoned his vigil and came up on deck to supervise the landing.

We did not leave the Air. Manoeuvring with difficulty in the darkness, our tiny fleet moored a hundred metres out from the Neo-Dieri camels and huts at the shore-camp, our wheels half-covered by water, with winch-lines fixed to posts hammered firmly into the hard pan, ready to haul our vessels to safety.

"How did you know?" Iain asked Si Akara.

The Neo-Dieri laid a finger along his temple. "The wind. The salt. The Star is here." He shrugged.

And that was the end of it, though there would be the scientific explanations—news of rains in the far north-east, a blocked or broken subterranean conduit to the Inland Sea, or accumulated waters from the sandstone catchment areas on the western slopes of the Great Dividing Range feeding through the water table, overloading the Great Artesian Basin underlying this most arid part of Australia.

When the sun rose the next morning, we were in the shallows on the edge of a glittering desert sea, with a strong warm wind blowing waves against the upper edges of our travel platforms and spray cooling our faces.

Out in that windswept expanse of water, the broken Airship wrecks were like strange ocean creatures, barbed, finned and vaned, their toppled hulls spired and arching in the bright sunlight. And in the distance, our scans showed the Chaness fleet swamped and stranded. Most vessels were in five metres of water at least and would never move again. Others, on hummocks of silt, could be given new travel platforms and other lives. But when the flood waters drained back into the hidden chambers of the earth, not one ship would be able to move from the lake on its own. Technically, they belonged to the lake now, though the Chaness were a powerful tribe and there would be negotiations with the arbitrators and special pleas made at the great corroborees, claims for Star dispensation. But most of the ships would stay all the same.

The Chaness had lost, and to the real kuddimudra of this waste, the enduring water spirit of this primeval inland sea.

We waited all morning, until the confirmation came through that the Chaness had forfeited and the Ajaro claim was to be upheld. Then and only then did our ships winch themselves ashore, the successful vessels helping to drag in the others until we were safely on the salt-pan before the sandridges facing the new sea.

An Airmen pirate ship, unseen in its ochre markings against the shifting dunes, suddenly came to life and, risking power, moved from where it had been recording our beaching activities.

This raider was not so lucky. The satellites were watching us closely and they received readings. There were flashes of hard light, the distinctive tearing sound of sky-born laser, and the Buchanan vessel exploded and rolled burning into the dunes, a final drama in all that had happened.

At 1400, we were checking out the electrics and cleaning *Rynosseros* down when Iain Summondamas and Si Akara came aboard.

"We should go," I told the new Prince.

He nodded. "My hand will always be open to you, Captain Tom."

"I value that greatly, Prince."

"Iain."

"Iain," I said, and smiled.

"One day," he continued, "I may send you a deck-boy, a younger son, to be taught the National ways. Will you accept this?"

"I will gladly, Iain."

Iain Summondamas nodded again. "One thing more. Your letter."

"You wish to know what John Stone Grey said to me?"

"No," Iain said. "While I do not know, my Prince still lives. He has something more to say. But you will read it when you leave here, while you can see the Ajaro-Dieri ships and the lake. Yes?"

"Yes."

We shook hands then, Iain first, then Si Akara, and as we did, the headman slipped something small and hard into my palm, his eyes telling me of its secrecy.

Then the Ab'Os turned and left *Rynosseros*. As they headed for *Jusu*, I examined what Si Akara had given me, then issued the order to move out.

We were running through the sandhills and fuming ridges under the hot afternoon sun when I drew John Stone Grey's letter from inside my djellaba. I broke the seal, opened it out and read.

Tom,

Win or lose, you have survived. I have survived in you and in Iain, for I must believe that he lives also and in great honour. Si Akara has given you a small thing, a stasis-flask with an authorisation. The flask contains some cells for cloning.

Grow me this andromorph. In three years he will be my age now, if the program is true: an unwed son's only chance, a father no other way. Let him earn his way on the Starship, where I learned what I needed. Call him Hammon.

I love you for what you have done, and wish I could be there now to tell you so.

John Stone Grey
Ajaro Prince
Anonymous Son
Hammon-Eagle.

I laughed and wept.

The Starship. Of course, the Starship. Airships and Starships!

Rynosseros moved at speed amid the dunes, with twenty kites in the sky and a strong lake wind at our backs. When I turned to look behind me, it was as much to hide the tears falling on to John Stone Grey's final words as to see *Jusu* and the tiny flashing mirror-figure of Iain Summondamas.

"Yes," I said. "Yes."

Everything we do is to complete our destiny—everything, word or deed—and as I held the stasis-flask firmly in my hand, it seemed that this fact could never be more true than at that moment, as we ran from the Air, safe again, full of the blessings of renewal and a sense of destiny at the Time of the Star.

Coyote Struck by

Lightning

HAVE YOU EVER looked at something and not seen it? Have you watched a street, studied a painting, looked through a window at a familiar landscape and only later truly beheld it for the first time, yet at first glimpse already had the sense, the premonition—somehow— of knowing it fully? Have you done this?

That is how it was that day on the coast outside Cervantes, with the rotors of the wind-farm turning—whoop whoop whoop—at the edge of town and the tribal people and Nationals bringing in their sand-dolls, and the smoke of bale-fires blackening the sky. It was Colios, a vital time, a pivotal time and, as so often happens, a largely unrecognised time.

The festival of Colios was a new thing, or rather a new-old thing, for its origins and workings were lost in memory and borrowed traditions. Like Koronai in Twilight Beach, like Tafa at Inlansay and Saralon at Port Allure, it fell during the first weeks of autumn. Every afternoon, every evening, there were bale-fires set along the outskirts of the town and up on the headlands where the desert met the sea, columns of black smoke streaking the sky, stealing the sky, linking up to form arches: roiling, surging cloisters through which the townspeople would come to add their votive dolls to the communal fires. The smoke of those fires became pinwheel vortices in the rotors of the wind-farm at the southern edge of town, became tangled, corkscrewed and flung away by the big ferris wheel at the carnival on Black Point.

It was all part of the payback of Colios, the new thanksgiving, since the Right to Fire, like the Right to Wind, Earth and Water, were all part of life's round. It was what you did. Rights had become rites, of course, the reasons for doing lost in the custom of doing.

So it was, a kilometre outside of the ancient town of Cervantes on the west coast of Australia that I followed the Line, allowed it to take me, directed it in fact so I could meet the Navajo semiologist-shamans from the university at Waso, here to study the newest skypainting in the A200 series.

They were down on the painting itself when I arrived at 1436, and when Ester, the local Council delegate, learned who I was, she couldn't help repeating the headline on the dailies back in town as she led me across to where they waited.

"They all have the same first name," she said, as if that were even more amazing than Navajo hatathalis being interested in these anomalies, even more amazing than the skypaintings themselves. "They're an old Amerind people. I never knew that."

"Ester, I know about the Navajo and Waso. I know about the first names."

"I just thought that being out on walkabout for so long you wouldn't—"

"Introduce us, please."

We walked out to this latest nazca, stepped onto the first scorch circle, sixteen metres in diameter, crossed it to the linking corridor, four metres wide, twelve long, reached the larger, thirty-two metre circle where three of the four Dineh stood holding their scanners and clipboards, watching us approach.

They had the same sanded mahogany skin-tones, the same obsidian gaze and tall, deep-chested physiques, with calm expressions on their rough handsome faces and, yes, though with different spellings, the same first names. And not Navajo, I reminded myself. Dineh. Their own name. The People.

I let Ester work through the introductions. John Dance and Jon Cipher, the older hatathalis, both had shoulder-length, steel-grey hair and badges of office in turquoise and silver pinned to their ochre-coloured university fatigues. John Mele, one of two younger field-service trainees and apprentice shamans, had his black hair back in a tight ponytail and wore Thunderbird and other yei motifs on his jacket. As Ester and I drew near, the fourth Dineh came towards us from the opposite end of the skypainting. This latest nazca was so large that it would easily take him a minute to reach us.

"*Ya eeh teh*, Hosteen Dance, Hosteen Cipher," I said when Ester was done, and to the younger man already with our group, "Ya eeh teh."

"*Ya eeh teh*, Captain," John Dance said, clearly pleased by the formal courtesy so far from home. "And first names here, Tom. Thank you for joining us. We know it is difficult for you now." He deliberately broke eye-contact and gestured at the expanse of the skypainting on which we stood, encompassing the fourth Dineh still on his way. "Again, scorching and staining both. Volatised pigments that possibly were not present before the manifestation, though how can we know? Many insist a chosen site is primed beforehand. What do you make of this?"

It was no empty question. "What you know. The usual thing. That it's Colios. New practices are being defined, meanings sought, as ever. The link to old crop circles is deliberate. But saltings, as you say. Fakery. A need for signs. John, I am no help here."

John Dance nodded and waited for the second apprentice to reach us, a most striking figure, I saw as he drew near, dressed less ornately than John Mele and the older hatathalis, just simple black fatigues, but an amazing sight with his long white hair and gaunt, scarred face, twenty years old made a hundred and twenty to judge by the head and face alone. It was a sight made more disturbing by the darting, sidelong glances he gave as he approached. Ester was clearly uncomfortable at the prospect of meeting him again; she excused herself and headed back to town.

"John," the older Dineh said, acknowledging him when he reached us. "This is Blue Tyson. The Tom Tyson we have spoken of."

"*Ya eeh teh*, Tom Rynosseros," the old-young man said, his gaze steadying. "I am John Coyote. Easy to remember."

"*Ya eeh teh*, John," I said, trying not to show any reaction to his appearance or the significance of such a surname for a Dineh. A coyote traditionally stood for evil and misfortune, for malicious pranks and things going wrong. Jass Lassi had mentioned this apprentice's name on his recent visit, had told me how four years ago, camping outside Teny in Dinetah, this young Navajo had been struck by lightning and survived. Only now did the connection make it more than a curiosity, another of Jass's stories.

Fortunately, John Dance read the moment and answered my earlier remark.

"Your three Madhouse signs are mental antecedents, we realise," the elder said. "Possibly placed within your consciousness by others. These are—as you say—no doubt saltings and fakery, but they mark the time. And, so that you know, Captain Tom, it is not the stigmata dreams of Totem Rule or your own signs that made us ask for you. Serafina images and Soul iconography have little to do with this."

"Then what, John? I'm at a loss."

"Let's say that it is your search among the world's symbol systems. Things like this." He gestured to where Cervantes stood beneath its pall of black smoke, to where the lines of its tribal and National inhabitants moved through the rising on-shore wind to add their dolls to the fires. That freshening wind made the pall curve over us even more than before. "We hear, too, that you have been assisting with various investigations."

"Hardly scientific, John. More the restless spirit."

"But intuitive and dedicated," Jon Cipher added. "Anything might help."

And, surprising the two elders, John Coyote spoke. "You are steeped in other signs now, Captain," he said, his gaze fixed on me. "Your medallion, your gun, your rhino head, probably that sword you wear. Even your Bladed Sun, so like our Zia sign—"

"Yes," John Dance continued smoothly, saving us from some old point of tension between Jon Cipher and this young, clearly precocious, strangely named man. It was there in how their dark gazes locked and held as the other senior hatathali spoke. "We accept these stainings, these skypaintings, nazca, whatever we call them, because they exist. Because of Colios and this re-focused practice of burning the sand-dolls on bale-fires. It is widespread now: during Tafa at Inlansay, Saralon at Port Allure. Even Koronai. Hosteen Cipher and myself see some pre-Tribation connection with the old European corn-doll rites. With similar autumn harvest festivals from all over the world transported and revived here, given new purchase. Even mixed up with the old plague practices of burning the dead."

"The Black Death?" I said, looking over at the line of bale-fires, at the happy if solemn parents and gleeful children bringing in what they had made to cast on the smouldering pyres. The westering sun turned them into silhouettes, shadow puppets, so many striking dolls themselves. "I've never thought of it that way."

"And similar plagues in history," John Dance said. "Smallpox plagues. Typhus. Cholera. Or the funeral pyres after any natural disaster: flood, famine, before the epidemics set in. Burning the dead during sieges. But all sorts of things. Rituals were often built around them."

"Burning the Guy as well," John Coyote added, making Jon Cipher's eyes lock hard on him again. He was clearly not meant to speak. "Old Guy Fawkes transplanted. Few dolls among the Nyoongar, Yolngu, Koori or other tribal ancestors, as far as we can tell, but clay dolls made so little girls could suckle them at clay breasts on the Mornington Peninsula—"

"Old customs always feed the new." Again John Dance continued as if the interruption hadn't occurred. "We accept these things because they exist. We accept you with no less wonder. Science may reveal it all."

"But patterning," I said, being careful because of the delicate situation here, because of the Line drawing to its end, because of how it had always been; needing to be careful because I had chosen wrongly in the past, made mistakes, committed butherum among the tribes as blundering National and bearer of a Hero Colour. Who knew what offence I might now commit among these Navajo shaman-scholars? These Dineh, yes.

"Patterning," John Dance echoed, and gestured at the skypainting on which we stood. "In all our legends there may be an answer for these."

Who really needs one?, I almost said, playing devil's advocate to myself, but the other elder spoke first.

"Be with us, Captain." Jon Cipher gave a wonderful smile, so much at odds with his manner towards John Coyote. "Share this. Let us talk. Anything."

And we all looked out at this corner of apocalypse: at the nazca leading off from where we stood, at the great cloisters of darkness building on all sides, creating the sense of being inside an immense black cathedral or within the fingers of a shadowing hand.

Or rather all but John Coyote did. I glanced back to find him watching me, his dark eyes filled with an alarming intensity, his face racked now and then by nervous tics. Here was a troublemaker, a maverick, someone quite possibly true to his namesake and probably worth speaking with alone. I nodded once, gift of sanction, then made myself study the skypainting again: the darker stained and scorched sand of the circles and the connecting corridor, noting the ancillary flourishes, the curious metre-wide swastika arms, two in the smaller circle, three in the larger. Overdone, if anything. Too much like the old twentieth and twenty-first century end-stage crop-circles before they were debunked. Trying too hard.

Jon Cipher might have read my mind. "We've been to Totem Rule, Captain. Guests claim to be having more stigmata dreams since the skypaintings. It's to be expected. We've seen the Image Books for the Soul and Ephemeris, talked to what mirage divers would speak with us. We know the iconographies for the Air and the Inland Sea. We've matched them to those from the Atlas Mountains and the Wadi Rum, from our own deserts in Dinetah."

"You must have considered the sats. Orbital strike."

"The obvious and most likely answer, but look at the precision, the detail. Not impossible, but improbable. Look at the colours—"

"Then something local. I hear that nearly all the nazca are on this side of the continent."

And John Coyote was there again. "There is a Gerias Kite tethered over near the rotors—"

Jon Cipher spoke in Navajo, quick guttural words, and John Coyote became silent at once. His eyes began their mad darting again, reading the landscape, refusing to settle.

"Excuse John, please, Captain Tom," John Dance said. "His youthful enthusiasm makes him forget our agreed protocols."

I nodded, and again deliberately scanned the distances of ochre and red sand that stretched to the horizon, again found myself marvelling at how these Navajo—these Dineh!—were out of Waso without the usual tribal supervision. The Waso concession was permitted under the strictest rules, the watch community there nearly fifty strong, but treated as if the Way of the Dineh, an amenable but contrary metaphysic, might disturb the local truths.

John Dance left me to my thoughts as we resumed walking across the vast shapes. After a few minutes, he spoke once more. "We know you are—outlaw now, whatever that means. Pirate. Privateer. We did not expect you to come. This might endanger you."

"I was never hiding, John. And they have never been far away."

"They're watching?"

"They will be watching, listening, yes. Have to, given what I am. As it is for you. You are watched."

"Yes," John Dance agreed as we neared the northern edge of the largest shape. The other Dineh followed several paces behind. "You will know why we're allowed Waso. They needed Teny in Dinetah, a place for looking back at here, for exploring the songlines and haldanes and Dreamings, all the Djuringa mysteries, away from this key locus. We requested the same, reciprocal liberties, to explore our Ways in due privacy, the curing and stabilising ceremonies we use to keep the universe in balance."

"*Hozho.*"

John Dance nodded, again pleased. "You know the word. Good."

"Superficially, John. There is so much to know."

"So we choose carefully, yes?"

"John Coyote mentioned a Gerias Kite."

"There is one tethered over by the rotors, yes. Someone has flown in for Colios, probably a Prince out of Lostnest to allow such a privilege. Such things are banned here, we know, but we're told that his small domain is off the coast, that there is a special dispensation. He could be the one. The only question is why would a tribal Prince create skypaintings?"

"What we said earlier, John. It's Colios. A new time, one still being defined, full of old things merged with the new. These are its forms, icons and sacred sites."

"Just people adding things to the mix, you think?"

"We're all desperate for meaning. You know that belief systems almost always start out simple and become complicated by the shrewder, more enterprising followers." I glanced back to make sure that Jon Cipher had the two younger shamans safely away from us. "John, I admit to being curious. Tell me about John Coyote if you can. A friend from Arizona once spoke of him. That name…"

The hatathali glanced over to where the other three were testing soil samples with their scanners.

"I promised he could speak with you, but it was to be after this first meeting. He is, well, unstable. We make allowances. He forgot himself and I apologise. The name Coyote he chose for himself after he was struck by lightning the second time—"

"Second time! John, I knew only of the once."

"You know of the spectacular thunderstorms we have in the high deserts of the American southwest. The first strike was when he was a boy. Burnt him, but he lived. The second was four years ago, very close to Teny. It turned his hair white, changed him in other ways, damaged his mind but focused him really, made a good thing out of what we feared would be a bad. That's when he took the name. He pleaded to come with us to Waso, the only thing he has ever asked of us really." Then John Dance glanced up into the sky, not as a spiritual or reflective act, but as a reminder that we would have listeners. "So, let me ask you, what do you know of the sand-dolls they burn here today?" He gestured, indicating the modest but unending lines of townspeople servicing the bale-fires.

"Only what I've heard from locals, nomads, sailors. It's a new thing, or another old thing made new. For five, six years it's been happening, all across the continent."

"What they told us in Cervantes, Tom. It's like the cluster of flags on Cervantes Island and along Old Ronsard Strand. Very important, everyone says, but ask why they are there? No-one knows for sure."

"So how should I play this? You say John Coyote wants to talk to me."

"You're both probably right about it not being the sats. So let him show you the kite. It is the most likely answer and you'll be gathering facts. We'll continue taking samples." And he smiled at the sky as if to say: Be circumspect for the watchers.

"Thank you, John."

"It is easy to give this, Captain. It matters to him and so matters to us."

Five minutes later, John Coyote and I were heading for the line of bale-fires, avoiding the main trail into town by turning south towards the wind-farm, to where a deeper shadow held within the pall, the dark shape of the kite swinging about its mooring stanchion.

John took on the role of guide, very earnest, very serious, his gaze darting this way and that, though everything he said seemed phrased as if to test whether I already knew what he was telling me. Every comment had its tiny payload of challenge and enquiry, though he started, predictably enough, by talking about the Colios festivities.

"This new custom of yours, Captain. Sand-dolls." His gaze swept the land, unrelenting. "You spend weeks making them, then bury them until harvest. You light the bale-fires, dig up the dolls and burn them, poke and prod at them with your forks, watch them fall apart. It's all so medieval."

I ignored the you and yours and the wildness in his eyes and played along, accepting that this was more protective coloration for the inevitable watchers and that his real purpose would be made clear in time. "As you say, John. I was telling the others. It's making virtue of necessity. Since we're in a desert, with only modest local crops, market gardens and hydroponics, it's less a localised harvest ritual now than a general plea for bounty and paradise, for any kind of flourishing viable future."

"Hence more urgent, more desperate, yes?" The kite was looming before us now, a great dark platform, a disk, an arrowhead shape hanging above the land.

"If you choose to see it that way. But thanksgiving just the same."

"With a sense of giving back for what has been given. Restitution." His gaze held mine.

I could only nod. What did this striking young man want me to say? But, thankfully, whenever I did leave a silence, John was quick to fill it.

"I notice that the National sand-dolls are makeshift, even half-hearted things compared to the tribal dolls. The Ab'Os know that stitched-up straw and soaked rags are not enough; you have to coat them with pitch, not just to represent tribal skin-colour but so they burn spectacularly and give off the smoke they require. They know that you need to build your temple in the sky."

The man was obsessed. "John, you're very taken with this? Is there a point you wish to make?"

"Always, but we're almost there. First let me show you the kite."

It was one more thing adding to the strangeness, the sense of portentousness. Here at the edge of town was a much-prized rarity: a Gerias Kite, tethered low to a three-metre stanchion like a crippled manta. Someone had flown a ritual bird up from Lostnest for the festival, a Prince or some other privileged tribal leader allowed the dispensation of flight so they could be here for Colios.

Flight! I could scarcely believe it. The votive kite strained at the iron support, pulling this way and that against its land anchors so the cables slackened and bowed one moment, then drew taut as the great arrowhead-shaped flying machine shifted, as if it were testing them. Tonight I shall escape.

I couldn't help but think of the aerotropts at Twilight Beach during that recent Koronai. This amazing craft was probably inert, probably didn't have a mind greater than function-dedicated comp systems, but it reminded me and I cherished it.

"This could do it," John said. "It can be programmed. It will have laser points, delivery systems for the pigments."

We stood watching the great shape nudging the stanchion, guy lines thrumming in the strengthening wind.

"See how the hull's patterned underneath," John said, his gaze checking the land about us, as if intent on everything but the hull patterning. "The polymer over the flotation nacelles has totemic striations. Very beautiful. It only looks dark like this because of the ash from the fires. There could very well be vents for releasing pigment payloads under there too, laser directed, then laser activated with appropriate allowances for wind dispersal."

And, taking his cue, suddenly realising what was intended, I moved in under the manta shape itself, avoiding the stabilising vanes.

When it covered us, creaking and straining barely a metre overhead, a vast ceiling, the young shaman held up his hand-set. "My scanner is dual function. But the hull screens us as well." His unsettling mannerisms had vanished just like that; his manic quality set aside.

"They'll send agents."

"But have to implement a suitable strategy." He spoke in a clear, low voice. "Discretion is important."

"Please, John, what is it?"

"In setting up Teny in Dinetah, the Ab'Os needed to bring in resources: necessary tech, search systems, all an acceptable risk, but a risk nonetheless."

"Go on."

"Such a relocation had to create logistical problems, the security problems of any such major undertaking."

"Of course. John, what are you saying?"

"That the Teny systems had little that was superfluous to the core task of studying the haldanes."

"So?"

"Your name was there."

"John!"

"Your profile. Your case. Coded, flagged highest security, but there."

"You hacked their systems."

"Acted according to my namesake, Captain. Coyote always plays a part. A troublemaker, true, but there is no civilisation without him."

"John, can we get back to—"

"Nothing is sacred unless we both agree it is so. People say things are intrinsically sacred, but no. That is a yearning, a projection, a need for things to matter. No pharaoh has been left untouched in his tomb, no Celtic chieftain, no Manchu potentate or Persian queen. Nothing has saved them. Nothing is sacred, unless we agree: not life, not even the land. Coyote exists to remind them of that by bringing chaos. It's his job."

I saw the change of tack for what it was, that this mattered, was what ultimately drove this man. "Tell me."

"He's the trickster, the mischievous, scheming outsider, the reviled thief and spoiler, the one who makes things go wrong to see what will happen." He spoke rapidly now, never raising his voice. "But he also sits in the doorway between this world and the other, between the spiritual world of the sacred hogan and the world out there. He keeps the door open, ultimately makes *hozho* possible by providing the chaos against which it is measured. He is Iai, the donkey-head in ancient Egyptian mythology who resists, who tests. The rebel. He is the fool without choice, ill-favoured, blessed and blasted, cursed and vital."

"John, what did you do? What did you find?"

"The others do not know. It's the real reason I am here, why I pestered them to let me come down to Waso. Because of what I learned there."

"Please!"

"You were made. Scribed DNA. They wanted a National Clever Man, as you've suspected. They had to know one way or the other. You are like Teny in Dinetah, only as a person: a way of looking back at here. Of looking at the tribal achievement. The Dreaming Way."

My gaze stayed locked on his. "The Dreaming Way?" But I understood. "What else?"

"You went to Tarpial?"

"I did."

"You met Seren S'lee, learned it was her face—"

"She put it there."

"Did she say why?"

"After a fashion."

"Don't be coy, Captain. It was an attachment."

"She said."

"She lied. She is your sister in a sense. The female part of the experiment."

"What!"

"Shut away in Tarpial. Working to bring you the truth."

"She's Ab'O!"

"Scribed to be that way. One more vital legacy of that ancient, splendidly co-opted Human Genome Project. Can you be sure you aren't scribed to be another?"

"You said—no, I can't."

"Exactly. You're National, deliberately that. But she was less clearly defined. She was temporised earlier too, brought into the world ten years before you. You were kept in the Madhouse."

"Do you know why?"

"I can guess. She was part of a great new experiment, the darling of the life-houses, smart, precocious, no doubt a deliberate prodigy. She earned their trust, won their confidence, and ruined the other part of their experiment."

"John—"

"Shut away in Tarpial she used what she could, found ways to circumvent their strictures. The Teny project was already underway. She linked to us in Tuba City; I agreed to act, a deformed outsider. I was already fated, had already been struck by lightning and spared. I was something of a pariah, a charmed yet blighted thing, even among my enlightened kind. I could easily assist. As Coyote, tradition sanctioned what I did. The bad things. The hard things."

"How did she ruin it? What did she do?"

"All she had time for. Something simple. Added a third image to the three. Her own face."

"Her face!"

"She knew something of scribing, had learned about keypoint insertions. She monitored your incept, added her own key template to the intended two when she could. Prioritised it."

"Then the Ship and the Star—"

"The other way round."

"The Star and the Ship."

"Together!"

"The Star—Starship!"

"Was the activation code. They sent it again and again, by tech, via the mindline—"

"On Lake Air." Thinking of Iain Summondamas and John Stone Grey, thinking of Arredeni Paxton Kemp and Anna, of Auer Rangan Anoki, all my confrontations with the Clever Men.

"But it never worked. You never became the full Clever Man they intended. Tartalen persuaded them to turn you out, to see what you would become, what would happen in situ. It was all they could do. They waited, tested, sent things at you."

Bolo May. Stoutheart Tiberias Kra. Naesé. A carefully laden torc at Pentecost. Ships on the Air. Mira Lari, an animate with that Face.

"Let the Tree give me Blue."

"No. That was something they didn't factor in. Couldn't."

It was good to have it confirmed. Needed right then.

"They've tried to kill me. Countless times."

"Factions. Tribal groups acting on their own, angered by the giving of the Colours, by the Haldane Order's reluctance to act. Even Kurdaitcha supposedly serving the life-houses. They see you as dangerous, as sacrilege."

"Others have died because of me. Other Captains. Traven."

"Then come in. Go public. Return to Twilight Beach. Or cross to Dinetah with us."

"Your colleagues from Waso will be at risk. They—"

"Captain, they are here to provide an excuse. We've been tracking you too, as well as we could manage. It was so we could talk."

"But Jon Cipher—"

"Resents the whole thing, yes. I have been struck by lightning. Ill-favoured. Unlucky. The risk to Waso and our people there concerns him. But a necessary part of the plan. They all know that whatever I tell you now is something we can give."

"You were struck twice. Outside Teny as well."

"Man-made lightning that time. There was a perimeter of angry hands."

"You tried to break in to Teny!" I could hardly believe what I was hearing.

"Three people in our cell did. Encountered difficulties. I tried to help."

"Your cell?" One thing after another.

"A group of Dineh and others trying to learn about the past. About the Tribation. It's an international movement, non-violent, full of Buddhists, Sufis and historians. Ours is a damaged, plundered world, Captain. Slowly healing."

"You think the tribes know what happened?"

"Some of it. Fragments. Information systems were the first to go during that terrible time. It's verifying everything that's important now."

"What do you have?"

John glanced at his scanner. "They'll be coming for us, Captain. We should get away."

"What did you learn, John?"

He didn't hesitate. "None of it is certain. But how there was too much information. Truths were lost. Basic knowledge. How the Information Revolution became the Reality Crisis, a saturation of the data-sphere coupled with an intended flattening of affect. Fiction and falsehood more eloquent, more persuasive than available truth. People didn't respond, didn't know how to respond. It's hard for us to conceive of it, to model it now. It got so the world no longer saw what was happening. Some insist it was more invasive, that waves of controlled microwave pulses brought down the global data-nets, isolated the nations again, that there were race-specific epidemics, ethnotropic plagues—"

"Culling."

"Culling, yes. We're almost certain. Culling and conditioning on a vast scale. Back and forth. Tom, we should go!"

The kite strained and heaved above us, lines creaking as it shifted with the wind.

But I couldn't leave yet. "It's why the arcologies were abandoned."

"Initially, yes. Or shut tight against the world."

"That didn't save them. They became dead cities."

"Many did, Captain. Many have."

"And those millions, putting themselves into cryo. All the Cold People in those storage vaults—"

"Against a better day, yes. Against plague viruses they knew were fixed term. But a logistics nightmare, you see. Now the revival tech just isn't sufficient—"

"The Ab'O, the Dineh—?"

"Not all peoples were targeted. It seems these angels of death were very specific. Minorities were exempted. The Maori, the Fijians, the Dineh, other Athabascan peoples—"

"The tribes weren't affected—"

"Captain, it's important we maintain our cover. We must get back to the skypainting, safeguard Waso."

"Of course."

I followed him numbly from under the striated hull, out past the mooring stanchion with its iron stairs leading up to the craft's flight-deck. John resumed his disguise of darting glances and fearsome intensity, and we let ourselves be seen to be chatting, gesturing, indicating things, making it seem as if we had been discussing the kite all along and its role in creating this new skypainting.

About us eddies of smoke from the bale-fires plunged and curled, caught up in the blades of the rotors to the south of the town, spiralling out from the great ferris by the Colios carnival on Black Point. For a moment it seemed like a corner of hell where dust-devils and willy-willies were made and set off on their courses, sent to haunt the emptied cities, sink charvolants and ruin lives.

Like Koronai so far away, Colios now seemed an even bleaker thing, a festival remembering a blasted, tragic time. Bring out your dead!

John Dance had been right. Not just some interesting re-location of corn-doll surrogates and harvest rituals, but a festival recalling the rest of it: wholesale slaughter, the burning of the dead. The more things changed...

"You! You there!"

We turned to see four tribesmen hurrying towards us, clearly more than festival custodians. They wore djellabas, had tribal sersifans and Japano swords. Two carried ritual woomeras for Unseen Spears.

"Tom, nothing I do should surprise you," John said, and with a wink, immediately let his scarred face and dark eyes become wild again. This is how he had played Coyote in Dinetah, how he had gained access to Teny.

"You are Tom Rynosseros," the leading tribesman said.

"I am the Blue Captain. Honour it!" I was tired, so tired of this.

"You are a pirate. An outcast," the Ab'O said. He had bands of deep orange painted on his dusky cheeks: proclamation of intent. His hands were on his swords.

"I am on walkabout and I stand for Blue. Who sent you?"

"What?" the young warrior demanded.

"Which group? Who is your sponsor?"

"I am a custodian here, pirate! It is my offcial task—"

"You are about to disgrace your totems and your clans," I said. "Mark the Colour and name yourselves."

I held him with my eyes, not daring to look away to see what John Coyote did, though I heard him muttering and gibbering at my side, playing the gifted sky-struck idiot.

It bought me seconds.

The young man glared, straightened. "This one is Aron Jarr Akita." The others exchanged quick glances with each other and followed suit, naming themselves in the lee of the Gerias Kite as at some embarkation ritual, John Coyote muttering all the while.

"We are allowed vendetta," Akita said. "We are—"

"Mark us!" I cried, looking up at imagined listeners, at the tribal scanners and their watch crews who had to be there, the ultimate reason for these men. "You see this bearer of the gun of Ajan Bless Barratin, commander of the Exotic ship *Gyges*. I wear the sigil of Auer Rangan Anoki, murdered Clever Man of the Chitalice. I carry the living sword, Sen, once owned by Mati of the Chialis. In their names, too, I claim the lives of these who now dishonour Blue." And to the waiting warriors: "Be ready!"

In unison, a dazzling, practised flourish, they drew their swords and stood waiting for me to draw, but frowning, frowning now because of what I had said.

Instead of drawing, I reached up, moved Anoki's medallion aside, and opened my jacket, then my shirt, revealed the cross-hatch of scars on my chest from where I had fed my sword.

I met their gazes then, saw the confusion and growing dread in their eyes, and imagined their thoughts. A living sword! What will be left of our lives for the noösphere, for the Dreamtime, for the ongoing? The living swords take everything.

Then, shocking us all, John howled and went rushing off for the wind-farm at the edge of town. It was an act that might have been misunderstood, might have triggered strike, but the warriors held. It gave more time.

"You want to keep Teny in Dinetah?" I said, ignoring the fighters and looking up at the unseen listeners. "Let anything happen to their divine fool and you'll lose it all. Waso will be withdrawn. Teny ends."

Decisions must have been made in seconds, relayed through implants, because the two young men with the woomeras sheathed their swords, turned and hurried after John, who had now reached the rotors and was cavorting among them, arms outstretched.

I faced the remaining two and drew my sword, did it slowly, purposefully. "You are both forfeit. You will feed Sen."

"Captain, there has been a mistake," Akita said. "We didn't know—"

"Of course you did. You would have agreed to it eagerly. Let's begin!"

"Please, we—"

"The Chialis do this all the time. Surely they are not braver. It's two against one. Begin!"

"We have been told not to engage," Akita said. "Ordered not to!"

"You've drawn."

"It's a command. We must obey."

"You've drawn. Your leaders know the forfeit."

"Why are you so determined?" Akita said, which made me ask it of myself.

Because of old anger, old grief and new. Because of rage and frustration. Because Traven was dead and a young woman had been left inside a triga ring, because of Mira Lari and Anoki and *Rynosseros* so casually slain, because some aerotropts had been murdered at Twilight Beach and, once, at far-off Trale, a hybrid life-experiment had reached out and sent a message, a star to match my Star because it found it there in my mind, possibly even recognised a piece of itself. Because. Because.

"Because sometimes I, too, believe I can win."

"What?" Akita said. "I don't follow."

"Of course you do, Aron Jarr Akita. Otherwise you wouldn't be here."

"I don't understand. You are mad! Both of you! You and that outlander!"

And my sword spoke, simple child words, but chilling to hear. "Sometimes I am mad too."

They were its first words in weeks.

The tribesmen stared, and their blades lifted, as much in terror as anything else.

"Captain, may I take their place?"

I turned to where the sun was westering beyond the colonnades of black smoke, saw a tall tribal woman in sand-robes, standing with two tribesman at her side.

"Lady Dusein!" Akita said. "We were—"

She stopped him with a gesture. "Excuse them, Captain. Let me blood your sword instead. Will you allow it?"

"No, Lady!" Akita cried, but she ignored him.

"Captain?"

"How is this your fight, Lady?" I asked.

"They are mine."

"Truly?" I said.

"Officially. Yes."

"Lady—" Akita began.

"Akita, enough! Officially, superficially, they serve Gerias."

"You are from Lostnest?"

She inclined her head. "Yes. Will you let them disengage?"

I felt foolish now, foolish again, reacting, overreacting. But Sen deserved it. This was all it knew. It had spoken. What happened now mattered.

"Of course."

She spoke in dialect, hard quick words that sent Akita and his companion rushing off towards the rotors to help secure John Coyote. She spoke again and her two bodyguards turned away as well, began walking back to the town.

Then she stepped closer, moved past me and turned so the sunlight lit her face and body, reached up and opened her sand-robes, opened her chemise, exposed her breasts, high and firm, the nipples erect with fear and emotion, perhaps just the cool wind from the ocean.

"Do it quickly. I am not very brave."

I laid Sen along her chest, angled between her breasts ever so lightly. The blood came, just enough, in the straightest, thinnest line on her dusky skin.

I sheathed the blade without wiping it.

"That was kind," she said, replacing her garments. "I gentled you."

"You did, Lady."

"You were so angry."

"You know me?"

"The Princes talk. Gerias is not so far away."

I glanced to the northeast. "You make the skypaintings."

"Sometimes I take the kite aloft. This was a chance."

"They're very fine. I'd like such a chance."

"To make a skypainting?"

"To go aloft."

"Where would you go?"

"Anywhere. Take the Line into the sky."

"Captain, I am wearing shielding tech. You can say it."

"Then back to my ship. Back to where the other Captains are gathering."

"But that's what they want. All the Coloured Captains together. You've been called to the Air."

"What!" A deep hard weight settled in my heart.

"It's true. A group claim. The elevation of Anna was too much."

"Then I must keep away so that can't happen. They need us all with our ships to make the claim. I would go back to Cape Bedlam then, so I can—"

"Tartalen is at Azira. At the life-house there."

"You know this?"

"Gerias is not so far away. I sometimes hear of Tartalen. I know Teny in Dinetah."

"What has that—?" I stopped. "You know Teny?"

"Of course. All the old stories of the Dineh. How Coyote was struck by lightning. Twice. And new stories of the tribes, now being made. How no Gerias Kite could cross the continent without being struck from the sky. Unless..." She hesitated, looking over at the town.

"Lady?"

"Let me show you the town."

"Lady, I know the town. I've been here before. Please finish what you were saying."

"It will be different this time, I promise. Let me show you."

It was strange to do, to go walking across the sand towards the chain of bale-fires with this Ab'O noble, towards the crusting of whitewashed buildings beyond the pillars of black smoke. To our left, the wind-farm rotors turned about themselves like great white birds never settling—whoop whoop whoop. Ahead, the black ferris pinwheeled against the golden sky like a stately old clock. On Pudding Hill coloured flags snapped in the wind on their tall poles. The pall of black smoke streamed into the sky above us, tipping over the land to the east, the black hand closing. And all the while the Ab'O townsfolk and Nationals came with their sand-dolls, feeding the fires.

"We shouldn't go too far," I said. "Especially now."

"Here will do. Captain, do you know the old Arabic word *moumia?*

"*Moumia?* Should I?"

"It means pitch. The tribal dolls are covered with pitch."

It was like resuming my conversation with John Coyote from twenty, thirty minutes before. It made me look for him among the rotors, but he was nowhere to be seen. No, there he was!—racing towards the carnival on Black Point, to the great ferris there, still pursued by the six tribal custodians.

"He's a diversion."

"He is. We're building an alibi."

"An alibi? And the other Dineh?"

"Are in on it too. Peripherally. They don't know everything yet."

"So, the tribal dolls are covered with pitch. To help them burn."

Again I waited. Again I let her guide me through this her way.

The Lady Dusein had brought us to within twenty metres of one of the fires. We stood watching as a family of Nationals: a mother, father and their two children, laid a daub, rag and wattle sand-doll on the pyre, obviously soaked with something highly inflammable because the doll flared and stood almost erect before falling back into ruin. The family then stood aside to let an Ab'O family approach with their contribution. Two men carried a long black doll between them, did a three-count together and heaved it onto the flames.

Dusein waited until it was done. "Did you know that there was a time in Egypt in the nineteenth and early twentieth centuries when finding burial pits was so commonplace that mummies were used to fuel locomotives running along the Nile? Wood and coal were scarce, and pitch had been used in the embalming, so they burned like bundles of dried sticks."

"What's this got—?" But I grasped it in an instant. "These dolls? These dolls are corpses?"

"Many of them. Most of them. From the old cryo crypts, Captain. The old failed forever crypts where so many Nationals went to escape the epidemics. The Cold People from when the arcologies were closed or abandoned. The spoiled ones."

"I knew there were crypts close by—"

"At least nine on this section of coast. Seven of them failed decades ago.

"Then Colios—?"

"Like so many renewal celebrations in history. Purging. Dealing with loss."

"But there were thousands of people! Hundreds of thousands!"

"Millions, ultimately," Dusein said.

We turned away from the fire, began walking back towards the Gerias Kite, not speaking until we were beside the mooring stanchion and the iron steps again.

"Thank you for revealing this," I said. "You are very brave to do it."

She gave a fleeting smile, humourless, grim, then cocked her head, listening to a data-feed. "They're bringing your friend. Are you serious about taking the Line into the sky?"

"Tartalen is at Azira, you said."

"Would you? Take it aloft? Fly to Azira?"

"How can I? It's like you began to say. No Gerias Kite could hope to cross the continent."

"Unless an abducted consort were aboard."

I scarcely believed what I was hearing. "You would risk it?"

"I risked your sword. That terrified me."

"You knew better."

"Hoped. You were very angry, very tired. You cared for your sword."

I had to smile. "Tell me the rest."

"Captain, I am here to risk it. I know John Coyote from Dinetah. I am in his cell."

Surprise after surprise. "His cell! But how—?"

"Tom, I suggest you draw your gun and sword and 'force' John and me aboard the kite."

It happened quickly then. The warriors arrived to see both gun and Chialis sword at their Lady's throat, obeyed her clear instructions to move away without daring to risk drawing their laser batons. John came leaping and dancing over to the stanchion where we waited.

"This becomes the top of the tower!" he cried, still in character, and clambered up the iron steps to the flight deck. Dusein and I followed.

In less than a minute, the land-anchors were free, the tether retracted, and the Gerias Kite was sliding across the land, shearing the nearest smoke column at three hundred feet as it swung about, all the while climbing, flight-comp using the heat of the bale-fires as well as the wind to lift clear of the town and the ocean, swinging away from Cervantes.

Perhaps farsight snipers could have hit us with the appropriate hi-tech, but we'd quickly donned matching flight coveralls with the hoods up and the masks in place, and John and I stood closely behind Dusein at the starboard rail so they dared not risk it. She was murmuring in dialect all the while, dissuading them from extreme action, insisting that she would be released unharmed once we had reached whatever destination I had in mind. The sats needed to be told, she repeated over and over. No sky-strike. Emergency privilege invoked.

The kite seized the sky like a live thing, lifting us away from the smoke-blurred coastline, from the dubious haven of Cervantes with its rotors and funeral pyres and hidden, emptying crypts: two sane madmen and this brave lady on their magic bird, their flying carpet, their desperate chance.

John Coyote had once again put aside his madness and stood at the control binnacle, as if the craft needed human assistance.

"I came from Dinetah on a dirigible," he said. "A great totemic whale of a thing. It felt like we were on the sky. This feels like we're in it. Does that make sense?"

I was at the port window, staring down, unable to look away. We were flying. "In it, yes. Part of it. I'm still coming to grips with it all."

"May you never," John said. "When this becomes commonplace, just a view, there is something wrong with the world."

And Dusein was there, veteran of such flights, though perhaps rarely so high.

"Your wish has been granted, Tom," she said. "You've taken the Line into the sky."

"Let's hope they allow it, Lady."

"Dusein."

"Dusein. It's not a precedent they will want. We can only wait and see."

John Coyote left the binnacle. "So let's go out and be in the sky."

"In a moment, John. The Lady—Dusein has something more to tell me. The rest of it."

John nodded, fitted his breather mask and left us, opened the cabin door and stepped out into the wind.

"Please," I said.

"Now you know what the sand-dolls are."

"What you said before. Mummies from the old crypts. The crypts that failed."

"Take it further."

"The tech failed. Was allowed to fail!"

Dusein nodded. "And one step more."

"Is being shut down even now!" I could scarcely believe it, could barely conceive of such a thing. Then, of course, could. It was so obvious, so inevitable. Settle the racial inequalities once and for all, everything from long-standing sovereignty squabbles over land-title and inheritance disputes to things like generational bank interest and the tenure of patents and copyrights.

Who authorised it?, I almost asked, but realised that it was something people always did. Just did. Out of envy, out of mischief and bravado, schoolyard dares and pranks becoming more, much more, getting even, part of payback, then clandestine policy. Custom. It was what John Coyote had said: no tombs remained intact from earlier societies; everything became scholarship, one man's grave was another's archaeology. What had he said? Nothing is sacred unless we both agree it is so.

Nothing sacred. Ultimately.

Then the other part of it grabbed.

A systematic shutting down of the Cold People facilities. At Cervantes. Across Australia. Throughout the world. The rest of the cull. The other part. All anticipated by the plague techs and program designers, the architects of the scheme.

Nowhere to hide.

I had been to Krombi, had read the histories. So hard to kill one or two or five or even ten when you had their faces in front of you. So easy to kill the thousands, the tens and hundreds of thousands when they were faceless, just lines of identical cryo sleeves stretching off in long dark vaults, strings of numbers on watch screens, so easy to switch off systems, use terms like rationalising resources, downgrading status, implementing cutbacks and shut-downs. You could put all sorts of edges onto words. Words took whatever you gave them.

"Tom?" Dusein asked.

There are times when it doesn't do to think too much. There are times when it's more important just to be.

"John Coyote's right," I said. "Let's go out and be in the sky."

Acknowledgements

"Nobody's Fool" copyright © 1991 Terry Dowling. First published in *Wormwood*, Aphelion 1991.

"Shatterwrack at Breaklight" copyright © 1985 Terry Dowling. First published in *Omega Science Digest*, July/Aug 1985.

"The Man Who Walks Away Behind the Eyes" copyright © 1982 Terry Dowling. First published in *Omega Science Digest*, May/June 1982.

"The Robot Is Running Away from the Trees" copyright © 1990 Terry Dowling. First published in *Rynosseros*, Aphelion 1990.

"The Man Who Lost Red" copyright © 1986 Terry Dowling. First published in *Aphelion*, Autumn 1986.

"The Only Bird in Her Name" copyright © 1985 Terry Dowling. First published in *Aphelion*, Summer 1985/86.

"The Last Elephant" copyright © 1987 Terry Dowling. First published in *Australian Short Stories* 20, Pascoe Publishing 1987.

"Spinners" copyright © 1990 Terry Dowling. First published in *Rynosseros*, Aphelion 1990.

"A Deadly Edge Their Red Beaks Pass Along" copyright © 1991 Terry Dowling. First published in *Wormwood*, Aphelion 1991.

"Privateers' Moon" copyright © 1992 Terry Dowling. First published in *Blue Tyson*, Aphelion 1992.

"Time of the Star" copyright © 1986 Terry Dowling. First published in *Aphelion*, Winter 1986.

"Coyote Struck by Lightning" copyright © 2003 Terry Dowling. First published in *Forever Shores*, Peter McNamara & Margaret Winch (Eds.), Wakefield Press, 2003 (as Part One of "Rynemonn").

THANK YOU

The publisher would sincerely like to thank:

Elizabeth Grzyb, Terry Dowling, Simon Brown, Jonathan Strahan,
Peter McNamara, Ellen Datlow, Grant Stone, Jeremy G. Byrne,
Sean Williams, Garth Nix, David Cake, Simon Oxwell,
Grant Watson, Sue Manning, Steven Utley, Bill Congreve,
Jack Dann, Stephen Dedman, the Mt Lawley Mafia,
the Nedlands Yakuza, Shane Jiraiya Cummings, Angela
Challis, Donna Maree Hanson, Kate Williams, Kathryn Linge,
Andrew Williams, Al Chan, Alisa Krasnostein, everyone I've
missed ...

... and *you*.

www.ingramcontent.com/pod-product-compliance
Lightning Source LLC
Chambersburg PA
CBHW031101030726
47496CB00002BA/333